ENEMY ARROWS

Toronto In The Year 1420

Will O'Hara

Copyright © 2013 by Will O'Hara
First Edition – August 2013

www.enemyarrows.ca

ISBN
978-1-4602-0930-1 (Hardcover)
978-1-4602-0928-8 (Paperback)
978-1-4602-0929-5 (eBook)

All rights reserved.

No part of this publication may be reproduced in any form, or by any means, electronic or mechanical, including photocopying, recording, or any information browsing, storage, or retrieval system, without permission in writing from the publisher.

Produced by:

FriesenPress
Suite 300 – 852 Fort Street
Victoria, BC, Canada V8W 1H8

www.friesenpress.com

Distributed to the trade by The Ingram Book Company

Table of Contents

PART I
The Bear Hunters 1

PART II
The Journey North. 115

PART III
Sight Of The Enemy 261

IN MEMORY OF
Bill O'Hara
(1924 to 1955)
A young man captured by enemy warriors during his first battle

To the Wendat people of Quebec
and the Wyendot people of Ohio,
Oklahoma, Michigan and Kansas,
all descendants of the great Wendat nation
of Southern Ontario
and to
my wonderful family

FOREWORD

ENEMY ARROWS takes place in fifteenth century Ontario, among the rivers and bays that are now called Toronto. By this time, the Wendat (Huron) people and their ancestors had lived beside the beautiful Lake Ontario for thousands of years, without any contact with Europeans. They had developed a prosperous society with trade routes stretching from Lake Superior south to Florida and as far as the Atlantic Ocean to the east. It was a matrilineal society where the Wendat women selected the chiefs and removed anyone who acted against the interests of the group.

The allies of the Wendat were the Algonquians who lived in the Canadian Shield to the north. The historical enemy of the Wendat were the Iroquois of the Finger Lakes region in what is now northern New York State.

In one sense the characters in this story are fictitious, since there is no written record of the people whose lives are described in *ENEMY ARROWS*. The only original records from this period consist of rock carvings and painted rocks. Early accounts from the French explorer Samuel de Champlain (c. 1567-1635) and the meticulous written descriptions by the Jesuits in the seventeenth century give us some idea of Wendat life, from a European viewpoint. The best source of information about the Wendat comes from the oral stories and traditions of their descendants, who live mainly in Quebec and the United States.

The next best evidence comes from the ground. The archaeological record in Ontario and New York State is rich with exciting stories. Dedicated archaeologists, archaeological anthropologists, linguistic archaeologists and historians have pieced together a reliable picture of Wendat life in those early days. Both writers and readers owe them a debt of gratitude. The people described in *ENEMY ARROWS* have been shaped from the fragments of pottery, post holes, petroglyphs, pictographs, and projectile points found not only across Ontario and New York State, but also far beyond modern provincial or state boundaries. The ancient Wendat once walked where their descendants walk today. They canoed on the rivers and bays that many of us know well. In that sense, the characters in this story are real.

ENEMY ARROWS is centred in a Wendat village on a plateau high above the Humber River, a few kilometers north of the Lake Ontario, in an area now called Baby Point in West Toronto. The village on the River of the Dawn was located above the Don River, with a spectacular view of the valley below, in what is now Broadview in East Toronto. The village at the Bottomless Lake is the reconstructed village at Crawford Lake Conservation Area, near Campbellville and Rattlesnake Point.

PLACE NAMES

The Bay	Toronto Harbour
Beautiful Lake	Lake Ontario
Bottomless Lake	Crawford Lake, near Campbellville, Ontario
Great Falls	Niagara Falls
Great Swamp	Holland Marsh, Ontario
The Islands	Toronto Islands
Lake of Islands	Georgian Bay
Northern villages	Orillia, Midland and Penetanguishine, Ontario
River of the Dawn	Don River in East Toronto
Stony Lake	Stony Lake near Petroglyphs Provincial Park
Thunder River	Humber River in West Toronto
Wide River of Many Islands	St. Lawrence River
Vast Cold Lake	Lake Superior
Village at River of the Dawn	Broadview near Bloor Street in East Toronto
Village at Thunder River	Baby Point in West Toronto

PEOPLE'S NAMES

Our People	Wendat (Huron) from Lake Ontario north to Georgian Bay
People from Across the Lake	Iroquois, from Northern New York State
People of the Lakes	Algonquian people from North Bay to the Ottawa River and including Algonquin Park

— *Enemy Arrows* —

MAPS

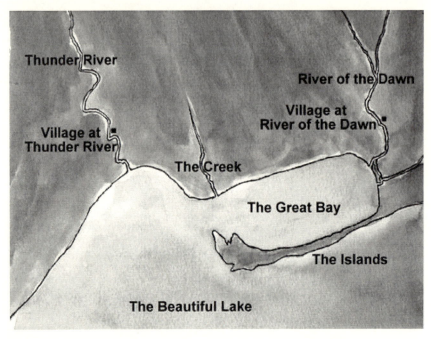

The rivers and bays of what is now Toronto

MAPS

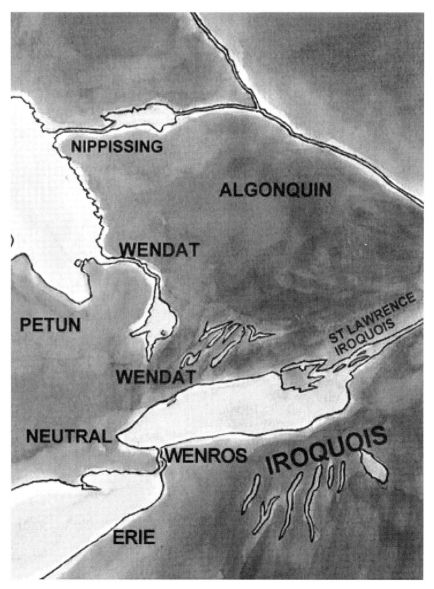

Homeland of the Wendat and surrounding nations

PART I
The Bear Hunters

– CHAPTER ONE –

Hunters with Pointed Sticks

Willow was the first to notice the bear prints in the snow, not far from the frozen lake. The tracks led out of the forest and into a gully where the bushes became a thick tangle of vines and thorny blackberry branches.

"Over here," he called to his friends, his breath visible in the cold winter air. "Look at the size of these!"

Otter and Loon rushed to his side.

"They're like snow shoes," said Otter in a low voice.

Loon put his moccasin inside one of the bear's footprints. "They're bigger than mine!" he shrieked.

"Not so loud," said Otter, pulling his friend away. "These are fresh. It could be nearby."

"Let's follow them," said Willow, heading off in the direction of the tracks with Otter and Loon close behind.

Halfway up the other side of the gully under some fallen trees was an uprooted pine tree. The tracks ended at a narrow opening under its roots, which had been plugged tightly with branches and leaves. There was no snow on the branches—they had been put there since the last snowfall only a few days earlier. Although the snow around the roots had been churned up by the bear, there were no tracks leading away from the trampled ground where the three young hunters stood.

Willow had his bow pulled back as far as it would go, with one pointed stick aimed at the opening. His face was tense with fear. "It's in there," he whispered to the others.

Loon took a step toward the bear's den and listened, but there was no sound from inside. Otter motioned to the others to move back. They climbed to the edge of the gully and squatted in the snow, staring at the bear's den.

"What do we do now?" asked Loon, his slight frame trembling under his bearskin robe.

"What do we do?" repeated Otter, running his fingers over the point of an arrow. "We came here to hunt and now we've found a bear asleep in its den—so close we could reach in and strangle it without waking it up." He was silent for a moment as he thought about their options. "What do we do?" he repeated. "We kill the bear and take it back to the village."

"And try to eat it before it eats us," added Willow.

"Before it eats us?" echoed Loon, his face contorted by the thought of imminent death.

"Yes—and it might," said Otter, squaring his wide shoulders. "This is the first time we've found a bear on our hunts. If we kill it, everyone will know we're real hunters, not just squirrel hunters."

"We *are* real hunters," said Willow, trying to keep his voice down.

"Except we only bring back rabbits and birds and bullfrogs," said Loon, looking back at the bear's den.

Otter continued. "What would they say if we went back to the village to get more skilful hunters to help us?" It was a question that needed no answer. The young friends thought silently about the dangers of hunting a bear on their own. They knew a sleeping bear is dangerous when disturbed from its winter sleep, and they all knew how ferocious bear could be. Still they couldn't stand to have others hunt it for them.

"We all agree then?" asked Willow. "We're going to hunt this bear ourselves?"

"There'll be enough fat for everyone in the village," said Loon, with a forced smile.

"And the hunt will be ours!" said Otter.

Loon let out a warbled call in celebration.

"Not so loud," said Otter, putting a wet rabbit-skin mitten over his mouth. Loon leapt to his feet to escape but Otter grabbed his foot, pulled him down and jumped on him, pummelling his shoulders while Loon tried not to laugh. Willow hurled himself on the pile, yelling at them to be quiet. By the time they stopped wrestling they were covered with snow.

Willow sat on the ground and looked again toward the overturned pine tree. When the others were still, he asked, "How do we get this bear before it gets us?"

They talked quietly about the best way to kill the sleeping bear. They discussed the possibilities of fire, water, spears and arrows. No idea was too far-fetched to consider. They talked until the winter sun had reached its highest point, and at last they had a plan.

Otter and Loon headed into the forest while Willow kept watch on the den. They walked until the bear couldn't hear them, and in a short time returned with a sapling pole sharpened at one end—as well as a heavy branch with a gnarled growth in the shape of a club. Loon carried the pole to the bear's den where he positioned himself amid the bear tracks. Otter and Willow stood silently on either side of the opening with their arrows ready and the branch by their feet. They glanced at each other to see if they were ready to go.

When Otter nodded, Loon began stabbing the sharp pole through the blocked opening, yelling his piercing loon call as loudly as he could. A thunderous roar came from the den that shook the oak trees to their roots. Loon dropped the pole and turned to them, but Willow and Otter shouted to be brave. He picked it up again and jabbed it toward the bear. Together they screamed at the trees and the sky—they yelled to frighten the bear more than it frightened them.

Suddenly, with a sound like a falling tree, the branches blocking the opening to the den were smashed to bits and flung toward

Loon. A huge black forepaw reached out of the opening, as Loon continued to jab with the pole. Then a hind paw crashed through the roots and frozen earth of the uprooted tree. When Loon finally pierced the hind leg of the angry bear, Otter and Willow let their arrows fly, but their pointed sticks only glanced off the bear's thick fur.

The young hunters pulled more arrows out of their quivers and shot their next round, but they had no effect on the thrashing beast as it twisted on its back, clawing wildly at the opening. As Loon tried again to impale the disoriented animal, it reached through the opening and grabbed the pole with its enormous black claws. Then its head shot out—its cavernous jaws opened wide enough to eat all three of them at once—as it slammed down on the pole, pulling it out of Loon's hands and snapping it in half. Defenceless and trembling, the young hunter reached for his bow and an arrow, stepping backward toward his friends.

At last one of Willow's arrows hit the bear's neck straight on and penetrated its flesh. Dark blood oozed out of the thick fur. The tiny stick rose and fell as the animal breathed deeply, caught upside down in the entrance to its den. Loon shot his first arrow, but his hands were shaking so badly he couldn't aim straight and the pointed stick was lost in the snowy underbrush. Otter's shot at close range pierced an ear and the bear roared, flipped itself over in one powerful move, and pushed its heaving body through the opening.

With one stroke an enormous paw ripped through the still air while Loon was trying to aim his bow. It tore a swath out of the boy's deerskin leggings as though they were made of spider webs. Otter and Willow let their last two arrows fly at their raging target and then turned and ran. Otter grabbed the club as they fled. The bear climbed to its feet, shaking its fur like a wet dog, snorting loudly and searching for the scent of the intruders—with Willow's single arrow still moving up and down, embedded in its bloody neck.

The hunters knew there was no good place to run from an angry black bear, since a bear can outrun the fastest runner, climb a tree like a squirrel, and swim like a beaver. They ran toward the frozen lake, more by accident than by design. Loon was far out in front, his wiry arms and legs flapping like bat wings under his cloak. The bear stormed after them. It couldn't see its enemies clearly, but it could track them easily by their scent.

When Loon reached the frozen lake he kept on going. The ice cracked around him. His winter moccasins slid on the smooth surface, but he ran until he realized what he was standing on—ice so thin it could collapse under him at any time. He stood still with his legs wide apart, his knees bent and his arms outstretched, as if he were standing in a canoe on a windy lake. He knew that the slightest movement could send him crashing through into the frigid water below. So far he was light enough to stay on the surface.

Willow followed Loon to the glistening ice, slipping as he went. He was taller and heavier than Loon and his weight made the ice groan. When he finally slid to a stop, it cracked with the sound of a splitting tree—but it held. He could see Loon farther out on the lake, holding his position. Behind him, Willow saw Otter running frantically in his direction, followed closely by the bleeding bear.

When Otter saw his friends standing motionless on the ice he ran out after them, but he was too heavy. He took only a few steps before crashing through into the freezing water, throwing the gnarled branch toward Loon as he fell. It spun through the air and crashed through the ice with a splash, not far from Loon. The bear bounded after Otter, sending shards of broken ice tinkling across the surface in all directions. When it broke through the ice, a sharp edge scraped its neck, ripping the arrow from its flesh. Blood now gushed from the open wound.

Stunned by the cold, Otter struggled to pull himself onto the ice, but each time he tried he broke through again, submerging himself in the icy water and cutting a path for the angry bear—a path that led straight to him. As the bear came closer, Willow stretched out on the ice and tried desperately to reach Otter. Loon yelled for him to climb onto the ice, but it was no use. The bear was too close.

Otter took one last look at Willow and then at Loon and his head disappeared below the surface. The bear brought down his huge jaws where Otter had been only an instant before, splashing ice and water high into the sky.

"No!" cried Loon as he watched Otter vanish beneath the surface. The bear turned its head toward Willow and charged at him, half swimming and half leaping through the water. Otter was under the ice and the other two were in danger of breaking through as the bear neared them. They had their bows, but no more arrows.

"Otter!" wailed Loon. His cries echoed from the rocky shore, but Otter didn't appear. In a rage, Loon pulled the gnarled branch from the hole in the ice and held it high above his head. Willow was now close enough to the bear to be showered by the shattering fragments of ice as the angry animal lunged after him. Willow carefully slid toward his friend.

Loon was so incensed that he forgot about the danger of breaking through. He slid toward the bear like a spider walking across water, holding the club high above his head.

A strangled voice called from behind him, but Loon didn't turn around. He sensed without looking that it was the spirit of the lake—and the spirit was angry. He could see Willow pointing in the direction of the cry with his eyes and his mouth wide open in disbelief, but Loon didn't dare look behind. Instead, he charged at the bear as it thrashed through the water toward Willow. With all his strength he brought the branch down on the bear's skull. Crack! The bear shook its enormous head and fell backward into the icy water, sending a wave over the ice. Loon followed it and again smashed the stupefied bear with the branch. Its head sank beneath the ice, but it soon rose up again, spraying water through its nostrils.

"Help me!" cried the voice from behind Loon, and this time he recognized the voice of Otter. He looked around to see Otter's head poking through the hole in the ice where the branch had crashed through. Turning back, he saw the bear sink beneath the cold water, bubbles rising from its black snout and dark blood pulsing from its neck with every heart beat into the icy water. Loon picked up the club again and moved carefully toward Otter.

— *Enemy Arrows* —

They ran toward the frozen lake.

"Help me, Loon," pleaded Otter. "Help me. I can't move."

Loon placed the branch across the opening in the ice. "You have to pull yourself up Otter," he begged. "You have to use your strength."

Otter lifted his frozen hands over the branch, but his muscular arms were too tired to pull his body up. He had swum under the ice to the hole and he was spent.

"Use all your strength," cried Loon. Otter's eyes rolled back in his head and closed. "Use the strength of your father and your ancestors," Loon screamed, as he attempted to reach Otter across the breaking ice. His desperate words echoed from the shore and the islands, booming back again at different intervals, sounding even more anguished than Loon himself.

But Otter didn't move.

"Move—before the enemy gets you," threatened Loon, looking toward the shore. Otter's eyes opened a little.

"There's an enemy warrior," said Loon in a hushed voice, pointing at the shore. "Here he comes now." A look of horror came over Otter's face.

"Listen to what he's saying," said Loon. "Listen!"

He cupped a hand behind his ear and faced the shore without moving. "He's going to throw your bones in the fire—after the dogs have peed on them."

Otter was moving in and out of consciousness, but the thought of an enemy warrior doing unspeakable things to his bones was far worse than drowning in the cold lake. Deep inside where fear turns to panic, he found the strength to grab on to the branch.

"Pull yourself up!" yelled Willow, as he moved away from the writhing bear. "He's almost here."

With the last of his strength and the vision of the approaching enemy, Otter slowly pulled his broad shoulders through the narrow hole in the ice. The branch spread his weight across the hole—and this time he didn't break through.

"Hold on!" Loon screamed, pulling the other end of the branch with all of his strength, hoping to ease Otter out completely. But all he did was slide himself toward the hole. Finally, Otter kicked his legs, slid onto the thin ice and rolled away from the hole where he lay soaked to the bone, frozen and motionless.

Willow was standing close to the open water where the bear had broken a path. Once more the beast rose above the surface and clawed at the ice. Loon pulled the branch from Otter's frozen grip and pushed it hard toward Willow. It slid, spinning as it went, and came to an abrupt stop against Willow's shin, almost knocking his legs out from under him. Lifting the branch high above his head, Willow delivered a devastating blow to the roaring animal as it lunged toward him. The huge head sank beneath the surface. When the water became still, the bear rolled over and floated on its back in the icy lake. Willow slid the branch back across the ice to Loon where Otter lay at his feet, beginning to turn blue.

"We have to get him to shore before he freezes," shouted Willow. "Push him with the branch."

Loon pressed the branch against Otter's waist and slid him in a trembling heap toward the shore, his head and arms dragging on one side of the branch and his legs on the other.

By the time Otter was on shore, Willow had found a sheltered place on the beach and cleared a place in the snow down to the sand. He stuffed some milkweed fibres under a small pile of twigs and birchbark and then tried to light it by striking a piece of chert against a sharp-edged rock. Loon dragged Otter close to the lifeless fire and ran off to get some dry sticks. Over and over again, Willow struck the chert, trying to get a spark, but it was too wet. He rubbed it against the dry lining of his cloak and tried again.

"Light!" he yelled. "Otter is freezing!"

Loon dropped the sticks by Willow's side and glanced over at Otter. "He's getting pale."

"I know. I can't get a spark." Again and again Willow struck the rock, but without success. In desperation he stopped to pull the fibres apart until they formed a loose web under the twigs. He started again. A spark from the chert shot into the snow and vanished. Again he tried. Finally, a feeble spark crept from the rock to the fibres and they ignited in an explosion of light and warmth, setting the birchbark on fire, and in an instant the twigs were alight. He carefully placed the larger sticks over the fire until there was a little flame. Willow added the branches one by one and before long there was a roaring blaze.

They hauled Otter closer to the heat and removed his wet robe so the fire could warm him. He lay on the snowy beach as the sun began to set, with his eyes closed and his chest barely moving.

– CHAPTER TWO –

Blood on the Snow

The night was still and a deep cold made the trees split with the crack of thunder. The ice on the lake would be thick enough to walk on by morning.

Lynx walked silently in the moonlight, skirting the shore of the frozen lake, keeping watch for anything that moved. His strong lean body was protected from the cold winter night by a long beaver cloak lined with rabbit skin and a hood of wolverine fur. Deerskin leggings and sleeves were secured in place by decorated leather straps. On his feet he wore deerskin boots with patches sewn on the sides. His beaver mittens gleamed in the light of the full moon. Since the snow was thin on the ground, he carried his snowshoes on his back. His bow and a quiver of arrows hung over his shoulder. Clouds of vapour gushed from his lungs into the cold air as he moved.

Lynx, who usually hunted alone by the light of the moon, was able to see in the dark like a cat and could walk through the winter forests unseen. He heard anything moving in the woods before it heard him.

The light from the setting moon cast blue shadows behind him on the snow as he returned along the lake to the village. When he came across the bear tracks he bent down to examine them.

"What is this bear doing out in the cold?" he wondered aloud. "All the others are asleep in their dens, waiting for spring."

There was just enough light to see the dark splotches on the snow, though he couldn't make out their colour. The tracks appeared to be a few days old and the blood had become thick and hard, like hot wax dripped on snow. As he followed the tracks in the direction of his village, the blood spots grew farther and farther apart. Lynx could picture the blood beginning to congeal on the bear as its wound closed.

He continued to follow the tracks in the darkness along the shoreline, listening and watching. The blood had disappeared. It wasn't long before the moon set behind the silhouettes of the naked trees. Soon the sun would rise behind him.

As Willow and Loon waited for Otter to open his eyes, a deer appeared on the shore not far away, bathed orange in the glow of the rising sun. It pushed snow from the frozen grasses at the edge of the woods and lowered its head to graze. Each time it raised its head, it looked toward the fire and the three boys huddled together.

Willow saw the deer turn its head quickly toward the sun, as if sensing movement, before bolting into the forest. Following the gaze of the animal, the young hunter could barely make out a solitary figure walking along the shore—as though it had emerged from the morning rays. He grabbed Loon by the arm and pointed at the strange sight.

"What do you think it is?" Loon asked. Willow didn't answer. They stared at the approaching being.

"It must be the spirit of the lake," said Loon.

Willow stood to face the spirit. Loon slowly rose beside him, clutching his bow.

"Who are you?" Willow yelled. There was no answer. He called again.

From the distance came a response: "Don't you know me?"

Willow immediately recognized the deep voice of Lynx, his father's younger brother from the next village. As he came closer, the hunters noticed a pair of white rabbits slung from a strap over his shoulder.

They ran to him yelling wildly about the bear, waving their arms and shouting as they described hunting and being hunted by the enormous animal. Lynx was astonished to hear of Otter's escape under the ice.

The sound of loud voices brought Otter back to his senses. He raised his head above the windbreak and was relieved to see Lynx's friendly face. Lynx went to the fire to examine Otter and noticed that his clothing was almost dry, although steam was still rising from his moccasins.

"You're still alive," Lynx whispered gently.

Otter moved his head, but was too weak to answer.

"Rest by the fire," Lynx said. "Your friends want you to live, and so do the spirits. Not many people could have done what you did."

Loon and Willow showed Lynx the dead bear with its huge paws frozen into the ice. Using sapling poles, they pried the carcass out of the ice and dragged it bit by bit on to the shore. Lynx lifted its head to examine the patch of congealed blood on its neck.

"I don't know why this bear was wandering about in the cold," he said in a low voice. "All the other bears are asleep, but this one had been wandering around wounded before it went to sleep under the roots. I followed its tracks along the shore."

He lowered the dead animal's head to the ice and sang a quiet song while the others watched. Then, wielding his sharp knife, he bled it and sliced through its fur from its jawbone to its legs. He slit each leg to the giant paws and, with the help of Willow and Loon, pulled the skin away from the flesh, removing the sinews as he worked. Then he carefully separated the fur away from the bloody patch on the bear's neck where Willow thought his pointed stick had penetrated.

"Look at this wound," he said to Willow. "You see how big it is—and how deep?" He sliced the thick layers of fat down to the warm flesh. "Your arrow didn't make this wound." He pointed to a small puncture on the other side of the bear's neck. "This is where your arrow went in."

He slipped his knife into the larger wound. Deep in the flesh it touched something hard. Lynx dug out a small, bloody triangular arrowhead with a fragment of gut still attached. He wiped it in the snow to remove the blood.

"It's an arrowhead, as I thought. But it's not one of ours. It looks like the arrowheads I dug out of my friends when we fought the People from Across the Lake." Lynx looked nervously behind him and scanned the shoreline both ways. "I don't like finding this so close to our villages."

"Where did it come from?" asked Willow.

"I don't know yet," he replied, dropping the arrowhead into his fire pouch. "After we get Otter home, I'll ask the arrowhead to tell us its story."

He continued to pull away the skin and before long there were two bear shapes on the ice—one a limp pile of black fur, the other a glistening mass of flesh with bulging eyes and bared teeth.

"We'll cut it up here," said Lynx, as he began to sever the hind legs from the massive body with his stone knife. "Then I'll help you get the meat back to the village. I know there will be a feast when you get home," he said with a deep laugh. "And it will be your feast!"

He put his hand on Loon's shoulder. "You gather some wood for a sled while we prepare the bear. Try to find some cedar to split for the runners. We'll have to make it big enough for Otter—he may want to ride next to the meat on the way back." Otter was still recovering beside the fire, staring listlessly into the coals. Loon nodded and went into the woods to find what they needed.

Willow held the bear's limbs in place while Lynx dismembered the carcass, singing hunting songs as he cut. Once the limbs had been removed he began separating the flesh from the bones and removing the thick, white tendons that held the muscles in place. He stopped and looked up at Willow.

"I remember when your father killed his first bear," he said with a faraway smile before going back to his work. "He was about your age and I was his snivelling little brother. Oh, I thought he could do anything!" His sharp knife scraped against a thigh bone and heavy slabs of meat fell into the blood-splattered snow.

"He found a young bear in the woods, not far up the river. That's right. He was hunting with his close friend, Moose. You know him well. Those two were fearless—foolish sometimes, but fearless. They chased the bear up a rotten tree and then pushed the tree over. When the bear crashed to the ground, it lay stunned for an instant—just long enough for them to lance it with a sharp pole. Moose was big even then, much stronger than anyone his age, and the two of them dragged the dead bear to the river and floated it to the village on a raft. What a celebration we had that night! My friends and I danced around the bear—naked except for our bows—and pretended to shoot it with pointed sticks. We knew our turn would come soon."

They turned the carcass over and Lynx began to strip the sinuous flesh from the ribs and back.

"From that day to the end of his life, your father was a great hunter—and the bravest warrior there was. He would have been happy to see you with your first bear, Willow." Lynx wiped his knife in clean snow, looking out across the lake. Long after the knife was clean, he continued to slice the blade through the snow while his mind wandered to distant events and places. In time a faint smile appeared on his face and he looked back at Willow.

"It's been almost ten winters since your father was killed by the enemy. You've grown from a suckling child into a bear hunter." He shook his head in amazement. "How does it happen so quickly?"

Before the sun reached its highest point in the sky they had cut up the bear and Loon had returned with enough wood for a sled. Lynx carefully cut the bear's penis bone away, while Loon writhed in mock pain. He gave the bone to Otter.

"Keep this Otter," he said. "You won't have to worry about evil spirits."

After they had built a sled they spread the bearskin over it, fur side down, and wrapped the meat in it. They tied the bones and skull on the sled beside the meat, ready for the journey back to the village.

"We'll eat before we leave for the village," said Lynx, hanging a thick slab of crimson liver above the fire. Then he sat quietly, gazing at the ice-covered lake.

"There have been strange happenings around here lately," he said. "This wounded bear with a foreign arrow fits the pattern."

Otter sat up beside the fire. The light had returned to his eyes. Lynx looked at the three fearless young hunters and continued.

"On the night of the new moon I was on the white bluff, high above the shore on the other side of the islands. I was on my way back to the village with some beaverskins. It was a bitterly cold night with stars so brilliant that they turned night into day. I thought no other living creature would be out. Then, from the top of the bluff, I saw three people walking along the shore. There had been a snowfall the day before so they were using their snowshoes. Since I didn't recognise them, I kept out of sight and followed them to the islands, beside the bay, and along the shore. When I checked their snowshoe tracks, I could see from the weave of the gut that they weren't our people. They were from across the lake." He threw a log on the fire, sending a stream of sparks shooting into the clear blue sky.

"I went back to the village and told my story to Old Chief. He gathered a scouting party to follow the tracks and they left soon after I arrived—but a strong wind came up from the west and blinded them with blowing ice. The scouts had to turn back before morning and never found the intruders.

"I tell you this because I saw it with these eyes," he said, touching a heavy mitten to his face. "And I've heard the same stories from others. There are too many of them—too many of the enemy coming into our territory. They send spies who watch what we do and see the way we build our villages." His eyes searched the horizon in all directions. "So they'll know where and when to strike."

"Are there spies in our village?" asked Willow.

Lynx stared into the fire before he answered. "There may be enemy spies near our village, but I've never seen any inside the palisades. Anyone who helps the enemy becomes my enemy. He threatens our villages and everyone in them. I don't know if there is someone like that among us, but if there is I will find him and drag him by the hair to the clan mothers. I know what they'll do to a traitor!"

The bear liver sizzled over the fire, dripping onto the coals. Each drop burst into flames, sending a strong scent of burning grease into the cold air. When it was ready, Lynx carved it into large pieces and gave chunks to each of the others, with the biggest piece going to Otter, who had watched the roast with the look of a ravenous dog. They gorged themselves until they couldn't move and then sat in the warmth of the flames, waiting for any remaining chill to leave Otter's bones. Lynx told stories of the great hunts from long ago. After a while he looked over at Otter's steaming clothing with a smile on his face.

"You swim like your otter brothers—underwater for long distances, even in the cold of winter. Tell me. Is it true you have webbed toes?"

Loon and Willow howled with laughter, as they pulled off Otter's moccasin to show Lynx his wrinkled toes.

"That one isn't webbed," said Lynx, still looking curious. "What about the other one?"

He laughed loudly when he saw the two bare feet, shrivelled from a night in steaming moccasins. But there were no webs between Otter's toes.

When the sun began to slide toward Thunder River, Lynx said it was time to return to the village. They moved Otter from the fire and placed him on the sled. Lynx and Willow hauled the heavy sled along the icy shore of the lake while Loon steadied the load. When they came to the mouth of the frozen Thunder River they rested briefly. Lynx stood quietly beside Otter, looking out across the snow-covered sand dunes.

"There's no better place anywhere," Lynx said with a look of wonder. "When I'm beside this river, I feel at peace. Even when the huge slabs of ice crash down the river in the spring, sounding like thunder, I feel at peace here."

He looked at his companions before he continued. The bear's severed head lolled on the sled at Otter's feet. Its eyes shone like wet pebbles from a stream bed.

"This river has a strong, generous spirit. It has cared for our people forever and I know it will always be here for us."

They turned the sled toward the village and hauled it along the ice. High tree-covered cliffs loomed over them where the river cut through the hills to reach the lake. Soon the sun was setting behind leafless trees.

"They'll see us from the village soon," said Lynx. "And you'll be mobbed."

– CHAPTER THREE –

The Arrowhead Speaks

As they approached the village, the dogs smelled the bear meat and came bounding through the woods, howling and sniffing at the carcass. Loon swung his bow to keep them away. The sound of madly barking dogs brought the children to see what was happening. When they saw the bear they screamed and shouted, jabbing at the skull with sticks to pretend they had been part of the hunting party. A few ran back toward the village shouting, "Lynx killed a bear! Otter was injured! Lynx saved him!" Their cries faded as they disappeared up the trail.

With that news everyone rushed down the steep hill to the river to get close. They touched the blood-spattered fur and the fresh-cut meat. They cheered when Otter raised his head. Willow's young sister, Wren, pulled at the wet clothing and asked Otter if he fell into the river.

"Lynx, tell us how you killed the bear," called one of the elders. Lynx looked at her in astonishment. He saw Otter struggling to stand so he lifted him off the sled, gathered Willow and Loon beside him, and raised his hand in the sign for silence. As soon as they saw the hunters standing still, the young children stopped shouting.

"You want to know how I killed this bear?" shouted Lynx.

The crowd began to cry out again. "Yes!" "Tell us."

He waited for the questions and calls to die down before he began.

"This bear was fierce," he said, opening his mouth to show his own strong teeth. "It had sharp teeth and long claws. It wanted to eat someone—and it put up a terrible fight." Lynx roared at a group of young boys who were poking at the bear and they ran squealing into the woods.

"How did I kill this ferocious creature?" Lynx paused and scanned the smiling faces of his friends and neighbours, enjoying the suspenseful silence—until Loon elbowed him in the ribs.

"I didn't kill it." His wide eyes stared at the astounded faces of the villagers. "My brave friends killed this bear long before I stumbled upon them. Willow, Otter and Loon are the bear hunters."

There was a look of disbelief in the eyes of the children. How had these squirrel hunters killed a bear with their pointed sticks? But the elders smiled broad smiles. Now there were three more brave hunters to provide for the people in the village. They all gave thanks for a successful hunt. There would be meat in many pots.

As the youngest children reached out to touch them, Wren hugged her brother around the waist, pressing her face hard against his bearskin cloak.

"You killed a bear! You killed a bear!" she yelled. "Will you tell me how, Willow? Will you tell me the story?"

He put his arm around her. "I'll tell you the whole story."

"Just us?" she asked.

"Just us," he answered. "Let's go home and I'll tell you from beginning to end."

They walked together up to the plateau where the thick wooden palisade surrounded the village. At the far end, they saw smoke rising from a fire where Old Chief often sat looking out over the river.

"We must tell Old Chief what happened," cried Wren, pulling Willow toward her. "Grandfather!" she called. "I've brought a bear hunter for you to see. You might have met him before."

Old Chief rose to meet his two grandchildren with his arms outstretched. He stood tall despite his age, though it took him some time to straighten up. His beaver robe covered deerskin leggings decorated with finely crafted porcupine quills. On his feet he wore tall deerskin moccasins lined with rabbit fur. An eagle skull amulet hung from his neck and eagle feathers decorated his long, gray hair. His face was marked with scars from the battles of long ago.

"Who has killed a bear?" he asked, to give them a chance to repeat the news.

"Willow and Otter and Loon. They killed a huge bear!"

Old Chief put his bare hand on Willow's arm. "Did the bear kill any of you?" he asked solemnly.

"Not me, Grandfather!" laughed Willow. "Not any of us. We killed it first."

"Tell us the story," pleaded Wren.

They sat beside the fire while Willow told them the story of the bear hunt from beginning to end. Wren sat close to her brother, holding his arm around her shoulders. Old Chief listened carefully with his eyes wide. An anxious look flitted across his face when Willow spoke about the arrowhead in the great bear's neck.

"Do you still have the arrowhead?" he asked.

"Lynx has it."

When Willow had finished the story, Wren held him by the arm. "Now he's a bear hunter," she said to Old Chief.

"He's a fine hunter," echoed Old Chief. "As I knew he would be."

Orchid came running across the snow with furs and skins flapping behind her. "Where have you been?" she cried. She grabbed Willow and held tight until he loosened her grip and stepped back."

"I'm not a child, Mother," he said.

"You're still my child when you're lost—where were you?"

"Hunting," he replied.

She quickly scanned his skin for injuries, turning him around to check the back of his head. "Was Loon with you?"

He nodded.

"He always gets you into trouble," she said. "What about Otter?"

"We saved him."

"Saved him from what?"

Old Chief stepped in. "Let's go back to the longhouse and you can tell everyone about bear hunt."

"Bear hunt?" shouted Orchid. "You're too young to hunt bears!"

When Old Chief moved toward the palisade, Orchid and Wren followed, smothering Willow with questions as they went.

There was feasting and jubilation in the village that night. The bear's head was hung on a pole beside a bonfire in front of the village lodge. The elders told stories of their hunts, being careful not to outshine the glory of the day, while the young children danced around the pole, shaking pointed sticks at the bear's head like real hunters. It would soon be their turn to hunt their first bear.

Inside the lodge, Lynx met with Old Chief, the clan mothers, and the elders. Beside them sat Moose, the War Chief, a massive man with huge hands and feet and a broad chest. His long black hair spread across his bearskin robes. Moose was Orchid's cousin, but he treated her as his sister and Old Chief as his own father. He was one of the strongest warriors in the village, known for his bravery and generosity, and he had earned the respect of everyone in the village. If they were going to fight the enemy, he would lead the way.

Lynx told them how he had found Willow, Otter and Loon beside the dead bear. He described the large wound in the animal's neck—a wound that could not have been made by pointed sticks. When he told them about the arrowhead he had dug out of its flesh, he drew the carefully crafted piece of chert from his fire pouch and placed it on the palm of his hand for all to see. There was no doubt that it was an enemy arrowhead. They had all seen them before, in painful times. A shudder spread through the lodge as the dark stone was passed from hand to hand. Moose spoke first, pulling his beaverskin robe over his shoulders. His voice was quiet, but forceful, with a resonance that shook the ground.

"There are only three ways that the arrowhead could have pierced the bear's neck," he said. "The bear may have been shot in enemy territory across the lake. Then it crossed the ice with the arrowhead already in its neck." A puzzled look came over his face.

"But Lynx says the wound was wide open and had not started to heal. And the ice on the lake was not thick enough to support the bear. The first way isn't possible."

A murmur of agreement filled the room.

"The second way," the War Chief continued, "is that an enemy warrior fired an arrow with a very powerful bow from far away—far across the lake. That arrow flew over the lake and hit the bear in the neck."

He slapped his hand on the side of his neck with a loud smack. The others laughed nervously. This second way was also impossible. So they all knew that the last way was the only possible explanation. Moose looked at Lynx in a silent request for him to continue.

"Or, an enemy warrior was hunting in our territory—just a few days ago," Lynx added. "This warrior must have forced the bear from its den and shot the arrow into its neck, but the bear escaped. Willow's arrow hit the bear, but the ice reopened the earlier wound. The bear died from that wound and from the blows inflicted by Willow and Loon."

"But where is the enemy now?" asked Moose. "He could be far away."

Old Heron, one of the most respected elders of the village, sat nearby, listening to Lynx and Moose, her rough hands skilfully weaving a basket lid. Her long gray hair swept across her pointed nose whenever she looked up from her work. When she spoke, she spoke slowly and deliberately.

"The enemy could be listening to our words from the other side of the palisade," she said.

"We have to root them out!" shouted the leader of the Deer Clan, turning his head toward the palisade. The others cried out until Moose raised his hands.

"The bear has brought us a warning," said Moose. "A warning that we can hold in our hands."

The others voiced their agreement. Moose continued. "But the enemy is days away from here by now. They are probably back in their own territory, sitting beside a fire, telling their own War Chief about our defences."

There were cries for revenge and retaliation.

"This isn't the time to do battle," said Moose quietly. "We'll go after the enemy when the time is right. And that time will come soon."

– CHAPTER FOUR –

Snow Snake

The late winter sun climbed higher in the sky each day, bringing its radiant warmth to the village overlooking Thunder River. The snow changed from the dry blowing dust of winter into a heavy mass that was perfect for rolling giant balls or packing fist-sized snowballs to hurl at unsuspecting friends. Snowball fights always broke out in the afternoons when the sun was at its peak—when the snow was heavy and easily packed. Conditions were just right for another game of snow snake.

In the late afternoon the young people gathered in the snow-covered cornfields not far from the village gate, laughing and joking and throwing snow. They stood near a sharp-nosed log, straight and smooth, the thickness of a man's upper leg. The members of the group pointed in different directions, talking loudly and moving their arms in a throwing motion, before agreeing on a path over sloping ground in the direction of the sun. Once they agreed, they rolled a few large snowballs, placed them in a row and shaped them into a long pile that began at knee height and sloped gradually to the level of the surrounding snow. Then they carved a groove across the top of the pile wide enough for the snow snakes.

Willow and Otter lifted the nose of the pointed log and tied two braided ropes around it. When the ropes were secure, the entire

— Snow Snake —

group hoisted the log into the trough and slowly pulled it down the slope and through the wet snow, leaving a long slithering snake track stretching across the field. A few of the young women and girls rubbed it with their mittens until it was as smooth as a frozen lake. It wasn't ready yet, but after a cold night it would be perfect.

Otter and some of the older boys stood beside the snow pile in the glowing light of the setting sun, pretending to throw things along the trough, while the younger boys mimicked their movements. Willow and Loon stamped out a circular track in unbroken snow for the fox and the goose game and they were soon joined by Otter and the others, chasing after each other around the circle, screaming and shaking with laughter, trying not to step off track and trying not to get tagged on it. It wasn't long before they shed their warm cloaks, fur hats and mittens and ran through the snow as if dressed for summer.

The evening air grew colder as the yellow-tinted clouds turned first to orange and then to red, but it was not until the colour had disappeared completely that they left the field and returned to their longhouses.

Loon had a large collection of wooden snow snakes spread out beside the fire inside the smoky longhouse. Some he had made himself. Others he had won. They were all different lengths, but most were about as long as his legs. Only a few reached his chin. No matter what length, they were all carefully carved and charred with geometric patterns to look like real snakes. His favourites were carved flat on the bottom, with bulges at one end to resemble the heads of water snakes and tails that tapered to a point. His most prized specimens had tiny shiny black stones hammered into the heads, giving them the searching look of real snake eyes. Loon considered himself one of the best snow snake carvers in the village, but his throwing didn't match his carving. He lost most of his collection each year when he played.

Otter had only a few snakes, all of them sleek and simply made and they always performed well. He pointed to one of Loon's most prized snakes.

"Those carvings look great," he said, "but the detailing will slow them down. Mine don't have any edges or cracks, nothing to catch on the ice. That's why I'm going to win."

"Yours are boring," replied Loon, holding a snake over the fire to make brown blotches along its entire length. "And they're no faster than mine."

"No? Feel the edges of yours," said Otter, running his fingers along the head of Loon's longest and most realistic snake. "It scratches my skin and it'll do the same to the snow. They're supposed to go far, not just look good."

"You make yours how you want, and we'll see who wins."

Otter shrugged. "Mine will win."

"We'll see."

"We will."

Willow joined them at the fire with an armful of snakes wrapped in a deerskin. He unrolled them at their feet and took out his best, a slender chest-high length of basswood stripped of its bark and sanded smooth.

"This beautiful creature will leave yours far behind, wondering what happened." Willow stroked its smooth white underbelly and smiled. "And this year I have a special treatment to make it go even farther."

Loon laughed aloud. "What? Grease? I tried that last year and it doesn't work. Real snakes don't have grease on their bellies."

"He's right. Grease just slows them down," added Otter.

"I'm not talking about grease," answered Willow. "It's a *secret* treatment. You'll see tomorrow." He pointed to the snake Loon was holding over the fire. "Do a good job with that one. I'm going to win it from you."

As the sun rose above the frozen fields the players and the spectators began to gather at the head of the trough. The cold night air had made the soft snow as hard and smooth as the polished slabs of limestone along the lakeshore. Before long there was a fire burning near the starting place, where the old people stood wrapped in fur robes to keep warm while they watched the contest. A few players

— *Snow Snake* —

took practice throws and made whatever last-minute changes had to be made to their sticks before the contest began.

Lynx was the first to step up for a real throw. He felt the smooth ice in the trough and smiled. He held his best snake, a creature almost as long as he was high, with few markings apart from some charring at the head and tail.

"Stand back," he called to the old people near the fire.

"Hurry up and throw," answered Old Heron.

He took ten long paces back from the pile and gathered his thoughts, practicing his moves over and over again until the voices by the fire yelled at him to go.

Willow, Otter and Loon stood together to watch his technique.

"Watch how he flicks his wrist at the last minute," said Otter. "He does the same thing when he skips stones across water. I've seen him practice for a whole morning until he gets it just right. He can make a rock slide over the surface like a toboggan on snow—hardly any skipping at all."

"He can skip better than anyone," answered Loon in a hushed voice.

Lynx held the snake's tail with his arm low by his side and made a quick sprint toward the trough. At the last minute he flicked his wrist and let the snake go, darting down the trough like a diving water snake, sometimes climbing up on the sides as it tried to escape, farther and farther, without losing speed, past the old men, clattering on and on until finally it coasted to a stop an arrow's flight from the start, barely visible to the cheering crowds. Lynx threw his hands into the air and let out the cry of a champion. At the far end of the path, an old man caught up to the snake and planted it, tail first, in the snow where it had stopped.

Lightning, one of the young men from the Bear Clan, stepped up to challenge Lynx's opening throw. He selected a long snake with a wide, heavy body and threw off his deerskin cloak, leaving his bare chest open to the cold.

"He always throws it like a spear," said Willow. "If he gets it in the trough, it goes a long way, but he usually misses."

Lightning held the snake above his head as he ran toward the snow pile. When he released it, the snake flew through the air before landing with a loud crash on the edge of the trough, where it careened from one side to the other before finally leaping over the side and into the loose snow. A young boy ran to it and planted its head in the snow to the scornful shouts of all. Lightning ran bare-chested and crestfallen to snatch it back.

"That never works," said Otter. "He can't skip a rock either."

Wren was next with a tiny snake she had made herself. She had peeled the bark off a birch branch and then dyed the white wood with blackberry juice, creating a purple snake unlike any other. She stood close to the trough, without bothering to take a run, and let her snake fly. It slid straight down the centre with hardly any sideways movement until it came to rest. Wild cheers filled the air and other young girls lined up to take their turns.

Old Chief stood next to Old Heron, watching the players take their turns. These young people would guard the village from enemy attacks when they were old enough to fight and they would look after any of the elderly who were unable to look after themselves. To the elders, the snow snake game was a time to see how the young people moved and how they interacted. They could spot the future leaders by the way they played their games.

"This little one has strong legs like her mother," said Old Heron. "Watch how she runs—with great long strides like a doe. She was almost as much help as her mother last harvest."

A young boy ran in front of the players and hurled an icicle down the trough, yelping like a dog when it smashed to bits.

"He's a handful," said Old Heron, as the young men swept away the broken bits of ice. "He makes his mother crazy."

Old Chief laughed. "Sometimes that's a good thing. He'll be fearless in battle one day."

"Perhaps," she replied. "But the fearless ones usually die in battle."

Old Chief pulled his beaverskin robes around his neck. "Or they're taken prisoner and forced to become the enemy."

— *Snow Snake* —

"Sniveling dogs!" snapped Old Heron, as she turned and spat in the snow.

Brown Bat, the adopted warrior, approached the snake track and bent down to feel how slick it was. He pulled a red snake dyed with bloodroot from his sleeve and held it above his head for all to see. There were cheers and jeers from every direction, as he walked back from the track.

"He's not a very good thrower," said Old Heron. "He learned from the enemy."

"He's one of us now," said Old Chief.

"Yes, I know. And he's respected by everyone in the village. But that doesn't mean he can throw."

Brown Bat raced toward the snake track and hurled his red snake so wildly that it missed the track altogether and disappeared under the snow.

"You see?" asked Old Heron.

"He has other skills," replied Old Chief with a smile.

Brown Bat didn't bother to find his red snake. He left it for the youngest boys and walked over to join Old Chief and Old Heron looking dejected.

"I'll get it right one day," he said with a sigh.

"You have other skills," laughed Old Heron.

"Moose," called Old Chief. "Where are your sticks?"

"You want to beat me again?" asked Moose, as he clasped Old Chief's shoulder. He smiled at Old Heron as she grabbed his arm and pulled him toward her.

"I usually let you win," laughed Old Chief.

"The young people will beat you both this year," said Old Heron. "Look. Here's Loon—one of the bear hunters."

Loon unwrapped his most decorative specimen and everyone pushed forward to see the beautiful and realistic creation.

"It's a real snake," cried a young girl. "He dug it up from the frozen ground!"

"He can't use a real one!" shouted Wren, as she touched its skin and rubbed its vacant eye.

Loon let out his piercing call—the sound of a solitary loon at dawn—and laughed to himself as he prepared for the throw. Though he was shorter than his friends and lighter, he was powerful for his size. He sprang forward like an arrow out of a bow, releasing the snake by his side. Straight down the trough it rattled before coming to a stop just past a group of young boys, who whooped and shouted as it went by. It had gone a long way, but it was still far from Lynx's stick.

"He's one who'll be fearless in battle," said Old Heron.

"He's already a fearless young hunter," said Brown Bat. "Those boys went out with their pointed sticks and came back with a bear."

"We came close to losing him to the bear," said Moose. "If he wasn't so light, he would have been eaten."

"Yes," said Old Chief. "And he and my grandson saved Otter from freezing to death. Here goes Willow now."

"He's got the same lanky shape his father had," said Moose. "He's like a snare—taut and ready to be sprung."

Willow moved up to take his turn. By this time the sun had started to melt the ice and the trough was beginning to glisten. He unwrapped his snake to reveal a two-headed monster with one at each end and no tail.

"Is that your secret?" asked Loon, laughing wildly. "Two heads? It won't know which way to go!"

Otter came over to look at the two-headed snake and saw that both heads were slightly raised, like a real snake.

"The tails slow them down," said Willow. "This one doesn't have a tail."

"How do you know which way to throw it?" asked Loon.

"You'll see." He stepped backward from the snow pile, counting his steps as he went. Not only was he a fast runner, but a champion rock skipper as well, and his long arms gave him a throw far more powerful than other young men with his build.

"Watch him," Moose whispered to Old Heron. "He throws just like his father, too. When he's a grown man, he'll be hard to beat."

"He plays stickball the same way," said Old Heron. "His feet never touch . . ."

Like a startled rabbit, Willow leaped into action with his long legs moving faster and faster and his knees rising higher with each step. At the edge of the snow pile he bent at the waist like a sapling, and with a deft flick of his wrist he fired off the two-headed snake. Above the ice it sailed before touching gently on the surface and blasting straight down the trough, without the slightest sideways rocking—past the sticks of the children and the old people, past the other sticks of young warriors bigger and stronger than him, until it finally slid to a stop—just behind Lynx's stick.

"The same throw as his father," said Moose.

"I thought he was going to beat Lynx," replied Old Chief. They watched as an old woman planted one of the two heads into the snow.

"I'm going to ask him how he does that," said Brown Bat, as he turned and ran toward Willow.

Otter and Loon caught up to Willow, hoisted him on their shoulders and ran in circles, with young children cheering and dogs barking. When they were exhausted they threw him into the snow.

"He and his friends will soon be old enough to join you when you battle the People from Across the Lake," said Old Heron.

"You're right. They're too young, yet," said Moose. "More trouble than they're worth. But in a year or two we may want to take them with us."

Old Chief looked nervously up at Moose. He leaned backward so he could see directly into his eyes. "They're just boys. How many winters have they had?" He made some scratches in the snow, reciting the events from the past as he did, and then counted them. "Is it twelve or thirteen winters?"

"At least thirteen," said Old Heron. "And they'll soon be ready to fight."

"The older I get, the younger they seem," replied Old Chief.

"You were in battle at that age," said Moose.

Old Chief shuddered and breathed deeply before he replied. "I was. But I was too young. I still have deep scars."

"We all do," said Moose, moving toward the snow snake track. Old Chief and Old Heron followed him for a close look.

Moose was the last one to throw. His snake was an unadorned pole, scraped down carefully to resemble a straight arrow the full length of Moose's massive body. It was by far the heaviest of all the snakes thrown that day. If he could land his stick accurately, he would certainly challenge Lynx. He ran to the pile and with an agile flip he launched the snake along the trough. It was so heavy that it bounced along the track, more and more violently until it leaped out of the trough, almost impaling an old woman standing at the edge of the track, before disappearing into the snow.

Moose laughed in his usual deep laugh and turned away from the snake. "The beavers will find it in the spring," he bellowed. He turned to Lynx and raised his hand. "Lynx is the champion again this year. He wins all the snakes!"

Lynx leaped onto the snow pile and shouted to everyone in sight. "I'm going to give my winnings away this year. Take back your snakes as my gift. Next year I may be on the losing end of this game."

With that, everyone ran past Lynx to collect their sticks and each one touched him or gave him a word of thanks.

"Let me see that two-headed snake," said Loon, as he snatched it from Willow. "I can't see how a tail could slow down a snake. Real snakes don't have two heads, and they can move fast enough. How did you get that to go so far?"

"Did you grease it?" asked Otter.

"Grease doesn't work," laughed Willow. "You know that."

"Nice throwing," said Lynx. "Next time you'll beat me for sure."

He looked at Willow with his two-headed snake and laughed. "Do you know that your father threw his snakes just the way you do, and he was usually the winner. You'll be the same way when you get some meat on your bones."

"Meat on his bones," repeated Old Chief, turning toward the village with Old Heron beside him. "He's just a boy."

"Boys turn into men," said Old Heron.

"I know," said Old Chief. "But I can't stand the thought of my grandson face to face with the enemy. He's too young."

As they neared the village he stopped abruptly and grabbed Old Heron by the arm. "What if he sees the hideous things I saw?"

– CHAPTER FIVE –

An Unwanted Message

Each day as the sun climbed higher in the sky, the air became warmer. Large cracks appeared in the frozen lake where water seeped through onto the ice. No person dared to walk there now, but the brave foxes still tiptoed across until it could no longer support them. One night a gale from the north smashed the last remaining ice into bits and carried it away. Although the rivers were still frozen, the lake was open again.

Every year at this time the Wanderer arrived at Thunder River. He travelled south in the cold season to gather special things that could only be found there, and then he returned to trade his goods. After a few days of rest he would head farther north to gather things that could only be found there. Everyone called him the Wanderer because he didn't appear to belong to any group.

With each journey the Wanderer dressed more outrageously than the year before. He decorated himself with long feathers of birds from far away and was tattooed from head to toe. He also spoke many languages. Most surprisingly, the Wanderer had no enemies. He traded with the People from Across the Lake as easily as he traded in the village by Thunder River. The village elders welcomed him every spring because of his goods, but mostly because he had so much news. He knew which areas had been hit by floods or famines—and he knew about wars in faraway lands.

The Wanderer travelled with his only known relative, his young dark-eyed daughter, Oriole. She had the Wanderer's power to remember everyone she met, along with everything there was to know about them, and she had her father's amazing ability with languages. She could change from one to another, as though they were all her mother tongue. Some said her true mother was the strange canoe in which she had spent her life—an unusually wide canoe, originally made of silvery white birchbark but patched now with yellow birch from the north and gray river birch from the south. There was even a section at the front of the canoe patched with elm, like the bark used by the People from Across the Lake. This patchwork was stitched together with spruce roots, its seams covered with pitch from distant pine trees. It was a collage of colours, textures and memories from a life on the move.

The Wanderer and his daughter arrived near Thunder River on a cold day soon after the ice had gone out. Wet snow had fallen all day. As they paddled toward the village, people left the warmth of their longhouses and ran to the shore to meet them. Oriole slipped out of the canoe into the shallow icy water to guide it toward a mud flat. Then her father stepped grandly onto the shore with a soggy mitten raised above his head to greet his many friends. With their help he unloaded his colourful canoe and gently lifted it to the low bank at the edge of the river.

Oriole stood quietly nearby, tired and wet after a long day on the frigid lake. She was tall and slender, except for her broad shoulders, sculpted by a lifetime of paddling. She wore an oiled deerskin cloak lined with black squirrel and decorated with paint and porcupine quills. Her legs were covered with beaverskin leggings, lined with the soft under-fur. They were soaked on the outside, but dry and warm on the inside. Her long black hair flowed down her back from beneath a soft white rabbitskin hat. She had dotted tattoos on her face and, as always, wore orange and black oriole feathers in her hair.

The Wanderer's goods were wrapped tightly in skins to keep them dry. Some of the villagers helped him take the packs up the hill, and everyone greeted him eagerly when he passed. Slowly he and his daughter made their way to the longhouse of the Loon Clan where they always stayed during their visits, even though they weren't members of that clan.

Sometimes the Wanderer told them about his own clan in the south named after a strange bird with long wings and a skin sack under its lower beak. He explained that the bird would never fly to a place where there was snow, so he had to be part of the Loon Clan when he was among them.

When the Wanderer and Oriole had eaten and changed into dry clothing they went to meet with Old Chief and the elders in the village longhouse. The Wanderer was decorated in his finest pink feathers and wore a long robe made of the skins of mountain lions. The elders seated by the fire smiled expectantly when he joined them. His visit was always a special event.

Looking at the elders, he smiled in his own odd way and placed a bundle on a cattail mat where he stood. Without saying a word he started singing in a high-pitched voice in a language they did not understand. As he sang he shuffled around the fire. Oriole watched from a distance, quietly singing along with her father.

Suddenly the Wanderer came to a stop with his arms held toward the sky. He stood silently before beginning his song again—this time in the language of his hosts—in a low soothing voice, shaking a turtle-shell rattle as he sang. It was a song they knew well, about the stars and the rain that fell from the sky. He sang about the gifts of the land and the rivers, once again moving slowly around the fire. One by one the elders rose to join him, singing and dancing in the flickering light.

Oriole sat in the shadows. Some of the young women in the longhouse approached her and stroked her white fox robe, its long fine hairs as soft as a rabbit pelt. They talked and laughed quietly as the elders sang and danced.

At the end of his song the Wanderer stood motionless until Old Chief motioned for him to sit down.

"You are very generous to take us in out of the rain and give us sustenance," said the Wanderer to Old Chief. "My daughter and I have travelled a long way."

Even though Old Chief was eager to hear the news from far away, he didn't rush. He preferred to savour his time with the Wanderer. He reached for his fire pouch and filled his pipe with tobacco for the occasion. It was going to be a good night.

"We've come from the warm south," said the Wanderer with a wave of his hand toward the lake. "The people who live there don't know how to make snowshoes." The elders laughed at the thought of such strange people.

"They don't know what a toboggan is," he added. The chiefs played along in mock disbelief.

"Of course, they don't need snowshoes or toboggans . . . because there is no snow there."

"No snow?" said the chief of the Wolf Clan. "They must have snow in the winter."

"No more than the dust on a path," replied the Wanderer. His daughter mouthed the words. She had heard them many times before, as had most of the elders.

"I have something for each of you," said the Wanderer, as he untied the bundle and spread it on a mat in front of him. He emptied a small bag to reveal a pile of gleaming pink discs the size of thumbnails, carved from conch shells, each with a hole drilled in its centre. The elders had rarely seen anything so beautiful. The Wanderer distributed a few shells to each of them as thanks for safe passage through their land, and the elders graciously accepted, knowing they would make wonderful gifts to pass on to others. They also marvelled at the green tail feathers from the jay with the blue face, and the long pink wing feathers from the pink herons in the south.

"I've been told that the southern herons are strange birds," said the Wanderer, holding a pink feather for all to see. "Their eggs are as white as snow and the chicks are white, too." He looked around to prompt the question.

"How do they become pink?" asked the chief of the Bear Clan.

"How does any creature get to be the colour it is?" asked Old Chief without waiting for the Wanderer to answer. "How do people in different lands get to be the way they are? That's the way the Creator makes them. Some creatures can change their colours, and so can some people. They can become other people, just as easily as a white bird can change into a pink bird."

The Wanderer laughed a knowing laugh. "That may be so," he said, passing the feathers to the elders. "When the chicks eat little pink crayfish they turn into pink birds."

"You are very generous," said Old Chief. "Tell us where you and your daughter are heading next."

"We will follow the lakes and rivers as the ice clears," said the Wanderer. "In three days we will take the overland trail to the Lake of Islands and then go by canoe to the Vast Cold Lake, far to the north, to trade with the people there. I know a place where they find copper in the ground and turn it into fishhooks and jewellery. In the autumn, after we visit the People of the Lakes, we will take some copper back to the warm south."

"Tell us news from the south," urged the chief of the Wolf Clan. "What wars have been fought there?"

The Wanderer looked concerned about the answer he would have to give. "Very few," he replied. The clan chiefs sat silent, waiting for him to continue.

"When I was young, the People from Across the Lake were at war all the time. They fought with the other people who lived near them on the far side of the Beautiful Lake—and lost many warriors. People starved or froze to death when their villages were destroyed in the winter. But that was a long time ago."

The Wanderer looked over at his daughter, who sat surrounded by the young women of the village. They continued to talk and laugh quietly so they would not disturb the elders. He lowered his voice. "That has changed. Now they have a pact of peace, like ours.

All the people across the lake—all five nations—have peace, and the peace is holding. They call it a 'league'."

He gazed at the clan chiefs one by one. "Now they are wary of people from outside the league. One nation guards the western door and another guards the eastern door. They meet together in the territory of the central nation on the shore of a Finger Lake. If they are attacked by people from outside the pact, they will defend as one. They assemble enormous numbers of warriors from every village within the league and overrun their enemies, forcing them to flee. Then they take over their territories."

"We have seen some strange things in our land," said Old Chief. "The People from Across the Lake are scouting in our forests—two or three together. We have seen their tracks in the snow. Three of our young hunters killed a bear that had an arrowhead in its neck, but it was not our arrowhead. It was the kind used by our enemies."

"Sometimes we cannot see them or hear them, but we feel their presence among us," added the chief of the Beaver Clan. "It feels like a thunder storm approaching and we know what the storm will bring."

Willow, Otter and Loon entered the longhouse quietly and stood beside a small fire near the entrance. Loon glanced at Oriole.

"What has she got on now?" he whispered. "She looks more like her strange father every time she comes here." He blurted out a loud laugh. Otter slapped his hand over Loon's mouth to stifle the noise. Old Chief glanced toward the source of the interruption.

"The bear hunters have arrived," called Old Chief. "Willow, come here beside me with your friends."

As they passed, Oriole turned to look at them. "Willow," she whispered to herself. Her eyes followed him.

The three young warriors stood in front of Old Chief, staring at the Wanderer's many tattoos.

"Willow, tell our guest about the bear you boys killed," said Old Chief. "Now speak well, so everyone can hear the story." Oriole left the other young women and stood closer to the chiefs so she could hear.

Stepping forward, Willow studied the faces of the elders before he began. He spoke slowly and clearly, reciting the events of the hunt from beginning to end. He stressed the heroic feats of Otter, swimming under the ice, and the bravery of Loon, attacking the bear with the club.

When he had finished, Old Chief asked Otter to tell how he had escaped from the bear, so the young hunter described the shock of the icy water and the darkness under the ice. The elders held their breath as he described how difficult it was to swim in his winter clothing and his agonizing search for an opening in the ice.

Next, Loon told about shooting the bear with a pointed stick and running to the ice where the bear couldn't follow. He described how he pulled Otter from the water and slid him to shore where they kept him warm beside a fire, and how Lynx cut the foreign arrow out of the bear's flesh.

"And now they are bear hunters!" said Old Chief. Willow, Otter and Loon retreated into the shadows. This time when they passed her, Oriole looked straight into Willow's eyes. Loon didn't miss the piercing stare.

"Why were you staring at her like that?" he asked Willow.

"I wasn't staring at anyone," he replied uneasily. Otter and Loon taunted him as they left the longhouse.

The Wanderer looked solemnly at Old Chief. "What will you do about these incursions on your land?" he asked.

Old Chief held up his hand before anyone else answered and signalled to the War Chief.

"We will continue to defend our homeland, as we have done since the beginning," Moose replied. "If they attack us, we will attack them—and we will always be more vicious to them than they are to us. We will chase them away. They will run from our lands—never to return."

The clan chiefs cried out in support of the War Chief. "Defend our people!" "Blood for blood!"

As the noise increased, Oriole slipped quietly out of the long-house and soon found Willow walking by himself. She ran through the puddles to catch up to him. Hearing footsteps, he turned around and was struck again by Oriole's immobilizing stare.

"You are Willow," she said.

"Yes."

"You've changed since last year."

He didn't respond.

"Your mother is Orchid."

"Yes."

Oriole moved closer.

Willow stepped back. "Why are you asking me these questions?"

"Don't be afraid," she laughed. "I have a message for you from far away, but you can't tell anyone." Willow looked at her blankly.

"Do you agree? You won't tell anyone?" she demanded, moving even closer.

"Why not?" he replied, leaning backwards.

"Don't be afraid," she said. "It's a message . . ." She hesitated. "A message from your father."

"Then you have the wrong person," he answered with a look of relief.

"No, I haven't. I can see his face in yours," she said, staring at him with her penetrating eyes. A light rain began to fall and droplets trickled down their faces.

"You're wrong. My father was killed by the People from Across the Lake when I was young. You have the wrong person." He turned and took a step, but she grabbed him by the arm and spun him around again. He had never been treated that way by a woman—young or old—and could not speak.

"Your father isn't dead," Oriole said bluntly. "He lives in a village across the lake where he was captured many years ago. Not killed—captured. He was adopted to take the place of a warrior who was killed in battle by your people." She let his arm go. "Do you want to hear the message?" she asked.

"No. I don't want to hear anything more. You're wrong about my father and wrong about me," he said forcefully, moving toward her. "And don't ever tell that lie to anyone again. He was a courageous warrior, not a coward. You can't destroy his memory by saying these things!"

He turned and ran through the puddles toward the village entrance, zigzagged through the gate, and headed down the hill to the river. He had to be alone to think about Oriole's hurtful words.

He followed the river upstream to the narrows. The river was still frozen on the surface but the water rushed violently underneath. The heavy rain had caused the level to rise and the ice was being pushed up in strange, sharp shapes.

How could Oriole come to his village and say these horrible things about his father? How could she accuse him of being one of the enemy? If this lie was repeated to anyone else, his father's memory would be destroyed forever. How could she be so cruel—saying these things to the son of a warrior killed in battle?

In the growing darkness he sat on a wet rock beside the river. Once again, the rain was coming down heavily and the air was cold and misty. He gazed at the river and saw cracks appearing in the ice with water gushing through. As the ice began to heave and groan, he watched for the spirit of the river—the spirit that always gave him strength. But a dark spirit continued to seethe deep inside of him. Oriole was wrong. He knew that. He had been told stories about his father all his life and was sure he could never be one of the enemy.

The river convulsed with a thunderous roar and a horrendous thought made Willow fall to the wet ground in a shivering mass. What if the words Oriole had spoken were true? What would happen if his father was a traitor, instead of a warrior who had died bravely in battle? Then what would become of him? He would be the son of a traitor instead of the son of a brave warrior. What would he do if his father was alive, trying to contact him?

With a sudden explosion, the ice on the river shattered into thick slabs that were hurled toward the narrows by the turbulent waters. Willow could feel the danger as the water level began to rise, and he realized that the spirit of the river was telling him to run to higher ground. The moment he stood up and moved away from the shore, massive slabs of ice began to block the narrows, damming the river. The flooding was instantaneous. By the time Willow had climbed up the hill, the entire river valley was underwater. Ice and water tumbled over the trees, crushing them like twigs. He stood watching in awe. Never had he seen the spirit of the river so angry. Never had he seen such destruction.

Willow's thoughts caused the same destruction inside of him. He had been trained to withstand torture inflicted by his enemies and he knew he could bear physical pain. But this pain was new to him. This was a kind of suffering he had not been trained to endure.

– CHAPTER SIX –

Frost Bite

The first blue heron arrived while the snow was still on the ground. It wandered through the soggy marshes near the mouth of Thunder River looking for creatures stirring in the frigid waters of early spring. The first person to see the heron was, as always, Old Heron. As soon as the snow began to melt, she was out roaming through the slushy hills above the marshes, waiting for it to arrive. When she finally saw the familiar long legs and slender neck, she returned to the village, beaming with pride, to share the news. A small group of women gathered around her in the muddy snow outside the longhouse, while she described the weary bird, looking tattered and thin after the winter.

"It will not be long now until we start planting," said Old Heron. "I know your backs are still sore from the harvest, but we have to get ready."

"My back is aching," joked Loon's mother, Moonlight, "but not from the harvest—from too much dancing!"

"We had far too many celebrations this winter," laughed Orchid, bending over with her hand on her back. "I may never walk straight again!"

Old Heron sniffed loudly and went on, "We have to make some new hoes this year. The old bones are worn out."

"My old bones are worn down to nothing," said Moonlight, to the guffaws of the other women.

"I wish you were that energetic in the fields," said Old Heron.

"Oh, I am," retorted Moonlight. "You should see me dance in the fields!"

The other women turned away, clinging to each other with laughter.

"Soon we will have to dig up the seeds from under the floor," continued Old Heron. "Let's hope the mice have left some for us."

"We can get our boys to dig them up," said Orchid, trying to be serious.

"You mean our *men*!" said Moonlight. "They're bear hunters now. We can't call them boys anymore."

"Yes, our *men* killed a bear," said Otter's mother, Water Lily.

"With pointed sticks!" added Moonlight, just as Willow, Otter and Loon came through the village gate. They saw their mothers gathered with Old Heron and ran over to them.

"We saw a blue heron!" the boys shouted at the same time. "Down in the marshes." They looked at Old Heron, waiting for her reaction.

"We were just talking about that," she said. "I wonder if it was the same one I saw this morning."

The young bear hunters looked at each other with deflated smiles. The other women tried not to laugh, but not Old Heron, who cawed like a hungry crow.

"Let's go," said Otter, and they ran inside the longhouse with the old woman's laughter ringing in their ears.

A large pot of corn soup stood beside the fire with bits of dried fish and roots floating at the top. The young hunters helped themselves to a small amount, since there was not much left. As they were eating, they heard a creak from a loft near the fire. The Toothless Hunter swung his legs over the edge of his bed and slowly lowered himself to the floor. He was dressed in a robe made of muskrat fur, tattered leggings, and undecorated moccasins. Although his ears were pierced, he wore no earrings, and no other jewellery of any kind. Deep valleys crossed his forehead and his eyes had the look of a hunted animal. His thin gray hair hung loosely down his back.

Without saying anything, the Toothless Hunter shuffled through the longhouse to the pot of soup where he took as much as Willow, Otter and Loon combined. He even reached his hand into the hot soup pot and tried unsuccessfully to snatch a piece of floating fish—until he burned himself. After he had licked his stinging fingers, he wiped his wet hand in his hair and wolfed down his soup. On the way back to his loft he tripped over a sleeping dog, sending it yelping behind a basket. As the boys watched, the Toothless Hunter belched, climbed back up on his loft, and disappeared behind a hanging deerskin.

"What makes him like that?" Loon asked in a low voice.

"My mother says he used to trade in faraway places," whispered Willow. "But he always came back empty-handed."

"He comes back empty handed now whenever he hunts," said Otter.

"That's true," said Willow. "I've never seen him bring back a thing."

"I've seen him accept gifts," said Otter, "but I've never seen him give anything to anybody. How can anyone live that way?" He looked at the others with a bewildered expression on his face.

"I wonder what spirits are haunting him?" asked Loon, as he gathered his bow and quiver. "Come on," he said, before they could answer. "Let's go outside."

Each morning for the next few days Old Heron went to the distant fields with other old women to see when they would be ready for planting. They could be seen poking sticks into the ground and squeezing the soil in their fingers. When the sun was high Old Heron wandered by herself into the woods beyond the cornfields, looking for the first flowers of spring.

As the days passed the snow melted and warm breezes carried earthy smells into the village. At night the oldest women gathered by an open fire.

"We'll be planting on the day following the full moon," said a withered old woman from the Turtle Clan.

"So will we," said several of the other elderly women.

"The full moon is only three nights away," said Old Heron in an anxious voice. "It is much too early to plant."

"The fields are ready," said an old woman from the Wolf Clan.

"They're still too wet," replied Old Heron. She looked around at her friends for support, but found none.

"If you wait too long, you will miss the season," warned a woman from the Beaver Clan.

"If you plant in three days, the frost will kill your corn," answered Old Heron. The others were not persuaded.

"I've already picked my best seeds," said the old woman. "I have them soaking near the fire. In a few days they will be sprouting."

"The dog-tooth violets are still blooming in the woods," said Old Heron. "We don't usually plant until after the marsh marigolds are out."

"There are a few by the river. There's no more danger of frost."

"I'm going to wait," said Old Heron. "I only have enough seeds to plant once."

Three nights later the full moon rose in the east above the trees on a cold still night, and a thin skin of ice formed in the bottom of footprints in the wet soil. Old Heron stood with Old Chief gazing up at the moon. Every mark of its face was visible. It seemed close enough to touch.

"The other clans are planting tomorrow," she said.

"Tomorrow?" asked Old Chief. He stared silently at the moon, but his fingers moved against his chest. "The time is right for planting," he said. "This is the fifth full moon past the day when the Great Turtle moved."

"We could still have frost," said Old Heron.

"I am sure they know what they are doing," said Old Chief. He turned to Old Heron and saw the weathered old face of the woman he had known all his life. She had been a close friend of his wife, who had died many years earlier. After a lifetime beside

Thunder River there was nothing about the land, the plants and the animals she didn't know. She had been a superb archer and she was one of the most respected elders in the village. Old Chief could not imagine her being wrong.

"Will you plant tomorrow?" he asked quietly.

"No, I will only plant once."

Old Chief stood beside her listening to the sounds of the river below. The river was still lined with large chunks of ice. On the opposite shore he could hear a beaver dragging wet saplings through the grasses. The two old friends basked in the light of the rising moon until the cold forced them back to the fire.

The next morning Old Heron waited for the women in the other houses to head for the fields, but they did not appear until after the sun was high above the trees. She watched them working, scraping the soil into low mounds, poking a hole in the centre of each one with a sharp stick, ready for the men to plant the seeds.

The women in Old Heron's longhouse watched with her from a distance.

"Don't you think we could at least prepare the mounds?" asked Fisher.

"We could, but the soil is still too damp and heavy," she answered. "It's like wet snow. Look at the way they are struggling. You saw how tired they were yesterday when they came in from the fields." Old Heron shook her head. "They could lose their entire crop."

– CHAPTER SEVEN –

Brown Bat and the Caterpillar

Willow was sitting alone beside the fire when the adopted warrior, Brown Bat, returned from a hunting trip with two rabbits hanging limp over his shoulder. When Willow made the sign of a successful hunt, Brown Bat cut the ties from one of the rabbits and handed it to him.

"Here you are, bear hunter," he said with a laugh. "It's only a modest catch, but it will give your mother something to add to the gruel you have been eating lately."

"You're a good hunter," said Willow. "We didn't see anything today."

"You and your family have always been good to me," he replied. "We help each other." Brown Bat slapped him on the shoulder and made his way to the fire pit. Willow skinned and cleaned the rabbit, threw it into the pot of thin soup warming by the fire, placed more wood on the coals, and waited for the soup to turn into a rich rabbit stew.

Not far away, Brown Bat sat roasting the other rabbit on sticks stretched above the flames. On an impulse Willow wandered over, sat down with his knees against his chest and crossed his long arms around them. Brown Bat looked at him with surprise.

"It's good of you to join me at my fire. Are you going to teach me how to throw a snow snake?" he asked. Willow smiled at him awkwardly, resting his head on his arms.

"My rabbit will soon be ready to eat," said Brown Bat, waiting patiently for his unexpected companion to say something.

Willow hesitated. "I want . . . can you tell me about your people?" he asked apprehensively.

"My people?" repeated Brown Bat. "What don't you know? You *are* my people."

"No," said Willow, raising his hand in the sign of 'stop.' "I mean your people—the People from Across the Lake."

Brown Bat nodded his head. "I thought you meant that," he said, turning the rabbit over on the sticks. "Ask me what you want. I'm not sure I can remember very much anymore."

"What do your people do with our warriors when they take them prisoner?"

"They do the same as we do with our prisoners."

"Do your people ever adopt our warriors—as we adopted you?" asked Willow.

"Yes."

"What happens to them when they're adopted?" continued Willow.

Brown Bat frowned. He avoided the question. "Why do you want to know this?" he asked.

Willow sat up straight before he answered. "I'm curious about the People from Across the Lake," he answered. "I've heard how brutal they are—how bloodthirsty and cruel. I can't imagine they would adopt one of us. Do you know that they do?"

"Yes, Willow," said Brown Bat. "I wasn't much older than you when I was captured in a battle on the islands near here. Several of us were caught that day. I was the only one who was adopted. I don't know what happened to the others." He looked at the smoke rising through the smoke holes on the roof of the longhouse.

"But that's not what you asked me about," he continued. "There were adopted warriors in most villages across the lake. I remember

— *Brown Bat and the Caterpillar* —

some of them. Most were grateful to be alive, as I am. Your people—now you're confusing me, Willow—*my* people have been good to me since I came here. It's the same with the People from Across the Lake. They're kind to the people they adopt."

"Do you want to return to your people?" asked Willow.

"I am with my people. This is where I belong. I have a beautiful, strong wife and a son. I wouldn't want to be anywhere else."

"Don't you miss the people you knew when you were a boy?"

A strange, peaceful look appeared on the adopted warrior's face. "I often think about the times I had as a boy and wonder about my close friends. They were as close to me as Loon and Otter are to you. We wouldn't be separated. We could talk to each other without speaking. And I often wonder about my parents and my family. I miss them all, but I try not to think about how much I miss them."

Willow sat quietly, trying to make sense of what Brown Bat was saying. He had one more question, but he wasn't certain how to ask it. Finally, he opened his mouth and let the words find their own way out. "Have you ever tried to send a message to the people you knew from across the lake?"

Brown Bat suddenly looked tense. He scanned the longhouse to see if anyone was listening and then moved closer to Willow before he spoke. "A caterpillar escapes from its cocoon as a different creature. It leaves the plodding world it used to know to live in the breezes—to flutter among the flowers. I have emerged from my childhood blanket to take on this new life and I can never live among the caterpillars I knew as a child. I live as the man I have become."

He put his hand on Willow's arm and held it firmly. "And remember, I prefer to have wings. Don't ever suggest to anyone that I'd rather be a caterpillar." And then Brown Bat got up to turn the roasting rabbit, not saying another word.

– CHAPTER EIGHT –

The Smell of a Field

The days passed without any work being done in the fields by Old Heron or the people in her longhouse. Instead, they made new pots for the fire from clay gathered by the river. As they worked they kept an eye on the women from the other houses who were busy in the cornfields.

Moonlight was more anxious than her sisters and began to pace through the village. Sometimes she would go to the fields and watch as the women from other clans formed the mounds and the men planted the seeds. These women added to her anxiety by asking what she and her family would do in the autumn while they were harvesting their corn.

"If you wait any longer to plant, your corn will never ripen," shouted a neighbour from the field.

"Old Heron knows what she's doing," Moonlight answered. "She says it will rain again tonight."

Despite her brave face, Moonlight was getting worried. After several days, she and her sisters spoke to Old Heron, as she sewed clothing by the light of the fire.

"I think we should join the others before we miss the time for planting," said Moonlight. "The other women are nearly finished and we haven't started."

Orchid stood listening to her sister. Old Heron also listened, but she rarely changed her mind.

"I think she's right," said Orchid. "We're going to miss the best time for planting, unless we start tomorrow."

"We can't wait all summer," added Fisher. "At least we can start soaking our seeds and put them in the ground when they're ready." Old Heron spoke to the women in a strained voice, placing her clenched fist on her heart.

"I know the others are planting now, but my gut tells me it is too early. I've felt this feeling before—a long time ago. It is a cold, strange feeling that warns me of danger." She drove her bone needle into the seam and placed the garment on a flat rock.

"I used to help my grandmother in the fields. She taught me how to grow more food than we could possibly eat—when to plant the corn, the beans and squash. She could smell the fields and tell when they were ready for the different crops. 'It is easy,' my grandmother would say, taking a deep breath in the evening when the air was still. 'Do you smell that? It is the smell of a field waiting for seeds. When you smell that you will know it's time.'

"The next year I smelled it—and the next. But the year after that I didn't smell the right smell. The others started planting anyway. I thought it was a mistake. All day long, I had a strange cold feeling in my gut—like I had swallowed shards of ice. Cold, sharp points jabbed into my stomach. It was awful and it did not go away."

Orchid clutched her stomach, as if she was in pain. Old Heron continued.

"Before long the corn seeds sprouted in the fields. They were about as high as fingers—little green leaves reaching for the sky—when a cold wind came in from the north. The chickadees sat in the middle of cedar trees with their feathers puffed up and the old women looked worried. When night came the stars were brighter than I had ever seen them.

"By the time the moon appeared, the frost was on the ground. The men built fires in the fields to burn the frost away and we spent the night gathering firewood to keep them going—but it was no use. Before dawn a heavy frost came in. It climbed up the mounds to the new shoots, freezing every leaf. By daylight the entire crop had been destroyed." Old Heron's eyes darted toward a dog licking a pot beside the fire, its long tongue reaching deep inside. "Get away from there!" she yelled, clapping her hands loudly until the dog disappeared into the darkness. Orchid placed the empty pot on a shelf out of reach. The old woman wiped her forehead with the back of her hand and then pushed her long gray hair away from her face before she continued.

"I remember walking through the fields with my mother and my grandmother in the light of the rising sun. The mounds cast long shadows across the soil and the withered leaves hung limp all around us. My grandmother wailed with grief. She knew what would happen—the winter would be lean. We would all be hungry.

"Her worst fears came true. We tried to plant more corn, but there were few seeds left—not enough for a crop. Then we planted the squash, but it rained all summer. They rotted in the fields. The crows got them all. Even the beans were woody and tasteless—like rabbit droppings." Old Heron paused. "So, the harvest was a disaster. The shelves in the longhouse were as empty as they usually are in the spring. We all knew we would suffer, but we didn't know how much. It was the coldest winter anyone could remember.

"For the first part of the winter we lived on dried berries and roots. Sometimes we had dried fish and meat. But as the cold lingered we spent more and more time in the woods, collecting any nuts the squirrels had missed. We had to boil the acorns over and over before we could eat them. I can still remember how bitter they were. I can't eat them now." Old Heron sat back from the fire and rubbed her eyes. She lifted her shoulders to ease the stiffness in her joints.

"We lived in a different place then, on a small creek along the lake. This was in the days when the People from Across the Lake were too busy fighting each other to bother with us very often. The men brought back a few deer and beaver. We even ate the

— *The Smell of a Field* —

long-bodied animals—mink and weasels. There was never enough to go around.

"In the darkest part of the winter we survived on bark—even lichens. The children were thin and listless. Some of the old people stopped eating. Not from lack of hunger—they couldn't bear to take food when the children were hungry. Many died of starvation. The rest of us nearly died of sadness.

"Sometimes I wandered by the river looking for goldenrods," she continued. "The little growths on their stalks had tiny worms inside, keeping warm in their little round homes. I would bite them open and pick the worms out. They were sweet and fleshy. They kept me alive.

"That cold feeling didn't leave me until spring, when I smelled the warm scent of a field waiting for seeds. I haven't felt it yet this spring. I go to the fields every day and take a deep breath. But I haven't smelled what I yearn for."

She reached again for the garment she had been sewing. "No, the fields are not ready. And they will not be ready until this ache leaves my gut."

At dawn Old Heron left the longhouse to stand in the fields, waiting for the signs she knew so well—but they didn't come. As the cold surrounded her, she wandered to Old Chief's favourite place above Thunder River and joined him by the fire.

"You're not ready yet, I see," said Old Chief.

"Not yet." Old Chief watched as she warmed her calloused hands, her lined face reflecting the glow of the coals. They sat silently together by the fire for some time until the Chief spoke in a low voice. "I have something I want to ask you."

"You can try," she sighed. "My thoughts are far away."

"Do you . . ." he began, pulling his robe around his shoulders. "Or . . . have you noticed my grandson acting strangely lately?" Old Heron peered at him through her small bird-like eyes. "He's a boy. They all act strangely."

"That may be," said Old Chief with a smile. "But have you noticed that his spirit seems troubled?"

"What makes you ask?"

"Brown Bat tells me he was asking questions about the enemy."

"Willow was asking questions?" she asked.

"Yes."

"What kind of questions?"

"Brown Bat didn't say."

"You didn't ask?"

"No." Old Heron sniffed the cool air. "I don't see anything strange in a boy asking questions about the enemy. He'll have to face them before long. It might be strange if he did *not* ask questions."

"Yes."

"Anyway," she continued, "I haven't noticed anything stranger than usual—but I haven't been looking. I'll keep an eye on him."

"So will I," replied Old Chief.

That night the stars shone more brightly than ever and a biting wind blew down Thunder River from the northern hills. Old Heron heard voices in the distant fields and when she looked into the starry night she saw fires burning in the cornfields. The ache in her gut told her what was happening. She called to everyone in the darkness of the longhouse to help with the fires, so the corn seedlings wouldn't be destroyed by the frost. In an instant everyone was heading for the fields along a path lit by starlight.

Willow, Otter and Loon ran into the dark forest for firewood, trying to avoid fallen logs, holes and pointed branches. There was little wood left on the forest floor, so in the dim light they searched the trees for dead branches. They carried whatever they could find to the fires.

"More wood!" the women screamed as they fanned the flames, trying desperately to spread the heat through the delicate corn shoots. The elders of the village walked among the fires, beating their drums and chanting to the Spirit of the Sky to help them. Rhythmic sounds could be heard in every direction.

It was difficult for Willow, Otter and Loon to hear the women yelling over the sounds of the rattles, drums and wailing elders, but

The Smell of a Field

they could tell what they were saying by the looks of distress on the their faces.

"Run faster!"

"More wood!"

As the night wore on and the stars rotated through the sky, the young warriors ran back and forth to the forest, groping their way through the trees and their twisting branches. They carried load after load of wood back to the fields, while the women pleaded for more. They could hear other panicked voices in the forest and the sounds of breaking branches.

With a pitiful yelp, Loon tripped on a stump and crashed to the ground. His angular face grazed a dead branch and he lay motionless until Otter and Willow helped him to his feet. Hunched over with his hands on his knees fighting for breath, he looked much smaller than he was. His narrow shoulders moved up and down until he could speak.

"Stop," he cried, spitting bits of rotten wood from his mouth. "I have to stop."

Otter and Willow remained beside him while they, too, caught their breath.

"These fires aren't doing any good," said Otter. "The heat is going right up to the sky. We're breaking our bones to heat up to the stars."

"We should plant corn . . . in the sky," gasped Loon.

"What can we do?" asked Willow. "We can't tell everyone to give up. They won't listen to us anyway."

"You're right," said Otter. "They'll fan those flames until the frost disappears or the last plant withers and dies."

Willow turned to look at the fires burning across the wide cornfields, their lights blinking on and off as distant figures rushed in front of them amid the sounds of frantic voices, drums and rattles in the cold night air.

"We're the only people standing still now," said Willow.

"One of us . . . will be impaled on a branch . . . before the sun comes up," panted Loon.

"We have to go," said Willow. "We have a big sky to heat up."

They disappeared into the forest to the sound of crashing branches and battered limbs. Old Heron was standing by a fire, fanning the heat toward the tiny plants, when she felt a gentle breeze coming from the direction of Thunder River. She looked to the west and noticed that the stars just above the horizon were hidden. Something was blocking their light.

"It must be clouds," she said to herself. "Clouds above the horizon—maybe I was wrong. How I want to be wrong!"

"More wood here, Willow!" she screamed. "Loon! Otter! Get over here with your arms full."

As the night passed, more stars disappeared. The eastern sky was beginning to turn a pale gray. Dawn was near. Before the frost had time to do its damage, low clouds and warm air came from the south and covered the cornfields with a soft blanket. As the young warriors raced by and dropped more wood on the fire, Old Heron grabbed Willow by the arm, stopping him dead. His friends stopped too, as though they were tethered to him. She held Willow without saying anything and pointed at the low clouds creeping across the sky.

With her head back, she took a deep breath through her nostrils, savouring the sweet smell of a field ready to be planted. A smile spread across her weary face.

"You can stop now," she said, and the three exhausted friends immediately collapsed on the ground beside her. "The spirits have saved us."

She took another deep breath before continuing "We'll plant today. The men will clear more land. Go home and rest now—you'll need all your strength."

– CHAPTER NINE –

A Rough Game

Moose made the best stickball rackets in the village, using the strongest hardwood he could find. He soaked the wood and heated it over a fire until it was as soft as a birch twig, then he moulded it around a frame to make a strong light stick with a loop at one end, ready to be strung into a pocket-shaped net. The champions of the game liked to use Moose's sticks because of their strength and beauty—but most of all because his sticks helped them win.

Willow watched as Moose gently bent the softened wood around the frame, slowly pulling until it had just the right curve. Then he tied it in position and left it to dry. When it was securely in place, he measured it against the length of his arm and then shrugged.

"This stick looks too small for me," he said, "but it's just right for you, so you can use it."

"I can use it?"

"I know it's not strung yet, but your mother can string it for you," he said. "She sings while she works and her songs are interlaced into the netting. Then it will sing to you as you play."

Moose stood back, brushed his long dark hair away from his face, and admired his work. The curved stick would be ready in a few days. "You have another, don't you?" he asked Willow.

"I have my old one."

"If you get it, we can throw the deerskin around."

Willow ran off and returned with a battered relic with frayed netting.

"That won't do for a young champion," laughed Moose. "This year or next you may be able to join in the games without getting killed, but you'll have to know what you're doing."

Moose went to his longhouse and uncovered a badly scuffed ball and a pair of finely made sticks. They were light but strong, and each pocket was perfectly shaped, like a cupped hand.

"This is what you'll have in a few days," said Moose. "It will fit you like your own moccasin." He led Willow into the fields behind the village and tossed the ball to him.

"You know how to catch and throw already, so I want to show you how to be as quick as a cat. You have the long arms of a great player. Now, stand by that tree and throw the ball to me as hard as you can."

Willow tossed the ball into the air a few times to get the feel of the stick. It was much longer than the one he had had since childhood and it sang to him as he swung it through the air. Moose was standing with his thick legs spread apart, ready for the ball. Willow raised the stick high above his head and whipped it at Moose as hard as he could. Moose snagged it and in one swift movement hurled it back. The ball was speeding toward Willow's head so quickly that he couldn't hope to stop it, so he ducked and let it soar across the field into the long grass.

"That was too fast!" he yelled, as he ran after the ball.

"Let's start again," said Moose. "Throw it to me and be ready when it comes back."

Willow put all his weight behind the ball and sent it speeding at Moose. This time Moose held it before he flung it back. They volleyed the ball back and forth, but each time Moose threw it he moved a step closer to Willow.

"Don't move backward," he called. The ball came back more quickly as the distance between Moose and Willow shrank. Soon they were only a few strides apart and Willow had to move quickly

— A Rough Game —

to keep up with Moose. Finally he caught the ball and threw it into the grass at his feet. "Stop!" he shouted. "I can't go that fast."

"You're as quick as a cat now," said Moose. "I won't be able to teach you much. Come on. We'll try passing in the trees."

They walked over toward a grove of tall, thin maples and again Moose tossed the ball over to Willow.

"This game is the little brother of war," he said. "All the skills you learn playing stickball will be used in battles with the enemy. The best stickball players are always the best warriors, so when you learn the game remember you're learning the skills for fighting."

Moose stood tall and still in the middle of the grove of trees. "You must be aware of everything around you when you play the game—and when you're in battle. Stand over there." Willow stood among the crowded grove of maple trees with their leaves high above him and Moose flung the ball.

"Send it back now."

Willow found a path through the trees and hurled it back.

Moose took a few steps and returned it.

"Follow me." he called. Willow took a step forward and whipped the ball back. "Good! Now keep up with me."

They walked on, throwing the ball between the trunks as they moved. "Keep up," urged Moose again, as he broke into a slow trot. Willow followed along not far from him. "Try not to crash into a tree," called Moose. "If you hit one, make sure it's smaller than you."

Willow launched a ball toward Moose. Whack! The ball hit a tree.

"Keep going," shouted Moose, as he scooped the ball out of the leaves and sent it flying through the woods to Willow. "Watch in front of you." At that instant Moose ran straight into a thin dead tree. The impact snapped it off just above his head and he crashed down on the lower part with his stick still firmly in his grip. The top part of the tree then came down like a spear and stuck in the ground by his feet.

"That could have gone right through me," he said. Before the dead tree stopped swaying, Moose was on his feet again, winded but not hurt.

— *Enemy Arrows* —

"You are doing well so far, Willow," he gasped. "Let's keep moving!" Moose led the way with Willow trailing behind.

"Good thing that tree was dead," joked Willow, "or I'd be carrying you back to the village."

Moose had just enough breath to squeeze out a laugh.

They ran through the woods, passing the ball. Moose ran faster and faster and Willow did his best not to trail behind, while keeping a close watch on the path ahead of him. At last Moose came to stop beside a small stream. They were both out of breath.

"Let's rest here," said Moose, leaning down to take a drink from the stream. Far in the distance they could see thin slivers of smoke from the village fires.

"I can see you're a fast runner," said Moose. "You'll learn to run like a swallow flies—with sudden turns and near misses, but never any accidents. Birds have eyes on the sides of their heads and can see everything around them. We have to use our forward-facing eyes to do the same thing."

He paused for another drink from the stream. "Sometimes we have to run blind through the trees. We glance ahead and remember what's there. Then we turn away to throw the ball and keep running without looking where we're going. We can't see with our eyes when we do that, but we can see with our memory. That's what you do when you play the game. You use your eyes to throw and catch—and you use your memory to guide you."

"Is that what you do in battle?" asked Willow. Moose breathed deeply.

"You need to think quickly when you're in battle to stay alive," he replied. "You have to be able to move without looking straight ahead because you're too busy watching for the enemy coming from the sides. You know where your friends are by the sound of their footsteps and you can read their thoughts."

He threw the ball to Willow again. "You'll be a great player like your father. You move the same way he did—with the same combination of speed and agility." Willow hurled it back at Moose. "And you'll be a great warrior like your father, too."

— *A Rough Game* —

"If my father was a great warrior, I'll do my best to be like him," said Willow, trying to push any lingering doubts from his mind.

"Oh, he was one of the best. One of the best! Don't ever doubt that."

"What's that?" whispered Willow, pointing to a distant figure moving in the trees. He crouched down and signalled to Moose to do the same. The shadowy shape disappeared behind a clump of trees.

– CHAPTER TEN –

Deadfall

Moose signed for Willow to follow him and they climbed up to a ridge, making their way along the high ground in the direction of the moving figure. They could see it disappear and reappear behind the trees, moving with an awkward gait. Because they were armed only with their sticks, they knew they couldn't challenge an armed intruder, but if this was a spy they would track him until dark and then ambush him while he slept. Moose moved through the trees, keeping low to the ground with Willow behind him.

"Down!" motioned Moose, as he collapsed to the ground. Willow fell without a sound. They lay silent and still in the cool forest. Moose slowly raised his head, trying to find the stranger, but he was gone from sight. He knew that the person they were stalking could be stalking them, if they had been seen. A cunning enemy could easily double back behind his pursuers and surprise them from behind. He scanned the trees and fields for any sign of movement but all was quiet. Only a few squirrels moved through the leaves.

"We've lost him," said Moose in a low voice. "He may have seen us when he turned around. We'll have to move ahead and try to find him. Keep your eyes wide open and look behind you in case he's doubled back. Remember, we're exposed and unarmed."

Moose glanced ahead for an instant and then ran through the trees, looking beside and behind him, heading in the direction where they had last seen the mysterious figure, but he couldn't see anyone. On the highest part of the ridge he suddenly came to a stop—so nimbly that Willow almost crashed into him. Below them, at the edge of a creek, was an elderly man lying under a precariously angled log. He saw Moose and Willow approach.

"Don't come any closer!" shouted the man. "Or I'll be flattened."

Moose put his arm in front of Willow. "It's Deadfall Hunter. He's under a trap." They didn't move. The man struggled out from beneath the log, pushed himself to his feet with his right arm, and walked toward them with a heavy limp. His left arm drooped by his side.

"You two came at the wrong time," he said with a wide smile. "I was just setting the trap. The log almost fell on my head. I was almost my own prey." He brushed some dead leaves from his leggings.

"You'd be a good catch," laughed Moose. "Lots of fat on those old bones."

"I saw a mink here a few days ago, so I brought a trout from the river to tempt it into my trap. The mink will be back soon. It can smell the trout no matter how far away it is. When it yanks the fish, the log will crash on top of it—as it nearly did on me—and I'll have another mink pelt to keep me and my beautiful wife warm in the winter." He led them over to a pile of furs draped over a log.

"Look at these," the old man said, holding the furs high. "I don't have to race around the forest after animals the way you do. They come to me." He laughed loudly.

"My wife is here somewhere," said Deadfall Hunter, scanning the woods. "She was gathering roots in the ravine." He cupped his hands together and made the sound of an owl. They listened in silence, but there was no response. Once more he hooted into the great expanse of the forest. This time another hoot echoed from the ravine.

"That sounds like her," said Deadfall Hunter. "She'll be back soon, and she'll be happy to see you both." He sat on a fallen log and offered Willow and Moose a few strips of dried deer meat, which they gladly accepted. Perched beside him, they gnawed on the tough, but delicious, brown meat.

"This is tasty after a long run through the woods," said Moose between bites. "We were practicing passing the ball through the trees. Willow is good. He didn't crash into any trees."

"That's because I'm learning from the best player in the village," said Willow.

"Yes, I only smashed one tree to pieces. It almost skewered me, too," said Moose with a squeamish look on his face. "I'm a little out of practice."

"It's a dangerous game, Willow," said Deadfall Hunter. "You won't believe it to look at me now, but I know how it feels to run like a deer as the other players fade into the distance, and the thrill of hurling a ball at the post. That is something I'll never forget!" He hesitated, as though he had lost his wind while racing through his memories.

"But it's dangerous," he repeated. With his good arm he rubbed a gnarled bump on the shin of his left leg.

"This happened in a match against one of the teams from the north. They're great players up there. I was just a few years older than you, Willow. Our village had one of the best teams anywhere. We travelled to the northern villages for a feast—and what a celebration it was! The deer were plentiful that year and the fish were bigger and fatter than they'd ever been before. Some were as thick as a man's leg. We ate until we couldn't move. Then we talked by the fire and played games until we recovered, and ate some more. This went on for days." He stopped to savour the memories.

"Ah, there is the brightest star in the sky now," Deadfall Hunter said, pointing to a large woman coming from the woods, carrying an armful of wood lilies, deep orange with dark spots, and a basket of lily bulbs she had dug from the thickets. "Come and sit with our friends, Bright Star. Moose and Willow are listening to my tales about the game. Sit beside me, my beautiful wife."

"The game," she said with a generous smile as she approached them. "So many tales about the game."

Moose stood up to greet Bright Star. She was a strong older woman with the bearing of a Clan Mother, dressed simply in a long-fringed deerskin cloak decorated with dyed bones and shells. A triangular pattern of beads adorned the fringe of her skirt. Around her neck she wore amulets of bone and horn dyed in bright yellows and reds.

"Moose," said Bright Star. She placed her basket on the ground and then straightened to look at his imposing figure. "The strongest man in the village. And Willow—the bear hunter," she said, looking at him from head to toe. "Are you men here to help me pick flowers, or help my husband with his traps?"

Moose replied with a laugh. "Your husband catches more than anyone else. He doesn't need our help. We were just hearing about his last game."

"Willow, you look more like your father every time I see you," said Bright Star, sitting on a flat rock beside her basket. "You don't need anyone to tell you about the game—you were born to play." She took a bone knife from her basket and began peeling the thin brown skin from the lily bulbs. "Go on with your story, my champion."

Deadfall Hunter smiled. "Everyone expects a few broken fingers and some bruised bones, but this game was rougher than usual," he said. "One of the biggest players on the other team intercepted a pass aimed at me. He batted the ball to the ground and scooped it up with his stick. Then he turned toward our goalpost and ran—straight at the goal. Anyone in his way was knocked flying. I ran after him, waiting for him to throw. As he came to our goal post, he lifted his stick over his shoulder—and that was my chance. I hit his stick from behind. The ball flew out and bounced on the ground. I caught it with my stick and hurled it to Eagle Talon. He never missed a pass. The ball went far above his head, but he leapt high—higher than any man can jump without help from the spirits—and snagged it with his stick."

Deadfall Hunter grabbed a broken branch and held it high above his head with one hand.

"One hand!" he shrieked. "He whipped the ball back to me before his feet touched the ground." Deadfall Hunter tried to show what he did, but without standing up.

"By then I was racing toward the post with the biggest players on the other team close behind me. I took a few steps with the ball in the pocket, darting back and forth to lose them, but then I lost my footing. I passed across the field to Charging Bear, rolled on my shoulder, sprang back to my feet, and kept running down the field to the post. Charging Bear was surrounded on all sides with the other players whacking at his stick. They were vicious. Somehow he was able to get the ball to Spider, who whipped it to Eagle Talon and in a flash he passed it to me."

Deadfall Hunter stopped to take a breath. He looked at Willow, as a wave of pride overwhelmed him. He lifted his head to the sky.

"Never was there better passing in any game, anywhere. You've seen an osprey dive from the sky to snatch a sleeping salmon. You know how fast it dives with its wings tucked behind it." Deadfall Hunter leaned forward in a dive position with his good arm close by his side, the other hanging limp. He stared at Moose and Willow with wide eyes. Bright Star stopped her work and looked proudly at her husband, waiting for him to tell his favourite part.

"Our passes were faster than a diving osprey," he said, sitting back with his chest expanded. "And like an osprey—right on target. The other players couldn't even see the ball!"

Bright Star smiled at her husband and continued slicing the roots.

"I ran toward the post with full force," said Deadfall Hunter. "Two of their guards stood in front of me. I dodged to the left and they slashed at my stick. I leapt to the right before they could knock the ball away. Then, right in front of the post, I let the ball fly with all my strength.

"Before I could see if it hit the target, I tripped over a stick and crashed right into the post. My leg hit first. The pain was . . . like being hit by lightning . . . unbearable . . ." He reached his hand to Bright Star, shuddering and unable to speak.

"You were heroic," she said, stroking his good hand.

He struggled to continue. "That's when . . . I heard the cheering."

Strength returned to his voice. "The ball had hit. A spectacular goal—the best anyone had ever seen."

Moose and Willow cheered together.

He continued, with his hand on his leg. "When I stood up to raise my stick, my right leg collapsed. I had shattered the bone like a green stick. A piece stuck out through the flesh."

Willow looked away from the injured leg. He noticed a scratching sound coming from a nearby tree.

"What's that?" he said, going over to find the source of the noise. At the top of a young maple tree, a porcupine was gnawing the bark down to flesh. Flecks of white bark floated through the trees, catching the rays of the sun as they fell. Willow thought of the succulent flavour of porcupine stewed with bulrush roots and wild garlic, but since they weren't there to hunt he returned to listen to the story.

"That was my last game," said Deadfall Hunter, looking down at his knobbly leg. "I thought it would be the last of my days, too. When the healers got their claws into me, I thought I would die. They pushed and pulled my leg, twisting the bones together. The crunching sound was even more painful than the break." He shook as he recalled the feeling of bone grating against bone.

"You were brave," said Bright Star, rubbing his twisted leg. "If you were in pain, no one knew but you."

"I passed out from the healing," he continued. "I dreamed I'd been captured by the People from Across the Lake. I was being tortured. It was a woman healer. I'll never forget her face—like a shaman's mask. But she saved my leg. It's a little shorter than my good one. Now I watch the young men play."

"You are still the best to me," said Bright Star.

"Everyone remembers you as one of the best ever," added Moose. "You won and did it with honour and courage. I was just a boy when you were on the field, but I remember the way you played. We thought you had wings."

Deadfall Hunter was about to respond when a loud thud made him struggle to his feet. The tail of a mink thrashed wildly under the deadfall trap and then fell limp.

"Another one!" he bellowed. "This is the best hunting I've had all year." He took a charm from his fire pouch and rubbed it against his chest as he hobbled over to the deadfall.

"The fur is still good," he said, holding up the limp remains.

"You are the champion of deadfalls," said Moose, stroking the tail.

Deadfall Hunter laughed a contented laugh. "No one is what he used to be, my young friends. Come now. We'll walk home with you."

Moose and Willow led the way back to the village with their sticks over their shoulders. Deadfall Hunter limped behind with the fresh pelts slung over his shoulder, and Bright Star followed behind him carrying her basket of lilies and bulbs. She sang in a low, melodious voice as she walked through the woods—forceful songs of great hunters, flowing songs of rivers and dreamy songs of rainbows in the mist. Her favourites were the ones of strong women who protected their people from harm.

When they came within earshot of the village, Deadfall Hunter joined in. He sang about victorious stickball games, capturing spies in the woods and raids on enemy villages, getting louder and louder the closer they came. As he limped through the palisade gate he hailed in the loud voice of a champion, "We burned their village to the ground!"

– CHAPTER ELEVEN –

On the Turtle's Back

Old Chief stirred in his loft near the end of the longhouse. He slid from his bunk to the creaks and groans of the knots holding it in place and stood facing the fire. The flickering flames and the orange glow of the coals reflected on his loose-fitting deerskin leggings and loincloth, giving him the appearance of a supple dancer, even though his agile days had long passed. Deep creases crossed his face, a long scar marked the side of his neck where an enemy arrow had sliced his young throat long ago, and a gray braid hung down his back.

Old Chief gathered his pipe and some tobacco and slipped them in his fire pouch. As he moved toward the few remaining stores of corn, the dogs opened their eyes and focused on his movements. They watched him wrap some fat mixed with boiled corn in deerskin and put it in his pouch. Through the smoke holes in the roof, they could see the sky beginning to lighten and knew it was time for another day. The younger dogs lifted their heads and yawned. The old ones didn't stir. They knew that Old Chief was always up before daylight.

Willow felt a hand on his back. He opened his eyes to see the wizened face of his grandfather smiling through the smoky haze.

"Come with me this morning," he whispered. "There's something I want you to see."

Willow propped himself up on one elbow and brushed the hair away from his face. Silently he signalled for Old Chief to wait for him and, still half-asleep, scanned the longhouse, taking his bearings. Then, with the suddenness of a bowstring being released, he sprang from his loft and landed on the floor near the fire.

As Old Chief moved toward the door with a few of the young dogs following, Willow grabbed the bow and quiver hanging beside his bunk and joined them. On the way out Old Chief hoisted the strap of a large basket filled with tiny corn cobs over his shoulder.

The eastern sky was turning gray and robins had begun singing in the low branches of the maple trees around the village as Willow and Old Chief passed through the entrance of the palisade, along the winding path and out to the open fields. In the dim light a pair of deer suddenly lifted their heads and bounded away. The young dogs raced after them, barking ferociously but staying a safe distance away.

"This is a special day," said Old Chief, walking through the dewy grasses with his grandson beside him. "We'll see sights that can only be seen on this day."

Old Chief walked steadily through the forest as they followed the trail toward the rising sun. Though he was old, his back was straight and his stride was long. His bare chest filled deeply when he breathed. It had once been broad and powerful, enabling him to run like a deer. Now his ribs were visible and the power had gone—but he still carried himself proudly. Willow had to step quickly to keep up with him.

As he walked, Old Chief sang songs of great hunts, travels to faraway places, and battles against the enemy. Willow knew most of his grandfather's songs and sang along with him when he knew the words.

"Wait," said Old Chief, stopping in the middle of the path. He squinted in the low light until he was able to spot a patch of strawberries shining in the morning dew. "I thought these might be ripe by now. Look at them."

He reached over to pick some berries, eating a few and giving the rest to Willow.

"I wait all winter for the taste of these berries," said Old Chief. "They have been ripening here, waiting for us to find them. They are a gift."

He looked toward the dawn. The pale orange sky had ignited into dark orange streaks. "We'll plant some berries on the way back," he said. "We have no time now."

They turned off the main trail through the forest to a narrow path leading in the direction of the Beautiful Lake. Old Chief moved quickly, looking over his shoulder toward the dawn. Eventually, he left the path and threaded his way through the trees to a small opening in the forest, which led to a low hill and a meadow filled with yellow flowers. In the centre of the meadow was a massive mound of earth, encircled by six large rocks.

"Follow me," he signalled, placing the corn basket on the ground. They climbed to the top of the mound where they found an empty turtle shell, picked clean by insects over the course of countless years. Willow stood looking at Old Chief, wondering what his grandfather wanted him to see.

"This is Turtle's Back," said Old Chief, as he sat down beside the turtle shell. "It is round like a real turtle's back. What are the six rocks surrounding it?"

Willow looked down at the rocks.

"That one's the head," he said, pointing to the largest. "And that small thin one—it's the tail," pointing in the opposite direction. "The others are the legs."

Old Chief smiled. "Which rock represents bravery?" he asked.

Willow pointed to a foreleg.

"Which one represents humility?"

Willow pointed to the tail.

"You know this well," said Old Chief. "You must remember the story about the turtle."

"I've heard it since I was a baby," said Willow.

"Yes," laughed Old Chief. "I've told it so many times."

He picked up the turtle shell. "Look around you" he said.

From the top of the mound, Willow could see the lake far below, calm and gray in the early light. In one direction, toward the dawn, he could see the tree-covered islands on the far side of the wide bay. At the end—out of sight—were the marshes and sand beaches where the River of the Dawn emptied into the bay.

In the opposite direction, he could see toward the mouth of Thunder River and the shore stretching off into a blur between the land and the water.

"The sky has given us a clear morning with few clouds," said Old Chief, pointing at the bright glow above the trees.

"Do you see that tall pine standing above the rest of the trees?" he asked, pointing to a distant pine tree. "You'll soon see it catch on fire."

Willow looked at the tree and then at his grandfather. "Why will it catch on fire?"

Old Chief smiled. "I have been coming here for a long time," he said, as though he were talking to himself. "In the winter and summer and all the times in between." He turned toward the eastern sky.

"I have seen the sun rise and set countless times. I can't decide which I like best."

Old Chief looked again at the pine tree and the smile left his face. He saw his grandson's eyes light up. Willow jumped to his feet and pointed excitedly. A sliver of gold light shone from behind the pine tree.

"Look!" he yelled. "It's on . . ." His voice trailed off as he looked down at Old Chief, who smiled at him with dark, playful eyes. "It's the sun," said Willow. "There's no fire at all." He sat down beside his grandfather. "How did you know the sun would rise behind that pine tree?"

"I've been here many times, Willow," repeated Old Chief.

"Does it always rise there?" Willow asked.

"Only on special days. It depends on where the Great Turtle is going. In the winter it's moving in a different direction and the sun rises over there." Old Chief pointed toward the lake and the distant islands. "At that time it stays very low in the sky all day and then sets over there," he said, nodding toward the bay where Thunder River flowed into the lake.

"You see the first point of land beyond the bay? The sun sets there in the winter. When it does, I know the cold will last only five more full moons. Today the sun will climb high in the sky and set over that cedar." Old Chief gestured toward a solitary tree in the direction of the village.

"I planted that tree long before you were born to mark the exact spot—it is my sunset tree. I've watched it grow over the years and it has always shown me where the sun sets before it begins its journey back. The change in the sun from one day to the next is so small that you can't see it, but as the year passes it becomes clear."

Old Chief arched his long thin arms in front of him. "Our world rides on the back of the Great Turtle, which is bigger than we can imagine. Slowly the Turtle moves in its own world across lands and waters that we cannot see. We know it is moving because we can see the way the sun travels through the seasons. It is the same every year—like the birds flying away in the winter and returning in the spring. They watch the movement of the Great Turtle just as we do and they know when the sun is low and when it is high. Perhaps they can see the world of the Great Turtle from the sky. If they do, they don't tell us about it—no matter how many times we ask them."

"The geese try to tell us every year when they come back across the lake," said Willow. "We can't understand their honking. If we could fly, we'd see for ourselves."

"If you could fly like the geese, you could understand them," replied Old Chief. "You know the story of how the world began?"

"Of course," laughed Willow.

"Then you can tell it to me," said Old Chief, leaning back in the grass.

Willow smiled and thought for a time before he spoke. There was no hurry that day. The sun moved at its own pace.

"There was only the Sky World at first. Like our world with lakes and forests and people, but it wasn't our world. Our world was nothing but water and air with no land. A young woman from the Sky World was chasing a bear when she fell through a great hole, down, down from the sky. Or maybe she threw herself in."

Willow noticed Old Chief's eyes becoming heavy, but he continued the story.

"However it happened, she fell until she was rescued by a flock of geese. They flew close together and caught her on their wings. They held her as long as they could. There was no land to rest on.

"When the geese were nearly exhausted a turtle appeared on the surface of the water. It called to the other animals to dive to the bottom to gather soil and pile it on its back."

Old Chief's eyes closed and a look of contentment came over his face.

"The animals—especially the beavers—dove to the bottom for earth to make an island. They tried and tried, but the only animal that could bring earth to the surface was a female toad. Before long, the toad had made an island on the Turtle's Back and the geese were able to lower the woman down. That's how this land was formed. All the soil and rocks we see around us were put here that day by our great-great-grandmother, the toad—and they've been here ever since."

Old Chief slowly opened his eyes and smiled at Willow. "My grandfather used to tell me that story, long, long ago. Now you, *my* grandson, tell it to me. That story always calms my spirit."

The golden sun had risen above the pine tree and a few thin clouds in the distance beyond the sun glowed red like the coals of a fire. Willow and Old Chief watched the sun change from a glowing circle into a blinding ball. They felt its warmth on their faces and bare chests as it moved across the sky toward the Beautiful Lake.

A light breeze moved the leaves and soon the smooth, gray lake rippled with blue and white, like the wing feathers of a blue jay.

The water was broken by small waves that reflected the sun in a glittering dance of silver and gold.

"We should go now," said Old Chief.

"Can't we stay and see the sun set over your sunset tree?"

"We can if you want," Old Chief replied. "First, I want to leave this corn in the swamp. When we return we can see how the strawberries are ripening."

He moved slowly down the mound of earth and followed a path toward a swamp at the end of the narrow lake, not far inland from the Beautiful Lake. Bullfrogs called out in the warm sun as they approached, but as soon as they sensed the presence of strangers they became silent. Only the hum of insects and the songs of red-winged blackbirds could be heard. Old Chief opened the braided lid of the basket to reveal tiny young ears of corn still wrapped in their delicate green husks. He smiled at Willow.

"These may be little stubs now," Old Chief said, "but they have the promise of greatness that comes with time. In the autumn they'll be pungent—ready to eat. I can share them with my friends. I'll save some for you."

He closed the lid and tied it tightly in place. Then he lashed a heavy rock to the bottom of the basket. After removing his fire pouch and clothing, he stepped into the murky water carrying the basket and waded through the clumps of bulrushes and water lilies until the scummy surface was up to his chest. He lowered the basket to the bottom and then pulled his way back to shore.

At the point where he emerged covered in mud, Old Chief blazed a nearby tree so he could find the basket when he returned in autumn. Then he collected his clothing and gave one last satisfied look at where his basket lay before making his way to the Beautiful Lake. In the cool clean water, he washed the muck from his body and dressed.

"Now we can spend the day eating berries," he said. They walked back up the hill and through the trees to the strawberry patch. Before eating any more berries, Old Chief buried a handful beneath the low grass beside the path. "There will be even more next year when we come back," he said with a broad grin.

Before long Old Chief had gathered enough berries for a meal. He sat down in the shade of an oak tree beside a small spring.

"This water is almost as good as the water in our village," he said, using his cupped hand to lift it to his mouth. He sang a song as he mixed some berries with deer fat and boiled corn and worked the mixture into a loose ball, which he shared with Willow. Once they had eaten, he stretched out in the grass and fell asleep in the shade of the oak tree, listening to the sound of the leaves whispering in the breeze.

Willow gathered more strawberries and then shot some of his arrows at a rotten birch tree, keeping watch as Old Chief slept. The sun was high in the sky—almost straight over his head.

Suddenly, a flicker of gray and white caught Willow's eye in the clearing beside him. He instantly recognized the drumming sound of a grouse taking flight. With his bow already in his hand, he pulled an arrow from his quiver, slipped it over the bowstring, aimed just ahead of the grouse, and released the arrow. The bird flew straight into the path of the arrow and fell flapping to the ground. Willow ran to where the grouse had fallen and found it tangled in the long grass, its wings still twitching.

– CHAPTER TWELVE –

A Roasted Grouse

"One arrow!" he said to himself as he picked up the bird. Its gray and black fan-shaped tail feathers were fully spread and a black ring encircled its neck. It wasn't a large bird, but it was beautiful, and it would make a good meal for himself and Old Chief. Willow admired the grouse, praising its wings and rapid flight, and then he plucked and cleaned it.

Before long he had a small fire burning. He skewered the bird on a pointed stick and placed it over the flames while Old Chief slept. As the sun fell lower in the sky, Old Chief stirred and took a deep breath.

"Do I smell the wonderful smell of a roasting bird?"

"Yes, you do," said Willow.

Old Chief let out a deep sigh. "Is that bird a grouse fattened on summer berries—the best bird of all?"

"Yes, it is."

"Oh, you are a good friend!" he said, pulling himself to his feet. "We will celebrate our day watching the sun.

"First, I'll get some water." Old Chief walked stiffly into the woods.

Willow sat by the fire, turning the bird over the coals. Old Chief soon returned with a roughly made birchbark container and filled it at the spring. When the grouse was roasted, Willow passed it to Old Chief on the pointed stick.

"This is a fine-looking bird Willow. Tell me how you killed it."

While the bird cooled down, Willow told his story, making them both hungry. Finally, Old Chief had the honour of dividing the bird with his knife. He gave the legs and tender breast meat to Willow and kept the back and wings for himself.

"Eat as much as you can, Willow. You've been busy hunting while I've been dreaming of roasted grouse and hoping my dream would come true." He gnawed on the wing bones, separating them to get every shred of meat.

"I have travelled far, but in all the lands I've been to, I have never tasted any bird that compares with the grouse in our forests."

Willow devoured the breast meat and stripped the flesh from the legs. When he was finished, he scraped whatever he could from the carcass and drank the cool spring water.

As the summer sun moved toward the horizon, Old Chief sat against a tree and pulled his pipe out of his fire pouch. He filled it with shredded tobacco, lit it with a burning stick from the fire, and began reciting quiet words of praise to the spirit of the sun.

"Where did you get that, Grandfather?"

Old Chief held the pipe out for Willow to see. It was made of dark stone with a wide bowl shaped like a turtle that faced Old Chief when he smoked—its four legs dangling over the edge of the bowl. The turtle's eyes had been drilled through the stone, so they lit up when the tobacco embers were hot. Each time Old Chief inhaled, the eyes glowed brighter.

"This pipe was given to me by the chief of the People of the Lakes—our friends from the north. It tells the story of the creation. This is the same turtle that holds the world on its back. That's what the chief told me, anyway."

"Where do they live?" asked Willow, finally abandoning the clean, white grouse bones on a rock by the fire.

"Have you never been to visit the People of the Lakes?" asked Old Chief. "They live where the winters are long and cold. The trail leading from the Beautiful Lake takes you past our own northern villages to the lake with many islands. The People of the Lakes live far beyond that lake, deep in the forests."

"What are they like?"

"I'm surprised you've never met them. Your father and I used to go there often. But they are different. They don't have villages like we have. They live in tiny huts and travel in their canoes from one lake to another, never staying in one place for long." Old Chief looked toward the setting sun before he continued.

"We have flat land here with deep soil for planting corn. They live in hilly lands with just a few trees clinging to the rocks. Most of them don't speak our language. They dress differently and act differently, but they are good people. We get our best furs from them because the animals there need thick fur to survive the cold winters."

He looked at Willow. "They don't grow tobacco either, but they love to smoke it. That makes for very good trading." He sat in silence, thinking about his days with the People of the Lakes, and then slowly stood up. "You must go to visit them, Willow. I will see to it."

Then Old Chief turned toward the trail. "The sun is getting low now. We should go back to see if it sets on the sunset tree this year." He led the way, talking to Willow as he went.

"Your father was our main connection to the People of the Lakes," Old Chief said. "We sent him there to learn their ways. When he was your age he spent a summer and a winter with their chief and his family. They traveled all the time, living in their canoes and sleeping beside sandy beaches. When he returned to us, he had so many stories to tell."

Willow and Old Chief walked into the clearing and saw the Beautiful Lake below them in the distance. "Your father learned to speak their language and he learned to think like them. Most of all, he learned to respect them as brothers—and they respected him." Old Chief stopped to look at the deep blue lake and the distant clouds hovering above it, now glowing orange like the setting sun.

— *Enemy Arrows* —

The wonderful smell of a roasting bird.

He turned to Willow. "When your father was older he would meet with their council. If there was a conflict between our people and their people, the council would find a way to end it. If one of their people killed one of ours, the council would decide how they could make it up to the family of the victim. He was a very good representative for us. We always had a close friendship with the People of the Lakes when your father was alive. You must go there soon."

– CHAPTER THIRTEEN –

Battle with the Enemy

Willow followed his grandfather and stood on top of the mound, looking out at the lake. He used to like to hear stories about his father, but now he sat uneasy, squirming to get comfortable.

Old Chief pointed across the lake. "One time when I was sitting here, I saw smoke coming up out of the lake. When the sun went down and the sky was dark I saw fire on the lake." He looked at Willow. "What do you think it was?"

"A burning log?"

"That's what I thought too, but no. It was a forest fire on the other side of the lake."

Willow's eyes widened at the thought of the People from Across the Lake being so near. Old Chief pointed to a faint wisp of orange mist that appeared to be rising from the forests beyond the lake, far in the distance.

"Have you travelled to the Great Falls yet?" he asked.

"Not yet," Willow replied. "But I want to see them."

"You can see them from here. That mist is from the Great Falls. You have to go there to hear them roar. There's nothing louder. The spray soaks everything with water and in the winter all the rocks and trees around them are covered with ice."

— *Battle with the Enemy* —

The sun had changed from brilliant orange to a deep red, suspended just above the sunset tree planted by Old Chief. They stopped talking and watched in silence until the last sliver of red disappeared beneath gold clouds at the base of the tree.

"The sunset tree marks the right place," said Old Chief. "Now the Great Turtle will move and the sun will start setting a little closer to the lake every evening."

He brushed a bug off his forehead as the air around them began to fill with a high-pitched hum from clouds of mosquitoes. Bats darted effortlessly across the darkening sky, feeding on the flying insects.

"No matter how thick and hungry the mosquitoes are up here, I know they'll be worse on the ground. There isn't a whisper of a breeze tonight," said Old Chief. The bushes and rocks at the base of the mound were soon lost in the darkness.

"Fireflies," said Willow, pointing into the darkness. Minute lights circled the mound, blinking on and off. "They can guide us back to the village."

"We won't head back to the village yet," said Old Chief. "Today has been a special day, but there is more to see. The bright stars are already out. There are stars in the south that can only be seen on this day. You will see them with your sharp young eyes before I do."

Before long a full moon began to rise in the east, just beyond the islands. As it made its climb above the lake, it appeared to be shining directly at Willow and Old Chief, and its shimmering reflection formed a trail directly to the shore below them. When the darkness became light, Willow looked into the illuminated face of Old Chief and forced out a question.

"Did you ever see my father in battle?"

Old Chief turned and peered into his grandson's eyes, noticing how much he looked like his father at the same age. His eyes were young and clear like a child, but at the same time they showed the fearlessness of a hunter and warrior. There was also a look of wisdom, which did not belong to someone so young. But of all the features that father and son shared, the most noticeable was the ever-present alertness of their senses. They both had the taut look of a bowstring ready to be released. Like his father, Willow was attuned to every cracking twig in the forest, every swish of a moving pine bough, every flap of a bird's wing. He caught even the most fleeting movement—the touch of a cool breeze in the spring, the scent of wood smoke, the taste of danger in the air.

"Your father was one of the bravest warriors ever," said Old Chief. "I saw him fight many times. One long night before you were born, we were on a mission of peace to the People from Across the Lake. Our people and theirs had been fighting for too long and your father and I were among a group sent to talk for the first time about peace between our nations. There was much tension and distrust when we met on a small island in the Great River that flows out of the Beautiful Lake. We had many differences, but we shared the wish to stop the senseless killing and capturing of our people.

"The first night was peaceful, but as dawn approached some of our warriors became tense. They imagined there was a plot to capture us on the island. On the second night, an argument over a careless shove between one of our warriors and one of theirs escalated into an ugly brawl and then into combat and they killed one of our chiefs. We were barely able to escape with our lives.

"The next new moon we took many people from our land by canoe and destroyed an enemy village. As your father set fire to the palisades, he was hit in the shoulder with an arrow, just above his protective armour—but he kept fighting. There were many killed that day. We captured four of their warriors when they tried to attack us through a gap in the palisade. We killed three of them, but kept one as a slave." Old Chief's voice grew strong when he told about their victories in battle.

"I was shot here," he said, pointing to a deep scar just below his ribs. "The arrow went in sideways—right through the slats in my armour. The enemy chased us to our canoes. Your father helped me escape—he almost carried me. As we headed into the lake, the enemy shot at us. We couldn't shoot back because we were trying

Battle with the Enemy

to get away from their arrows. I was hit again in the back. Your father was struck in one arm and had to paddle with the other."

The moon rose higher above the lake, casting long shadows in the clearing in front of Willow and Old Chief. The only sound above the constant hum of the mosquitoes was the screech of the nighthawks flying low to the ground.

"The enemy chased after us. Although we had ripped holes in most of their canoes before we attacked, two of them came after us from the other side of the village. We could not distance them because so many of us were wounded and we could not shoot while we paddled. We had to stop in the middle of the lake and fight—even though we were running out of arrows. We gathered the arrows that rained down on us. We pulled them out of our canoes and out of our limbs—even out of our dead.

"One of our arrows hit an enemy warrior in the forehead. He stood up in his canoe screaming, trying to pull it out. He fell backward on the edge of the canoe and flipped it over. While warriors in the other canoe tried to right it, we shot at them until we had nothing more to shoot. Finally, they returned to the river where they had come from, and we fled across the lake." Old Chief gazed up at the moon for several long seconds. "Yes, your father was a brave warrior. I was not fighting with him when he was killed by the People from Across the Lake, but I have heard from others that he was courageous to the end of his life."

"Tell me again what happened when he was killed," asked Willow, as calmly as he could.

"I wish I could tell you what I saw with my own eyes, but I can only repeat what I was told. Our warriors attacked the enemy in a large village with a double palisade surrounding it. Your father was the first to get near the wall, but he was hit by a rock. It shattered his protective armour and knocked him to the ground. He pulled himself up, but was hit in the face by an arrow that deflected from a tree. I heard from others that the arrow hit him in the eye. That is what they told me. He fell to the ground and didn't move.

"The battle continued all day, but he didn't move. Our warriors couldn't get near enough to rescue him. Finally, at night, one of our warriors tried to get to him. Who was it? No . . . I can't recall now. Anyway, he crept in beside the palisade where your father lay, but your father wasn't there. The enemy had taken him along with two others. Wait, the man who tried to rescue your father was the warrior from the north. Your father lived with him and his family whenever he stayed with the People of the Lakes. They were like brothers . . . his name escapes me now.

"Next morning our warriors were about to attack again. In the dawn light they saw the naked bodies of three warriors hanging from the palisades. The enemy had mutilated them in the most horrible way.

"Your father's friend, Grosbeak . . . no, Gray Jay . . . no . . . what was it? Anyway, he crept up to the palisade to get a closer look. Wait! His name was *Shrike*, of course—the man with red hands. Shrike saw one of the bodies with a scar on his back—where your father had a scar. Yes, Shrike thought it was your father. They were like brothers. Then he was hit with a hail of arrows and had to get away. His guardian spirit was with him that day. Shrike was fortunate to escape with his own life.

"When the battle was over, our warriors tried to negotiate with the enemy to recover the bodies, but they refused. That's what Shrike said. I was in the village when they returned and told us what had happened. It caused so much grief, especially for your mother. And to intensify the unbearable pain, we all knew that your father's bones would not be buried with our bones.

"Yes, he was fearless when he fought the enemy, but with his own people he was kind and respectful. He hunted and traded so he would have enough to give to others. The feasts he held were famous in our land and in the land of the People of the Lakes. There was great sadness at the news of his death."

The moon had risen high above the Beautiful Lake. The rocks and trees were visible again in the pale blue light.

"Was Shrike certain it was my father?"

Old Chief looked perplexed. "I don't know. You must ask him yourself."

"Does he ever come here?"

"Not for a long time."

Willow stared silently over the moonlit lake, as if trying to see the far shore and the land where the battle had taken place.

"Does this talk of the battle upset you, Willow?"

"No."

"Is there something else troubling your spirit?"

"I don't think so."

"Nothing at all?" Old Chief prodded.

Willow took a deep breath before he answered. "Someone told me a lie. I know it's a lie, but it makes me angry. I'm trying to forget about it."

"Do you want to tell me?"

Willow looked away from his grandfather. He wanted to tell him about what Oriole had said. He wanted to hear Old Chief say it wasn't true, but he couldn't bear to dishonour his father by repeating her words—even as a lie. His father was not living with the enemy on the other side of the lake. He had died bravely in battle. If he allowed himself to repeat Oriole's lie, even to his grandfather, his father's memory would be tarnished by doubt—like the green corrosion eating into copper jewellery. Copper can be made to shine again, but not the memory of a dead warrior. Once the lie was out, the doubt would remain forever. No matter how badly he wanted to tell Old Chief about Oriole's lies, the words wouldn't come out of his mouth.

"I can't," he said.

"Then we can head back to the village with the light of the full moon to guide us," said Old Chief. "We can talk of the past when you are ready."

– CHAPTER FOURTEEN –

Taking Flight

Willow soared high above Thunder River with his arms stretched out beside him and his legs and arms as straight as arrows. All of his limbs were covered with feathers from the tips of his fingers to his pointed toes, like a turkey vulture. He soared on the breezes with the wind brushing his gleaming black hair away from his face.

Far below, he could see his village on the high plateau above the river. Tiny figures carried wood from the forest and weeded the fields, while a few canoes glided toward the river mouth. His shadow crossed the fields beneath him, faster than any runner.

The sun felt warm on his back, despite the cool winds blowing past him. An osprey sped past, turning its head to see the strange creature in the sky. Willow laughed at the bird and veered away. There was something he had to do.

Higher and higher he spiralled until the village became a small dot beside a thin strand of winding light. He could see the Beautiful Lake from one shore to the other, sparkling with the sun's reflection on the waves. Soon he would be high enough to see the Great Turtle—and the world beyond.

As he continued to climb, he noticed the birds had disappeared. He had left them far below. Why didn't they climb to see the Great

Turtle? He soared in wide circles, getting nearer and nearer to the clouds until he could almost touch them.

The nearest one was a dark, billowing mass moving majestically across the sky. Willow moved his feather-covered arms and glided toward it. As he was about to touch it, the sky shook with the sound of thunder and a bolt of lightning shot from the towering cloud, striking him like a burning coal, singeing his feathers, and knocking him from his flight.

He struggled to stay aloft, like a grouse struck by an arrow, but began to plummet from the sky. As he fell, his feathers were ripped off one by one and he was transformed from a soaring bird into a young warrior thrashing wildly toward the earth. He had come so close to seeing the Great Turtle and was not going to give up.

"The Turtle!" he cried as he fell. "The Great Turtle!"

He crashed in a heap with his eyes closed and lay still on the ground, thinking the impact had broken his bones. Slowly, he opened his eyes and looked around. To his astonishment, he was inside the dark longhouse beside his own loft. In the darkness, he looked up at the roof, but couldn't see where he had crashed through. Orchid rushed to him—followed by Old Heron, who had been sleeping at the far end of the longhouse.

"What happened to the boy?" demanded Old Heron.

"Lie still, Willow, lie still," sang his mother in a soothing voice, pushing the dusty hair from his eyes.

"He's not well," said Old Heron. "Look at his eyes. He's far away. He must have landed on his head."

Brown Bat, the adopted warrior, emerged from the darkness and crouched beside Willow until he was able to move by himself. Then he helped Willow back to his bed.

"What happened to you?" he asked quietly.

At first Willow didn't speak, but slowly he tried to answer.

"I fell from the sky," he moaned.

Old Heron shook her head.

"I did fall from the sky," Willow protested in a weak voice. "I was hit by lightning."

"I saw no lightning," said Old Heron, turning to the others.

"He needs to sleep," said Orchid. "We can talk about the lightning in the morning." She pressed gently on his shoulders until he was lying down again and then began singing a low, haunting song about geese flying in formation across the forests and the lakes before disappearing behind the moon. With his mother stroking his forehead as she sang, he soon fell asleep and the smoky longhouse was quiet again.

Morning comes early in the short nights of summer. No sooner had Willow stirred than Old Heron approached him with her sharp eyes close to his face.

"What was all that noise last night?" she asked.

"What noise?" he replied.

"You don't remember?" she asked. "You were shouting about falling from the sky."

Willow was suddenly overcome by the memories of flying high above the village. They flooded over him like water from the river in a spring melt—and he recalled the dark cloud and lightning as well as his fall to the ground. But he didn't know how to describe the wonder of his adventure to Old Heron.

"I don't know," he said.

"You fell to the ground," she said.

Willow looked at her with a start. "Yes, I did—I was among the clouds."

"Was this your dream?" she asked.

"No," replied Willow, staring at the old woman. "It was too real. I was there."

Old Heron stared back at Willow, trying to see his thoughts in his anxious eyes. A birch log on the fire crackled behind her and then its bark ignited in a flash of light. The longhouse glowed with the white light of the flames.

"Of course you were there," she repeated. "You have had a difficult journey. Try to be still today." Old Heron looked at him with pity and disappeared to the far end of the longhouse.

Willow lay on his bed, staring at the roof above him in the dawn light. There was no sign of the hole where he had fallen through. The smoke holes were open, but they were too far away. He knew he had been flying, but couldn't understand how he had crashed where he did. Slowly he sat up and looked around. The longhouse was the same as always, filled with bundles of precious things stored high in the rafters, with bedding and clothing piled on the lofts around the perimeter and large storage baskets crammed in the spaces below the lofts.

Scattered everywhere were the living footprints of his family—wood chips from carvings strewn beside the fire, dyed quills drying on a rock, feathers here and there, scraps of rabbit skin, bits of brown corn waiting beside the grinder for the mice to find them. It was all so familiar that it made his memories of flying among the clouds fade away.

Slowly and stiffly, he climbed down from his loft and looked up through the smoke hole. Far above, he could see the brilliant sky and knew the sun would be rising over the trees. Grabbing his bow and quiver, he went outside to search for his friends. They would believe him.

– CHAPTER FIFTEEN –

Wings Like a Bird

Not far away, Orchid knelt beside a fire making cornbread, so he went to her and sat quietly on the ground.

"Take some," she said, handing him a piece. "You fell out of your bed in the night," she said smiling, as she shifted a large flat rock in the fire. "I had to sing you to sleep like a baby."

Willow squirmed uneasily. He was a warrior and a bear hunter. He didn't deserve to be talked to like a child. When he had finished eating, he replied.

"I was flying like a bird—but higher than any other bird. Then a bolt of lightning struck me and I fell out of the sky. It was awful to fall so far. I was on the ground beside my bed, but I can't understand how I landed there."

"You slept in your bed last night," Orchid responded. "It was raining, so you came inside."

"But it was real," he said. "I was flying!"

"I've had dreams like that before," she said, spreading some cornmeal on the hot rock. "They seem so real that you could spend the rest of your life in them." She handed him some water. "You don't know it's a dream until you wake up and you're back in this life."

Willow rubbed his forehead. "How do I know I'm not in a dream now?"

"You could be. You can never tell."

She sang to herself while she worked. At the sound of approaching footsteps, she looked up to see Loon and Otter coming toward the fire and smiled at them.

"Was that you making all that noise last night?" shouted Loon as they approached.

"We heard you laughing, and yelling about a turtle. What were you doing?" asked Otter.

"I'm not sure what happened," answered Willow. He stared into the fire, remembering the thrill of flying. His friends waited for an answer, but Willow jumped to his feet. "Aren't we hunting ducks today?" he asked.

"Here, take some of this to lure them in," said Orchid, handing chunks of cornbread to Loon. "Make sure they're nice and plump before you bring them home."

"There won't be any left for the ducks," laughed Loon. "We're hungry—and they're already fat enough."

The three hunters headed out the gate and followed the path to the river. On the bank, far away from the sleek birchbark canoes used by the elders, were the three canoes used by Willow, Otter and Loon. In the spring they had found them broken or abandoned and had restored them. One was an elmbark canoe, which had been nearly rotten when they found it overturned in a swamp, covered with spruce boughs. Old Chief said it had been hidden by warriors from across the lake, so they towed it back to the village and replaced the rotting bark and a few broken ribs. When they finished, it was heavy and leaked badly, but it did float.

They had been given the other two birchbark canoes when they seemed to be beyond repair, but had restored them with new ribs, bark, and on one, a new nose. Now they were good enough for hunting ducks on the river—and no one else ever wanted to use them.

Down the river, not far from the lake, was a small marshy bay lined with dead trees. Red-winged blackbirds swayed in the bulrushes, singing to the three hunters as they paddled toward them, and an oriole whistled its melodic tune from the top of an elm tree on a nearby cliff, its brilliant orange plumage shining in the morning sun.

The bay was filled with ducks and geese of every colour and size, and large, mud-coloured turtles swam beneath their canoes.

"Let's spread out so we don't frighten them," Willow said in a low voice.

"Keep low," signalled Otter.

The three old canoes glided in different directions. They used the silent stroke, slicing their paddles through the water like feathers on the return stroke, instead of lifting them out. They knew the ducks could hear the sound of water dripping from a paddle. A pair of mallards flew low above the water and skidded on flat feet across the surface before coming to a splashing stop. Noiselessly, Otter eased his bow from the bottom of his canoe and pulled an arrow from the quiver on his back. The ducks were close to him, but not close enough, so he paddled with one arm to get closer, holding the bow and the arrow in place with his other arm—never letting his paddle scrape the side of the canoe.

He moved as silently as a floating log, but despite his quiet approach, the ducks became suspicious and swam away, their brilliant green heads turning nervously to look at the large shape pursuing them. Otter knew that their retreat would send an alarm signal to the other birds, so he slowed and let them escape. He would have to get closer to the flock if they were to take any ducks home.

On the far side of the bay a light breeze drifted down the cliff, sending ripples across the water. Loon took advantage of it to slide effortlessly into the reeds, keeping one hand on his paddle to steer toward a flock of pintails. The silver backs of the males shone like snow in the moonlight and their tiny black eyes glowed like polished stone. They crowded into a narrow opening in the reeds as the canoe approached. Loon let his paddle slip silently from his hand into the water and then nocked an arrow to his bowstring. The brown-flecked females were swimming in circles, becoming more and more agitated. He knew they were about to fly, so he aimed his arrow just above the water and waited.

The three hunters headed out the gate.

The large male pintail nearest the canoe let out a warning whistle and suddenly the bay was filled with webbed feet churning the water and flapping wings. Whistling and quacking noises echoed across the water. Loon shot his arrow into the midst of the rising flock and quickly grabbed another arrow. Ducks scattered in all directions, except for two brought down by his arrows.

The noise from the pintails alarmed a pair of geese grazing at the base of the cliff. Willow was ready with his arrow when the two large birds took flight, honking loudly as they lifted their heavy bodies into the sky. He could see their long black necks and white cheeks as they flew above him—and his first arrow brought down the larger goose. He grabbed another arrow and shot at the smaller one, but it escaped.

Willow then looked behind to see Loon, paddling his canoe with his hands to the place where he had let his paddle slip into the water. It was floating on the surface like a water snake basking in the summer sun.

"Two pintails!" Loon yelled to Willow.

"A fat goose!" called Willow.

"My ducks escaped," laughed Otter. "They said they'd bring their friends next time."

The three hunters headed to the shore at the base of the cliff, pulled their canoes up and sat in the long grass to admire their catches. Insects buzzed around their heads and the warm sun beat down on them, as Willow carefully spread the wings of the dead goose across his legs, its long neck hanging limp by his side.

"I had a dream last night," he said quietly. "Or maybe it really happened. I don't know." His friends waited for him to continue. "I was high above the village. My arms were outstretched like this and covered with feathers. Even my body was covered with feathers. I climbed up to the clouds. I could fly!"

Otter spread his arms and pretended to soar like a bird.

"It's easy when you're on the ground," joked Loon.

"It's not so easy when you fall," continued Willow. "I was close enough to touch the clouds, but I was hit by lightning. Then I fell and fell and couldn't stop. The last thing I remember was when I hit the ground—and found myself next to my bed."

"That's what the noise was last night," laughed Loon. "Did you come through the roof?"

"I thought I had, but I couldn't see a hole."

"What were you doing in the sky?" asked Otter, his large head tilted to one side.

"I wanted to see the Great Turtle."

"The Great Turtle!" cried Otter and they laughed together at the calls of "turtle" in the middle of the night.

"How many people have bad dreams about turtles?" cried Loon, holding his ribs with laughter. The three rolled in the grass with their eyes closed, laughing and yelling, until they couldn't breathe. Then they lay on their backs surrounded by goldenrods and chicory, trying to catch their breath.

"I'm not sure what the dream means," said Willow, still holding his sides.

"Why did you want to fly over the Great Turtle?" asked Otter, sitting up.

"My grandfather told me about it," Willow answered. "I wanted to see for myself."

"The dream means you want to fly," said Loon, leaping to his feet. "We'll help you fulfill your dream." He disappeared into the woods, laughing as he went. The sound of breaking branches shattered the stillness of the bay before he reappeared with two dead branches as thick as his arms and as long as his legs. As Loon and Willow looked on, he took the branches over to a flat meadow beside the river, placed them on the ground, and signalled for the others to join him.

"Come here and lie down on the branches, Willow," he called, pointing to the branches on the ground. "You're going to fly again."

Willow gave Otter a bewildered look, but then he hopped over to the meadow, flapping his arms on the way.

"Lie on your stomach," said Loon, pointing at the branches.

Willow lay across them with his face in the grass—the two branches sticking out on either side.

"Now spread your arms," said Loon, squatting beside Willow. "Come on, Otter. Grab the other ends—one in each hand—and lift!"

Otter did what Loon asked. They lifted Willow awkwardly to knee height.

"Spread your arms, Willow," repeated Otter, "and keep your body straight. Here we go!" They staggered across the meadow carrying Willow until they came to the bank of river. Then they turned around and stumbled back again, Loon struggling to keep up with Otter. Willow kept his arms out and his body straight, trying hard to recreate the thrill of flying—but he knew the difference between soaring high above the lake and being carried on branches just above the grass.

"Put him down," panted Loon. They lowered the branches into the grass and Willow rolled off while Loon and Otter regained their breath.

"How was that?" asked Loon breathlessly. "Was it just like flying?"

"Was it the same?" echoed Otter.

"It was a good ride," said Willow. He knew they were trying to help. "But flying is different." He thought about the best way to explain it to them. "Flying is spectacular. You can see everything. You imagine where you want to go—and you go in that direction without effort. It's magic. And it doesn't bruise your ribs like a ride on branches."

Otter laughed. Loon looked disappointed.

"If that didn't work, we'll have to find another way," said Otter.

"How do we do that?" asked Loon. "Push him off a cliff?"

"I don't know," replied Otter. "We'll have to think about it."

As Willow looked up at the steep cliff behind him, a gust of wind rippled down the river toward the lake, shifting the canoes on shore. "Why not push me off a cliff?" he asked. Otter and Loon stared at him as though he had lost his senses.

"Because we don't want to kill you," answered Loon.

"Then I can jump on my own," said Willow. "I'll cover myself in feathers and run as fast as I can. If I flap my arms like a goose I'll be able to fly again!" He searched the faces of Otter and Loon for signs of excitement, but saw only disbelief.

"Did you land on your head when you fell from the sky?" asked Loon.

"We can make wings now," said Willow. "We can pluck the feathers from the goose I shot and stick them on my arms with pine gum. I'll be just like a bird."

Otter elbowed Loon in the ribs. "Let's go back to the village and tell everyone, Willow. I'm sure they'll want to see you fly, too."

"No," said Willow impatiently. "I want to fly now."

Otter walked to the canoes with Loon whispering to him, while Willow scanned the high cliff behind him.

"We have to get him back to the village," Otter said to Loon. "Some bad spirits are haunting him—or maybe he's been cursed. Whatever it is, we have to stop him."

Loon agreed. "Come with us, Willow," he called. He and Otter gathered the limp ducks, slipped their canoes into the water and began to paddle away. To their relief, Willow came after them.

"Something isn't right," whispered Loon before Willow caught up to them. Otter shook his head.

– CHAPTER SIXTEEN –

An Old Man's Eyes

In the face of a wind that whirled and twisted through the river valley, they had to struggle to control their empty canoes. Otter's was the biggest, built originally to transport trade goods throughout the endless lakes to the north. Now it was a cumbersome shell that caught the wind like a milkweed seed.

Without a word Otter steered it to the riverbank and carefully stepped out, placing one foot into the shallow water. With his other leg holding the canoe in place, he lifted a heavy rock and lowered it gently into the front. Willow and Loon held their canoes steady while they waited.

"I'd rather have the weight of a skinned deer or a bear to hold my canoe steady," laughed Otter. "But today I'll be happy with a rock. At least we won't return emptyhanded."

They paddled together upriver to the village, where they lifted their old canoes onto the shore and flipped them over. As soon as they reached the longhouse Willow began plucking the goose and the two ducks, placing the feathers carefully in a small basket. Otter and Loon found Old Chief in his favourite place, sitting by a fire outside the palisade, staring at the river and the trees below. Some of the elders sat beside him. When Old Chief heard the young hunters approach, he signalled to them to sit down beside him.

— *An Old Man's Eyes* —

"I saw your canoes on the river," he said. "Was that Willow in the third canoe?"

"Yes," replied Otter. "He followed us—instead of jumping off the cliff."

"Jumping off a cliff . . ." repeated Old Chief, looking from one to the other. "Why would my grandson want to jump off a cliff?"

"He wants to fly," blurted Loon. "He fell from his loft last night. Now he thinks he can fly like a bird."

"He had a dream last night," explained Otter. "He said it was real. He wanted to fly high enough to see the Great Turtle and the world beyond. Now he's at the longhouse plucking feathers from a goose to stick on his arms and legs, so he can jump off a cliff and soar through the sky—just like his dream."

Old Chief thought about what he had just been told, as Loon and Otter flicked sticks into the fire, waiting for him to respond. Then he scanned the faces of the elders beside him.

"Do we want our young warriors to jump off cliffs?" asked Old Chief.

"I think we should see what he is thinking," said Hummingbird, a frail old woman from the Bear Clan. The others nodded in agreement.

"Ask Willow to come and see us," said Old Chief.

Otter and Loon ran off and soon returned with Willow, smiling broadly with white feathers stuck in his hair.

"Will you sit with us for a while?" asked Old Chief, motioning to a place in front of him. Willow sat down with Otter and Loon behind him.

"Your friends tell me you want to fly like a bird," said Old Chief. Willow turned to Otter and Loon before he answered—but instead of returning his glance, they stared into the fire.

"Yes," he answered with his eyes beaming. "I'm going to fly!"

The elders sat silently with puzzled expressions on their faces while Old Chief explored Willow's thoughts.

"You had a dream," continued Old Chief. "Tell us about it."

"I don't think it was a dream, but I'll tell you what happened." Willow spoke slowly and clearly, describing every detail from beginning to end. He tried to convey how far he could see from the sky, how thrilling it was, and ended by describing his plan to put feathers on his body and jump off the cliff.

Hummingbird pointed a bent finger at Willow. "What do you think your dream meant?" she asked.

"Flying in my dream made me want to fly again."

"Why do you think that?" she asked.

Willow thought for a time before he answered. "What else could it mean?"

The lines deepened on the old woman's wizened face. "It could mean many things," she said, looking around at the other elders. "Do you want to fly away from something?"

"No."

"Do you have something to fear?"

"What do you mean?"

"Do you have a secret?"

Willow suddenly thought of the untrue things the Wanderer's daughter had said to him. He glanced quickly at Old Chief before he answered.

"I have nothing to fear."

"If you had a secret, would it trouble you?" continued the old woman.

"I don't know," Willow answered.

"No," responded Hummingbird, closing her eyes.

After an awkward silence Old Chief spoke. "Would you like to go to faraway places, my grandson?"

"Yes, I would," answered Willow. "I would like to touch the clouds again and see the Great Turtle."

"Perhaps your dream means you will travel far away. You and I have talked about visiting the People of the Lakes. Is that what disturbs your spirit?"

"I want to go there, grandfather, but first I want to fly again," Willow said, turning to his friends. To his disappointment, they continued to stare into the fire.

"What cliff do you plan to jump from?" asked Old Chief.

"The cliff overlooking the marsh."

"If you fly from there, you will be above the most beautiful place on the Great Turtle's back," said Old Chief enviously. It was the place he gazed upon day after day. "But if you can't fly, you will land on the shore and be killed by the fall."

"I don't think I'll fall," said Willow confidently.

"You don't have any feathers," observed Hummingbird.

"Bats don't have feathers," said Willow. "Neither do bumble bees."

"But you don't even have wings," added Old Heron.

"Flying squirrels don't have wings," Willow answered with a hint of laughter in his voice.

"But squirrels don't fly like birds," said the leader of the Beaver Clan. "They glide—like falling leaves."

"I'll have feathers all over my body," said Willow springing to his feet. "And I'll use my arms as wings."

Old Chief slowly stood up and moved toward Willow, putting his leathery hands on the boy's shoulders. "You are a brave warrior and bear hunter. You make your own decision. We will not prevent you from doing what you must do." His gnarled hands squeezed Willow's shoulders.

"But listen to me, Willow, and try to see through the eyes of an old man. You and your friends are the future of this village. We depend on you now and we will depend on you even more as the years pass. We can't lose any of you—not to bears, or the enemy, or jumping off cliffs."

Willow looked into his grandfather's kind eyes and tried to imagine he was behind them looking out. He imagined his own gnarled hands squeezing the shoulders of a young warrior who wanted to jump off a cliff. He thought of the days and nights he had spent talking to the young man and teaching him the skills he would need to survive. He tried to imagine watching the young warrior leap with feathers attached to his body.

"I can see through your eyes," said Willow. "Can you see through mine?"

"I can," replied Old Chief, releasing his grip. "Don't forget, I was young once—you have not been old yet. I want you to be old one day."

"I hope you'll be there to see me fly, grandfather."

"I will be with you, and I will always be with your spirit, wherever it soars."

– CHAPTER SEVENTEEN –

The Last Flight

The next morning was clear and windless, just as it had been in Willow's dream. The children of the village watched as he and his two friends gathered pine gum and stuck the goose feathers onto his body. Every part was covered except his head and the soles of his feet.

"You look like a goose that's been caught by a fox," cried Loon.

Willow raised his arms above his head. Long brown and white feathers hung from his arms. The older children screamed at the sight and the little ones ran away.

"I know I'll be able to fly!" he said. "When you see me circling above, you'll want to join me."

"I'm going to see how you do it first," said Otter.

Old Chief appeared with Moose by his side. They admired the feathers and the careful way they had been stuck to Willow's body.

"When will you fly?" Old Chief asked.

"I'm ready now," replied Willow.

"There are people waiting to watch you," said Moose. Willow was stunned.

"What? Where are they?"

— *Enemy Arrows* —

"Near the mouth of the river—across from a steep cliff. The water is deep at the base of the cliff," said Old Chief. "They've cleared a path at the top, so you can run fast before you leap."

Willow was astonished by the sudden change. The day before, everyone in the village seemed to doubt his plan. Now they were helping him.

"They're waiting for you," said Old Chief.

Otter and Loon took Willow to an old canoe waiting by the river. They sat him at the front, with his arms apart like a giant bird drying its wings. His friends sat behind him making loud remarks about the cormorant in the front of the canoe, but Willow didn't pay any attention. Moose and Old Chief followed behind in Moose's sleek new canoe.

When they rounded a sharp bend in the river, Willow saw a crowd of people sitting on the bank, waiting to see the spectacle. Most of the village was there. Someone in the crowd spotted Willow and everyone yelled, causing birds to fly from the trees in every direction.

Otter beached the canoe near the cliff and Willow stepped out carefully, keeping his arms stretched out. Old Chief led the human bird up a path to the top of the cliff, overlooking the river and the villagers on the opposite bank. When Willow looked down, he could see the river running far below. The cliff seemed much higher from the top than it had from the river and he remembered what Old Chief had said about living to be old—but his excitement soon overshadowed his fear.

As Old Chief had said, a long path had been cut through the trees to the edge of the cliff, so Willow could run at full speed before soaring over the river and people—and up to the clouds. Today he would see the Great Turtle and the world beyond.

Now the villagers were on their feet, yelling for Willow to fly. For a few seconds he stood there with his arms outstretched, listening to their cheers, then slowly he walked back along the cleared path, away from the edge, until he could barely see Old Chief. He raised his arms higher.

— *The Last Flight* —

"Go when you're ready!" signalled Old Chief.

Willow started toward the cliff at a slow run, going faster and faster as he neared the cliff, his knees high and his arms extended as he sped on, leaving a trail of feathers twirling in the air behind him. Old Chief stepped back as Willow launched himself over the cliff with his arms flapping to gain height.

With the cool wind on his face and the familiar sound of air rushing past his ears, he looked down to see the trees and the river far below—and for one glorious instant he flew through the air as he had in his dream. He knew again what it was like to soar with the birds.

Then he plummeted to the water below—a flapping mass of arms, legs and swirling feathers followed by a huge splash.

He was so badly winded by the fall that he couldn't breathe when he surfaced, his featherless arms thrashing in the water. Fortunately, when he sank below the surface, strong hands immediately grabbed his hair and pulled him up. Otter and Loon hauled him into their canoe with the soggy remnants of broken quills and pine gum stuck to his body and Otter began paddling toward the shore.

"I flew!" Willow gasped. "Did you see? I flew!"

"I saw you soar like a bird," shouted Otter. "Like a bird!"

On the shore, people cheered and screamed for Willow. "He flew like a bird! Willow flew in the sky! Willow!"

When Old Chief called to him from the top of the cliff, Willow looked up and signalled the sign of a successful kill.

"I flew!" he yelled to his grandfather. "I knew I could."

"You did!" cried Old Chief.

When Willow arrived on shore he was mobbed by the entire village. As the crowd continued to cheer, some of the warriors joined hands and threw him into the sky again and again.

"Willow is a bird!" chanted the children, as he was thrown high above their heads. They raced around him, shouting and flapping their outstretched arms.

Old Chief stood with Moose on the shore, watching the celebrations from a distance. He spoke to Willow but in a low voice, far too quiet to be heard over the celebrations. "You will remember this day, Willow, for the rest of your long life." Moose nodded his head.

That evening a thin layer of clouds covered the sky, temporarily obscuring the setting sun and casting a dreary gloom over the land. But as the sun set, a flash of red suddenly appeared beneath the clouds, creating a warm glow, like coals in a fire.

Old Chief, who had been speaking with Lynx, stopped to admire the splendour of the summer sunset. They sat together watching the sky turn from orange to red before fading to the colour of darkness, with no stars in sight.

"When are you leaving for the north?" asked Old Chief.

"As soon as I've packed all my gifts—probably in a few days. I want to get some more packs of tobacco from our friends to the west and a large bag of pink shell disks. They're a favourite of the People of the Lakes. Everything else is ready."

"Would you like some help carrying your packs?" asked Old Chief.

"I wouldn't ask you to carry anything," answered Lynx. "But you're welcome to come with me."

"I am not offering my own back," said Old Chief with a laugh. "Would you consider taking three young bear hunters with you?"

Lynx sat up straight and forced his elbows back until his spine cracked. "Do you think they're old enough to make the journey?"

"I think they are," replied Old Chief. "They are young, but getting stronger every year—and they know how to hunt."

"That's true," answered Lynx. "But are they ready to represent our people? Do you think they can strengthen the bond with our allies?"

"I don't know for certain. They do odd things, as you know, but this could help them gain wisdom. They will see new places and experience other ways of thinking."

"Wisdom . . ." repeated Lynx thoughtfully.

"Apart from that, I want Willow to meet Shrike. He seems to be tormented by questions about his father's death at the hands of the enemy. Perhaps Shrike can help him answer those questions."

"I know Shrike," said Lynx. "He was with Willow's father when he was tortured and killed. I've heard him talk about the battle—it still causes him pain. Those two were close friends. What does Willow want to know?"

"I'm not certain, but something is distressing him."

"I've seen some glimpses of that, too. I'll do what I can do to help." He stood up and stretched, looking down at the dwindling fire. "Yes, I'll take them. With some experience they might become good envoys."

PART II
The Journey North

– CHAPTER EIGHTEEN –

The Northern Lakes

Dawn arrived early after the short summer night. In the shadowless world just before the sun rose, a falcon soared high above Thunder River in search of smaller birds. Far below lay the village surrounded by its towering palisade, with thin trails radiating from the gate in every direction. The falcon turned its head to see four small figures heading north away from the village.

Lynx sensed movement in the dim light and glanced toward the sky to see the wings circling above. For the long journey in the heat of summer he wore a loincloth and moccasins, with a string of wolf teeth and small purple shells around his neck. His fire pouch was slung over one shoulder, a quiver filled with arrows over the other. He held his bow in his right hand.

On his back, Lynx carried a large pack filled with tobacco, shells, and an array of gifts for the People of the Lakes. A smaller pack held his finest ceremonial attire for the celebrations to come. Since he had done the trip many times before, he knew there would be feasts, dances, and speeches for days.

Willow, Otter and Loon followed behind him, each carrying his own heavy load. When they saw Lynx glance skyward they looked up, too. The bird rolled its wings and veered toward the river. For Willow the memory of being high in the sky with nothing beneath him sent tingles through his feet as he trudged along the trail under his heavy pack.

The four soon passed beyond the village cornfields and scattered trees into the forest. All morning they walked, pausing only for water where the streams crossed the trail. When the sun was overhead, they stopped by a small lake to eat some of the corn and dried fish they had brought for the journey. Before they set off again, Otter and Willow jumped into the lake for a quick, cooling swim.

As the day grew hotter their heavy packs began to stick to the skin on their backs. The trail was more uphill than downhill and the hills seemed to get steeper. But none of this bothered the young warriors, who were excited to be going to a place they had never seen. Also, they knew the long journey would give them a chance to show their strength.

At dusk they reached the top of Skunk's Back, the highest land on the trail, which then began to slope downhill. This was the usual resting place for travellers to the northern villages. From here they could see the vast swamp in the distance, stretching from where the sun rose to where it set. The swamp was a natural barrier that kept the northern villages safe from enemy invaders. Few of the southern raiding parties ever came this far—and no one ventured into the great swamp without a guide. On the far side of the swamp the land climbed again to the north.

Skunk's Back was a barren, rocky area covered with low blueberry bushes. When the travellers arrived they could see a mother bear and her cub rooting for berries, but the mother quickly picked up the human scent and bolted into the woods with her whining cub close behind her. The hunters let them go. They had no need for large animals while travelling.

A light breeze blowing across the area kept most of the insects away, so Lynx decided to camp there for the night to avoid the clouds of mosquitoes near the swamp. The well-used Skunk's Back site had a fire pit, a small bark-covered hut, and a pile of firewood for anyone to use.

— *Enemy Arrows* —

While Lynx started the fire, Otter gathered more wood, Loon picked berries from the patch where the bears had been—he knew they always found the sweetest, juiciest berries—and Willow went to hunt rabbits. By nightfall the four weary warriors were resting by the fire enjoying a stew of corn, blueberries, and dried fish while a skinned rabbit roasted on a stick over the fire.

"This is one of my favourite places to camp," said Lynx, extending his arm to turn the spit. "We're close enough to the stars that we can pluck them from the heavens. In the winter you can often see coloured lights travelling across the sky, wave upon wave. Some people say they're the spirits of the dead racing around the moon before the sun chases them away. I'm not sure about that. I've seen them on nights with no moon at all."

"How long will it take us to reach the People of the Lakes?" Willow asked.

"We'll get to the northern villages of our own people tomorrow. First, we'll have to cross the Great Swamp, but that shouldn't be too difficult, if we can find some unused canoes that don't leak too badly. After a few days with our clans, we'll push on through the lakes. You'll know some people from the northern clans from their visits with us. You may even know some of the People of the Lakes who've travelled to our village."

"I've seen some of them," said Loon. "They talk strangely, especially when they try to speak our language."

"What are they like when they're in their own land?" asked Otter.

"They have different ways from us," answered Lynx, as he checked the rabbit. "They see spirits that we don't see. They don't grow much corn and no tobacco, because the frost stays late in the spring—and returns early in the fall. They live the best way they can in the land where they were born."

Willow could see the silhouettes of bats flying in front of the stars. "Why were they born there?" he asked.

Lynx placed another branch on the fire. "I don't know. Only the spirits can answer that question."

The Northern Lakes

As he lay on his back to stare at the brilliant stars, Lynx could see the faces of his companions in the starlight. "The People of the Lakes say there are more stars in the sky than there are grains of sand on all the beaches of all the lakes in their land. I wonder if that's true."

Lynx was up at first light preparing a meal of corn and berries. He knew they might have a difficult journey ahead through the swamp. A light drizzle started to fall just before they left Skunk's Back—and it soon turned into a downpour, making the downhill slope slick with mud and running water. It was a struggle to make it to the bottom.

Before long, the overland trail ended in a clearing at the edge of the swamp where several abandoned canoes had been pulled up and turned over with battered paddles lying beneath them. Lynx selected two canoes strong enough to carry them through the swamp to the open lake, lifted one over to the open water, and motioned for the others to follow him with the other canoe. By now, heavy rain was falling in drops as big as chickadee eggs, causing a low roar throughout the swamp, so he had to yell to the others.

"Otter and Willow can take that canoe and Loon and I will take this one. They're not the best, and they probably leak— but in this rain it won't make any difference. They should get us to the open lake and we'll find better canoes when we get to the village. Otter, Willow, try to stay close to us."

Lynx pushed the canoe into knee-deep water and lowered the packs carefully onto the wet ribs lining the bottom of the canoe. When Loon was settled in the front, he pushed off from the shore and slipped gracefully into the back as Loon began to paddle.

Steering with his paddle, Lynx followed the shallow channel through the reeds and bulrushes. Turtles hovered until the canoe came close and then slid under water and swam away, and thick, black snakes slithered over the lily pads. The rain was so heavy that even the redwing blackbirds were silent. All the birds had taken shelter.

— *Enemy Arrows* —

With Lynx as the guide they followed the winding channels through the swamp. Somehow he was able to keep his course through the maze, even though the sun was hidden. As the rain continued to fall, water collected in the bottoms of the canoes and Lynx was thankful their packs had been well wrapped to keep the tobacco dry.

"Watch where we go now," called Lynx over the sound of the rain. "Remember these channels, because you may have to come through here by yourselves some day. People have been lost in these marshes."

Otter and Willow followed Lynx's canoe as closely as possible as it meandered through the swamp. The branches of dead trees fringed the passageways. At last the group came to a wide channel. For the rest of the day they paddled steadily through its stagnant water until, just as the evening was turning to night, they could smell the faint scent of wood smoke and see the dim lights of distant fires. Finally, the shadowy palisades of a northern village loomed ahead of them.

Lynx was soon being given the welcome of a long-lost champion by his clan. He introduced his three companions and everyone celebrated with a feast of deer meat and fresh fish under a shelter beside the fire, protected from the rain.

While Lynx was telling their hosts about his recent travels, he described in great detail how he had come upon his three young friends one day during the winter, soon after they had killed a bear. Everyone listened eagerly—and the three bear hunters noticed a different level of respect from their hosts after their tale was told.

The rain and the stories continued long into the night.

The next morning the travellers woke to the rising sun, which revealed a wide bay opening into a large lake. At a beach, also hidden in the darkness of the previous night, they found two overturned canoes. The biggest one needed pine gum to close some leaks, but the other was in good shape.

For breakfast Otter netted delicious, fresh fish while Lynx, Willow and Loon worked on the larger canoe. First, Lynx scraped some hard pine sap from the trees into a birchbark container and

The Northern Lakes

melted it beside the fire. He stirred in a dollop of bear grease and some ground charcoal and before long he had a gooey liquid that could be spread over the canoe's cracks to plug the leaks. Then, they turned the boat upside down, rested it across two logs, and Willow crawled beneath to look for any glimmers of light coming through. Once the larger holes had been found, they were easily repaired.

The tiny invisible leaks were more difficult to locate. Leaning across the overturned canoe, Lynx placed his lips over the bark seams and sucked—as if he were trying to draw air through the space between his fingers. In most places the seams were tight, but in a few the air came through, so he covered them with gum. By the end of the day both canoes were ready for another long journey.

Early the next day Lynx leaned down and frantically shook Otter to wake him up. As he opened his eyes, Otter could hear the strain in Lynx's voice. Soon Willow and Loon were awake too, wondering what was causing Lynx such anxiety.

"I had a clear dream last night," he said with a shudder. "It was horrible—almost too horrible to tell."

"What was it?" asked Willow. "Tell us."

"Tell us," echoed Loon, ready to hear the worst. Otter could feel his skin tighten, sensing that the dream involved him.

"I must," said Lynx solemnly, standing above them. Casting his gaze across the village, he took a deep breath and spoke slowly. "We awoke at this place—on a day just like today. The four of us were here—just like this. We set off in the canoes—those same canoes." He pointed to the canoes they had repaired.

"We followed the route along the shore of the Lake of Islands, as I have done so many times. We passed a large cave—one I've passed often, but this time an enormous black serpent—the length of a longhouse with a head as big as a moose's—came charging out of the cave and across the water straight toward us. Its eyes were dark and empty. I yelled to you, Otter, to turn your canoe around and paddle for your life, but the serpent snatched you and disappeared underwater with you in its jaws. The water churned and boiled—and then it went still."

— *Enemy Arrows* —

Lynx looked into Otter's eyes. "We couldn't do anything to save you. There was nothing we could do." He lowered his eyes to the earth.

The pale morning light heightened the look of distress on their faces. They knew the dream was an omen. Otter could see that Lynx was reacting as if he were mourning his death. He reached out and touched the older man's shoulder. "Lynx," he said quietly. "The serpent didn't get me. I'm still alive."

Lynx raised his eyes. A look of recognition flickered over his face. He clasped Otter's arm.

"Yes . . . you *are* still alive." He sat down by the fire, took some tobacco from his fire pouch and sprinkled it onto the coals, as he sang to the spirits of the deep waters. His young companions rose from their places on the floor and sat beside him.

"This dream was a warning," said Lynx. "A clear warning. If we ignore it we'll pay a terrible price. I don't know what will happen if we continue our journey as in my dream, but I don't want to find out. It's too dangerous."

"I don't want to find out either. You must go ahead without me," said Otter.

"But we want you to be with us," said Loon. "I'm not afraid of a serpent with a head as big as a . . ." His voice trailed off before he could finish and he stared nervously at the still lake.

"I think Otter is right," said Willow. "He should stay in the village and wait until we return. We have to go on to the People of the Lakes, since Old Chief asked us to meet with them."

Lynx stood up and pondered the options, wincing again as he recalled his hideous dream. He spoke directly to Otter. "I don't want to see anything like that happen to you. It's best if you stay here with your clan. You'll be welcome until we return."

"I'll stay," replied Otter, trying hard not to show his disappointment, "but I want to hear all about the People of the Lakes when I see you next. Save your stories for me."

"You'll hear them all," said Lynx, grasping Otter by the shoulders. He turned to the others. "Let's load up now—we'll just take one canoe. The sun is almost up."

– CHAPTER NINETEEN –

Preparing the Pigments

Two days later the three travellers were cutting through the blue waters of the Lake of Islands in the large canoe with Lynx in the back, Willow in front, and Loon in the middle. The canoe moved quickly with three paddlers.

When they passed the cave where the dream serpent had emerged, it was nowhere to be seen, but Lynx veered far away from shore to be safe. They hugged the shoreline until they passed the endless islands and then followed a river east into the homeland of the People of the Lakes. Gone were the low meadows of the south. This land was jagged and rocky. They saw no one growing crops, no open fields and few people.

On the eighth day of their trip they encountered a family camped beside a beach where the river opened into another large lake. Lynx steered the canoe to shore so he could speak to a man repairing a canoe. When the man saw them heading in his direction he stood and waited. Behind him was a house made of poles covered in sheets of birchbark with a piece of moosehide over the entrance. Two young boys standing naked beside the door also watched the canoe approach—until the man said something to them in a strange language and the boys disappeared inside.

— *Preparing the Pigments* —

"Look at that sorry pile of sticks," said Loon quietly, pointing to the hut.

"Where canoe?" called the man. It was clear from those words that he could speak little of their language.

"What did I tell you about the way they speak?" said Loon, leaning forward to whisper into Willow's ear. Lynx allowed his paddle to catch the surface on his back swing, sending a splash of cool water across Loon's back.

"We are headed to the gathering place to meet with your people," replied Lynx slowly.

"Gathering place," repeated the man.

"Do your people gather there now?" asked Lynx.

The man didn't reply. He looked blankly at Lynx as the canoe approached the rippling sand beach.

Lynx repeated his question again, this time in the language of the People of the Lakes. The man's face lit up with the sound of his language coming from the mouth of a stranger. He responded excitedly, pointing across the lake.

Two small heads peeked out from behind the door until the hide flew open and a large woman stepped out wearing a deerskin skirt and carrying a bark container. When the man called to her she rushed across the beach into the shallow water and handed the container full of sweet raspberries to Lynx. He ate a handful and said something to the couple, who glanced at Loon and Willow sitting in the canoe and then looked at each other and smiled. The woman said something slowly and precisely and beamed a broad smile as Lynx translated.

"She said to be on your guard when you get to the gathering place. The girls are both strong and beautiful." Lynx waved his hand at the couple and swung the canoe away from shore.

"Paddle hard my friends," said Lynx. "Show your strength." With a few bold strokes they were off again, slicing quickly through the still waters with only the slightest hint of a wake.

For two days they paddled past the towering pines and through rocky islands until they came to the last lake on their journey. This was the place where their people met the People of the Lakes after crossing into their territory. They prepared a camp a half-day's paddle from the gathering place, even though the sun was still high in the western sky, and spent the late afternoon hunting for rabbits.

At dusk Willow and Loon went fishing. They stood silently like herons, holding their pointed poles above their heads, ready to spring at any fish swimming in the shallow water.

"What are we going to do tomorrow when we meet these people?" Loon asked in a hushed voice without moving. "They can't speak to us. We can't understand them. What will we do?"

Willow glanced at Loon for an instant, but didn't answer. He looked back at the water for any sign of movement.

"We've come all this way," Loon continued. "But now that we're almost there, I wonder why we came. Why are we here surrounded by these rocky lakes?"

In the dim light, Willow lowered his spear and waded slowly through the water to Loon. He could feel the ridges of the sand on the soles of his feet.

"You know why we're here, Loon. You heard what Old Chief said when we left our village. These people are our allies. We trade with them and sometimes we fight alongside them. You and I will be their allies if the enemy starts another war with us. We have to keep strong ties with them."

"But what can we do? What do we know about keeping alliances strong? We have to meet them tomorrow and I'm not sure what to do."

Willow didn't answer immediately. He thought of his village and family so far away and longed to see them again. He knew that Loon felt the same way in this strange land, but he remembered what Old Chief had told him.

"We have to keep our eyes wide open and listen carefully. Old Chief will want to know everything we see and hear, so keep a lookout for strange things and tell Lynx if you see anything unusual. Also, it would be good if we could teach some of these people how to speak our language, so we can understand them. We might even learn some words in their strange language."

"Anything unusual," repeated Loon with a forced laugh. "I'll tell Lynx if I see anything that *isn't* unusual."

They walked back to shore where Lynx sat singing to himself beside a low fire, surrounded by wood smoke and the scent of burning tobacco and bear grease. He turned toward them and grinned as he mixed portions of coloured pigments in small bark containers.

"We'll rise at first light tomorrow, my young warrior friends, and prepare to meet with the People of the Lakes. They already know we're here and they're expecting us to arrive at their camp before the sun is high. Of course, they won't know you at all." Lynx let out a loud satisfied laugh, as he continued to stir the pigment. "You won't even know yourselves!"

– CHAPTER TWENTY –

The People of the Lakes

A heavy rain fell during the night forcing Lynx, Willow and Loon to seek shelter under the overturned canoe. The sound of drops falling on the bottom of the canoe brought back memories of the clatter of rain on the longhouse roof and gave them a feeling of being home, though they were so far away.

Before dawn the rain stopped, leaving the smell of wet leaves in the still morning air. The new day arrived with brilliant orange clouds in the east against a sky of robin's egg blue.

Lynx was awakened by the laughing call of a loon drifting in the water close to the camp. He looked out to see the bird's red eyes peering from its black head and knew immediately that the loon was calling them to prepare for the meeting with its people— the People of the Lakes. Out from under the canoe he rolled and walked slowly to the shore where he spoke to the loon, thanking it for bringing the dawn. The feathered black and white spirit called once again in reply, its haunting sound echoing across the still lake. When the loon turned its head to listen to the echoes the white band on the back of its neck reflected the orange light of the rising sun.

Lynx watched silently as the bird glided beside the shore. Sometimes it dipped its black head into the water to listen for fish.

Then, as if being called by the spirits, it threw its head back and emitted a shrill, lingering cry. In a flash of black and white wing feathers amid a glistening spray of water, it rose up and raced across the surface of the lake, using its webbed feet as tiny snowshoes and its wing tips as paddles until it lifted into the brightening sky.

"Don't be impatient," said Lynx, as he watched the bird fade into the distance. "We'll be with your people soon."

Lynx unwrapped a bundle containing sacred decorations and then waded knee deep into the still lake facing the rising sun. Using a frayed twig and looking at his reflection in the still water, he spread pigment of red ochre mixed with bear grease over his face. He swirled the edges of the paint to form spirals and long pointed bear teeth, bending closer to the water as he drew the finest lines. His practiced hands worked with the skill of an experienced envoy who had prepared for many meetings with the People of the Lakes.

A small fleck of pigment fell from the twig into the water, causing a shimmering ring of red oil to spread across the surface in all directions like a brush fire, obscuring his reflection. He stood up straight, waded through the water away from the oil and continued to prepare himself for the ceremony with different pigments—bright greens from copper, vivid yellows from lichens, rich browns from black walnuts and deep blacks from charred wood. He decorated himself all the way down to his knees, peering into the water as he worked.

By the time he had finished the sun had risen above the trees. He took one last look at his reflection and waded to shore to wake his companions. It was time to get them ready for the meeting, too.

He leaned over the sleeping boys and gave their shoulders a gentle shake. Willow was sleeping too soundly to awaken, but Loon opened his eyes to see a brilliantly coloured mysterious figure looming over him. His eyes widened and he gasped at the sight of this strange vision.

"Lynx!" he cried, sitting up and looking frantically around the site for his friend. "Help me, Lynx!"

His shrieks woke Willow from his deep sleep. When Willow saw the strange figure beside him he tried to scramble away on his hands and knees, but Lynx grabbed an ankle and held it tight.

"Wait," said Lynx in a soothing voice. "I'm right here. It's me you see."

Once the panic had left them, Willow and Loon stood up and checked him to make sure he was really Lynx.

"I can see who you are now," said Willow, with a weak laugh, admiring Lynx's colourful decorations. "But you frightened us. How did you get like that without waking us up?"

"Come and I'll show you," Lynx answered.

Before long Willow and Loon were sitting by the fire eating smoked whitefish, watching as Lynx knelt down and unrolled another precious bundle of ornaments. They had prepared for other ceremonies from an early age and knew the meaning of each colour and shape that would be painted on their bodies, as well as the symbolic trinkets they would wear.

"You dishevelled muskrats are going to be transformed into eagles," said Lynx. "You're the representatives of our great people now and you must arrive at the gathering place in splendour." He surveyed Willow and Loon from head to toe with a frown on his face.

"This will take some time," he said, as he unwrapped a bark container and handed them each a small ball of bear grease. He gave Loon a thin comb carved from a deer antler.

"First, rub this through your hair until it shines like a beaver's coat. Then comb it straight. After that, we can paint you to look like the brave hunter you are."

He turned toward the ornaments and began to chant about the animals that had given their bones, teeth and feathers for the grandeur and teachings of his people. As he sang, he sprinkled dried tobacco leaves on the fire and fanned the smoke over his collection. Then he rose and danced solemnly in a circle around the flames—and around Willow and Loon, busy combing the grease through their hair.

Once his dance was over, Lynx helped his young friends paint their faces and decorate their bodies in shapes and colours indicating their status as young warriors and envoys. He covered their foreheads with red and black lines and their arms and chests with green and yellow. When Lynx finally stood back to admire his work, the frown had left his face.

As the paint congealed he added the final touches, giving Willow and Loon necklaces of white shells and beaver teeth.

"These are from Old Chief," Lynx said. "When the People of the Lakes see them, they'll know you are his representatives." He added copper earrings decorated with shells and a bear-tooth necklace. "They'll know you've killed a bear," he said proudly. Then he gave them each a pair of ankle bracelets adorned with shells. "And these will show that you can run as fast as the wind."

Next, Lynx unwrapped several sacred eagle feathers and attached one in the hair of each of his companions before putting three in his own hair. At last, he looked at his friends with a smile. Willow's long slender arms and legs and his natural poise were accentuated by the vivid colours and the ornaments he wore. His narrow face looked longer than usual because of the vertical lines of red and black on his cheeks, and the yellow paint on his prominent nose. The single feather in his hair gave him the bearing of a towering tree.

Yellow and blue circles painted around Loon's arms and the green lines across his chest brought out the toughness of his smaller physique and emphasized his solid chest, while bright colours on his face made his teeth shine like a full moon.

"Good," said Lynx with a broad smile. "Very good. Now you are eagles!"

Willow and Loon looked at each other in amazement. For the first time in their lives they were eagles.

A serious look came over Lynx's painted face. "Remember, my friends, why we're here. We have work to do for our people, and we'll do it well."

Willow began to dance with excitement, jangling the shells on his ankles. His spirit had been freed from his imprisoning thoughts.

He had forgotten about the Wanderer's daughter and her poisonous lies about his father.

When the sun was near the high point in the sky they set off for the final part of the journey to the People of the Lakes. The clouds had disappeared, leaving a brilliant blue sky and a gentle breeze. The lake was studded with tiny islands and pine trees clinging to cracks in the rocks. Across the water they could see the antlers and head of a bull moose, swimming from one island to another. If they were hunting they could have caught it with ease, but they stuck to their course.

A breeze guided them to their destination—the gathering place on a beach at the east end of the lake where the wind always blew. Willow could see several birchbark canoes on the sand and a handful of low huts in the narrow meadow just beyond. A group of men and women stood silently not far from the water.

"We can stop paddling now," Lynx said. Willow rested his paddle on the edge of the canoe as Lynx back-paddled, bringing the canoe to a drifting stop close to the shore.

"What are we doing?" asked Loon, turning around to Lynx.

"We have to wait until they invite us to join them," he replied in a low voice. To keep the canoe from drifting into shore, he feathered his paddle, slicing it back and forth through the water without lifting it. Willow looked at the strangers, who smiled back. Their eyes showed excitement, but they didn't speak.

At last, a thin old man dressed in a simple loincloth walked forward across the sand and motioned to Lynx to come to shore. With that the others began to yell out to Lynx. The older women pointed to Willow and Loon and called excitedly to a group of young women, who, Willow noticed, were beautiful—just as he had been told. At the back of the crowd, a small group of young men looked at the newcomers apprehensively.

Once the visitors were on shore, Grackle, the thin old chief of the People of the Lakes, welcomed them to the gathering place and introduced them to the other leaders. Willow and Loon couldn't understand what he said, so they smiled and responded in their own language. The young men, dressed like their chief, gathered closer to inspect Willow and Loon and examine their ceremonial dress.

"I don't think these simple people can understand our language," said Loon quietly to Willow, amid the strange sounds coming from everyone around them.

"Some of us can," replied a young man standing behind him. He was the same height as Loon, but far more muscular, and his huge rough hands looked strong enough to strangle a bear. He looked Loon straight in the eyes with a penetrating stare until Loon turned away.

"I'm Willow, and this is my friend Loon," said Willow, stepping forward. "We live beside Thunder River—close to the Beautiful Lake."

"Do you play stickball?" asked the young man, whose hair was tied back with a strip of deerskin.

"Yes, we do," answered Willow. "How do you know our language?"

"Do you play well?" he asked, moving closer. Willow didn't know how to respond.

"We are the best!" Loon interjected. Willow winced at his friend's exaggeration. He knew they would be put to the test.

Several other young men pressed in closer. They listened to the words, though they couldn't understand what was being said.

"I'm Falcon—and these are my brothers," said the young man turning to his friends. They were also dressed for the woods in loincloths and moccasins, just as Willow and Loon had been when the day dawned. Some were decorated with tattoos and earrings, but they certainly weren't clothed and decorated as envoys of their people.

As Falcon talked, small children came forward to touch the ornaments worn by the honoured guests. The youngest rattled the shells on Loon's ankles and laughed with delight, since they had rarely seen such opulence. Loon stepped back out of reach.

— *Enemy Arrows* —

"We'll see what your best is when we play tomorrow," said Falcon, looking into the canoe. "You didn't bring sticks. Don't worry, we'll find some for you."

Falcon scanned Loon from the single feather on top of his head to the moccasins on his feet. He said something to his friends and then left with the others following behind. They were soon visible on the far reaches of the beach, playing stickball with breathtaking speed and agility.

The welcome celebration began with a feast and continued with singing and dancing late into the night. Lynx exchanged gifts with the elders and chiefs of the People of the Lakes. They were especially grateful for the tobacco and corn, as they had used up their stores from the fall harvest and it was too early to trade for the summer's harvest. They were also pleased with the gifts of flint from the cliffs near the Great Falls. The women prized the purple and white shells from distant lands to the east.

Of all the gifts given by Lynx, none was welcomed more than the fishnet made by the women in his village. The People of the Lakes marvelled at its perfectly formed holes and length. They pulled at it—gently at first—to test its strength. It held fast.

Then Willow and Loon watched in amazement as the People of the Lakes showered Lynx with gifts of rare furs and presented them with beautiful silver beads.

When the festivities were over the elders sat with their guests around the fire, speaking in the language Willow and Loon couldn't understand. Sometimes Lynx would translate for his companions when the talk was about great battles, or to repeat jokes made by their hosts—leaving the young warriors to laugh after everyone else had finished. Lynx looked directly at Willow when they talked about Shrike, who had been with his father in his last battle with the enemy, and all eyes turned to Willow.

The chief of the People of the Lakes spoke to Willow in the language of his visitors. His heavy accent made it difficult for Willow to understand.

Lynx clarified his words. "Your father was a great friend and brother to us. He lived with us and became one of us. We hope you will become our friend as well."

"Yes," added the chief, as he reached over to clasp Willow's arm.

"I know we will become friends," answered Willow.

Talk then turned to the enemy from across the lake and the new pact of peace that had joined all of the warring enemy nations into one nation. Deep creases formed around the eyes of Grackle, the thin old chief, and the discussion continued late into the night.

– CHAPTER TWENTY-ONE –

Testing the Strength of the Allies

Late in the morning, after sacred chants by the elders, the stickball game began. The playing field took up the entire beach—from the water's edge to the rocks and huts behind the sandy meadow. The canoes had been moved to the shore beyond the goal posts planted at each end. A cool breeze blew off the lake.

Falcon gave Willow and Loon two battered sticks to play with. Their moosehide netting was tough and hard and they showed the marks of many years of hard play, but they were light and well balanced.

"You be on my side," Falcon said to Willow. "Your friend will be on their side." He looked at Loon and pointed to a knot of players at the far end of the beach.

"I always play with Willow when we're at home," said Loon.

"You're in our home now," said Falcon with his piercing stare.

Willow gave Loon a nudge. "Play well, Loon—but not too well. Remember we're the guests."

"No, no. Don't hold back because you're guests!" Falcon protested. "You say you're the best. We want to see for ourselves."

A pair of old women put out the breakfast fires on the beach and cleared away any loose branches. Then they joined the other women sitting on the rocks overlooking the beach with the children and elders, who were waiting excitedly for the game to start, yelling and clapping their hands.

It was going to be a small game with only twelve players on each team. Willow was introduced to his teammates—men and youths of every shape and size and age. Falcon spoke loudly to them, getting more and more boisterous, until finally he raised his stick and yelled wildly at the sky. The others raised their sticks and yelled even louder.

At the far end of the beach the players on Loon's team yelled back, brandishing their sticks above their heads. The spectators joined in the cheering, whacking broken branches against the rocks to add to the noise.

Grackle, the chief, stood at the water's edge, midway between the two posts, holding the ball. When he raised his hand above his head, the game was on—and both teams ran toward him at full speed. Just before they collided he threw the ball high. It arced near the sparkling blue sky and came down toward Loon. He raised his stick above his head to make the catch, but a heavy player from the other team knocked him to the ground before he could touch the ball. Then a mob of players ran over him while he lay face down in the sand.

Willow charged to the far end of the beach after Falcon and the rest of his team. Although he was a fast runner, he wasn't used to playing on sand. The other players darted from side to side across the beach, but he couldn't keep up until he moved onto the grassy area near the huts.

"I'm in the open!" he cried to his teammates. "Pass it to me!" No one did. Instead, the ball whizzed back and forth among the other players on the beach.

Loon attempted to intercept the passes without success. At one point the ball flew past his head and splashed into the lake behind him. He raced to scoop it out of the water, but another player landed on him with full force—and then another—and another. He was buried under water with the wind knocked out of him. Finally, someone grasped the wet ball and hurled it toward the post at the far end of the beach. The mass of players lifted themselves off Loon's flattened body and sped after it.

Falcon caught the soaked ball, twisted in mid-air, and passed it to Willow before he touched the ground. Willow made the catch, but the force of the wet, heavy deerskin surprised him. The ball pushed his stick aside and kept going until it was caught by an opposing player, who raced down the beach and slammed it at the post. It left a dark blotch before falling on the sand with a thud. The spectators screamed and beat their branches on the rocks. Willow looked down the length of the beach at Loon's teammates and noticed Loon vomiting in the lake nearby.

Lynx sat beside the chief on the rocks above the beach with a smile on his face. He wasn't cheering for either team.

Falcon came up behind Willow and slapped him hard on the shoulder, pushing him forward. "Good try for that catch," he said, as he dashed off in the direction of the ball. Willow ran after him, trying desperately to follow the play.

Out of nowhere, a long pass came from the knot of players at the end of the beach. The ball hit the ground at Willow's feet, spraying him with sand. He scooped it up and ran toward the post. Two opponents stood between him and the goal and there was no one on his team nearby. Instantly the two players charged him. As Willow lifted his stick to hurl the ball over their heads, his stick was hit from behind. He turned around to see Loon's stick raised above him. The ball flew into the air and was snatched by one of Willow's opponents who headed down the beach—with Willow and Loon on his heels.

Willow turned to see the ball hurtling past his head toward Loon. This time it was his turn to knock it away from his friend. He swung at Loon's stick, but missed, so Loon kept running ahead—right into the path of Falcon. When he dodged to his left Falcon followed. When he leapt back to his right, Falcon jumped in front of him again. With nowhere to go, Loon held the ball above his head and ran straight at Falcon with Willow on his tail. Falcon crouched low like a tree stump and sent Loon tumbling over him.

— *Testing the Strength of the Allies* —

Willow and Falcon bolted after the ball toward the far end of the beach, leaving Loon gasping for breath in the sand. An old man sitting on the rocks turned to Lynx and smiled the toothless smile of a seasoned stickball player.

As hard as he tried, Willow couldn't catch up to the passes of the opposing team. The ball seemed to go all around him, but he was never close enough to intercept it. He was getting dizzy from running and was having trouble telling the teams apart. Then the ball rolled past him into the water. He scooped it up with his stick and paused ready to throw, trying first to read the play and observe the position of the players.

His nearest opponent was charging toward him. Falcon and two others on his team were racing toward the post at the far end of the beach with sticks held high, ready to catch a long, long pass. They were in the clear. The rest of the opposing players were approaching him with looks of glee on their faces. He could tell they wanted to shove him under the water as they had done to Loon.

In a flash he recalled what Moose had said about running from memory. He thought of the time he had raced through the forest with his eyes closed, trying to remember where the trees were. In the instant before the opposing players landed on him, he hurled the ball high into the sky, so it would land behind the thundering mob.

To his relief they stopped and looked up for the ball—but they couldn't see it beside the blinding sun.

He lowered his head like a buck and charged through the squinting, staggering group. Most of the players were heavier than he was, but catching them off guard he sent them rolling in different directions, all the time keeping the path of the ball in his memory. Without looking, he pictured the ball arcing beside the sun and falling toward the beach somewhere close to him.

Then he saw the shadow of the ball on the sand ahead. It fell directly on its shadow with a thump. Willow scooped it up and hurled it to the far end of the beach where Falcon had been standing—but Falcon had moved. The ball was caught by an opposing player who leaned back and hurled it with all his force to the other end of the beach, where one of his teammates caught it and slammed it against the post. Willow saw his brilliant play go up in smoke.

Then a mob of players ran over him.

— *Testing the Strength of the Allies* —

Whoops of joy came from the spectators on the rocks.

"Good play!" shouted Falcon to Willow as he flashed past. Willow saw Loon struggling to walk toward the far end of the beach and ran toward him.

"You took a bad fall," said Willow.

"I didn't fall," he replied, breathing heavily and shaking his head. "I was ambushed."

"Are you hurt?"

Loon stopped walking and leaned close to Willow's ear. "I'm having trouble keeping the teams straight," he said, gasping for breath and spitting sand as he spoke. "I know you and I are on opposite sides, but I have a feeling all the other players are against us. Something isn't right."

"They *are* against us. We're from a different team. We know it and they know it."

"They want to kill us!" yelled Loon over the cheering.

"I think they just want to injure us," answered Willow. "Play your best."

The ball whizzed past Loon's head at the speed of an arrow. "They're going to kill us!" he shrieked, as he shot after the ball with Willow following close behind him.

"Your warriors play with determination," said the chief to Lynx.

"Yes, they do. And they will learn from your warriors," replied Lynx. "Soon they'll have the skills to match their determination. When they return home they'll be unbeatable."

The chief received the compliment with a satisfied sigh. "There's much they can teach us as well."

The game lasted through the afternoon. No one cared about the score. It wasn't as important as the heroics of the players. There were few serious injuries. Willow cracked a finger when a player on the other side slashed at his stick, but he played on like a champion. His eyes shone with the thrill of the contest and his spirit soared.

Loon suffered another punishing fall on the wet sand by the shoreline and two large players landed on him one after the other. He was dragged out of the game by an old woman, who screamed at the players and jabbed her finger toward their eyes. Loon wasn't conscious and couldn't hear her. Willow heard, but couldn't understand. Lynx heard as well and knew exactly what she said.

"She's right," said the chief.

"Yes," answered Lynx.

The game ended with loud cheers from both sides.

At dusk someone spotted a canoe at the far end of the lake. It was heading toward the gathering place, pushed by a light evening breeze, with two figures paddling in unison. A few people straggled out to meet them under the darkening sky while everyone else gathered around a fire on the beach. The bruised and battered players lay flat in the sand looking up at the brilliant stream of stars crossing the sky. Few of them could move.

In the dim firelight two young women sang a haunting melody that Willow didn't recognize—in a language he didn't know. They opened their arms to the sky and swayed like branches in the wind. At times the older women joined them, then their voices would fade away. Drifting in the world between waking and sleeping, Willow thought he could understand some of the words. He could picture the singers' lips forming the words and the soothing sounds of the unfamiliar words communicated their meaning to him. The closer he came to sleep, the better he understood them. Far in the background he could also hear sounds coming from the canoe and the people who had gone to meet it. They were calling to each other across the water. Soon the visitors came ashore in the dark, but by then Willow had fallen asleep by the fire. Loon lay next to him, twitching and groaning in his sleep.

By the time Willow opened his eyes again, the sun was up. His cracked finger throbbed with pain. He lifted himself stiffly from the sand, groggy with sleep and aching from the brutal game, and headed toward the rocks to pee. As he passed one of the huts, a head popped out from behind the deerskin cover and a young woman crept out. She stood up in front of him and stared at him. Willow noticed her, but saw only an obstacle to avoid on his way to the rocks. She said something in her language, but he smiled at her and kept going.

"Wait," she said in his language. "I know you."

He squinted with the sun in his eyes, but didn't recognize her.

"Yes, I do know you. You are the little snapping turtle," she continued in his language. "But you're not so little anymore."

"Why do you call me that?"

"Because you hide in your shell when you're afraid and you strike like a snapper to protect yourself." She gave a gentle laugh that showed her white teeth. "And you have a vicious bite."

Willow looked at the young woman. Her arms and face were covered with tattoos and a small pendant of orange and black feathers dangled from her neck. Her voice was familiar, but in his dazed state he couldn't remember where he had heard it before. He only knew that her melodious voice sparked a feeling of panic deep inside him—like a fire racing through a dry forest.

"I don't know you," he said, looking into her dark eyes. He stepped around her and headed for the rocks at a slow trot. As he heard her calling to him, he wanted to run into the forest to hide in his shell like a turtle.

– CHAPTER TWENTY-TWO –

Monsters in the Lake

Late the next morning, the net ceremony began under a gray sky. As a strong wind blew from the lake toward the beach, pushing low clouds overhead, a young girl was led toward the shore by the women of her clan. She stood barefoot in the sand adorned with necklaces and feathered earrings, smiling apprehensively and looking to her mother for reassurance. A robe of white rabbit skin hung over her shoulders and down past her knees. The women danced around her, singing quietly, moving from the waves to the beach and back, in and out of the water.

A shaman walked toward the girl carrying the net Lynx had brought as a gift to the elders. He held it high above his head and sang in a deep voice that contrasted with the gentle voices of the dancers. Before long, the men of the village began to dance too, going in the opposite direction to the women, circling both the girl and the fishing net.

While Willow and Loon stood near the dancers, wondering what was happening, Lynx stood among the elders of the People of the Lakes. Once again he spoke with them in words Willow and Loon couldn't understand.

"There you are!" said someone behind Willow and Loon, slapping them hard on their backs. "You two played hard yesterday—beyond fear. We like that!" They turned to see a broad smile on Falcon's face where his scowl had been the day before.

"We thought we had drowned you a few times," he laughed, looking at Loon.

"I thought you had, too," said Loon, without returning the laugh.

"Don't worry," said Falcon. "We wouldn't drown you. We might make you feel like it, but we wouldn't do it really." He looked pleased with himself as he added, "We would only drown you by accident!"

"What is happening to this girl?" Willow asked, wanting to talk of other things.

"She's getting married," replied Falcon.

"Who's she marrying?" asked Loon.

"She's marrying the net your people gave us. You see how the shaman carries it above his head? He's keeping it away from the sand and the water, so it can marry the girl. Then our men will use it for fishing."

Loon looked askance at Willow.

"Do you mean she'll have to live her life with a fishing net, feeding and taking care of it? Will she have to bear its children?" he asked.

Falcon responded with a perplexed look on his face. "You ask so many odd questions. Watch and see what happens."

The dancing stopped and the shaman threw the net over the young girl. She stood motionless, like a frightened rabbit. Then he raised his hands high, chanting as he moved, and wrapped the net around the girl before leading her into the waves. The dancers followed, still swaying and singing. When the girl was in water up to her waist the shaman turned her around to face the people on shore. She smiled again and the people on shore threw berries and flowers into the lake beside her.

"Now they're married," said Falcon. "The spirit of the net has a beautiful young wife. It will tell the fish that they'll be treated well, and it will catch many fish."

"But is she . . ." Loon stumbled. "Is she the wife of a fish net?"

"Only for this season," replied Falcon. "She won't be allowed to be with anyone else until the spring. Then she'll be free to marry whenever she's ready. The net will marry another young girl next spring and the spring after that."

The girl was led through the waves back to shore and the dancing began again, followed by feasting and singing and more dancing until the sun had set and the fires burned low.

By nightfall the wind had died and the sound of waves lapping on the beach had faded into silence. The night sky cleared to reveal a wide sparkling river of stars stretching from one horizon to the other, while fireflies blinked in the grass and sparks from the fire rose to mingle with the stars.

A small group of chiefs and elders gathered around one of the fires on the beach to listen to Lynx talk about recent attacks by the People from Across the Lake. Nearby, Willow and Loon sat with the other stickball players, talking and laughing about the game. As Falcon translated between the visitors and his own friends, Willow listened carefully, trying to pick up some useful words.

"When did you learn to speak our language?" he asked Falcon.

"I was young. I went with my father and mother to spend a winter in the south. I remember that your people lived in big houses in a village surrounded by walls. I made friends and we played together all winter long. We tracked animals in the snow and pretended to hunt with spears, but we were too young to catch anything.

"Sometimes my friends would take me inside their homes," Falcon continued. "I remember how huge they were—and how many people lived in them. Most of all I remember the shafts of light that came through the smoke holes. They seemed to move slowly from one side of the big room to the other, pointing together in the same direction—always at the sun. Once I thought I could climb up a shaft, all the way to the sun. I tried, but fell on my face."

Willow and Loon laughed at his foolishness, even though they had tried the same thing when they were young. When Falcon repeated his story to his friends in their language, they laughed and made joking comments that Willow and Loon couldn't understand.

"We stayed there beside the village until the days became longer," Falcon said. "When the spring rains came, we returned to our own lakes, but the next winter we did the same thing. I spent two winters among your people."

One of Falcon's friends said something to him and then looked at Willow.

"He wants to know why your people live behind walls. How can you live without seeing the forest?"

"We can't see the forest unless we go outside the palisade," answered Willow. Falcon translated and his friends reacted with frowns and murmurs.

"Our houses are behind walls because our enemies sometimes attack us. The walls protect us," Willow continued as Falcon translated.

"Who are your enemies?" asked Falcon.

"We call them the People from Across the Lake. They call themselves something else. We live on Thunder River on the northern shore of a huge lake, the Beautiful Lake. It's so wide it takes our strongest warriors a day and a night to cross by canoe—and that's in calm weather. But it's usually too dangerous to cross. We follow the shoreline to get to the south side where our enemies live. They've always been our enemies. They attack us mostly in the spring and the fall, but they can appear any time. Without the palisades to protect us, we'd be massacred in our sleep."

"We fight them, too," said Falcon. "Some of our warriors have joined your people on raids across the lake."

"Shrike fought with my father long ago," said Willow. "We're going to see him."

"I know Shrike," said Falcon. "His painted images watch over the lakes."

Someone else asked a question and Falcon translated.

"Why do you keep your villages in the same place all the time? You'd be safer moving around as we do."

Loon laughed out loud at the question—to the displeasure of Falcon and his friends.

"We can't move our villages like you. Our longhouses and palisades are surrounded by cornfields. They don't move easily. We only move when the fields are tired and the firewood has been used up."

Falcon asked Loon another question. "Why do you grow corn if it forces you to live in villages you can't move?"

Loon looked shocked at the question. He turned to Willow for help.

"Why do we grow corn?" Willow repeated. As he did, he noticed the Wanderer's daughter appear in the light of the fire where she sat down quietly near the elders. Falcon and his friends noticed her, too. Willow felt a gnawing pain in his stomach as he attempted to answer the question. He wanted to slip into a shell.

"We grow corn because it's our life," he said, leaving time for Falcon to translate. "It allows us to get through the winters without starving. Most of all, we can carry it on hunting trips, or when we go to war. We can travel farther and faster than anyone else because we don't have to hunt on the way, and we trade it for things we don't have." He looked over at Lynx who sat listening with the elders on the other side of the low fire. Lynx nodded back at him imperceptibly.

"I have a question for you," Willow said to Falcon. "Why don't your people grow any corn? Why do you trade with us to get it?"

Falcon repeated the question to his friends. They talked excitedly among themselves for some time, waving their hands for emphasis. Finally, when everyone was silent, Falcon answered.

"Because we're hunters."

Willow wasn't satisfied with the answer. "We hunt, too," he said. "But we grow our food as well. Why don't you do both?"

He waited for Falcon's response, but Loon interrupted. "Yes, we're hunters," said Loon. "We killed a bear this year before the snow melted." He held out the bear tooth strung around his neck for everyone to see. Falcon and his friends wanted to hear more, so Loon told them about killing the bear with pointed sticks.

By now, the attention of everyone around the fire had turned toward the younger men and Lynx described how he found the three young hunters beside the lake and how they got Otter home before he froze to death.

"These two will be known as great hunters," he said proudly. "Just like their fathers."

"Who is your father?" Grackle asked Loon. Loon told all about his father and his great hunting skills, pausing now and then to let Falcon translate.

"You must bring him with you next time you come," said Grackle.

Falcon turned to Willow. "And who is your father?"

"My father was Gray Fox, a great warrior and hunter."

"Your father was a strong and generous man," said the thin old chief. "We welcomed him whenever he came to see us. One year he brought a beautiful young woman with him. I think her name was Orchid."

"She's my mother," said Willow.

"Ah, yes," replied Grackle with a smile. "She is a strong woman. How old were you when your father was killed by the enemy?"

"I was small," said Willow.

The chief continued. "I remember he had a tattoo on his chest—a beautiful tattoo with different colours. It was a bear, I believe. I wanted one like it."

"I remember it, too," said Lynx. "But I thought it was a beaver."

"I thought it was a bear," said the chief, turning to Willow. "You must know."

"I don't remember," Willow answered. "I was too . . ." He was interrupted by a soft voice coming from behind the elders.

"It was a running deer."

All eyes turned toward Oriole, who sat staring into the fire. Her dark hair shone in the firelight and the orange feathers braided into her hair trapped the warm glow of the coals.

"Yes, it was a running deer," exclaimed Grackle. "Of course, it was. He was a champion deer hunter."

"That's right," echoed Lynx.

Willow's eyes flashed from Lynx to Oriole and back. How could she know it was a deer? He could feel the anguish he'd felt days before churning inside him again. With only a few words, she had bound his spirit in tight ropes and twisted them until he could barely breathe.

"Your father knew Gray Fox?" Lynx asked Oriole.

"I don't know," she answered nervously, looking up from the fire.

"Then how did you know?" Lynx pressed.

Oriole smiled a strained smile. She glanced at Willow for an instant and then turned to Lynx, but before she could respond, the Wanderer appeared from the darkness.

"There you are Lynx, my old friend!" he yelled, appearing in the light of the fire. "I heard you were here." Lynx stood to greet the Wanderer and they admired each other in the flickering light.

"Yes, you're still as strong as ever," said the Wanderer.

"And you'll outlive your own grandchildren," replied Lynx.

They sat down on the sand and talked about the times they had spent travelling together. Lynx regarded the Wanderer as a reliable source of news about the movements of friends and enemies alike. Once the talk turned away from Oriole, she stood up and slipped into the darkness.

The Wanderer and his daughter left the next morning before dawn.

Lynx was repairing his canoe on the beach in the rays of the rising sun when the chief approached him.

"Are you leaving us?" asked the chief.

"Not yet," replied Lynx. "I want to find someone before I return home. You know Shrike?"

"Of course I do. He's the man with red hands."

"Where is he this time of year?"

"Probably at his mine," replied the chief, pointing to the northeast. "Falcon knows the way. He can take you whenever you're ready to go."

"He's a strong young man," said Lynx. "We'll be grateful to have him as our guide."

"He can keep you away from the monsters," said the chief ominously.

"Monsters?" repeated Lynx. "What monsters?"

"They live in the lake where Shrike has his camp."

"Have you seen them?"

"No, but I know they're there. Everyone knows they're there."

– CHAPTER TWENTY-THREE –

Battle on the Wide Bay

As the nights passed, the moon changed from a thin sliver to a bright orb, round and full like a droplet of dew on a spider web lit by the morning sun. With the full moon the People of the Lakes left their gathering place in small groups to follow the plentiful gifts of the land. Each group knew when the different types of berries would be ripe, and everyone had their favourite spots to camp while enjoying the harvest. At the same time, the small bands followed the fish from stream to stream, lake to lake, so they would be at the right place when the catches became most plentiful.

Lynx, Willow and Loon set off with Falcon as their guide to find the camp of the man with the red hands—the man who had been with Gray Fox when he was killed by the enemy. The young warriors watched in wonder as Falcon took them through the mazes of lakes and rivers and portages. Falcon and Willow paddled in one canoe while Lynx and Loon followed in the other. As the days passed Falcon tried to teach Willow his language and the customs of his people. They talked of many things as their canoe sliced through the still waters of the northern lakes.

"I wonder what they are talking about all the time," Loon said to Lynx one afternoon while they listened to the animated voices coming from the other canoe.

— *Battle on the Wide Bay* —

"This is why we're here, Loon," replied Lynx patiently. "Old Chief and the elders want to keep these people as friends and allies. That takes time and effort. Willow's making the effort to get to know Falcon."

"The more I know Falcon, the less I want to know him," laughed Loon, but with a serious tone in his voice. "He almost killed me in the first stickball game we played."

"I remember that."

"Then he said he would only drown me by accident." Loon stopped paddling, as he carefully chose his words. "That makes it hard for me to respect him."

Lynx raised his eyebrows.

"Apart from his threats to me, he's disrespectful to us," Loon continued. "He speaks down to us. He thinks we're stupid because we don't know the routes through lakes we've never seen before—and he eats like a starving wolverine. Do we really need Falcon as an ally?"

Lynx remained quiet. He paddled without missing a stroke.

Loon turned in the canoe to look at him. "Do you think you can trust him as an ally?"

"Yes, I do," replied Lynx firmly.

Loon continued to stare at Lynx, as if waiting for him to say more.

"Keep paddling, my friend," said Lynx. "We're almost at our camp and there'll be plenty of fish to fill your empty stomach."

They paddled to a flat rock on an island near the mouth of a stream where the trout were plentiful, and before dark they had netted enough for a feast. After cleaning and roasting their catch, they ate together in the fading light of the summer sun and then fell asleep by the fire.

At dawn the sky was filled with streaks of crimson from distant clouds and the air was unusually still. Lynx netted some more trout and cooked them on hot rocks by the fire before the others stirred. When the red sun appeared above the horizon, he roused his friends with the promise of fresh-cooked fish.

"We have a long way to travel today," said Falcon while they ate. "There's a wide bay between us and the river where we're going. If we paddle hard, we can get to the other side before dark and from there it's not far to Shrike's camp. If it's too windy we'll have to go around it. It can be dangerous."

Willow and Lynx nodded. Loon appeared not to hear what he said.

"My canoe was leaking yesterday," said Lynx, putting his arm on Willow's shoulder. "I want to do some repairs before I set off. You're good at repairing canoes, Willow. You can help me. I'm sure we can catch up to Loon and Falcon without too much trouble," he added with a hint of challenge in his voice.

Loon didn't react. He had no desire to paddle with Falcon and no interest in joining forces with him in a contest against Lynx and Willow. Falcon felt the same.

"Why don't I help you with the repairs while they go ahead?" Falcon suggested.

"They don't know the route," answered Lynx.

Falcon turned with a disgruntled look on his face and began loading Loon's gear into the canoe they would take.

"Let's get moving," he said sharply to Loon.

"I'll help you with the repairs, Lynx," said Loon, irritated by Falcon's sharpness. "I know how to repair leaks as well as Willow."

"I've seen Willow do this before," replied Lynx. "I want his help today."

When Falcon and Loon had loaded their canoe, Falcon signalled for Loon to sit in the front.

"I'd rather be in the back," said Loon.

"You're lighter," responded Falcon.

Loon glanced over to Lynx for support, but he knew the lighter person always sat in the front. There was no way to avoid it. He would be in a canoe controlled by Falcon. They set off without another word.

— *Battle on the Wide Bay* —

Through the mazes of lakes and rivers and portages.

"We'll catch you soon!" yelled Lynx, as they paddled away. Before long he and Willow had turned their canoe over and were carefully

— Enemy Arrows —

checking for loose seams. Willow put his lips against the seams and checked for leaks, but couldn't find any.

Lynx took a pitch stick from beside the fire and began to dab the melted pitch on the canoe at random.

"I don't see any leaks in this canoe," said Willow.

"No," said Lynx. "I guess there aren't any. I think we've fixed the problem. Let's see if we sink or float."

He flipped the canoe on to his shoulders and carried it to the water, leaving Willow to puzzle over what he had said.

Falcon and Loon paddled silently along the shore toward the bay with Loon setting a regular rhythm. He had the sense that Falcon's strokes were always slightly ahead of his own, as though he was trying to set the pace instead of Loon.

"Doesn't he know to follow my stroke?" Loon wondered to himself, keeping his rhythm steady, no matter how hard Falcon pushed him. A web of mutual distrust hung over the canoe like a wet fishing net.

When the sun was high Loon and Falcon rounded a rocky point to see the lake open into a vast bay. The wind was coming up and a few whitecaps dotted the waves. Loon could barely see the opposite shore where they were headed. Only the faint outline of distant trees was visible. He wondered how they would get there. If they took the direct route across the mouth of the bay, they could be on the far side before dusk, but if they followed the shoreline they would arrive long after dark. Falcon swung the canoe in toward the bay to follow the shore.

"Where are you going?" demanded Loon.

"We'll follow the shoreline," replied Falcon.

Loon turned around to see if Falcon had lost his senses.

"But we can go straight across," Loon said with a bewildered laugh.

"Not me—it's too windy."

"Not you! Then let me sit in the back and I'll take us across."

Falcon didn't alter his course. He kept the canoe close to the shore.

— Battle on the Wide Bay —

"Why don't you cross?" insisted Loon.

"It's too dangerous," said Falcon. "If the winds get worse, they'll blow us into the open lake and we'll never be seen again."

Loon couldn't understand what Falcon was saying.

"My people wouldn't hesitate to cross this bay," he said.

"You must lose many friends—and many canoes," answered Falcon.

"My people are strong enough to get across a bay like this—and smart enough to know when the wind isn't dangerous."

"Are you saying your people are superior to us?"

"We'll see who gets to the other side of the bay first," laughed Loon. "I know Lynx will go straight across—and then we'll know who's superior." He laughed uncontrollably at Falcon.

With a sudden thrust of his paddle that nearly threw Loon out of the canoe, Falcon whirled the canoe away from the shore and headed directly across the vast bay.

"This may be your last day, Loon."

Loon dug his paddle deep into the lake and pushed the canoe ahead with all his strength. He would soon be proven right and teach Falcon how to treat him and his people.

They weren't far across the bay when Falcon looked back to see the other canoe—a small speck in the distance—following the shoreline of the bay. He didn't turn back, despite the growing wind, the ripples on the water and the dark clouds forming at the end of the bay. He pulled hard on his paddle, thinking it could be his last day.

By the time Falcon and Loon reached the midpoint in the crossing, where the distant hills on the shore behind them were as small as the hills ahead, the wind was blowing hard from the bay out into the boundless lake. Large waves began hitting them broadside, pushing them away from their path. The edges of the heavily loaded canoe were too close to the water to keep the waves out.

"You'll have to paddle harder than that!" yelled Falcon.

"If you weren't lily dipping, we'd be there by now," cried Loon into the wind.

— *Enemy Arrows* —

He paddled with all his strength, but the point they were trying to reach was getting farther and farther away from them. Low clouds raced above their heads, almost close enough to touch, and it was getting darker as the sun faded from view.

"Harder!" shouted Falcon above the roar of the wind. "Is this how your people cross wide bays?"

Loon didn't reply. He looked in the direction the wind was pushing the canoe. There was no land in sight where the bay opened into the endless lake. He knew they would be blown into the pounding waters of the lake if they didn't get across. Loon stopped paddling long enough to bail water from the bottom of the canoe and rest his aching arms. He couldn't tell whether the punishing waves were filling the canoe or it was leaking.

"Never mind that," screamed Falcon. "Paddle—or we'll be at the bottom of the lake!"

As the wind grew steadily, it became impossible for Falcon and Loon to make their way along the troughs between the waves without rolling over. Falcon quickly turned the canoe directly into the waves, so they wouldn't be blown too far away from land. The unrelenting wind kept pushing them back backwards. If the spirits stayed with them, the wind would die down before nightfall and they could paddle to shore—on one side or the other. But the wind grew stronger and the waves continued to swell.

Finally, Falcon had to yield and bail out the canoe, even though it meant being pushed backward toward the open lake. As darkness descended a sense of despair settled over the tiny craft. Both young men had reached the point of exhaustion, but they continued to paddle, knowing they were far from land and the crashing water was weakening the seams of their canoe. In these brutal waves it wouldn't be long before the spruce roots holding the bark to the ribs began to break apart.

Falcon threw out some of the gear to lighten the load—their heavy weapons and clothing, even their food—but the waves continued to roll over the sides. Their legs were submerged in water

Battle on the Wide Bay

and their arms and shoulders ached with fatigue as they tried to keep the canoe pointed into the wind.

A white gull soared over their heads at the speed of an arrow, twisting and rocking in the turbulent wind. Just above it, dark clouds whipped across the sky toward the open lake—toward the landless horizon where they would never be seen again. Dark gray waves rolled in the same direction with white foam blowing violently from crest to crest slashing at their bare chests. The wind roared like continuous thunder.

"Over there!" yelled Falcon over the deafening noise. He pointed to a patch of frothing water not far away, directly across the path of the wind. "We have to get over there. Paddle to save your miserable skin!"

Loon couldn't see what Falcon was pointing at, but the cold breath of imminent death gave him new energy to paddle. With the last of their strength they forced the canoe across the waves toward the roiling water, and as they got nearer, Loon realized there was a shoal just below the water with waves breaking over it. No matter how hard they tried to reach it, the wind kept pushing them past the submerged rocks.

"Paddle, Loon. Paddle! The spirits have taken pity on us."

They both strained on their paddles in the broken waves downwind of the shoal and slowly made their way to the rocks. Loon jumped out of the canoe and landed chest deep in cold water with the waves crashing over him. He held the canoe firmly so Falcon could leap out. Falcon tried to get out, grasping his paddle, but he slipped on the jagged rocks and slammed his head on the canoe before sinking beneath the waves. His paddle shot out of the water like a leaping salmon and disappeared in the unrelenting waves. Falcon was nowhere to be seen.

Loon reached into the water and groped in the darkness for Falcon, while trying to hold on to the canoe. When he felt his hand brush against a few strands of hair, he grabbed them and dragged Falcon toward the shoal, spewing and coughing until he was able to breathe again. When he finally regained enough strength to raise his weary body, he and Loon stood together clutching the canoe. It was damaged, but still in one piece.

And they were alive.

Before the sky became completely black, with no moon or stars visible behind the dark clouds, they stumbled over the submerged rocks until they found a small plateau where the water was only waist deep and the biggest waves would pound against them without knocking them over. Standing in the darkness in the middle of the lake, they held the canoe tightly, keeping it pointed into the wind with the remaining packs tied to the thwarts. When the driving rain began they flipped it upside down on their shoulders and used it for shelter.

Loon held his paddle tightly, knowing it was their only means of getting to shore—if they survived the night. As the rain pelted down on the bark skin of the canoe he thought again of his longhouse so far away.

– CHAPTER TWENTY-FOUR –

The Will of the Spirits

Lynx and Willow arrived at the campsite at the far side of the bay long after dark, after following the shoreline. They had seen Falcon and Loon cross the mouth of the bay, but didn't risk going after them. As Lynx had said to Willow, if the wind came up, they'd be blown away and never seen again. They both feared their friends had been lost, and Lynx was already dreading the time when he would have to tell their families and clan leaders what had happened.

He and Willow sheltered from the heavy rain under their canoe. The small fire they built nearby struggled to stay alive in the driving rain, but it was finally extinguished by the downpour, leaving them in darkness.

"What made them try to cross the bay?" asked Willow, not really expecting Lynx to know the answer.

"They both knew better," Lynx replied gravely.

"Where would they go if they were blown away from shore?" Willow continued.

"I don't know. This is a huge lake with a bad temper. People have canoed around it, but not many have tried to cross it. In waves like those it would be impossible to cross," he said, pointing to the lake. Because the wind was blowing from behind them toward the water there were no waves crashing on the beach where they sheltered—but they both knew it would be violent on the open lake.

Enormous waves struck the shoal where Falcon and Loon stood facing each other in the darkness under the canoe. Loon was standing at the end of the canoe that took the brunt of the waves and was hit repeatedly from behind by the massive swells. When he lost his balance, he would hold on to the canoe, leaving Falcon to support him. When Falcon lost his balance, he would rely on Loon to stay upright.

"If we both slip at the same time, we'll be back in the lake," yelled Falcon over the din of the rain and the howling wind. "We'll never find this shoal again in the dark."

"I'm trying not to slip," yelled Loon. "But the waves . . ." He was too cold and exhausted to finish his words. The skin on his shoulders was being rubbed raw by the wood on the gunnels and his hands were aching from grasping the thwart and his paddle. Standing with his knees bent and his body braced, waiting for each wave to strike, he could feel the movements of Falcon at the other end, who was also trying hard to keep his balance against the walls of water crashing against him. As the night dragged on and on the wind grew even stronger.

"Will the sun ever come up again?" yelled Falcon after an eternity of being bashed by the cold waves in the darkness.

"I think we've moved to torture time," answered Loon weakly. "Things take longer when you're in pain." He managed a feeble laugh.

"We should sing to the spirit of the lake," said Falcon, and he began to sing loudly in his own language. Loon tried to sing along, but didn't know the words, so he sang another song in his own language at the same time. Though their songs clashed, they sang together in the darkness, trying to be heard over the noise around them. They sang until the rain became drizzle and they sang louder still until it stopped completely.

"Let's take this canoe down," shouted Loon.

"Over!" said Falcon, as they flipped it off of their aching shoulders in one graceful move.

The two warriors held tightly to the bounding canoe, still singing into the darkness. As the wind became less violent the waves turned from jagged mountains to rolling hills that were soon visible in the faint light of dawn.

"My paddle is gone forever," said Falcon.

"Unless someone finds it on the far side of the lake," laughed Loon.

"It's good you held on to yours. At least we can try to paddle to shore when the waves die down."

"You can bail while I paddle," replied Loon. "The canoe took a beating, so it's going to leak like a fishnet."

"We can take turns paddling," said Falcon.

Loon recognized Falcon's humiliation at the thought of being paddled to shore in his own lands by someone from far away. He also knew he was too fatigued to reach shore all by himself.

"Yes."

Loon gazed at the glowing sky surrounding them and then looked pensively at Falcon in the dim light—a wet, cold, exhausted young man standing on a shoal in the middle of the lake with a battered canoe. Loon knew he must look just as fragile.

"Falcon," he said. "We wouldn't be here if I . . ."

Falcon held up his hand to stop him.

"It's not what you did or what I did that brought us here," he said. "It's what we both did." He stared at Loon as though he were seeing him the same way Loon had just seen him. "If we get back to shore alive after this brutal night, we can look back at what we've both done to stay alive." Loon nodded. He knew there was nothing more to say.

As dawn lightened into day, the rolling waves gradually began to subside. In the distance they could see the shoreline of the vast bay where Lynx and Willow would be waiting and assuming the worst.

"Do you think we should try to get to shore yet?" asked Loon.

"Yes, the waves have lost most of their power."

They tested the strength of the canoe and turned it over to empty it. Though it was badly beaten, it would have to do. Loon held the battered craft steady while Falcon climbed in, and then he followed with the precious remaining paddle and sat facing his fellow survivor. They headed for the distant point of land at the end of the bay, with Loon paddling and Falcon bailing water with his cupped hands.

On the far shore Lynx and Willow continued to wait, looking out over the empty bay. As the sun began to rise in a cloudless sky, the lake lost its fury. "Are we going to look for them?" Willow asked.

"Where would we look?" replied Lynx.

Willow had no suggestions.

"Will we wait for them?" asked Willow.

"We'll wait for a bit, Willow," replied Lynx solemnly, "but I don't expect them to return."

Willow scanned the lake searching for floating debris.

As they slowly crossed the water, Falcon and Loon encountered branches from trees battered by the storm, as well as leaves and weeds pulled from the bottom of the lake, floating in tangled clumps on the waves. When Loon was exhausted he turned the canoe around to face the open lake and handed his paddle to Falcon, who continued toward shore while Loon bailed. The canoe was leaking badly and they had to bail constantly to get the water out faster than it came in.

Willow spotted them first. He saw only one person paddling, since Loon was sitting too low to be seen.

"There's a canoe!" he shouted. "Someone's in it."

Lynx leapt to the top of a boulder.

"Which one is it?"

"I can't tell," answered Willow. "It doesn't look like Loon's stroke."

Lynx jumped down and raced to their canoe. In an instant he and Willow were charging out across the lake.

"They've seen us!" cried Falcon.

Loon sat up to look.

— *The Will of the Spirits* —

"There's the other one now!" shouted Willow. "There he is. They're both alive!"

"How can it be?" said Lynx to himself, wondering whether he was seeing a mirage—or the ghosts of dead warriors.

Loon cupped his hands to make the piercing sound of a loon, as Lynx and Willow raced toward them.

"We thought you were at the bottom of the lake!" shouted Willow.

"We were," said Falcon.

The two canoes came together far from shore with the clasping of arms and cries of jubilation. Lynx tied Loon's leaking canoe to his and he and Willow towed the battered survivors to shore. As soon as they were out of danger, Falcon and Loon collapsed in the bottom of their canoe, too exhausted to paddle. When they arrived at the camp they stepped out of their canoes onto the beach. Falcon fell to his knees, scooping wet sand into his hands and rubbing it in his hair.

"For a while in that awful night I thought I'd never feel sand in my fingers again."

"You were as frightened as I was," Loon gasped.

"Yes, I was frightened," said Falcon. "We nearly lost our lives." He poured the sand over his head and felt it drizzle down his face. "It took all our strength and the will of the spirits to overcome our foolishness."

"We're so strong we can be as foolish as we want," laughed Loon. "We can survive anything."

Falcon lifted himself from the beach and stood in front of Loon with grains of sand stuck to his face and hair. He held Loon by the shoulders. "But will you be in my canoe the next time I do something foolish?"

"I'll be with you whenever you do anything foolish," howled Loon.

"Then I hope the spirits will be kind to us again." Falcon staggered down the beach and collapsed in the soft sand.

– CHAPTER TWENTY-FIVE –

Monsters and Spirits

There was nothing for Lynx and Willow to do the next day but repair the battered canoe while Loon and Falcon rested beside the fire. They didn't have to pretend to look for leaks or broken ribs this time. The canoe had been badly damaged. But with cedar boughs at hand for the ribs and an endless supply of white birch and pine gum, the canoe was soon repaired. The freshly-split cedar even gave it the fragrant scent of a new canoe.

The last part of the journey to Shrike's camp took them upriver past quickly flowing rapids with Loon and Falcon in one canoe and Lynx and Willow in the other. When they came to a waterfall they portaged along an overgrown trail until they came to a lake surrounded by tall, rocky hills with sheer cliffs plummeting into the water below. Unlike the clear lakes they had passed through, the colour of this one was brown and opaque—as if it had been stirred by a giant stick. Some people said it was inhabited by monstrous underwater creatures, rarely seen but often detected by the bubbling, churning waters that would suddenly appear on its placid surface, even on a windless day.

In a secluded cove at the base of a granite hill they found the bark-covered hut where Shrike made his camp. The rocks beside his fire were still warm. Falcon said he was probably out digging for ochre. They waited beside the hut for him to return. Just before sunset Falcon spotted Shrike's canoe and called to let him know they were friends. Shrike paddled his canoe to the shallow beach and stepped onto the fine white sand to greet his visitors.

He wore only a loincloth. His long black hair was tied back in a braid to keep it out of his face while he worked. Although he wore no tattoos or jewellery, his hands and knees were stained dark red, like sumac cones. In the bottom of his canoe were two fresh pickerel and several small baskets of reddish powder. Shrike immediately recognized Lynx and grabbed him by the shoulders, holding him firmly.

"You've changed since I saw you last," he laughed, holding him tight. "Now you have muscles on your arms and real meat on your chest where you had nothing but ribs." He looked over at Willow and Loon.

"And who are these young men? They remind me of you when you first came to visit us. This one even looks like you," he said, as he placed his red hand on Willow's arm and squeezed it firmly. "Stay here for the summer and we'll fatten you up."

"No wonder he looks like me. He's my brother's son, Willow," said Lynx.

"Gray Fox?" stammered Shrike. "You're Gray Fox's boy?"

"Lynx tells me that you and my father were close friends."

"Not friends," replied Shrike, raising his hand. "He was my brother, just as he was Lynx's brother. We grew up together on the lakes and rivers, travelling from one end of our land to the other, hunting and fishing whenever we needed to eat. When he arrived here he was thin like you, but he left as strong as Lynx." He laughed loudly at what he'd said.

"I don't get many visitors here," he added. "If I don't laugh at my own jokes, no one will." He laughed even harder at that, until he realized he was the only one laughing. "Yes, we were brothers. I have so many wonderful memories of our times together."

Then a dark cloud passed over Shrike's face, dissolving his smile, and he held Willow tighter. "I was with him at his final battle. I'm sure you know that."

"And this is Loon," said Falcon. "He can stand in the middle of a lake all night long and still have the strength to laugh." Falcon recited the story of their close call while Shrike made a fire on the beach and hung the fish over the flames. Before long they were eating fresh pickerel under the stars, telling stories and laughing about the many foolish things they had done.

As the stars rotated through the sky the talk turned to the great battle where Gray Fox had been killed by the enemy. Shrike described it just as Old Chief had, but with details that could only be related by someone who was there. He seemed to be remembering an event from the previous day, talking about the direction of the wind, the cool night air, the smell of wet leaves and the stains of blood on the rocks. Willow listened intently as the man with red hands described his father's first injury—close to the enemy palisade—and how his protective armour was splintered by a rock. Shrike spoke about the bravery of Gray Fox, how the wounded warrior lifted himself slowly and painfully from the ground, holding his ribs. When he described how Gray Fox was hit in the face by a deflected arrow, he became agitated, his voice growing tense and shrill.

"All day he lay there," he cried. "He couldn't move and we had no way to reach him. My brother . . . he lay there dying and we couldn't help him."

"He didn't move at all?" asked Willow.

"Not the slightest movement, not even a moan to tell us he was alive."

When Shrike placed a thick branch on the fire the leaping flames seemed to calm his spirit. He waited until they were high before he continued.

"We tried over and over again to rescue him, but we couldn't get near him. When it was dark I slithered over the ground like a snake to find him, but by that time he was gone. He'd been taken away by the enemy. I spent a long painful night wondering what had happened to him and feeling like I'd lost my arms and legs.

"The worst was seeing him at dawn, hanging from the palisade with two other bodies—hanging like dogs by their wrists. They had all been tortured. Their bodies were covered with blood. I wanted to charge through the gate and destroy the entire village, but my friends held me back. It took four of them to hold me. He hung like a dog," he repeated with his red hands covering his face.

"You tried to get the bodies back," said Lynx.

"Someone else tried. All I wanted to do was burn the village to the ground, but we couldn't get close enough to do any damage. And they wouldn't return the bodies."

Shrike told them about the journey back to Thunder River along the shores of the Beautiful Lake and the grief that spread through the village like a cold fog with the news of Gray Fox's death. He described how Orchid had collapsed in front of him when he told her the painful news and how he had to carry her back to the longhouse convulsing with grief.

Shrike and Lynx both told stories of growing up with Gray Fox and his ability to do so many things effortlessly. He was one of the fastest stickball players and the best hunter in the village. He seemed to be able to call the animals to him. They talked long after the young warriors had fallen asleep—and still hadn't run out of stories when the sky began to turn gray.

Willow awoke when the rays of the rising sun warmed his face. He opened his eyes to see the low rays shining through birch trees, as an onshore breeze began to ripple the lake. He noticed two canoes resting on their sides in the sand surrounded by tightly wrapped packs. Nearby, a red fox skin stretched over a circular frame swayed gently in the light air. At the shore he saw Lynx, Falcon and Loon fishing with a small net. He closed his eyes again and watched the patterns of light dancing on his eyelids, as the birch leaves flickered back and forth in front of the sun's rays.

A strange grating sound came from Shrike's hut and before long the man with red hands slipped out holding an ochre-stained basket and two small ceramic pots. Willow raised his head to see what was happening.

"You're back from the dream world," called Shrike. "Welcome again to my home. You can help me today while your friends fish. I have something to do that takes two people."

He carried the baskets and pots to the fire and added some twigs to the ash-covered coals. When he had a fire going and a green stick ready to hang a fish above the flames, he called to Lynx and signalled for his other guests to join him.

They ate fresh roasted fish while Shrike told them of the best spots on the lake to find bass and trout eager to be caught. But he warned them of the underwater monsters and drew a picture in the sand of the places they should avoid for fear of having their canoes tipped—and being devoured in one bite. With the point of his stick he drew a fearsome monster with a long tail, ridges along its back and huge jaws filled with long sharp teeth.

"Have you ever seen one of these creatures?" asked Loon.

"Never," answered Shrike.

"Then how do you know what it looks like?" pressed Loon.

"How do I know?" he repeated with his stained hands sweeping the hair away from his face. "Everyone knows what they look like. We've heard stories about these beasts since we were infants. Falcon can tell you what they look like, too."

Falcon stuck his finger in the sand, piercing the body of the monster as though stabbing it through the heart. "They look just like that."

"But if you haven't . . ."

Falcon interrupted Loon before he could finish his question. "How do you know what the Great Turtle looks like if you've never seen it? How do you even know it's there if you've never seen it?"

"Everyone knows it's there!" retorted Loon. He turned to Willow for support, but his friend was lost in thought.

"Willow," Loon said, poking him in the ribs with a stick. "How do we know what the Great Turtle looks like if we haven't seen it?"

Willow brushed the stick way. "I don't know," he answered. "I guess we believe what people tell us."

"That's it," said Loon. "That's why everyone knows."

"And that's how we know what the monster looks like," said Falcon, leaping to his feet.

Lynx stood up and headed for the canoe with Loon close behind.

"Willow," said Shrike. "Are you going to help me today?"

"What can I do?"

"I'll show you. I know your father liked to leave his mark on the cliffs, so bring those pots to the canoe and grab your paddle. I'll bring the rest."

– CHAPTER TWENTY-SIX –

The Sound of a Cliff

Under the brilliant morning sun Willow and Shrike followed the shoreline into deep bays and past tree-covered islands that leaned out over the water as they passed. On the far side of the lake, near a hidden portage leading to another series of lakes, was a rock cliff that grew taller and more massive as they approached. Shrike paddled to the base of the cliff and studied the rock face. While moving the canoe from place to place, he shouted at the rock and listened for the echo, over and over again until he found what he was searching for.

Then he followed the shore to a narrow gravel beach where they unloaded the canoe and started a fire. Moving with the swiftness that comes from a lifetime of experience, he emptied a handful of red ochre into one of the ceramic pots, trying not to spill any on the beach. Then he handed Willow the powder-filled pot along with a smooth rock shaped like a thigh bone and a thick stone bowl.

"You can grind this a bit more while I prepare the oils. The finer the better. Just crush a little at a time against the base of the bowl. When it's as powdery as wood ash it will be ready."

While Willow ground the ochre, Shrike heated some sturgeon glue and oils in another pot beside the fire, stirring the mixture constantly with a flat stick as he worked. Every now and then he added flecks of ash to the oils and then some of the finely ground ochre, testing the mixture by lifting the stick out of the pot and watching how the gluey substance dripped.

When it had become a paste—like the yolk of a goose egg—he set the pot on the ground and took a small amount of tobacco from his fire pouch, crumbled a few bits into the mixture, and stirred it again. Then he wrapped the pot in deerskin.

"It won't be long now," he beamed.

On the way back to the rock cliff, Willow sat at the front of the canoe holding the warm pot while Shrike paddled. Without any effort he located the precise spot on the cliff where they'd been earlier and manoeuvred up to the towering mass of granite.

"This is where we'll make our marks," he said proudly. "You can hold on to the cliff while I work and later we'll trade places. Put your fingers in that crevice and hold on tight. You should sit as low as you can because I'm going to be stretching high."

He moved slowly to the centre of the canoe and unwrapped the pot. Holding it in one hand, he lifted himself up until he was standing straight, balancing himself against the rock. He smiled at Willow, who sat holding the canoe as tightly as he could.

"You can see why this needs two people." With the sun on his back Shrike dipped his hand in the mixture and reached as high as he could on the warm rock. His fingers left a streak of red paste on the cliff when he slid his hand over the surface, trying not to push the canoe away from the rock face. Again and again he applied colour to the rock with his hand or with a frayed stick until shapes began to appear—crooked edges and long, winding, reed-shaped forms of red.

Willow watched from below, straining to hold on to the crevice, as the shapes joined to create a monstrous-looking creature with a long tail, a jagged back and huge jaws filled with sharp teeth.

"This will appease the spirits in the lake," said Shrike, lowering himself to the bottom of the canoe to rest. "Now take me out farther and we'll see how it works."

— *Enemy Arrows* —

As Willow paddled the canoe away from the cliff, the spectacular image stared down at them with its jaws wide open and its teeth ready to rip them apart. Not far from the cliff, Shrike began to shout at the monster and each time the monster shouted back.

"It works well," said Shrike. "The monsters will be calm now." He looked inside the pot and gave the mixture another stir. "Let's go back and finish it." Willow turned the canoe and paddled toward the creature on the rock.

"Your father always wanted to do this when he was here. You may see some of his images on your way back." When they approached the cliff, Shrike held on to the narrow crevice in the rock face while Willow stood up in the canoe.

"Can I make anything I want?" he asked.

"Whatever you can think of. Reach high or the ice will scrape it off in the winter."

Willow dipped his hand in the sticky mixture and slathered a long stripe down the rock beside the monster. "That looks good so far," said Shrike with a grin.

Willow spoke as he scooped more of the mixture out of the pot. "Shrike, I want to ask you something."

"Ask me what you want—I'm not going anywhere."

"It's about when you saw my father's body hanging from the palisade," the young man said, his hand covered in the red paste.

"What more can I say?" Shrike asked.

"Could you see his face?"

"I could see the back of his head."

Willow added a narrower stripe to the rock. "Could you see the tattoo on his chest—the running deer?"

"I saw his back."

"You said he was covered with blood."

"Yes, they'd all been tortured, covered with blood."

"His back?"

"Yes."

Again Willow painted a narrow stripe on the cliff. "What scar could you see on his back?"

— *The Sound of a Cliff* —

Willow watched from below, straining to hold on to the crevice.

"Your father had a scar on his shoulder blade. I thought I could see it from where I was."

"Under the blood?"

"There was blood all over his back. I couldn't see it very well."

Willow placed his paint-covered hands on the rock and made hand prints at the end of the long stripes. Working silently, he added a neck, head, and two thin legs and soon a long hanging figure appeared on the rock beside the monster. He handed the pot to Shrike and sat down in the canoe facing him.

"What do you think it is?"

"It looks like your father to me," answered Shrike without hesitation. Willow's eyes narrowed. He twisted uncomfortably.

"How can you be sure it was my father you saw hanging from the palisade?" he asked, staring into Shrike's eyes.

"How can I be sure?" repeated Shrike. "I know Gray Fox was badly injured and I saw a body that looked just like his. I know he didn't return with us and has never been seen since. I know that everyone in your village grieved for him, as I did myself. How can I be sure? I'm sure about the spirit of the sky and the eternal hunting grounds in the stars. I'm sure there are monsters in this lake and I know what they look like."

He took a deep breath before he continued in a hushed voice. "Can I be sure it was your father I saw hanging from the palisade? I've always wanted to be sure, because the alternatives are too horrible to imagine. That's what makes me certain. I don't think it does any good to doubt what everyone knows."

Willow saw the anxiety in Shrike's eyes and wondered whether he could tell Old Chief about this when he returned home. He couldn't tell if Shrike was remembering what he had seen, or what he wanted to remember. Willow's hands suddenly felt cold and his innards started to churn. He had to ask Shrike one more thing while he had the chance.

"Then it's not possible my father lived?"

Shrike let go of the crevice and dipped a red hand into the water before wiping his eyes. He sat still looking at Willow in the drifting canoe until he could respond.

"There are bad spirits invading your thoughts, Willow. If you don't chase them away, they will certainly cause you harm. The man

— The Sound of a Cliff —

I saw was dead. They were all dead, and no one would adopt a dead warrior—no matter how brave he was."

This was the answer Willow wanted to hear, so he tried to press for more. "But if it wasn't my . . ." he began. Shrike immediately signalled him to stop.

"You're causing me grief now, Willow, and I can't listen to any more. He was my brother." He leaned forward and held Willow by the wrists, looking at his ochre-stained hands. Closing his eyes, he sang a mournful song that Willow could not understand, and then looked solemnly at Willow. "You must fight these spirits, Willow. Drive them away—or you'll never have peace."

He moved the canoe back against the cliff and motioned to Willow to hold it in place while he added images of fish and birds and lightning around the figures of the hanging man and the monster. When all the paint was finished he moved away and shouted again at the images, as they shouted back.

"This will do well," said Shrike. He turned the canoe from shore and set off across the placid lake toward the late afternoon sun without the slightest fear of monsters.

The pair reached Shrike's camp as the sun fell below the trees. Long before they could see the other canoes on the beach or hear the sound of their friends calling to them, they could smell wood smoke from the fire mixed with the delicate scent of smoked trout. They knew it would be another night of feasting, stories and laughter under the stars.

Just after dark the air became still and thick enough to taste, and they realized they wouldn't be sleeping outside. Before long they could hear rumbles in the distance, while lightning illuminated faraway clouds with vivid white tinged with gray and yellow. As the night passed, the thunder became louder and the lightning changed from glowing shapes to jagged lines. When the rain started they all squeezed inside Shrike's hut and covered the smoke hole with bark to keep the wind and water out. The fire outside was soon doused by a deluge from the sky.

Inside, the hut was grim and sticky with five people crammed in a space made for one. It was hard to breathe in the close, airless hut and no one could move without kicking someone else in the darkness. Whenever lightning lit up the sky, they could see themselves vividly—wet figures crowded together, staring into the darkness and looking uneasy.

The storm moved slowly in the still air, but when it reached their camp it seemed to hover directly over them. Thunder and lightning exploded at the same instant, making the ground beneath them shake, while the rain poured over them as if they were sheltering beneath a waterfall. The sounds of thunder and rain on the bark roof were far too loud inside the hut for them to talk or sing.

Then out of nowhere a squall came up. They could hear shallow waves skipping across the beach and the hut began to creak and shake.

"The canoes!" shouted Shrike above the din. He shot out through the tiny opening followed by the others. One canoe had already been lifted up and was tumbling across the beach in the flashing light of the unrelenting storm. Shrike and Lynx chased after it while the young hunters carried the other canoes into the forest and hid them under low boughs.

When the canoes were safely stowed they rushed back to the hut amid flashes of lightning, but found nothing but a few poles sticking out of the wet earth and bits of bark strewn among the bushes. With a deafening crash, a bolt of lightning shattered a pine tree behind them, splitting it from the highest needles to the roots. Both halves of the tree teetered in the wind before crashing to the ground, sending the warriors scattering in every direction.

Willow found a safe place to hide under a cedar tree. The others took refuge under the canoes where they spent the rest of the night wet and cold. There were no stories that grim night—and little laughter.

– CHAPTER TWENTY-SEVEN –

Spirit Rocks

Dawn came after an eternity of driving rain and warmed into a steamy day of heat and humidity. The visitors said goodbye to the man with the red hands and Falcon guided them back through the lakes and rivers to the place where his people had camped.

Lynx and Willow were the first to arrive on the beach at the gathering place. Grackle, the thin old chief, and the clan leaders welcomed them back with questions about their travels. Falcon and Loon were not far behind. The chief watched as the second canoe sliced through the water with a flawless rhythm.

"I see they learned to paddle together while they were away," he said to Lynx.

"The spirit of the lake was good to them," replied Lynx. "They'll tell you their story."

Loon jumped out of the front of the canoe and held it steady while Falcon stepped on to the sand, barely getting his foot wet. With a broad smile and a wave of his hand, Loon gave the chief a greeting in the language of the People of the Lakes. The old man replied politely and then turned to Lynx with a look of surprise on his face. "They've learned more than paddling," he said.

With each passing day the sun reached lower in the sky. Shadows in the forests grew longer and the nights became cool. It was time

— Enemy Arrows —

to return to Thunder River. The serious trading between north and south took place during the last days that Lynx, Willow and Loon spent at the gathering place. Lynx filled a small canoe with the finest furs from the cold northern forests. In exchange for the tobacco, chert and colourful shells he had brought from the south, he was given fox pelts, dark robes of fisher and wolverine. He stuffed the canoe with packs of beautifully crafted moccasins, mittens and all types of winter clothing made by the People of the Lakes, along with large quantities of shining copper beads that came from the far west. All of these treasures were carefully wrapped in beaverskin packs, ready for the rapids and long portages ahead.

The night before the visitors were to depart, the chief held a feast. Willow and Loon laughed with Falcon as they remembered the times they had spent together. Loon and Falcon retold the story of being swept out into the stormy lake and how they spent the night holding the canoe over their heads. The young men who had played stickball so violently wanted to see if Loon could really breathe underwater. Loon retorted with a few stinging words in their own language that left them stunned and speechless, to Falcon's great delight.

After the younger people had left the fireside, Lynx and the chief talked late into the night about the strength of their alliance and pledged to continue the friendship of their people—and fight together against the enemy.

Early the next morning, as the travellers were getting ready to leave, Grackle stood on the beach in the cool air wearing a deerskin cloak and leggings. The chief sang a song asking the river spirits to keep the travellers safe while he burned sweetgrass for the spirits of the sky. Willow stood nearby, watching him and listening to his words. A large crowd gathered to wish them well. When the chief had completed this ritual he spoke quietly to Willow.

"You are welcome here—just as your father was. And your own sons will be welcome here in time. Your visits with us strengthen the bond between our two nations." Grackle paused and looked

— Spirit Rocks —

closely at Willow. "There is one thing that has been troubling me since you arrived. Maybe you can help me understand."

"If I can," replied Willow with a smile.

"Tell me then," the chief continued. "How did the Wanderer's daughter know about your father's tattoo?"

The smile left Willow's face and his mouth became tense and angular. He picked up a small flat rock from the beach and skipped it across the still water before he answered, watching it bounce over and over until it skidded to a stop and sank into the lake.

"I think she's bewitched," Willow said in a whisper. "She sees the dead. She disturbs me as much as she troubles you. I can't help you, because I can't stop wondering myself."

"But how did she know?" the chief repeated.

Willow responded as calmly as he could. "Someone must have told her."

That was all he could say. He thanked the chief for his kindness—in Grackle's own language—and walked into the shallow water where Lynx and Loon waited in the large, fully loaded canoe.

Falcon and the young men of the village gathered to see them off. They laughed and joked as they readied their own canoes. Willow slipped the loaded canoe off the sand and guided it into the shallow water before stepping in. A chorus of voices called to them and wished them well, and the young men of the village accompanied them across the lake before yelling their good-byes.

"Come back next summer," shouted Falcon. "We can be foolish again!"

The loaded canoe was caught by the current of a river leading to another lake and was soon out of sight. They were on their way home.

The single canoe with three paddlers raced through the lakes and rivers to the Lake of Islands and down the jagged eastern shore until they came to the lands of their own people—where Otter was waiting for them, looking fit and strong after fishing with his clan for more than a full cycle of the moon. He had made friends with everyone in the village and introduced Loon and Willow to most of them.

Otter was also respected for his ability to fish and swim great distances under water. When he had told the villagers that this was because he had webbed toes, the young boys began to follow him wherever he went—asking to have a look.

One night by the fire, after Lynx, Willow and Loon had arrived, Otter told the boys he would show them his webbed feet. But before he did, he and Loon wrapped thin membranes of fish guts around his toes. The boys gathered close to Otter near the glowing fire—and when he spread his toes apart to show his webbed feet, they jumped back in amazement. Like a flock of swallows, they raced through the village shouting "He *does* have webbed feet—like a beaver—like a frog! We've seen them! He *does* have webbed feet!"

The visitors spent several days among the northern clans feasting, exchanging news, telling stories and talking about people they knew. Then it was time for the journey to the Beautiful Lake and Thunder River.

Instead of travelling overland as they had come, they decided to return by water because of the weight of the packs. They found a second canoe and made it ready for the trip. After a long night of celebrations and more good-byes, the two canoes pushed off—past the villages, past the beaches lined with canoes and fishing weirs, and along the narrow lake into a larger one filled with whitefish and pickerel.

On the eastern shore a small river led to the chain of lakes and rivers that would eventually take them home. The four paddled upriver past forests and meadows, past the villages and places where villages had been. Before long they reached the end of a narrow stream where the water became impassable. It was the first long portage.

They carried their canoes and their many packs along a well-used trail through the forest until they reached a long lake surrounded by low hills and hardwood forests where they set up camp on a beach of fine white sand.

— *Spirit Rocks* —

"I'm always happy to reach this lake," said Lynx. "We've climbed the rivers to get here, but from this place the water flows down all the way to the Beautiful Lake. There are rapids ahead to test our skills, and we'll race through the water faster than a diving osprey. At a bend in the river you'll meet the Two Sisters," he said, looking at them with raised eyebrows. "You'll never forget them."

The next day they followed another small river down its winding path until they came to a waterfall. On the other side of the portage they came into a lake dotted with islands and large stones sticking out of the water.

"This is Stony Lake," said Lynx. "There is a magical place near here that I want to show you."

They paddled along the rocky shore, past silent forests and narrow streams that emptied into the lake. Giant pine trees towered high above the water, their strangled roots clinging for life to the rocks along the shore. Deer stood silently in the dark woods watching the canoes go by, while moose grazed in the still marshes, oblivious to the rhythm of the travellers.

At dusk they came to a large flat rock with animals and spirits carved into the stone. One image showed a strange figure on two long legs, with arms holding its long neck. At the end of its neck was a giant eye where its head should have been and lines resembling rays of light shining from the eye. Herds of oddly shaped animals with pointed bones jutting from their heads were immobilized in the rocks, like frogs frozen in the winter ice. Twisted and distorted faces loomed out of the granite and leered at them in silent agony.

Lynx told them stories about the rock carvings, moving from one shape to the next. As he spoke his hand brushed across the figures as if to draw words from them.

"Who made these marks?" asked Willow.

"They've always been here. Our ancestors created them."

"What are they for?" asked Otter.

"They're guides of the forest—and guides of the spirit world. They show us things we can't see in this world," he said, as he stroked the image of a giant underwater monster with fangs and a serpent's tail. "This may be the monster in the lake where Shrike lives."

That moonless night they camped beside the carved rocks and the haunting images. It was as dark as a cave until coloured streaks of light began racing across the sky. Blues and greens whirled around them throughout the night, moving in every direction, obscuring the stars and forming images like the shapes carved in the rocks. Serpents loomed above while distorted faces peered at them from the darkness.

"I think we've angered the spirits of this place," said Loon, adding more wood to the fire. "I don't like it here."

"We'll leave at first light," said Lynx, watching the images forming and dissolving before his eyes. They tried not to sleep for fear of evil spirits invading their dreams—and by the time the eastern sky showed a tinge of gray, the swirling lights were gone.

– CHAPTER TWENTY-EIGHT –

The Elm Canoe

All morning they paddled along the winding river, still haunted by the spirits and images in the rocks. Loon often looked over his shoulder to make sure they weren't being followed. Although Lynx didn't look back, he watched Loon's face for signs of danger. By the time the sun was high, Lynx turned the canoe toward a narrow beach just above a waterfall where a carrying trail led from the beach into the woods.

"We can eat here before making the portage," he said, as Willow stepped out of the canoe into the shallow water to guide it to shore. They unloaded the canoes and turned them upside down on the beach beside the wrapped packs. Lynx passed a chunk of smoked fish to the others and they stretched out on the soft sand to eat and rest. This had been a challenging morning and it would be a long time before they stopped for the night.

"I didn't like that place," said Loon without looking at the others. "There were too many spirits there." He stripped the backbone and ribs from his fish and then returned the bones to the water before continuing. "I had a bad dream there."

"What was your dream?" asked Willow, leaning back into the sand on one elbow.

Loon looked toward the clouds before he answered. "It was more of a flash of lightning than a dream," he replied. "I wasn't really asleep—and it was over as soon as it began." He lay back in the sand with his eyes closed before describing his dream.

"I was standing on the shore beside a rough stretch of rapids. The sound of the water was like thunder, and there was a canoe trapped at the foot of a waterfall with someone in it." As he took another bite from his smoked fish, the others waited for him to continue.

"What happened then?" Willow asked.

Loon raised his hand and signalled for them to wait while he picked a bone out of his mouth.

"There was nothing more," he mumbled with his mouth full. He got up from the beach, walked slowly into the river and bent down with a cupped hand to drink while the others watched and waited for more. When he'd quenched his thirst he straightened up and wiped his mouth with the back of his arm.

"Then it was over," he said. "I saw the spirits racing across the sky again." Loon waded to shore and collapsed on the sand.

Lynx watched him for a moment, thinking about the meaning of the dream. He stood up and stretched with his hands behind his head, his elbows pointing to the sky, before walking along the beach to a small fire pit surrounded by smooth rocks. He leaned down to put his hand on one of the rocks.

"This rock is warm," he said. He stirred the blackened coals and raised a wisp of smoke. "Last night," Lynx added, looking down river toward the waterfall. He studied the tracks in the sand and then headed quickly to the beached canoes. When he grabbed a canoe and flipped it over his head the others sprang to their feet. Otter quickly hoisted the second canoe on his shoulders and Loon and Willow followed with the packs. The portage trail meandered up the side of a wooded hill, past the waterfall and down to a quiet pool below the rapids.

A single line of footprints marked the path. Whoever was ahead of them had portaged his canoe and all of his gear in one trip—while they had to return along the trail several times to move all of their gear. The stranger's prints were soon buried under their many steps.

They put their canoes in the water and paddled through the whirling currents below the rapids into a wide river bordered by reeds. Red-winged blackbirds clung to the bulrushes swaying in the breeze and a loud buzz of insects pierced the stillness. Before long the river opened into another wide lake dotted with heavily treed islands. By this time the breeze had grown into a strong wind that blew toward them over choppy water.

"We should stay close to the shore," said Loon, jabbing his paddle toward the gray rocks on the shoreline. Otter smiled and with a powerful stroke turned the canoe toward shore, with Lynx and Willow following. On a rock ledge above the water, out of the wind, a large water snake sunned itself with its head resting on its coiled body. When the travellers passed by, the snake raised its head and stared at the intruders, flicking its tongue. Slowly it unwound, dropped from the ledge into the lake with a splash, and swam away under water, its striped body undulating back and forth until it disappeared into the depths.

All afternoon they paddled along the shore, sheltering from the wind when they could. By the time the sun was setting behind them, they had reached the out-flowing river. A string of submerged boulders blocked the way, leaving only a narrow channel for the canoes to pass. Lynx headed toward the opening and plunged into the fast-moving current. Willow and Otter followed close behind, veering around the boulders and between the high, tree-covered banks on either side. They followed the river through the forest and into a small lake rippled by the wind. Lynx pointed to a stand of pines on the opposite shore.

"We'll stop there for the night," he said.

That evening beside the fire Otter told his friends about fishing in the weirs with his clan. The others stared in awe when he described the baskets full of fish they carried from the river every day and the long smoking racks where the fish were preserved for the winter. He told them about the tireless young women who tended the fires while turning the fish—and how they cooled themselves in the river when the heat became unbearable. The others listened intently when he described how their long gleaming hair clung to their backs as they waded toward shore. Otter told them he wanted to return to live with the northern clans next summer and his friends said they would go with him.

There was no moon in the sky to dim the stars that night and the spirits were quiet. As a warm breeze blew in from the lake, the mosquitoes disappeared and the bullfrogs sounded their deep croaks, calling and answering, calling and answering, from a nearby swamp.

"Tomorrow we'll run the rapids," said Lynx, his wide smile illuminated by the fire. "They are long, fast—and dangerous, but not deadly at this time of year. I've been here in the spring when they're impassable. If we make it through them tomorrow, we'll save a gruelling portage up the side of a cliff. Actually, this is my favourite part of the journey."

"If there's a danger of not making it through, I'll take the portage," said Loon quietly. "I've spent enough time clinging to overturned canoes."

Lynx laughed, but at the same time he recalled the empty, dismal feeling when he thought Loon and Falcon had perished in the wide bay, and the unbearable prospect of telling Loon's parents how their son died.

"Don't worry. We'll scout the rapids first. If you hear the spirits calling, you can take the trail."

"I can hear them already," answered Loon quietly.

At dawn Lynx was up checking the repairs on the overturned canoes. When he was satisfied that they could handle the rest of the trip, he called the others to join him for a look at the rapids. They left the canoes on the shore and walked along the jagged rocks to a ledge overlooking the noisy, swirling water. Lynx shouted to be heard.

"Stay on this side of the river when you come down and watch out for that rock just under the surface in the middle of the current."

"What rock?" yelled Loon.

— *The Elm Canoe* —

"Look for the shape of geese flying up river," answered Lynx, holding his fingertips together so his arms formed an angle of geese in flight. "The rock is always under the leading goose. Two streams of white water flow out on either side, like the other geese following in formation. You can't see the rock, but you can tell where it is."

Willow pointed to a sharp bend in the river ahead. "What's around that bend?" he asked.

"That's the most dangerous part of the rapids," shouted Lynx. He motioned for them to gather close to him. On a flat rock he sketched the course of the river using a green stick.

"The Two Sisters live here," he said, making scrapes on the rock. "Two large round rocks that stick out of the water. You can't see them from here. They're very friendly. Stay between them and you'll get through," he said. "But if you go to the side of one, the other will become jealous and rip out the bottom of your canoe, sending you bouncing from rock to rock all the way down."

"I want to see for myself," said Loon. Without waiting for a reply, he started down the rocky shore with Lynx and Willow following quickly behind, picking their way through the spray and the broken, wet rocks.

Otter stayed where he was. "Tell me what you find!" he yelled.

On the shore beside the bend in the river, Loon stopped suddenly and shouted to the others, pointing at the river and signalling for them to hurry. When they caught up to him, Lynx and Willow saw a thick pine log wedged in the gap between the Two Sisters— just above the rushing water. At one end of the log was a tangled mass of broken roots sheared off to form points, each as sharp as an awl.

"I hear the spirits calling me," said Loon, pointing to the log. Lynx gasped at the sight of the Two Sisters fouled by the log.

"I hear them, too," he said with a haunted look in his eyes. He put his hand on Loon's bare shoulder. "This would have been a disaster. We can't go around it and we can't go through it. We'll have to portage." He stood silently with Loon, imagining what would have happened if they had come across the spiked barrier by surprise.

Over the thunderous roar of the rapids Willow heard the sound of Otter's distant voice. He looked back, but couldn't see anyone. Then he saw a glint of light reflected from a swiftly-moving paddle. "Look! Up there!" Willow yelled, pointing to the head of the rapids.

The others spun around to see a lone paddler shooting down the river toward them in a strange, gray canoe. He skilfully stayed in the deep water on their side of the river and avoided the hidden rock beneath the leading goose. As he flew through the water toward them, Lynx stumbled across the broken rocks, waving his arms like a hummingbird, shouting above the roar of water to stop. But it was too late.

– CHAPTER TWENTY-NINE –

Enemy Arrowheads

When the paddler rounded the bend in the river and saw the log across the Two Sisters he tried to veer away, but the current pulled him sideways to the gap—and the pine log lying across it.

With a fearful yell he reached out his hand in a futile effort to avoid a crash. As he did, his canoe flipped over, hurling him against the log. He clung to it with both arms, like a man hanging from the edge of a cliff and, at the same instant, his overturned canoe shot up from the churning water behind him and pressed against his back, pinning him against the log. The rushing water pushed against the canoe, squeezing the breath from the trapped man and threatening to drown him. He clawed at the log with his fingernails in a hopeless effort to stay above the water.

Lynx grabbed a dead branch and tried to reach out to him, but it was impossible over the swiftly running water.

Far above the desperate scene, Otter stumbled across the rocks to see what had happened. When he saw the trapped, drowning man, he rushed back to the camp to get a canoe. At the same time, Willow disappeared into the river just above the Two Sisters before anyone could stop him. Lying on his back like an otter, he plunged feet first down the rushing river toward the stranger.

When Lynx saw Willow in the raging river he raced to save him, yelling and holding a branch out to him, but Willow flew past, pulling his arms backward like a bat to slow himself down. When his feet crashed against the log beside the trapped canoe, he kept his legs and back straight and rode over the rushing water like a duck skidding to a landing on a pond.

In one quick movement Willow grabbed the front of the stranger's canoe and pulled it toward him. The powerful current caught it at once and tore the canoe into bits that swept away beneath the log. Immediately the man was pulled under the log and disappeared beneath the surface. Only his hands could be seen above the swirling water, grasping at the air above. Taking a deep breath, Willow slipped beneath the log, caught the man by the arm, dragged him into an eddy behind a boulder and then pulled the man to the rocky shore.

Lynx and Loon raced after them across the broken rocks.

Willow could see that the stranger was young—not much older than himself. He lay face down on the rocks, rolling his head from side to side, coughing violently and spewing water from his mouth and nose. He was tattooed on his forehead and his lips and a long earring dangled from one earlobe. The other earlobe, freshly torn, dripped blood on the rock. The strap to his fire pouch was twisted around his neck, so Willow loosened it and put the pouch on the rock beside him.

With a sudden shudder the young man's body convulsed and water trickled from his open mouth. When Willow raised the man's head, more water escaped. Then the young man vomited violently before he began to breathe in shallow, laboured gasps.

Lynx and Loon clambered down the rocks. "Is he alive?" yelled Lynx as he approached.

"Who is he?" called Loon at the same time.

"He's alive," answered Willow. He lay the young man's head down on the rock and stood up to get a better look at him.

"You saved his life," said Lynx, breathing heavily.

Enemy Arrowheads

"I was upriver from him," answered Willow. "I knew I could reach him. You couldn't."

"You risked your own neck."

Willow shrugged. "I couldn't just watch him drown."

"You could have," said Lynx, as he examined the stranger's fire pouch. "But you have a generous spirit. I hope you encounter generous spirits when you travel to enemy lands." He pulled out a sharp bone knife, some wet tobacco, a bone awl, a piece of chert, a matted clump of white fibres, several arrowheads, and a small piece of rolled birchbark with charcoal lines on it.

"He's from across the lake," said Lynx, brushing hair from his face. "I could tell by his canoe. These arrowheads make it certain."

"He's the enemy," yelled Loon, waving his arms over his head. "A spy—we saved an enemy spy!"

Otter came from behind them. He stared at the young man, breathing heavily before he spoke. "Our canoes have holes in them," he said. "Someone cut them with a knife."

"He wrecked our canoes," exclaimed Loon. "And we saved him!" He turned away in disgust.

"Help me carry him to the trail," said Lynx, stooping to lift the unconscious young man.

Loon turned back around. "What are we going to do with him?" he asked. "He's the enemy. We should throw him in the river."

Lynx turned to Loon and spoke slowly and quietly. His voice could barely be heard above the rapids. "Then help me throw him in the river." Loon reached down and grasped a leg, but Willow held his arm.

"Wait," he said. "I just pulled him out of there."

"He's a spy!" repeated Loon.

"There's still life in him," said Willow, staring at the young man's heaving chest.

"A spy who wrecked our canoes!" shouted Loon.

"He is a captured spy," said Lynx. "He can't harm us now." He began to gather the contents of the young man's fire pouch. Meanwhile, Loon unrolled the birchbark and tried to decipher the strange markings made in charcoal. They made no sense to him, so he threw the bark into the river.

"We should throw him in after it," he said to the others.

"Look at him," said Willow, raising his voice above the roar of the water. "He's just like us—doing what we may be doing in a few summers. He was nearly killed in the rapids that could have killed us. We can't throw him back into the river like a dead dog."

Lynx motioned to the others. They lifted the moaning figure by his arms and legs and carried him slowly over the slippery rocks to the carrying trail. They placed him on his stomach and then tied his hands behind his back with a length of braided rope. The young man twisted and coughed up more water. He struggled to lift himself to his knees, but collapsed again on the trail.

"Leave him here," said Lynx. "He won't go far. We'll come back for him after we repair the canoes."

Not only had the spy slashed the birchbark skin of the canoes, he had also driven a pole through the cedar ribs of one canoe. They spent the rest of the day repairing them in silence. No one spoke of the young man who caused so much damage.

Before they left, Lynx built a stone cairn at the top of the rapids to warn other travellers of the dangers that lay ahead at the Two Sisters. Then, as the sun moved behind the trees, he and Willow carried the two canoes over the trail beside the rapids, past the young man lying face down where they had left him. Loon and Willow carried the gear over the portage.

Each time they passed the spy he seemed more alert. By the time they had taken the last load he was fully awake, so Lynx helped him to his feet and walked him along the trail to the foot of the rapids where Otter had built a fire. The young man collapsed to his knees beside the fire. Around him stood his enemies—the people who had saved his life. He had an expression on his face like a whipped dog waiting for the next beating. When Lynx offered him a cut of smoked fish he turned away.

"Where is your home?" Lynx asked. The young man didn't reply.

"How did you come to this place?" he asked. Again, there was no reply. Lynx looked to the others standing beside the fire.

"I know how we can make him answer," said Loon, pulling out his knife and pointing it at their captive's neck. A look of defiance replaced the fearful expression on the young man's face. It was clear that he was ready to deal with any pain they could inflict, but Lynx stood between Loon and his potential victim.

"Put your knife away," Lynx said calmly. "Take him over there and tie him to the tree. We'll make him talk tomorrow." Loon and Otter led the captive to a pine tree and tied his hands around it.

"What are we going to do with him?" Willow asked Lynx in a whisper.

"I don't know," replied Lynx. "He'll only hinder us." He hesitated before he spoke again. "This wasn't part of Loon's dream."

As the stars circled in the sky, they sat beside the fire talking about what they would do with the stranger. Loon wanted to torture him to find out what he had learned from spying. Willow said they should take him to the next village and leave him there so the people he had been spying on could decide what to do with him. Otter wondered if they could use him in a captive exchange.

Lynx was uncertain. He told about his own journey as a spy in the lands where the enemy lived. He talked of travelling blindly through the night in unknown foreign places, knowing he could be captured at any time and tortured to death. He tried to explain the deep sense of isolation he felt and the overpowering fear that his bones would be buried far from the bones of his ancestors.

They talked into the night, watching the movement of the stars—and their prisoner.

When it was time to sleep, Lynx went to check the captive's ropes. In the dim light of the fire the young man watched him fearfully, perhaps wondering where his bones would be buried. His eyes followed Lynx when he returned to the others.

Willow sat on the ground beside the fire while the others fell asleep one by one. Through the night he watched the young man frantically twisting and working the knots. When the fire burned

— *Enemy Arrows* —

down he added more wood so he wouldn't lose sight of the captive. He wondered as the night passed if he could talk to the captive at some time to find out what his people did to their prisoners. Perhaps he knew something about his father. How had he died? Or was he still alive? He thought that the young man would either be tortured to death or adopted by a village that needed a strong warrior. Willow struggled to keep his eyes open as he thought about the enemy from across the lake, listening to the sound of rope scraping against bark.

As the fire burned high it illuminated the trees around him, making them twist and sway with the rhythm of the flames. The captive, too, seemed to move with the flickering flames and his struggle to undo the ropes became more like a dance than the desperate contortions of a doomed man. Everything around Willow began to sway as one in the firelight. As his head fell backward, he began to feel himself moving.

The rhythm overtook him and he saw himself tied to a tree, trying desperately to get free, swaying with the trees and the flames. His movements blurred while he watched himself from a distance—and his mind raced back to the Two Sisters and the sight of the young man pinned against the log by the rushing water. In a flash he saw him being dragged down the river by the current.

He could no longer hear the scraping of the ropes against bark, only the crackling of the fire.

Willow heard a snap in the darkness like a breaking bowstring. He saw a dark figure pull his arms away from the tree and stand up. The figure turned to face the low fire with his knees bent and the severed rope in his hands. Willow stared at him with half-opened eyes. The blissful comfort of sleep turned into terror when he realized it was the enemy standing in front of him poised to strike. As panic surged through his body he yelled to the others. For an instant the young man paused, then he raced to the river and slipped into the darkness without a splash.

Lynx jumped to his feet when he saw that their captive had escaped, shouting wildly to the others, and ran to the shore to search for him, but he was gone. It was too dark to search. Willow and Otter stood by the fire in a daze, wondering what could be done, while Loon ranted about the escaped spy and what he would do if he found him again. Lynx tied the canoes to a tree and moved the paddles close to the fire. He knew it would be a night with no sleep.

For the rest of the night Willow fed wood into the fire without going back to sleep. He listened for sounds in the forest with Lynx and Otter lying awake near him. When the sky turned gray, Lynx looked again for tracks, but there was nothing to be found. Without a word about the captive he put a canoe in the river and loaded it for travel. The others were soon with him on the water again.

The sun was bright and warm that day as they passed through the lakes and rivers leading to the Beautiful Lake. They ate in their canoes, speeding through the waterways and looking for signs of the escaped captive. Just before nightfall they found part of their enemy's elm canoe drifting down the river, nearly submerged—its bark broken and its ribs crushed. The rest of the canoe was nowhere to be seen. They put a large rock in the broken shell and watched it sink slowly into the mud. As the bubbles popped on the surface, Willow thought how close he had come to having his own ribs crushed during the night.

After two more days on the chain of lakes they arrived at the long carrying place, a small clearing on a sandy shore with a trail disappearing into the forest. From there, all rivers flowed like the roots of a tree toward the Beautiful Lake. Two days later they reached the long narrow bay on the Beautiful Lake that opened toward the rising sun. Not far from there a trail led through the woods to the setting sun—toward Thunder River. Lynx stopped at a sandy beach beside the trail.

"This will be our last portage," he said. "It will take us to the wide open lake, only a few days from our home."

The last portage took them across a narrow neck of flat, grassy land to a white sand beach. Even before they could see it, they could smell the sweet waters of the lake—the scent of wind blowing over water and sand and through the grasses and fragrant flowers on the shore. It told them of the abundance of birds and fish and plants that had fed their people forever.

On the beach, at the far end of the carrying trail, the endless expanse of the lake opened before them, bathed in the glow of the setting sun. It had been many days and nights since they had seen such boundless space where the shoreline faded into the distance and the clear waters touched the sky. They would soon be home.

– CHAPTER THIRTY –

Return of the Warriors

As soon as the sky was gray, the four travellers launched their two canoes into the Beautiful Lake and followed the shore in the calm, windless time before dawn. For three more days they paddled through light winds and the warm sun of late summer until they caught sight of the towering red bluffs and familiar islands near the River of the Dawn. Beyond the islands they entered the wide crescent-shaped bay at the mouth of Thunder River—the river that led to their village.

"We're home at last," said Willow. "Old Chief will see us coming up the river." As he paddled the final leg of his journey, he wondered what he would say to his grandfather about his time with Shrike—the man with red hands—especially his vivid memories of the battle when his father was killed.

Although Willow's mind had been eased by Shrike's strong beliefs about his father's brutal last hours, he still had several unanswered questions. Had Shrike remembered what he had actually seen with his eyes, or simply what he wanted to remember? Willow knew Shrike's images of the captured warriors hanging from the palisade seemed as real to him as the unseen monster in the lake, but he also knew that Old Chief would ask him for more details—and he had no idea what to say. There didn't seem to be a right way to answer the questions he would be asked.

Perhaps, before telling his grandfather about Oriole's lies, he would ask Wanderer how the enemy fighters treated their prisoners, since he always seemed to know about the enemy. If Wanderer couldn't help him understand, he would have to tell Old Chief about Oriole's lies—and hope that his father's memory was not destroyed by his own attempt to ease his mind. Willow felt like a beaver dam pushed to the breaking point by a spring thaw. If he couldn't stop the pressure soon, he imagined he would burst wide open and wash down the river in a churning mass of mud and broken sticks.

"Willow," said Lynx, getting no response.

"Willow!" shouted Otter. "He's waving."

"Who?" asked Willow, as if waking from a trance.

"Up there!" shouted Loon, pointing toward the village.

High above the river in his favourite place, Old Chief stood waving his bow with an outstretched arm. He was the first to see the two heavily laden canoes appear on the river and he shouted to the others in the village.

Soon there was a parade of friends and relatives rushing down the path to the river. Orchid and Wren were calling to Willow even before he could be seen. He shouted back to them from behind a bend in the river. Loon let out his familiar shriek of a loon call to the delight of his clan, while Otter and Lynx pulled hard on their paddles.

As soon as the canoes were in shallow water they were mobbed by friends. Willow hadn't even stopped paddling before his sister leaped on him, almost overturning his canoe. His mother and Wren grabbed him as he stepped into the shallow water and held him tight.

"I'm so happy now!" Orchid cried. "You're back—you're back in one piece."

Willow stood awkwardly, unable to move, until he gently loosened their arms and reminded them that he was a warrior now, not a child. But they didn't care. They held him all the way up the path and into the longhouse, showering him with questions as they went.

That night Old Chief held a feast around the central fire in the village longhouse to welcome the envoys back from the north. There were endless quantities of fish, so plentiful in the river in late summer, and freshly cut squash, and beans boiled with corn and apples to make a sweet stew.

After the meal and celebrations Lynx distributed gifts of furs and clothing from the People of the Lakes to clan leaders and the elders. To the young men in the longhouse he gave moccasins, hats, and mittens, and to the young women he gave robes of red fox and white rabbit. They laughed and talked excitedly as they wrapped themselves in the gifts—each one trying on every robe at least once. The children were given small copper beads that shone like fire when they were rubbed.

Lynx saved his own gift, the fisher robe—a rare and beautiful garment—for Old Chief, who then praised him for his skills as a hunter and warrior, but most of all for upholding the clan's tradition of generosity. Everyone agreed.

Willow, Otter and Loon shared gifts they had brought. Theirs were smaller and less spectacular than Lynx's gifts, but they were accepted with gratitude just the same.

Later, as they sat around the fire, Lynx told stories of their travels to the north. He spoke about the near drowning of the young man at the Two Sisters and Willow's heroic efforts to save him. He then described the man's elm bark canoe and showed them all the enemy arrowheads from his fire pouch. When he told how the captive had escaped in the night, there were calls for revenge against the enemy and their spies.

"Moose will want to hear every detail about this intruder when he returns," said Old Chief.

Willow then described the fearful night they spent beside the rock carvings with angry spirits racing across the sky—while Wren sat close to him clutching his arm. Once again Loon told of his harrowing night in the open lake, to the amazement of his friends and family. Most were distressed that Falcon would put Loon in so much danger. Others knew that the spirits had saved Loon and Falcon from their own foolishness. Otter told everyone about Lynx's frightening dream of the black serpent and his times fishing with the northern clans. He was pressed endlessly for news about friends and family in the great villages in the north.

Old Chief signalled to Willow to follow him and the two slipped out the south-facing door into the fading light of the full moon setting over the river.

"It was a memorable trip, Willow," said Old Chief.

"Yes, I saw things I'll never forget—and people I'll never forget. They're good people in the north—once you get used to their ways."

"Are they your friends? Do they treat you like a brother?"

"Yes."

"Good. You will make a fine envoy—just like your father."

Willow nodded, not knowing what to say, and not knowing whether this was the time to talk about his meeting with Shrike. Old Chief put his hand on Willow's shoulder. He seemed to have to reach higher than he had in the spring.

"Willow, did you meet with—I have forgotten his name—the man with red hands?"

"Shrike? Yes, I helped him paint enormous images on a cliff," he replied.

Old Chief moved closer. "Did he answer your questions?"

"In a way," said Willow, without adding more.

Old Chief waited for him to continue, and then asked, "Did his answers give you peace?"

Willow took a deep breath before he replied. He had been wondering how to describe Shrike's words to his grandfather ever since he'd left the lake with the water monsters. "Shrike was there," said Willow tentatively. "He told me what he saw—but I think he believes what he wants to believe, so I'm not sure what to think."

"Can I help you to find out?" asked Old Chief, probing his thoughts.

"Maybe." Willow turned away to look at the first light of dawn, thinking about what to say. In time he answered. "Do you know . . ." He stumbled on his words and started again. "Can you say if Wanderer's daughter knew my father?"

Old Chief looked at the dim stars as he tried to recall. "She's about the same age as you, Willow. Or a bit older. Perhaps she knew him as a small child, but she would not remember him."

"No?"

"No," replied the chief.

"Then I don't know what to think," said Willow.

Old Chief noticed a slight quaver in his grandson's voice and a subtle drooping of his shoulders. He waited again for Willow to speak, then finally asked, "Why does that trouble you, Willow?"

"I can't say."

"I may be able to help you find what you are looking for," said Old Chief, trying not to push the young man too hard.

Once more Willow was torn between his desperate need to talk to his grandfather about prisoners and adopted warriors and his fear that his own father might be a traitor living with the enemy. He couldn't bring himself to destroy his father's memory by repeating the lie. The words would not come out. He felt like a coward whether he remained silent or forced himself to speak.

"I can't tell you yet—maybe later, but not yet. I'm still trying to find some answers."

"Then tell me when you want," replied Old Chief. "I will always be here."

– CHAPTER THIRTY-ONE –

A Hidden Stash

Late the next day, Willow and Wren walked through the village to visit the homes of people who were especially close to him. After a summer of new faces and strange places, he found comfort in the fact that so little had changed while he was away. The same cooking smells came from the longhouses and the same children roamed the village looking for excitement. They tugged on his arms, pleading with him to tell more stories of his travels until finally he sat with them in the grass and told them of his adventures. They listened with wide eyes as he described rock painting with the man with red hands—although he didn't mention Shrike's distressing words.

While Willow had been away the corn in the fields had grown almost to the height of a man and the beans had climbed their way up the corn stalks, twisting around the husks. Large flat squash leaves on the ground kept the roots of the corn and beans cool, and ripe sunflowers hung their heads toward the ground.

It was a good harvest, despite the frosty planting in spring, which seemed so long ago.

Willow and Wren found Orchid working in the fields where she had been most of the summer. Wren helped their mother cut corn and gather squash, as Willow answered more questions about his travels.

— A Hidden Stash —

Finally, when the time felt right, Willow told Orchid about meeting Wanderer and Oriole while he was in the north. He described the young woman's odd remark about the running-deer tattoo on Gray Fox's shoulder. Orchid froze with her knife poised against the neck of a large squash while she listened to the story. When Willow told his mother about Wanderer and Oriole disappearing into the night, Orchid spat on the ground and sliced the neck off the squash. It rolled across the field before coming to rest at Willow's feet.

"Stay away from Wanderer," she warned. "Stay away from his daughter, too. They have so many secrets they can't tell the truth from a lie."

Willow thought carefully about his mother's advice. There was certainly something about Wanderer's daughter that upset him and disrupted his thoughts. It was more than her horrid lie about his father, but he couldn't say what. Even though he tried not to think about her, she seemed to haunt his thoughts.

At sunset Orchid returned to the longhouse and Toothless Hunter soon appeared at her shoulder.

"There's too much corn and squash," he said loudly. "We can't live here anymore."

"We've had a good harvest," she replied. "I don't mind that. In a few days we'll bury the corn in a safe place."

Orchid turned to Willow and pointed to the floor near her loft. "You can dig a pit around here and we'll bury as much as we can—away from the reach of mice and squirrels." She spoke again to Toothless Hunter. "This will be out of your way soon. It will be the same as it was."

"There's no room for it here," repeated Toothless Hunter anxiously.

From out of the darkness Old Heron appeared and spoke firmly to Toothless Hunter. "She told you it will be the same as it was."

He grunted and retreated behind a deerskin curtain. "Don't dig near my loft," he added in a weak voice.

Willow began digging a storage pit the next day after Toothless Hunter had left the longhouse. He scraped the ground with a hoe made from the shoulder bone of a deer and piled the soil in baskets to be spread on the ground outside. When the hole was knee deep, his hoe struck something hard, which broke a large chunk off the hoe.

When he continued to dig, Willow found a stone axe head, several beautiful stone knifes, clay pipes, arrowheads, furs, and a large beaver pouch filled with valuable shells and jewellery of every description. He pulled all of this from the pit and spread it out near the fire. Then he called to Old Heron.

"Where did you get this?" asked Old Heron.

"Near Toothless Hunter's loft," he replied, pointing to the hole in the ground.

"We feed him . . . we take care of him," she said sadly. "What does he do in return?"

Willow continued digging the storage pit, hoping he wouldn't unearth any other treasures. Just before dusk Toothless Hunter returned to the village from a hunt—empty-handed as usual. Old Heron met him at the entrance to the longhouse and spoke to him about the hidden stash.

"This is not our tradition," she said patiently. "Even a squirrel shares with its family."

Toothless Hunter looked about him, hoping that no one else had heard of his hoarding, but he knew it was too late.

"I want you to come with me and speak to the other elders," said Old Heron. "They will want to help you with this. Will you come with me now?" she asked.

Toothless Hunter lowered his head. He knew that everyone in the village was aware of what he had done. He also knew that his clan had helped him through the lean years when he couldn't provide for himself or anyone else. They would be disturbed to find out that he had so much wealth that he hadn't shared.

"I'll go with you," he said feebly.

"Come with us, Willow," she added.

— *A Hidden Stash* —

A group of elders was inside the main village longhouse, listening to Lynx describe the northern journey to Moose and the War Chief, when Old Heron entered with Toothless Hunter and Willow. They welcomed her as one of the most respected elders in the village, but wondered why the reclusive Toothless Hunter was with her. She told them about the hoard of valuables Willow had found and how she and the others had always cared for Toothless Hunter when they thought he had nothing. The elders listened sympathetically, shaking their heads.

As his actions were being revealed, Toothless Hunter remained silent, staring at the ground or glancing occasionally in the direction of Old Heron. He felt a strong sense of betrayal, but couldn't tell whether he had been betrayed by someone else—or by his own greed. Now and then Old Heron met his glances with a powerful stare. She knew how important it was for the entire clan that the elders deal quickly and firmly with his loathsome selfishness.

When Old Heron had finished, Old Chief spoke quietly to Toothless Hunter. "Is this true, my old friend?" he asked.

"I bury my possessions in the earth," he answered. "We all do."

"You can bury whatever you want," replied Old Chief. "But is it true you take for yourself—without giving to others? Can that be true?"

Toothless Hunter looked at him without answering. He glanced at Willow standing near the door. After a long silence Old Chief rose and walked slowly to him. He stood very near and looked deep into his eyes. He spoke to the others, as though Toothless Hunter couldn't hear.

"Look at him. He is toothless now—old and frail. He hunts, but never returns with anything. Once he was a good hunter who contributed what he could." Then he spoke to Toothless Hunter.

"What has happened to you?"

The old man remained silent, staring at the ground.

"Why are you silent? Are you unwell?"

Toothless Hunter lifted his head and answered defiantly. "Those things are mine. I have them because I'm a good trader. He shouldn't have dug them up," he said pointing to Willow.

"Don't turn on him," retorted Old Chief, with his eyes narrowed. "He did nothing except stumble on your hoard."

"I want to know what makes the old man this way," said the mother of the Deer Clan. "What makes you keep these valuables for yourself? You can't use them all. You can't even see them when they are buried."

He didn't respond.

"What joy is there in taking without giving back? What respect do you get? What honour is there for a man who takes more than he needs?"

"How does it help you?" asked Old Heron. "How does it help your clan?"

Toothless Hunter looked around the longhouse at the people he had known all his life. He saw the strained looks of concern and pity on their faces, but he couldn't answer. Nothing he could say would change their minds.

Instead he left the longhouse and made his way through the village, aware of the silence that followed him, aware of the pain of being shunned.

As soon as the Toothless Hunter had left, Moose called out to Willow. "Willow, my friend, come and tell me about your trip to far-away places." He moved over to make a space on the log. "Sit down here. Did you see Grackle? Did you play stickball? I want to know everything from the beginning to the end—but first tell me about the elm canoe and the man you pulled from the water. We were just talking about that."

Willow sat down beside Moose and described the events from his first sighting of the elm canoe to the young man's escape into the river. The elders listened carefully to every word. When he was finished, Moose asked him detailed questions about the man's torn earring, the contents of his fire pouch, the age of his canoe, the calluses on his hands, and the shape of his paddle. Nothing was overlooked. Nothing was too trivial. When Moose finished his questions he turned to Old Chief.

"My chief, I think we should have a meeting of everyone in the village to warn of these spies. They are becoming too common. We all have to be on guard."

"This is a matter of war, so I will follow your wishes. We will meet in two nights."

Later that night, when Toothless Hunter returned to his loft, he saw the piles of corn that had not yet been moved and the large hole in the floor. Beside his loft for all to see were the possessions he had secretly buried.

For two days Toothless Hunter didn't ask for food, and none was offered. He sat by the fire in the longhouse—alone.

At the end of the second day, as the sun was setting beyond the valley below, Moose spoke to the village about the presence of spies in their territory. He told them of the young man in the elm canoe who had been saved by Willow and then escaped into the river. He reminded them of times in the past when enemy warriors had been seen on the frozen lake. Old Chief listened silently at the War Chief's side.

"The enemy want to drive us from our land," said Moose. "They are too near and there are too many of them. We must be careful at all times."

On the evening of the third day, under a waning moon, the village medicine man came to talk to Toothless Hunter. He appeared in the longhouse wearing a wolverine robe, his white hair combed back from his tattooed face, his dark eyes shining with the wisdom of many years of healing. The medicine man spoke quietly so that no one could hear, while Toothless Hunter continued to stare silently at the fire. After some time and many words he gave the distraught old hunter a bowl of broth mixed with soothing herbs, which he quickly drank. Slowly a calm came over Toothless Hunter and he began to speak in a low, mournful voice about the battles he'd been in and the hideous sights he'd seen. When night came the medicine man led his patient into the forest to a small sweat lodge.

— *Enemy Arrows* —

For several days the medicine man cared for Toothless Hunter, giving him herbs, roots, and dried mushrooms. He heated rocks in a fire outside the sweat lodge until they glowed red from within and then carried them inside, holding them tight with split branches shaped like snake tongues.

In the darkness he poured water over the glowing rocks until the rising steam was thick enough to cut with a knife. Outside, a heavy mist hung over the sweat lodge deep in the silent forest, marking the place where Toothless Hunter was learning to see clearly again.

One by one during the day, the clan leaders joined the medicine man and Toothless Hunter in the lodge where they bathed in the magic clouds produced by the most important elements of the earth—rocks, water, and fire. As poisons and harmful spirits oozed out of their skin, the visitors spoke to Toothless Hunter about his life, sometimes laughing when they recalled events from long ago.

Early one morning, Moose sat with Old Chief in his favourite place overlooking the river and the autumn trees, talking about the need to send spies into enemy lands. Their peace was shattered when a pair of stickball players came running toward them across the open field, whipping the ball quickly and accurately from one to the other. Old Chief was the first to point out how fast and agile they were. He was about to ask who they were when they both heard the maniacal call of a loon.

"That's Loon!" cried Moose. "And Willow." He looked at Old Chief in amazement.

"Where did they learn to play like that?" asked Old Chief.

"From the People of the Lakes," answered Moose, squinting as the whirl of shapes and colours disappeared into the forest.

"There is nothing more I can show them about the game," said Old Chief with a smile. "Perhaps they can show us some of their lightning moves."

As the days passed the people from Toothless Hunter's longhouse came to see him in small groups of two or three to show their respect for him, despite his selfishness. They asked him to return

— A Hidden Stash —

when he was ready to live among them again and he responded kindly—asking them to be patient with him.

At last, when the full moon was rising above the forest, Toothless Hunter returned to the village with the medicine man. He was welcomed by his clan as a friend returning from a long and difficult journey. His hoarded possessions had been carefully placed in baskets under his loft, and when the old hunter saw them lying there undisturbed, he was suddenly overcome by shame.

The next morning Toothless Hunter announced that he would hold a feast for everyone in the village—and that he would no longer be a bloodsucker, taking more than he could use. From then on he would try to regain his honour by being generous and helpful.

There were looks of disbelief among his clan members. Old Heron listened quietly, watching his movements carefully as he spoke. She noticed that his shoulders, which used to be hunched like those of a beaten dog, were now straight and square. The crouch had gone from his knees. Instead of staring at the floor when he spoke, he looked at the people he was addressing.

Most of all, his strained, halting voice was now as clear and flowing as the river that ran near their village. The medicine man stood beside Old Heron, watching her and looking at the reaction of Toothless Hunter's clan as he spoke. He was hopeful that the cure would be successful.

Toothless Hunter did give a feast for the entire village. He had little food to give away, but he was determined to share whatever he had. All the valuables that he had hidden under the floor of the longhouse—and in several other hiding places around the village—were distributed among his clan members and the rest of the people in the village.

After the feast he turned to Willow, who was standing beside Orchid near the fire.

"You were the one who found my hoard," he said. "I was angry then, but now I'm grateful to you. I want you to have these arrowheads. I know they'll do more for you than they ever will for me.

You can use them to defend our people, or maybe you can bring down another bear."

Willow accepted the gift with a feeling that it came from a different person than the troubled old man who had greedily hidden everything he had managed to accumulate.

By late that night Toothless Hunter had nothing left but the moccasins on his feet and the loincloth around his waist—and one other gift, which he had saved for Old Heron. Standing by the blazing fire before his guests, he gave her a necklace of jagged purple stones, which had been buried in the ground for many years, speaking bravely with the voice of a respected elder.

"This is the last of my hoard," he said to Old Heron. "I give it to you because your strong words brought me to my senses. I felt the emptiness that came from my greed, and the weight of my possessions was crushing my spirit. Now that they're gone I feel strength returning to my spirit. Perhaps one day I will regain my honour as well."

Old Heron received the gift and the praise graciously. She would protect the people of her longhouse from dangers outside and within. If Toothless Hunter stayed true to his humble words, he would no longer be a threat to the clan. She would believe him for now, but she would watch his shoulders and knees for signs of illness, and listen carefully to the sound of his voice.

– CHAPTER THIRTY-TWO –

To the Bottomless Lake

An autumn crispness was in the air. Squirrels had filled their houses with enough nuts to last the long winter and the waterfowl had flown south in their arrow-shaped formations. In the dense forest where no one lived, the deer were gathering together in herds, fat from a summer of grazing on sweet grasses and succulent berries. Their reddish coats were fading to gray for the winter and the growing fawns had lost their spots.

Sturdy bucks and graceful does wandered through the forests listening for the sounds of danger. When threatened, they lifted their white tails and bounded through the trees to safety. No predator was fast enough to catch a fleeting deer by itself, but, as wolves knew well, there were other ways to bring them down. Instead of speed, wolf packs relied on co-ordination. When planning a kill, they moved as one.

Even the fastest deer could not escape.

In the early morning light a group of canoes rounded the last bend near the mouth of Thunder River and moved into the wide bay and calm waters of the Beautiful Lake. The sun was climbing at the far end of the lake as the last one appeared. Then, the group turned like a flock of birds and headed west along the shore with the sun behind them. A light breeze from the east pushed the canoes past the sand beaches and open fields, past the forests plunging to the water.

Some of the paddlers gazed across the lake where the distant mighty river fell into a gorge. They could see a plume of mist caught by the morning sun, forming an orange cloud that hung high above the Great Falls like a spirit.

Orchid sat in the centre of one canoe on a pile of mats and coils of twine with her back resting against a basket of dried fish. She smiled a contented smile at the sight of the lake in the quiet of a new day. At her feet were large clay pots full of fresh beans and corn from the harvest. She had brought a paddle, but kept it beside her most of the time. Whenever she wanted to move her body she would take a few strokes, feeling more like a helpful passenger than an idle traveller.

Lynx paddled in the back of the same canoe with the power of several men. He was surrounded by tools for cutting trees, each wrapped carefully to avoid damaging the bark at his feet. Because of his strength, there was no need for Orchid to paddle at all. At the front, Willow scanned the shores for signs of animals—though they would not stop to hunt this time.

Orchid sang travelling songs while they charged through the water. She sang about the rhythm of the paddles and the spirits of the lake, about the sun and the wind. Her songs always made the trips go faster.

"This is my favourite season of the year," she said. "The corn is in from the fields and the longhouses are full. Now I can rest and get ready for the winter festivals."

She looked behind her at the others skimming across the water. "It was a long hard summer and I'm glad it's over." She turned her head toward Lynx. "It seems to get harder every year. The corn we grew when I was young was much lighter to carry," she said with a laugh.

"You're just as strong now," he said.

"Just like you, Lynx. Age has only made you stronger." She leaned forward and patted Willow on the back. "Age is making

— To the Bottomless Lake —

you stronger, too, my handsome son. Look at you now after your summer among the People of the Lakes. They fed you well." She paused to admire Willow's strength and agility as he pulled his paddle through the water and thought about how quickly he had gone from a helpless infant to a young warrior.

"Yes, you'll make some wide-eyed fawn a good husband."

"I would tell you about some of the other things we did in the north," he answered, "but not now. You'd fall out of the canoe."

Orchid dipped her hand in the cool water and splashed his back.

"Do that again," laughed Willow. "I can take any torture you give me."

Orchid sang a song about young love. She lingered over the words about the young couple hiding in the cornfields and her voice became louder.

Willow jammed the blade of his paddle between his knees and held his hands over his ears. He howled like a wolf to drown out his mother's song. "No more!" he pleaded. "No more. I can take torture, but I can't take that."

Lynx laughed at his suffering. He knew that mothers had a way of turning the strongest warriors into whimpering pups, because they knew just the right words to use—and kept them ready in case their sons lost their humility. Lynx had been humbled many times himself.

Old Chief paddled in the centre of the canoe that cut through the water next to them, pulling hard on his paddle, showing he hadn't been weakened by age, although his arms looked thin compared to the huge arms of Moose behind him. When he heard Willow howling he turned with a wide smile. He always smiled on the way to a deer hunt.

Otter sat in front with a puzzled look on his face, wondering why Willow had stopped paddling on the way to the hunting grounds. In a distant canoe, Loon accompanied Deadfall Hunter and his wife, Bright Star. Deadfall Hunter beamed with the joy that comes from hunting with others. In the thrill of the moment Loon cupped his hands together and mimicked the boisterous sound of a loon, which echoed from the shore.

The route to the deer-hunting grounds was along the northern shore of the Beautiful Lake to a winding stream that led into the hills and then, when the water became too shallow, through the forest by foot. By the time the sun was high, the travellers could see their hilly destination moving closer and closer as they followed along the shore. Lynx kept a close lookout for enemy canoes emerging from the south, since their group was not well armed. With several women and elders in their group, he knew they would have to retreat into the forest if the enemy approached. Battle would be impossible.

By late afternoon the travellers left the open lake and followed the narrow stream as far as they could before pulling up their canoes and hiding them in the woods. They would camp for the night at the foot of heavily treed hills before making the long trek to the deer hunting grounds.

As soon as the canoes were unloaded, Orchid sprang into action and before long she had pots full of corn and fish warming over a fire, with fresh herbs to enhance the flavour. Watching Orchid's quick movements, Lynx and Moose placed loads of firewood nearby.

"I don't think she knows how to rest any more," said Lynx.

"This morning in the canoe was the first time I've seen her sit still since the spring," replied Moose.

Lynx laughed at the thought of Orchid being idle. "I remember her running through the village as a child, talking to everyone she met. She knew everything about everyone."

"She still does," said Moose, adding wood to the fire.

At dawn, Lynx, followed by Orchid and Willow, led the way along the trail north through the forest to the hunting grounds. Even though Lynx and Willow were laden with equipment and supplies, they had their bows in hand in case of an ambush. There had been enemy raids in the past, though they both knew an attack was more likely on the way back to their canoes when they had meat from the hunt.

— To the Bottomless Lake —

The trail continued for a day's walk through the woods and up a cliff to a small village beside the deep, blue waters of the Bottomless Lake. At dusk the travellers arrived at the village, where they were greeted by their friends and members of their clans.

The chief was a tall man with long straight hair on either side of his head. A narrow strip in the centre of his scalp was cut short and it stood upright like the quills of an angry porcupine. His ears had been pierced in several places and from each hole hung a strand of coloured beads made from hollow bird bones dyed different colours. A jagged scar ran from his nose to his earlobe, and around his neck he wore a collection of teeth, bones, and rocks. Each trinket had a story, which the chief was always anxious to tell. He was called Porcupine because of his slow, thoughtful way of speaking.

At the eastern end of the lake were a few small huts where a breeze usually blew the mosquitoes away. The lake itself was small enough for a strong archer to shoot an arrow from one side to the other, but so deep it seemed to have no bottom. It was also clear enough to see any crayfish or water snakes that swam out of the dark blue depths, or the large snapping turtles that glided through its still waters.

On a rise above the lake was the village, with five completed longhouses and an outline of poles to mark where a sixth one would be built. The houses were surrounded by broad fields where crows searched for kernels of corn. Stunted corn stalks piled in rows in the fields showed all the signs of a poor harvest—the result of late frosts.

The next day when the sun was high, Porcupine, his neighbours, and their visitors met beside a longhouse to plan the hunt. Then they walked through the shady forest until the darkness again gave way to light at the edge of a cliff. There they stood looking out over a narrow valley, which opened onto more wide forests spreading south all the way to the Beautiful Lake sparkling in the distance. On the far side, another cliff faced them with large, gray rocks jutting out toward them. High above their heads, turkey vultures soared in the light breeze, their black wings lifting up on either side of their bodies.

As Willow, Loon and Otter stood at the edge of the cliff, Loon kicked a rock over the edge and watched it cascade to the boulders far below. When it landed it shattered into pieces with a sound that echoed among the hills.

"This is where the jump will be," said Old Chief. "We will join together to make this the best hunt yet."

Porcupine answered slowly. "We have already started building some fences. You can see one side through the trees." He pointed to a line of brush where there were tall poles planted in the ground, starting at the cliff edge and disappearing into the distance.

"The other line of poles will be built from here," he said, marking the spot with a stick. "It will follow the same path into the forest. The two lines will meet, just as the wings of a soaring vulture meet its body, but there will be a narrow gap—right here at the cliff."

Porcupine peered over the rocks below as he continued. "We'll build a small jump here, low enough for the deer to leap over, but not so low that they'll be able to see beyond it. There will be two or three hunters at the bottom with sharpened poles, but most deer will die quickly when they hit the rocks."

Because most of the hunters had chased deer over these cliffs before, they knew how it was done—and were anxious to get started. They spent the next two days felling trees and constructing the other wing of the fence, which spread the length of the cliff. At the gap where the two wings met, they built a narrow jump and covered it with branches and leaves. It was built to look like the only escape for the trapped deer and was the only place where the sky could be seen. The deer would race toward it like fish to a torch on a dark night.

That evening a light breeze blew while the hunters gathered around a fire at the north shore of the Bottomless Lake. The women who had come for the hunt sat nearby. They had been busy preparing food while the fence was being built, but they knew that the hard job would begin the following day, when they helped butcher the deer and collect fat from their carcasses.

Porcupine told stories of hunts from past years and of spirit hunters chasing deer among the clouds. Late in the night the village shaman rose beside the fire, looked out across the dark lake and raised his hands to the sky. Old Chief stood up and moved beside him. They walked slowly toward the lake, chanting in strong voices as they went.

The shaman sang first to the spirit of the Bottomless Lake, throwing bits of tobacco leaves into the water, and then to the spirit of the sky, so it would give them good weather and guide the deer to the jump. As he sang, Old Chief sprinkled tobacco on the fire and fanned the smoke upward, the scent spreading through the air.

Several women then rose to sing in praise of the deer, which would soon face death. They shook rattles made of turtle shells and called to the deer to jump bravely over the cliff. Orchid sang with the excitement of someone who had seen many hunts and skinned many deer.

The singing and dancing continued late into the night, with the young hunters leaping excitedly toward the stars. When it was over Willow, Loon and Otter collapsed on the grass overlooking the lake under the swirling sky.

Orchid was among the first women to wake before dawn. Soon she had a large pot full of soup warming beside the fire and corn bread heating on a flat rock. When the sky became brighter she could hear the sound of other voices around fires by the lake and from behind the palisade of the village beyond.

Orchid walked to the lake to fill a pot of water. As she passed Willow, lying under a small canoe, she called to him softly. When he didn't move, she sat down on the grass where he slept and whispered his name, brushing the hair from his face, but still nothing. Otter and Loon were also asleep, far away in their dreams.

Sitting beside Willow, smoothing his hair, she wondered what kind of man he would be. She hoped he would be a strong warrior, kind and generous to his own people, but fierce and ruthless against the enemy. He looks so much like his father, she thought, the man she missed every day. Orchid's daydreams were interrupted when Willow unconsciously brushed his hand across his forehead to swat away whatever was moving in his hair—and hit her hand. It was something much larger than he had expected. Shaking his head violently, he sat up and opened his eyes—only to see his mother on the grass beside him, laughing at his sudden start to the day. Willow looked at her in surprise and stood up.

"It wasn't an insect," she said with a quiet laugh. "It was just me, a mother watching her child sleep. Watching and wondering."

"I'm not a child," he responded.

"You're right," she said, as she stood up beside him. She had to look up to see into his eyes. "You are a strong warrior—strong enough to fill this with water for me."

Willow looked around and saw that his friends were still sleeping, so he took the empty pot and filled it in the lake.

– CHAPTER THIRTY-THREE –

Over the Jump

The hunt was to start at dawn. As the sun crept above horizon the people in the village and the hunters from Thunder River gathered beside the Bottomless Lake. There was silence as Old Chief spoke.

"Most of us have done this before, so we will do what we always do. There will be two groups of beaters. Both groups will start here and fan out on either side. One by one you will drop behind so that each hunter will be within yelling distance of the next, but don't start yelling. As you walk through the forest, you must be silent!" he said emphatically.

"Do not speak," he continued. "Do not even step on a twig or frighten a bird or the deer will hear us and run away from our trap. We want to surround them like fish in a net and then draw the net closer. Anyone who has not been on a hunt before should stay near an experienced hunter. Deadfall Hunter will stay out of sight beside the jump to make sure all goes well at the edge of the cliff."

Porcupine spoke next. "Old Chief will lead one group and I'll lead the other. When we're in position the net will be closed. That's when we'll start yelling and keep going until we're hoarse." Holding the palms of his hands downward to signal silence, he continued in a low voice. "But not yet. We'll all be hoarse soon enough."

— *Enemy Arrows* —

The faces of the young hunters glowed with excitement and anticipation. The hunt was about to start.

"When you hear me yell—start yelling too!" said Old Chief. "Walk toward the gap in the fence. Draw the net in tighter and tighter, so the deer will run toward the fence—and then to the gap. Lynx and Moose are at the bottom of the cliff now. They have spears to kill any deer that survive the fall."

"We'll keep the same groups as always," said Porcupine. "My group can come with me now, and stay as quiet as salamanders," he said with a grin, looking at the younger hunters in his group.

Old Chief led his group in a line silently through the forest with Willow, Otter and Loon following immediately behind him. As they moved away from the Bottomless Lake he stopped and signalled for the last person in the line to drop off and hide in the bushes. Then he continued through the forest, always keeping an eye on the position of the sun through the trees. Each time he stopped another hunter hid in the bushes.

As they walked, Old Chief pointed into the trees with his hand, making the sign of a deer. The hunters behind him squinted into the empty forest, looking for anything alive, but only once did they see a white tail fleeing in the distance.

"He can see in the dark, too," whispered Loon. Willow turned to smile silently at Otter and Loon. As he did, Old Chief stopped in his tracks and Willow crashed into his back. Though he was old, Old Chief stopped his grandson like a standing tree.

"He has good hearing, too," whispered Old Chief with a stern look on his face. "The deer have even better hearing." He signalled down the line for silence and then walked on.

As Willow took a step to follow, he stepped on a dead branch. A loud *crack!* rang through the forest, sending a grouse flapping noisily through the trees. Old Chief squatted close to the ground and the others followed him one by one. Willow didn't dare to breathe—and Old Chief didn't need to say anything. They remained rigid until Old Chief stood up, signalled again for silence, and then moved on.

— *Over the Jump* —

As each hunter dropped behind, the line became shorter and soon there were only four left, Old Chief, Willow, Otter and Loon. They knew the yelling would start soon. At that moment Porcupine appeared through the trees a short distance away and signalled to Old Chief. The net was complete.

"Spread out," yelled Old Chief. "We are about to start!"

Willow, Otter and Loon backtracked through the forest. Old Chief signalled to Porcupine that all was well. He let out the howl of a wolf, and in an instant the silent forest was filled with the din of yells, howls, and branches beating on trees. Birds screeched in terror as they tried to escape.

Slowly the hunters stepped through the forest, heading toward the gap in the fence.

"Deer!" shouted Otter, pointing to a large buck bounding through the trees toward the jump. The sun cast a dappled light on its back, like the spots on a fawn. A fat porcupine slowly shinnied up a birch tree to escape the noise.

At the jump site, the Deadfall Hunter crouched out of sight between the fence and the edge of the cliff, carrying a heavy stick. He peered through slits in the fence, looking for the first approaching deer. Far below him, he could see Moose and Lynx standing with their spears ready.

Above the cliff, turkey vultures circled in the morning sun, gazing down at the smaller birds scattering in panic from the noisy forest. They saw bobcats cowering in swaying treetops—but the vultures were not afraid. They had heard this noise before and knew it meant endless feasting for the meat-eating scavengers of the forest, so they spiralled lazily in the breezes above the jump, waiting for the carnage.

Deadfall Hunter caught a glimpse of a young doe. Her head spun wildly back and forth as if trying to locate the source of the noise—the direction of the danger—but it came from everywhere. She ran to the clearing in front of the jump and froze. High fences blocked her escape on either side. As her wide eyes scanned the trees for signs of movement, her ears swivelled back and forth and her nostrils opened and closed. Perhaps she recognized the scent of the hunters coming through the forest. Her head turned from the jump to the noise and back. She looked behind again and then raced to the jump. Over the logs and bushes she leapt—through the gap between the fences—and plummeted to the rocks below.

A pair of bucks stampeded through the clearing after her without hesitating. Over the jump they went, crashing in a heap close to Lynx and Moose.

Deadfall Hunter watched through a narrow opening as a graying buck hobbled from the woods into the clearing. The old buck had a broken antler and its rear leg showed the marks of a recent fight with a sharp-toothed predator. It stood with its injured leg raised, snorting and stomping its hooves on the rocks in front of the jump. The noises it made thundered throughout the forest, warning the other deer of imminent danger.

The old buck limped forward and stood before the wall of brush as though wondering whether it could clear such a height, but the yelling was getting closer and the noise more frightening. With a clumsy kick, the old buck leapt at the jump—only to fall among the branches. It thrashed and tried to kick its way over, but was soon caught fast in the logs.

The more it struggled the more it became entangled.

Deadfall Hunter could see a frantic cluster of bucks coming toward the clearing, trying to escape the hunters. They were snorting with fright at the noise from behind and the sight of the thrashing buck in front. Deadfall Hunter limped out from his hiding spot to free the injured buck. He grabbed it by the antlers and pulled, but he couldn't move it. The bucks behind him were pounding the ground and whirling in circles with their antlers down for protection. They couldn't go forward and they dared not go back toward the noise.

With one mighty pull, Deadfall Hunter freed the wounded buck and hauled it away from the jump. At the same instant a large young buck raced for the opening with its antlers down, knocking the Deadfall Hunter through the remnants of the barrier. The buck

— *Over the Jump* —

and the Deadfall Hunter soared through the opening together and plunged down, down to the rocks below. The rest of the crazed deer followed before Moose or Lynx could get to the Deadfall Hunter.

The turkey vultures circled lazily above, waiting for the feast to begin.

"Stop the deer!" boomed Moose, as he scrambled over the rocks. His voice echoed down the valley. "Stop!" he cried, but no one could hear him above the yells of the hunters far above—and the deer kept coming.

The cliff was far too high to climb, so Lynx raced along the base of the cliff to a place where a wall of rocks had collapsed into the valley. He struggled to make his way up the pile, yelling as he went to anyone who might hear him above the noise of so many others.

Moose stayed at the bottom of the jump yelling to stop the deer. Far above, in the forest at the top of the cliff, Old Chief stopped to listen. He could hear a sound in the melee that didn't belong.

"Willow!" he yelled. The young hunter turned to Old Chief and saw him signalling to come quickly.

"There is something wrong at the jump," said Old Chief. "Run and see what is happening—and come back as fast as you can."

Willow raced toward the place where the jump had been. When he arrived he saw that it had been smashed, leaving the edge of the cliff visible. Frantic deer stood in the clearing, not daring to leap over the cliff to escape. Deadfall Hunter was nowhere to be seen.

"Stop!" Moose's voice echoed from the bottom of the cliff.

Willow carefully slipped through the gap in the fence, holding on to a cedar tree until he could see below.

"Willow," Moose screamed. "Stop the deer! Deadfall Hunter has fallen over."

Willow stared down at the pile of deer carcasses at the bottom of the cliff. Although he couldn't see any sign of Deadfall Hunter, he signalled to Moose that he understood—but as he turned to go back through the gap in the fence, two does launched themselves over the cliff, nearly taking him with them. They fell through the air just as Moose climbed on to the pile to search for the Deadfall Hunter.

— *Enemy Arrows* —

"Moose!" he shrieked. The hunter below looked up in time to see the animals falling toward him. He threw himself from the mound of carcasses and landed on a pile of boulders, where he lay without moving. Willow turned toward the snorting, frantic deer. He waved his arms and charged at them, hoping to chase the panic-stricken creatures away—but they were being driven toward him by people making far more noise.

And even more deer were rushing out of the forest.

He ran back through the frightened deer to tell Old Chief what had happened. By this time the hunters were almost in sight of the jump, squeezing the deer closer to the edge—tightening the net.

Old Chief reacted instantly.

"Run that way and tell everyone to retreat back into the forest—let the deer escape. Go quickly!"

Willow ran first to Otter and Loon, who also began running down the line telling the hunters to fade into the woods and let the deer escape. Meanwhile, Old Chief and Porcupine ran to the fence behind the deer and with loud shouts drove them back into the forest.

The hunt was over.

Lynx appeared at the top of the cliff, scraped and battered from the climb. He and Porcupine led the way down into the valley and the mound of carcasses where they searched until they found Deadfall Hunter—but it was too late. He had been crushed by the fall.

By then Moose was standing again with dried blood caked on the back of his head. He limped toward the others.

"We must carry the body back to the village," said Old Chief, looking at the remains of Deadfall Hunter.

"He'll have to be buried today," said Lynx.

"Bright Star will be overcome at the thought of her husband being left here in the ground," said Old Chief, "but we can't risk angering the spirits."

"Let me tell Bright Star," said Moose, sitting on a rock, rubbing his head. "I know her well." Old Chief nodded in agreement.

— *Over the Jump* —

Porcupine knew they must move quickly. "The deer must be butchered right away," he said. "I'll go back to village with Lynx and tell everyone to bring their knives. We'll be busy before the sun sets—before the wolves move in. But first I'll round up some strong men to carry the body back to the village."

As he began to leave, he turned to Old Chief. "You may want to come later with Moose. He's not able to walk by himself, yet."

On the way back to the village, Lynx and Porcupine met a group of hunters who wanted to know why the hunt had been stopped. When he told them what had happened they rushed to the valley to help carry the Deadfall Hunter's body back to the village.

When Moose was able to walk, he and Old Chief returned to the village, with Willow and Loon following behind them, to tell Bright Star her husband had been killed. They found her with Orchid, cutting up squash beside the Bottomless Lake.

Willow and Loon moved back from the lake so they couldn't hear what was being said. They saw Bright Star greet Moose and Old Chief with her warm smile, and watched as her smile twisted into a look of alarm. Then the word of her husband's death hit her like a falling tree. She staggered backward with her hands on her head and fell to her knees on the rocks.

Willow and Loon could hear her crying for her husband, as though they were standing right next to her. They watched as Orchid rushed to comfort her friend, but Bright Star was inconsolable. Moose and Old Chief remained with Bright Star while women from the village gathered around her.

Suddenly, Bright Star let out a gasp and cried out to Moose. "Will he have to be buried here?"

"Yes," answered Moose solemnly.

"Away from his people?" she cried. Moose turned to Old Chief.

"Yes," said Old Chief. "We can't anger the spirits. He must be buried here."

Bright Star howled before collapsing unconscious on the rocks, overcome by grief. Moose and Old Chief called to Willow and Loon, and the four deer hunters carried Bright Star to the village.

Her arms hung by her sides and her fingers dragged in the leaves. Before sunset Deadfall Hunter was buried in a field behind the village, far away from his people. Bright Star was too grief-stricken to travel, but the others prepared their packs for the return journey.

They set off early the following day for Thunder River. Each person carried a heavy load of deer meat down the trail toward the Beautiful Lake, where they had left their canoes. Before the sun was at its highest they found the canoes beside the stream, but they saw at once that they had been disturbed. Two had been punctured and one was missing. The rest were untouched. In place of the missing birchbark canoe was a badly worn elm vessel with a deep gouge running along the underside, as though it had run over a sharp rock. It was useless.

Moose and Old Chief were the first to see the damage, followed by Lynx and then Willow, Otter and Loon. They dropped their packs, knowing they would be there for some time. As the others arrived, a sombre crowd gathered beside the wreckage.

"That's the same as the canoe we saw at the Two Sisters," shouted Loon. "We should have let him drown."

"It's the same bark," added Lynx, peeling a strip from the torn bottom.

Moose looked at Otter, who silently signalled "Yes," and then at Willow.

"It's exactly like the wrecked one we saw downriver from the Two Sisters," said Willow. "But it can't be the same one—the other one was broken in half."

Lynx smelled the strip of bark. "It's an old canoe," he said. "Three or four winters at least."

Moose kicked the broken shell over to reveal a badly worn relic, scuffed and dented from years of use. A few strips of deerskin dangled from the thwarts.

"There are too many of these canoes in our land," said the War Chief. "Too many spies."

"What do we do now?" asked Old Chief.

"We repair the canoes and return home, just as Lynx and our young envoys did before." He looked into the trees as if trying to find an intruder, and his eyes narrowed. "It's time to take revenge."

– CHAPTER THIRTY-FOUR –

Squirrel in the Longhouse

Moose called the war council together shortly after the deer hunters had returned home from the Bottomless Lake. They met on a cloudy afternoon outside the palisades beside a fire where the deer meat was being smoked for the winter, filling the cool air with the scent of fat dripping into the coals. It was the smell of a successful hunt and a plentiful harvest.

Moose and Old Chief sat together with the clan leaders and elders surrounding them. Willow, Otter and Loon sat far enough away from the council to show their respect, but close enough to hear some of what was being said.

"This year we may be able to go with them," Otter whispered to his friends.

"I'm ready to go now," said Loon. "Everything I need is ready—a new bowstring and stone-tipped arrows."

"So am I," added Willow. "I've made a pouch full of arrowheads. We can't take pointed sticks this time." He raised his hand. "Listen—Moose is speaking."

"We all know there have been too many spies in our nation," said Moose. "They are like bats flying over our heads at night. We can barely see them and we never catch them. If we do, they escape.

"The only way we can get rid of these spies is to attack their villages and force them to move farther and farther away, until they stay away from us."

The council members and elders murmured their approval. When they were silent again, Moose continued. "We must take all the warriors we have and cross the lake."

Willow elbowed his friends and repeated Moose's words. "*All the warriors we have*—that means we'll go!"

"The only thing we have to decide is when we will attack," said Moose. "It will be winter soon, so we must go before it gets cold, or wait until the spring—and I say we go soon."

Again, there were sounds of agreement.

"We have plenty of corn and meat now," he added. "Our longhouses are full. We won't have to stop until we reach the enemy villages."

"Then we'll burn them to the ground!" shouted the leader of the Deer Clan.

The others clan leaders and elders joined in with shouts and battle cries.

"Revenge!"

"Drive them away!"

Loon grabbed his friends by the arms and shook them. "We're going to be in battle!" he cried above the noise.

"We'll be warriors!" shouted Otter.

Old Heron sat quietly amid the excitement, until finally she stood up. One by one the others noticed her and stopped shouting, and when it was quiet she began to speak.

"The method of war is for the War Chief and the War Council to decide—once you have decided it is necessary to go to war. You know how to go about it and we trust you to make the plans.

"I ask you to take a step backwards and consider whether it is necessary to go to war at all."

The members of the war council were stunned by Old Heron's words.

"The forests are full of spies!" shouted one.

Old Heron continued despite the cries. "Every time we try to drive the enemy away we seem to attract more spies. And each time we do, we lose warriors. Think of the fathers, sons, uncles—the good men who will not return. Think of the women here who will be crushed by the loss of their loved ones.

"I ask you—all of you—to think again about whether the presence of a few intruders in our land should force us into the darkness of loss?" Old Heron searched for sympathetic eyes, but found none, so she sat down again.

"How can she say those things?" whispered Loon. "We *want* to go to war!"

Moose looked over to Old Chief, as if to signal to him to respond.

"As always, Old Heron speaks with courage and wisdom," said Old Chief. "We value every word she says. We should not rush into war, for all of the reasons she has given us." Old Chief looked at her and then glanced at Moose in an effort to read his reaction. Then he continued. "I think we should go to war with the enemy, but I suggest we consider what Old Heron says and meet again tomorrow, when we will reach a decision. One day will not affect our plans." Again he turned to Moose.

"Yes," said Moose. "We should all consider Old Heron's words. If we decide to attack the enemy, we will still have time. If we decide not to, we will have time to strengthen our defences. Think about this carefully and we will meet again tomorrow."

With that, Moose and Old Chief got to their feet and the council meeting was over. The three young hunters sat on the ground wondering how the opportunity to go to war had slipped through their fingers.

"I'm not sure we'll be in battle this year," said Otter.

"Why, why, why did she say those things?" stammered Loon.

"We were almost warriors," said Willow.

That night the scratching sounds of mice and chipmunks could be heard throughout the longhouse. They, too, had waited all summer for the harvest and were ready to gather and store as much of the corn and as many of the beans as they could. The mice scurried across the poles from one side of the huge room to the other with cheeks bulging, while the chipmunks stayed close to the ground, nibbling at any basket within reach.

Squirrels came into the longhouse through the smoke holes in the roof and scurried around the smoky rafters until they had to run outside for air. The scratching of little claws and the crunching of corn could be heard all night long.

The noise woke Willow late in the night. He looked around in the low light of the fire, which had dwindled into glowing embers. No one else was awake. Even Old Heron, who never slept, was lying quietly on her bed. A few visitors from a nearby village slept on mats beside the fire.

Willow tried to sleep with his hands over his ears, but the noise was too much to bear. He slipped out of his bunk and moved silently to the woodpile. Choosing a heavy birch branch, he placed it in the embers. The bark ignited instantly and the fire was alive again.

A large black squirrel stood on a pole above his head, poised to leap to a reed basket perched precariously on a platform high on the opposite side of the longhouse. Only the reflection of the fire in its eyes and the sheen of its fur could be seen in the darkness. Willow watched the squirrel as flames began to rise higher. With a mighty push, the animal launched itself into the darkness, its tail waving back and forth like the tailfin of a salmon as it propelled itself forward toward the basket, gliding on its outstretched arms. As it neared the other side, it dropped its tail and grabbed the basket, clinging like a bat on a cave wall.

For an instant the basket teetered from the impact, but then the weight of the squirrel flipped it off the platform toward the fire. It spun in the smoky haze as the squirrel tried to jump free, but then the basket bounced off a rafter, releasing a landslide of dried milkweed pods and crashed into the blazing fire.

The dried pods ignited and the longhouse was instantly bright with flames leaping toward the smoke holes in the roof. At the same time, white tufts of milkweed floating toward the fire, were set alight by sparks. Some of them fell on the dry birchbark containers and reed mats—and they burst into flames.

Willow screamed to wake everyone.

"Get out! Get out everyone!" cried Old Heron with terror in her voice.

"Take the corn," yelled Orchid, waking to see the fire spreading toward the full baskets. Panicked faces flashed in the bright light of the fire and children ran out empty-handed. Some people at the far end of the longhouse were able to grab the baskets, while others gathered things of value or simply close at hand—a comb, a pouch filled with fresh tobacco, a child's toy. The fire spread so quickly through the aging longhouse that there was no chance to save winter clothing, snowshoes, or axes, let alone the precious costumes worn for feasts.

As the flames licked up the outer walls, shouts were heard from neighbouring longhouses and people came running from every direction carrying pots of water and long poles to beat out the flames. But this fire was too big to smother. Corn, pots of oil and deer fat, and the cedar bark covering the walls fuelled the conflagration. Nothing could be done to save the building—or the precious corn that took so much effort to grow.

The best they could do was tear away the walls of the longhouse and throw the burning slabs of bark toward the open spaces where they could burn harmlessly. There was just enough distance between the burning longhouse and the adjacent buildings to keep the flames from spreading on that windless night. Everyone knew they could survive if they contained the blaze, but if the fire spread and the entire village was destroyed, they would all face starvation.

Only a few of the bravest warriors could stand the heat of the fire long enough to throw water on the walls. Together Willow, Otter and Loon carried a large pot full of soup and poured it on the blaze between the houses. Then they filled the pot with water to pour on the nearby houses again and again until their hair was singed by the heat.

— *Squirrel in the Longhouse* —

Thick gray smoke rose from the storage bins as the corn, squash and beans were destroyed. There was a sickening, acrid smell of the burning skins and furs abandoned in the panic. Everyone seemed to be screaming over the roar of the blaze. Dogs barked wildly to match the frantic screams of the people, adding their voices to the chaos.

But no amount of effort could save the burning building.

Once they had escaped, the old people huddled well away from the fire as their shadows danced on the palisades behind them. Few had anything left to keep themselves warm except the heat created by the destruction of their home and their winter supply of food.

As the flames grew higher and the heat became more intense, chunks of burning bark were carried up in the sky above the longhouse by the rising heat. Some drifted back down and landed on the neighbouring longhouses, but men and boys used long poles to beat them out immediately. The village had no chance of containing the disaster if other houses caught fire.

An old woman holding two young children stared at the flames from a safe distance. "I saw this happen before—when I was your age," she said softly amid the yelling, crashing, and barking. "The wind was strong then and the houses burned faster." She didn't say that most of the people in the village lost their homes and harvest, and she didn't describe the winter of starvation they endured by eating lichens, wild roots and the bark from saplings.

Nor did she mention how the People from Across the Lake had come to attack the village when they learned of the great fire.

The flames had soon destroyed all the bark covering the longhouse, leaving only a skeleton of burning poles. The tops of the poles had been tied together to form arches for the curve of the roof, but when the strapping burned through they collapsed, sending hot embers raining down on the other longhouses.

"Willow! Otter!" cried Moose, rushing through the inferno of the flames licking at the longhouse. He grabbed them each by the arm with his huge, steaming hands and motioned to the top of a nearby longhouse that was not yet on fire.

"Get up on the roof and tear away any burning bits of bark. Throw them far away from the houses. Get up now and don't stop—this fire could destroy us! Loon, come with me." He disappeared in a wall of smoke and flames with Loon trying to keep up with him.

– CHAPTER THIRTY-FIVE –

Fire on the Roof

Willow and Otter knew from past experience that the best place to climb up a longhouse was at the ends, above the doors. They had been scolded for climbing on the fragile bark when they were younger—even though they had tried to climb carefully. This time they ripped and kicked at the bark to get to the roof as quickly as they could. If the building was to be saved, it was going to be severely damaged in the process.

Willow reached the top first and helped Otter onto the arched roof. They lay flat on their stomachs to avoid breaking through, as a fall from that height would mean serious injury. Through the smoke at the far end they saw other figures climbing up, too.

The heat from the fire was intense at that height and the screaming and commotion on the ground seemed even more chaotic from above. Cinders and flaming bark rained down upon them.

"Over there!" yelled Otter above the roar of the blaze. He pointed to a small fire taking hold in the centre of the roof, just beside the middle smoke hole. They scrambled like spiders to reach the burning bark and with their bare hands pulled out the flaming slabs and threw them into the open spaces.

"Back behind us!" Willow motioned silently to the sky where a large cinder was floating down. It landed on the lip of the roof where they had just climbed up and immediately ignited a thin strip of bark. In an instant they were there, ripping away the bark and flinging the bits away.

Crash! A long, blazing pole smashed against the side of the longhouse. *Crash! Crash!* Someone on the ground was trying to beat the wall where a large section of bark had caught fire just below them.

"We have to get to it," cried Otter.

"I'll climb down," signalled Willow, as he slid along the sloping arch of the roof toward the fire. Below him to one side was the smoking rubble that had once been his home. Otter slid down the slope just above him. They punched holes in the bark roof, trying to grasp the supporting beams.

"Hold my leg," yelled Otter. Willow grasped his ankle and moved down to the fire. With his free hand Willow yanked the burning bark away and threw it to the ground. Just beyond his reach was a small flame beginning to spread over the roof. He swung his legs toward the flame, kicking at the smouldering bark.

"Hold on tight," screamed Willow, "or we both go into the flames!"

"I can't hold it," replied Otter quietly. "My hands are going to slip."

The bare toes on Otter's free foot scraped at the bark to find a hold. A knothole in the bark or a lose strand of rope was all he needed to take some of the weight from his failing arms, but there was nothing.

"I can't hold on," he mouthed again in silent warning.

Willow flailed at the smoking bark with his legs while clutching Otter's ankle. He twisted his head upward to look at his friend and knew from the strain on his face that he was about to let go. He also knew that Otter wouldn't kick him loose to save his own life. If Otter let go, they would perish together.

Willow could reach all of the burning bark except one smouldering sliver just beyond his most contorted stretch. As he reached up to grasp Otter's other ankle he heard a loud crack on the roof

— Fire on the Roof —

beside him that sent panic through his exhausted body. He clawed at the side trying to pull himself up Otter's legs.

"I can't hold on!" shouted Willow over the roaring flames.

Suddenly Otter's grip failed and he slipped down the side of the curved roof. Willow let go of Otter's leg, clutching at the threads of basswood twine used to hold the bark on the frame. Otter was trying desperately to find another hold, but he couldn't find anything and was slipping backward down the roof.

They heard a deafening crack as a log pole split the bark at Willow's feet. At the other end of the pole Moose was yelling to Willow, but the flames raging behind him drowned out his words. Instinctively, Willow put his foot on the top of the pole and stopped his slide. As Otter slid past him, Willow grabbed his outstretched arm. Now it was his turn to save Otter from the flames.

With another loud crack, a second pole smashed against the side of the longhouse beside Otter. The young man grasped it tight against his chest, as he clawed his way up the roof. Then, in one powerful surge of strength, Moose and two other men raised the poles and hoisted Willow and Otter higher until they were able to scramble to the top, where they collapsed on the flattest part of the roof.

The poles disappeared beneath their feet and continued to bash at the flaming walls.

In the narrow space between the burning house and the one next to it, Loon ran back and forth carrying pots of water to throw against the walls to prevent the next house from catching fire. The smoke was so thick he couldn't breathe. He could only hold his breath and race into the blinding smoke. Loon felt the fire singeing his hair each time he went in, and the skin on his back began to sting from the scorching heat. But each time he came out of the smoke-filled alley—gasping for air—there was another pot thrust into his hands. Sometimes when he came out he grabbed the pot and poured water over his head to make sure he didn't ignite first. And in he went again, throwing water on the wall that was not yet burning.

Willow searched the far end of the roof for the other people who had been putting out the fires, but they were nowhere to be seen. He looked down at his blackened hands and wrists. Although he knew he had burned them, the sight and smell of the burnt flesh was more than he expected. The pain he hadn't felt before came in searing throbs, wave after wave. But he was a warrior and a hunter. He would try not to show the agony he felt.

When Otter saw the contorted expression on Willow's face, he examined his own hands and saw that they were shredded and bleeding. He looked at Willow's bleeding knees and feet, then at his own, and the pulsing agony started. He struggled to raise his head.

"Let's get down from here," Otter said with a weak smile. "I think they need our help on the ground."

Willow raised a burnt hand and together they slid across the roof and slowly, painfully climbed down to the ground, where Loon was waiting for them—his hair burnt and his face covered with soot. Heat blisters covered his back and shoulders, some oozing a clear liquid.

"We're alive," Loon said.

"We'll heal," answered Otter.

Willow repressed the pain, but couldn't reply.

The longhouse burned until dawn and by then there was nothing left. What had once been a home for several families was now a heap of glowing embers. Smoking piles were the only traces of the massive stores of corn and beans that had filled the longhouse. In a few piles at the edge of the blackened soil were hardened scraps of skin and fur that had escaped the full force of the flames. Everything above the ground was gone. Only some of the buried stores of corn could be salvaged.

The people of the village continued to pour water on the smouldering ruins until not a trace of smoke could be seen. There was nothing else to do. The fire was out and the flames that had threatened the other longhouses had been beaten down. Now was the time to stare at the blackened remains, to marvel at the power of fire and contemplate the near destruction of the entire village.

Everyone knew how quickly a forest fire could destroy the trees of the forest, along with the nests of birds and the homes of animals. Often the charred carcasses of the slower animals were left on the ground. Scorched porcupines could sometimes be seen at the bases of trees they had climbed for safety. On rare occasions, cooked fish had been found floating upside-down in shallow ponds. They could swim quickly—but had no place to go.

Those who stood looking at the charred ruins experienced the same anguish they felt walking in the wake of a forest fire, although this time there had been no loss of life. As Old Chief approached the wreckage, where the heat from the baked soil could still be felt, the village elders gathered beside him to console those who had lived in the longhouse. He then surveyed the nearby dwelling with the chunks of bark ripped away from the frame and looked over at Willow, Otter and Loon. Brown Bat had given them warm beaver robes to put over their shoulders.

Slowly Old Chief walked through the crowd to the three young warriors. When he stood in front of them he saw their blackened hands and blistered skin. He took Willow's forearm in his withered hand and stared at the burns.

"You almost fell into the fire," he said, before turning to Otter.

"And you—you were almost pulled into the fire." With his other hand, Old Chief held Otter's arm and looked at the scrapes and cuts on his hands and wrists.

"Loon was able to stand the smoke longer than anyone possibly could."

He stood holding the weary young men, looking at one and then the other.

"You have youth," he said to them quietly, "and you are as agile as cats." He put up his hand to signal 'No' and added, "You are more agile. A cat could not have done what you three did." He cast his eyes around at the villagers, who were listening silently.

"We are grateful to the sky for guarding you—and we are grateful to you." Slowly Old Chief turned and spoke to the elders and clan leaders.

"We will eat and rest for a short time and when the sun is high, we'll meet in the council house. We have so much to do and the snow will be here soon."

Willow, Otter and Loon were taken to a healer to have their wounds treated. Her coarse gray hair hung down past her waist, covering undecorated deerskin. Long silver earrings hung past her shoulders and necklaces made of shells and bird bones were draped in layers around her neck.

She sat Willow and Otter on a log beside the fire and soaked their hands in warm water held in a birchbark bowl stitched with spruce root. When their hands were completely waterlogged, she picked out the largest splinters and cinders and then submerged them again.

"Leave them there," the healer told them, as she added balsam fir resin to warm water, stirring constantly and turning the liquid into a sweet-smelling tea. Then she poured the mixture over their hands.

While their hands were soaking, she soothed Loon's blistered skin by spreading cool clay over his back and shoulders. His body trembled with the cold, but he didn't show any pain.

"One by one, now," said the medicine woman sitting on the floor beside Otter. "This may hurt—more than it hurts already."

"It doesn't hurt," said Otter weakly, looking first at his friends and then at the medicine woman.

"No," she said. "I don't suppose it does—just a few torn bits of flesh." She took his hand out of the water and turned it over, looking carefully at his injuries. "And a few slivers digging into the bone." She lifted her head and studied Otter's face before starting her work. "We'll be finished soon."

With a sharp blade made from chert, the medicine woman began to slice burnt bits of skin from the young man's hand. Her knife flashed as she made her cuts, but Otter didn't wince. Only once while the medicine woman was pulling slivers from his knuckles, she heard a faint murmur, but his face showed no sign of discomfort. She didn't hesitate for fear of being seen to recognize his pain.

While Otter stared straight ahead over the medicine woman's head, Willow turned away to examine his own burnt and blistered hands, knowing that the medicine woman would want to cure him the same way. The clay on Loon's back began to dry, forming tiny cracks as he breathed.

After the medicine woman had removed the tattered bits of skin and slivers from Otter's right hand, she moved quickly to his left, drawing little blood. When this was complete she rinsed his hands, smeared them with balsam fir resin and wrapped them in soft deerskin.

"Hold your hands high until I tell you to put them down," she said, turning her attention to Willow.

"Your burns don't hurt either," she whispered when she lifted Willow's right hand from the bowl. She sang quietly as she removed the dead skin from his blackened hands, taking care not to cut into the healthy tissue. His face showed no sign of pain, apart from a few drops of sweat dribbling down his forehead into his eyes. Like Otter, Willow stared straight ahead while the medicine woman did her work.

The healer turned to see Otter. "Keep your arms up," she reminded him, as Otter's failing arms began to wilt toward the dirt floor.

Then she rinsed and dried Willow's hands, again covering them with resin and wrapping them.

"Put your hands up too," she said, as she carefully gathered the bits of skin from the deerskin on her lap. She then took the scraps outside and dug a small hole beside the longhouse where she buried them in the ground. Before going back inside she sprinkled the area with tobacco.

"You can put your hands down now, Otter." He dropped his throbbing hands by his side.

"Don't use your hands for anything," the healer said. "Not even for peeing." She looked kindly at him to make sure he understood. "Come back tomorrow and I'll make sure they are healing well."

Willow's arms began to slip downward. "Keep your arms up, Willow!"

Loon sat silently beside the fire, trying not to shiver as the old woman put more clay on his skin. "You can use your hands, Loon, but you won't be able to lie down for a few days." She placed a rabbit skin shawl over his clay-coated shoulders. Bits of clay crumbled and fell to the floor.

She sat down on a log by the fire and sighed. "You've all seen the soft skin on the antlers of a young deer. It looks like it's never been touched—it's so soft and perfect." She didn't look at them, but kept speaking quietly, staring into the fire.

"You've felt the softness of a new-born baby's head when it is still wet from birth." The young men looked at each other with a puzzled look. "Maybe you haven't—you would remember if you had. But listen carefully. You must keep your wounds protected like the most delicate skin. Keep them dry. Don't scrape or rub against them, and you will heal. Soon you'll have hard calluses again like the hunters and warriors you are."

"You can put your hands down, Willow," she said. He dropped his aching arms.

"Come here tomorrow before the sun goes down." The medicine woman stood up and smiled as they left.

"She expected us to wince with the pain," said Otter.

Willow laughed. "Then she doesn't know us."

"She knows us now!" cried Loon, cupping his hands in an effort to make his loon call. But no sound came out.

"The loon will be silent for a few days," laughed Willow.

The wounded warriors walked through the village together, stopping to talk to anyone who asked about their injuries.

– CHAPTER THIRTY-SIX –

Out of the Ashes

As Old Chief inspected the charred longhouse remains, he stood back to study the position of the surviving houses nearby. Had they all been too close together, he wondered? Should they rebuild farther away, or on the same spot? While thinking about the new building he did a slow, shuffling dance through the blackened cinders, giving thanks to the spirits for not taking any lives. Heavy, black ashes rose around his moccasins. Then he noticed Moose by his side looking beaten and bruised. His dark hair was singed on one side and his forehead was still smeared with soot.

"What does this mean for the raid on the enemy?" Old Chief asked.

"I don't think we can leave the village like this," Moose replied with a sigh. "We have to rebuild. There are too many people without shelter."

"I think you are right. But now we have other decisions to make. Do you think we should move the village?"

When the sun neared its high point in the sky, Old Chief gathered with the clan leaders and elders to decide whether to attack the enemy and what to do about the destroyed building. They met on the grassy field just outside the palisade—high above the river, looking down the valley toward the Beautiful Lake. The trees in the

— Enemy Arrows —

valley were glowing with reds, yellows, and oranges—the colours of the fire that had brought disaster the night before. Soon the leaves would turn brown and fall, covering the forest floor before the snow arrived.

Old Chief wore a gleaming black squirrel cloak, which matched his soot-covered moccasins. The small group of leaders and elders sat in a semi-circle beside him, facing the noon sun and looking down at the blaze of colour in the valley beneath them. A few stickball players stood in a circle in the open field nearby flinging a ball back and forth.

"I want to hear from each of you," Old Chief said. "What do we do about the longhouse? Should we rebuild?" He turned to look at each of the elders beside him. "Do we have any other choice?"

The leader of the Hawk Clan spoke first, slowly and deliberately.

"This village is close to the end of its natural existence. It can only live for so long. Bears live longer than chipmunks because they are bigger and stronger, but it's not the same with villages. Larger ones like ours have shorter life spans than the smaller ones, because it takes more trees to build our houses and we use more bark and firewood. Most of the trees nearby have been stripped and chopped down, so each year we have to travel farther and farther to find what we need.

"Our fields are tired, too. Everyone can see they produce less each year. The women say they have to work harder to produce a good crop, and they are becoming as tired as the fields."

He stopped to select his words while the others waited patiently for him to continue.

"In the past few years we have been getting ready to move the village. We should move next summer, and if we do, what sense is there in rebuilding a longhouse that will be abandoned after one winter? Those who lived in the destroyed longhouse can live in other houses this winter. We will all help them.

"I have talked to my clan brothers and sisters and most agree that the longhouse should not be rebuilt on this site. Instead, we should rebuild next year at a new site."

He looked at Old Chief to signal that he had made his point.

Old Chief turned to an elder from the Deer Clan. He was old, wiry, and covered by many ancient battle scars. Despite the cool weather, he wore only a loincloth, leggings and moccasins. A bear tooth hung from a cord around his neck.

"We all know we have to move the village to a new location—but it will take time. In the meantime, we will have to build a new longhouse so our friends can have somewhere decent to live. If we want to save work, we can use the logs from the old palisade to make the new one when we move."

"That would leave us unprotected," said Moose, the War Chief. "There are too many spies in the forests to do that. As soon as the enemy learned we had only part of a wall around the village, they would be on their way to attack us—and they would take many lives. We can't move the village until a new palisade is built, ready for all of us to live in safely. I say we rebuild the longhouse on this spot and plan our move to a new place in two years or three—when we're ready."

"I agree," said the leader of the Wolf Clan. He was a large man of few words. "We cannot move next summer. We won't be ready."

"And if we can't move next summer," added the leader of the Deer Clan, "we have to rebuild for the people who lost their house. They can't live scattered in other houses for two or three years. They need their own. It may be a waste to build a new dwelling to use for only a few years, but it has to be done."

Loud urgent shouts came from the stickball players. "Ball!" they screamed. The clan leaders and elders didn't hesitate to see what the trouble was. They knew the warning shouts that signal a runaway ball. As they dove for cover, sliding through the dust and dry grass, the speeding ball crashed in their midst like a bolt of lightning, scattering sticks and small stones. It bounced and crashed against the palisade, knocking a chunk of bark to the ground.

While the elders slowly returned to their former positions, brushing off the dust and spitting bits of grass from their mouths, a young boy ran through the group, scooped the ball from the ground with his stick and hurled it toward the circle of players. He beamed a wide smile at Old Chief. "We'll play somewhere else!" he said, with an embarrassed laugh. Old Chief returned a strained smile, and the boy raced away with the others to a distant field.

Broken Arrow, one of the oldest members of the village, rose to speak as though nothing had interrupted them. He pulled his bear robe tight around his frail, teetering body. Although his legs had grown wobbly, he had been one of the best runners in his youth. Some said he could outrun a deer when he was at his best, but now he could only outrun a porcupine—and only if the porcupine was chasing him.

"We all know there have been too many sightings of the enemy in the past few years. They are as bold as mice. If we did not have that fire we would be attacking them before the next full moon."

He adjusted the bearskin around his shoulders and brushed off more dust. "As you all know, we have been clearing a new site for the village up the river. We stripped the bark off the trees two winters ago and now they're starting to lose their branches, so there will be plenty of firewood for everyone when we move there. But the new site is close to where we are now—perhaps too close. The enemy can easily follow us—and attack. I think we should move farther inland. We should start clearing another site far away from the lake and abandon the one we have cleared nearby. It is too dangerous."

The clan leaders and elders looked at each other to see what their reaction would be to the thought of abandoning the new site they had been preparing for so long.

Old Chief spoke first before the thoughts and words of the leaders strayed too far. "You may be right, Broken Arrow. We will have to consider won't have said. If we move the village to a site farther away from the lake, we will have to begin clearing the trees soon or we won't be able to move for several years. But if we are here for several more years, we will have to rebuild the longhouse. Do you agree, Broken Arrow?"

"Yes," he replied. "We have to rebuild now and then decide where to locate the new village. Whether we move as we had planned in a year or move somewhere else in three years, the people who suffered from the fire must have a home."

"Do we all agree?" asked Old Chief. He looked at the faces of the leaders. Everyone appeared to agree. Old Chief then looked down the river valley toward the lake.

"This is a wonderful place. We have everything we need here and we have the serenity that comes with beautiful surroundings. Wherever we go, I'll be sad to leave this place."

Old Chief asked the leaders what their clans could provide for the rebuilding. Everyone was quick to offer as much as they could to show their generosity.

"Well, we have a house to build before the snow comes," said Old Chief. He stood up, looked once more down the river and walked back through the gate, followed by the clan leaders and elders.

Inside the palisade a crowd had already gathered. The men and boys carried newly ground axes, ready to rebuild as soon as Old Chief assigned the work. He stood beside the ashes of the old longhouse and the people waited to hear him speak.

"We have work to do, my friends!" Cheers rang out through the village.

"We'll make this house like we've made so many others—and we'll make it quickly," Old Chief continued. "If we all work together, it will be built before the snow falls." Small knots of people in the crowd started jumping and bobbing in excitement.

Old Chief outlined the plan. "The Bear Clan and the Deer Clan can cut poles for the new house. It will be the same size as the last one. The Fox Clan will gather slabs of bark for the outer shell. If the cedar bark does not come off the trees easily this time of year, get whatever bark you can find. The Wolf Clan will cut saplings to keep the bark in place and build the support frames—as it was before. Everyone bring whatever twine and rope you can spare. We will need it all. The Loon Clan can dig the remains of the old poles from the ground and dig holes for the new poles. The women of

— *Enemy Arrows* —

all clans will gather enough baskets of corn, beans, squash and dried fish to restock the new longhouse. Dig up your buried stores and bring what you can."

He paused a moment. "Before we go we must give thanks to the great spirit of the sky for keeping us from falling into the flames." Old Chief held a clay pot full of embers high for all to see, and the village became silent. When he placed a clump of dried grass into the embers, a puff of white smoke rose to the sky. Holding the smoking pot high above his head, he chanted words of thanks, as a light breeze spread the sweet scent of smoke through the village.

"Before long the new longhouse will be built and we will celebrate with a feast to tell our grandchildren about!"

The village began to pulsate again with dances and song. Clan members gathered around their leaders to talk about the work to be done. Soon the men left the village with their axes held high.

Willow and Otter stood near Old Chief. He had told them he had something special for them to do, since they couldn't use their hands.

"How are your wounds today, Willow," asked Old Chief. "Is there much pain?"

"No. There's no pain. I should be with my clan getting poles," he answered.

"And you, Otter? You have no pain either?"

"My hands are stiff, but not painful."

Old Chief knew they were in pain, but he also knew they wouldn't show it. They had been trained well and would be fine warriors one day.

"Where is Loon today—our friend who walks through fire?"

"He's gone on a trading trip with his father. He said he'll be away for a few days," answered Otter.

"Well, I'm sure you two can help me. I want you to be my messengers," he said. "You won't have to use your hands—only your feet." He sat on the ground and motioned for them to do the same. Then he picked up a burnt stick and drew a curved line on the ground.

"This is Thunder River," he said. "It flows here—to the Beautiful Lake." He drew a similar line toward Willow. "This is the north shore of the lake where you killed your first bear, and here are the islands on the far side of the bay."

"That's where I nearly drowned under the ice," said Otter, pointing to the spot in the sand.

Old Chief continued drawing. "This line is the River of the Dawn that flows into the far end of the bay. Up the river—about here—is the village you visited last spring for a stickball match."

"We caused some bruises in that game!" said Willow with a look of satisfaction.

"I want you to take a message to their chief, Wolverine. There's no need to go by water this time. You have nothing to carry except a message, so take the trail overland," he said, drawing a straight line in the earth from their village to the one on the other river.

"Tell Wolverine about the fire. Let him know that we can use help rebuilding our longhouse, and ask him—and anyone who wants to help—to come to the feast we will have when the new house is built."

"We will!" Willow and Otter replied together.

"It should take you the rest of the day to get there," said Old Chief. "The trail is well marked, but be on guard for the enemy. A stranger was sighted near the bay during the last full moon—probably a spy."

"Should we try to capture him?" Willow asked.

"No, not today. You went through enough last night. Just protect yourselves. Stay at the village for the night and return with the others in the morning."

Old Chief saw that Willow didn't have a bow or quiver. "Take my bow until you can make a new one. It may be big for you, but it always hits the mark." He gave Willow his long bow, charred and decorated with carvings of wild cats, and a quiver filled with stone-tipped arrows.

"This bow was a gift to me from People of the Lakes," Old Chief said, admiring the carvings on the bow. "Now, tell your families where you are going and keep your eyes open on the trail."

Willow returned to the remains of the longhouse and saw men and boys from the Turtle Clan digging up the corn stores. Some of it was scorched, but most was still edible. At the same time, the Loon Clan was digging the burnt poles from the hard-baked ground.

Willow found his mother standing beside the blackened patch of ground where her family's home had been the day before. Her face and hands were dusted with ashes and her moccasins were black with soot. She held a pointed stick that she had been using to stir through the ashes. When she heard her son's voice she turned. Tears had streaked the ashes on her face, giving her a frightening look—but when she smiled at him the mask disappeared.

"There is nothing left in there," she said. "I was searching in the ashes . . . trying to find a necklace your father gave me when we were young."

"I don't know what you mean," said Willow.

"No, you wouldn't. I haven't worn it for many years. It was made of copper beads from far away. They shone like the sunset when they were rubbed. Your father brought it back from the People of the Lakes. I know it's in this pile of ash somewhere, but I'll never be able to find it. Perhaps it melted into nothing."

Willow looked at his mother's streaked face. "Old Chief asked Otter and me to take a message to the village on the other river. We'll be back tomorrow. Will you be all right?" he asked.

"Yes. We'll be fine. Wren and I will live with Moose until the new house is finished. You and Otter can stay there, too, when you get back. Go now. You must do what Old Chief asks."

Willow met Otter at the gate. Each carried a bow and a quiver of arrows, even though their hands were wrapped and unable to use them. An old woman from the longhouse they had saved from the fire approached and gave them a small bag of corn meal and dried blueberries. She thanked them and then sang a song to the spirit of the sky for stopping the fire before anyone was badly hurt.

Her song faded in the distance as Willow and Otter left the village enclosure and followed the overland trail across the empty fields toward the River of the Dawn. Along the way they encountered members of the Wolf Clan heading back to the village with the first of many loads of saplings for the walls of the new longhouse. As they passed each other, there was an air of celebration with laughing and jokes from both sides.

"You'll miss all the work!" called a young man with an armload of saplings.

"Don't worry. We'll be back in time for the feast," replied Otter. "Save some meat for us!"

– CHAPTER THIRTY-SEVEN –

The Broken Bow

The trail to the River of the Dawn soon led toward the edge of the forest, where dead and dying trees stood amid piles of fallen boughs. As Willow and Otter neared the brightly coloured forest, they could hear the ripping sound of trunks being stripped of bark for the new longhouse. Under a canopy of yellow leaves they saw Moose chopping down a tree. His heavy granite axe shattered the trunk as he pounded over and over, leaving woodchips littering the ground at his feet and bits of the tree stuck to his arms and face.

The chopping noise made by Moose's powerful hits echoed through the forest, mixing with the calls of others working nearby. Before long there were only a few white strands of wood to keep the tree upright, and after one last mighty thump the tree started to tremble. The last remaining wood groaned and shrieked before it finally gave up. Moose stepped back and yelled a warning as leaves and dead branches began falling to the ground. While the tree lurched forward and fell, he stood admiring its straight trunk and narrow branches. Everyone else stopped their work to watch. The tree gracefully twisted sideways, with a whoosh of leaves arcing through the air, and crashed to the forest floor, flipping like a beached fish until at last it came to a dead stop.

Moose began stripping the branches as soon as it was still. Then he cut the top off, leaving a straight, limbless pole. As he worked he sang an old song that promised the tree it would be away from the rain and snow, surrounded by singing and dancing and warmth. He called to the others to take the naked pole back to the village and, without taking a breath, began to look for another.

Continuing on their way, Willow and Otter walked through the forest along the narrow path. Sunlight filtered through the red and orange leaves, projecting moving dots of light on the forest floor. They could hear the usual background sounds of birds singing, squirrels leaping in the woods around them, and deer bounding through the dead leaves in the distance. These were all sounds they knew and expected. Even the whisper of a snake slithering across the trail was too familiar to attract their attention.

The two young warriors were listening for noises that were out of place—the loud crack of a breaking branch, the quiet snap of a twig, the frantic wings of frightened grouse—the sounds that signalled danger. They walked through the forest with their hands bound, bows slung over their shoulders, and their arrows close at hand—even if they couldn't hold them.

The trail was straight and level most of the way, with only a few ravines and shallow streams to cross. When the sun was getting low in the sky, the trees opened to reveal the River of the Dawn below, with cleared fields on either side of the wide valley. Above the fields on a plateau they could see a palisade surrounding the village, where smoke rose from fire pits.

While they stood quietly surveying the scene, they heard a sudden thrashing of leaves in the forest behind them. Immediately, they bent low and kept their heads down. Willow groped for Old Chief's bow, but his wrapped hands couldn't hold it. He dropped it at his feet, where it wedged between two large rocks on the edge of a ravine. From the corner of his eye he could see a frightened doe leaping from her hiding place behind a spruce tree and disappearing into the woods.

— *Enemy Arrows* —

At this, Otter moved quickly to grab his bow, but as he reached for an arrow he struck Willow on the head with his elbow, knocking him over. Willow fell to the ground and landed on the bow lodged between the rocks, snapping it in two under his weight with a loud *crack!* that echoed through the forest. One of the rocks was sent crashing down the ravine, causing loud thuds each time it hit a tree.

Otter stared in horror without moving, while birds took flight from nearby trees.

"You broke Old Chief's bow!" he said, helping Willow to his feet. "That bow was like an arm to him."

Willow picked up one end of the broken bow, while the other dangling lifelessly from the gut bowstring. He stared back at Otter in shock. "We'll have to tell him," he said. "He'll never be able to use it again. If our hands were free this wouldn't have happened."

"It's not good to break a chief's bow," said Otter. "I don't like this. I don't want any harm to come to him."

"We'll have to do something about it," said Willow.

"We even missed the deer!" said Otter. His expression changed from discomfort to amusement. "If you hadn't fallen, we probably would have shot each other."

"I want my hands back!" cried Willow, waving his arms over his head. He accidentally batted Otter on the shoulder. Otter elbowed him back and then ran down the hill toward the river with Willow chasing him, brandishing the broken bow above his head. "Here come the clumsy hunters!" he yelled in the direction of the village. "Hide before it's too late!"

The trail ended at a shallow place where the river could be crossed easily. They held their pouches and wrapped hands above their waists as they walked through the cool water. On the other side, a woman and young girl sat on the bank gutting fish while screaming gulls hovered in the sky, waiting for them to throw pieces of flesh into the river.

— *The Broken Bow* —

"Who are you?" called the girl. Her black hair was tied back from her face with strips of deerskin and her hands were covered with the slime of fish guts mixed with silvery scales.

"We've come from the village on Thunder River. We're looking for your chief," answered Otter, looking at the woman instead of the girl. "Can you help us find him?"

The woman stood up to answer. Her hands were bloody and her knees and feet caked with clay. She pushed her hair away from her face with her forearm and pointed to the village at the top of the hill. "He was repairing the palisade with some others when we came down. You should find him by the gate."

The girl looked at Willow's wrapped hand. "What happened to your hands?" she asked.

"I burned them," he replied. "We had a fire."

"What happened to your bow?" she asked next.

Willow and Otter glanced at each other. Then Willow looked at the broken bow and sat down in the long grass beside the river.

"You have so many questions. Where do they all come from?" he asked.

The girl's mother answered for her. "She gets it from me." The woman stepped into the water and began rinsing the blood from her hands and wiping the clay from her legs. "Who is your mother?"

Standing impatiently, Otter motioned to Willow that it was time to go.

"My mother is Orchid," said Willow. "Our Clan Mother is Old Heron."

"Ah, yes. I know them. I know most of your family. What's your name?"

"Willow."

She stepped out of the water and looked into Willow's eyes. "Yes, I see it now. I knew your father. He came from here. I remember how he could play stickball—like a swallow. We checked him every game to see if he had wings!" she said with a deep laugh.

As the girl stared at Willow, Otter signalled at him once again.

"Who is your friend and why is he in such a hurry?" asked the girl. Otter turned to leave.

"His name is Otter," replied Willow.

"Wait," said the woman. "You are the hunters who killed the bear with pointed sticks?" She didn't wait for an answer. "I'll take you to Wolverine myself." She turned to gather her fish. "Come, my daughter. Grab what you can. These hunters want to see our chief."

The woman sang as she climbed the path toward the village. Suddenly, she stopped and looked at Willow. "How long has it been since your father was killed by the People from Across the Lake?"

"It happened just after the last Feast of the Dead in our village," he replied.

"Has it been that long?" she exclaimed. "It can't be true." She turned and continued up the trail, brooding about the loss of Willow's father so long ago.

"We should go across the lake to that village of murderers and *burn it to the ground*," she yelled. "Take them all prisoner . . . and torture them slowly!"

She had an agitated way of speaking that made Willow wonder if she had ever seen the horror of torture. He noticed how the girl repeated her mother's words—almost with the same vehemence—until the strain of the hill left the mother breathless and silent. The girl took the opportunity to shower Willow and Otter with questions about their village and families, as they followed behind her to the village on the top of the hill.

Bathed in the orange glow of the setting sun, Wolverine sat outside the palisade looking out at the long sloping fields that led to the river below. The village was smaller than the one Willow and Otter knew, and the palisade surrounding it seemed frail compared to theirs. Willow thought how easy it would be for the enemy to breach the defensive wall just by pushing it over.

Wolverine was talking with a strange-looking man who wore unusual feathers and coloured shells unlike anything Willow and Otter had seen before. The woman and her daughter stopped out of earshot of the two men sitting on the grass and motioned the

— *The Broken Bow* —

young warriors to approach them. As they did, they heard the man speak with a lilt in his voice.

"These peace talks are the first sunbeams breaking through the clouds after a long rain. They've brought light to the villages across the lake and they will cause . . ." The stranger cut short his speech when Willow and Otter came near.

"These two warriors have come to speak to you," announced the woman from a distance. "They killed a bear with pointed sticks," she added in a loud voice. Wolverine looked curiously at Willow and Otter at length, seeing two young warriors with bound hands and a broken bow. When he was finished he motioned them to sit beside them.

"What bear?" he asked when they were settled. "And what sticks?"

"We've come with a message from Old Chief of the village on Thunder River," said Otter respectfully. "He sends you his greetings."

"And my greetings to him," replied Wolverine. "What bear are you talking about?"

"We're not talking about a bear," said Willow. "We have a message for you."

The stranger laughed and said to Wolverine in a low voice, "This must be an important message. Old Chief sent two strong warriors, so we should listen to what they have to say."

Wolverine held up his hand. "Tell me your message."

Willow spoke. "Old Chief sent us to tell you that we had a fire." A look of alarm spread across Wolverine's face.

"We lost a longhouse, but no lives," continued Otter. "Old Chief asks for your help and invites you and everyone who wants to help with the building to come to our village and stay for the feast we'll have when the new house is complete."

"What happened to your hands?" asked Wolverine. Otter told him how they had scrambled to the roof to prevent the fire from spreading.

"You are brave warriors," said Wolverine. "I should not have doubted Old Chief." He noticed the broken bow in Willow's hand.

— Enemy Arrows —

"That's your chief's bow," he said, looking at Willow. He put out his hand and gently took the two broken pieces with the dangling gut. "Yes, I know it well. I've hunted with your Chief and fought beside him. This bow is like no other."

"What happened to it?" he asked, as he returned the pieces. Willow told Wolverine how he fell on it when they startled the deer. Wolverine put his hand on Willow's shoulder and shook his head.

"We'll help you all we can. Your chief and your people have always been good to us. You've given us food when we were hungry and shelter when we were attacked. You even let us win at stickball . . . though not very often," he added, turning to the stranger with a smile.

"When the sun rises tomorrow, we'll be on our way to your village with rope and twine and cedar bark. We'll give you knives, tools, and pots—and plenty of food for the feast. What else can we do to help?"

"Old Chief said we need people to tie the bark on the frames," said Otter. "He said he wants people with nimble fingers."

"He'll have more fingers than he can keep busy!" said Wolverine triumphantly. He called to a group of men who were coming out through the gate to assemble everyone in the village for an important meeting. Then he turned to Willow and Otter and held his hand out to the stranger.

"This is Turkey Vulture. He comes from the Wide River of Many Islands." He noticed a puzzled look on Otter's face. "It flows out of Beautiful Lake—at the far eastern end," he added, waving his hand in the direction of the rising sun. "He wants us to have peace with the enemy."

PART III
Sight Of The Enemy

– CHAPTER THIRTY-EIGHT –

Enemy Arrow on the Trail

Wolverine led Willow and Otter through the gate into the village, where they immediately recognized friends from past stickball tournaments and the feasts the two communities had shared together. Everyone welcomed them and wished them well.

There were only five longhouses inside the palisade, and Wolverine showed his guests into the one nearest the gate. A sign above the door marked it as a house of the Wolf Clan. Inside, clouded by smoke from the fire pits, was the picture of abundance after a rich harvest—sunflowers and corn hung from the rafters, piles of brightly coloured squashes filled the spaces under the bunks, and skins stretched on wooden hoops.

Everywhere there were signs of preparation for winter. A woman and her two daughters were making clay pots for the fire, while another was twisting twine from the inside layers of basswood bark. Nearby, an old man drilled a smoke hole in what would one day be a stone pipe. Stopping their work, they greeted Wolverine with affection and welcomed his three guests. Soon a withered old woman with long, gray hair approached Wolverine and held his arm close to her, smiling toothlessly.

"Our friends are hungry," said Wolverine. "I told them we have the best fish stew on the lake." The old woman made a signal with her hand and turned to a pot beside the fire. She then began to serve large portions of a hot stew, which Willow and Otter devoured after their long hike.

After they had eaten, Otter told Wolverine and Turkey Vulture the story of the bear, as a small crowd gathered around to listen. They were amazed by the bravery of Willow and the strength of Otter and Loon. Wolverine looked worried when he heard about the arrowhead lodged in the bear's flesh.

"What did the arrowhead look like?" he asked. "Was it one of ours?"

Otter told him what Lynx had said—it had come from across the lake.

"We have seen too many tracks of strangers in our territory," said Wolverine. He turned to Turkey Vulture. "How can we talk of peace with these hideous people? They want to enslave and torture us. They want to burn our houses." He placed an oak log on the fire and watched it smoulder before bursting into flames. "They are loathsome," he said to himself.

Wolverine slapped his hands on his knees. "Come now!" he shouted, as he sprang to his feet and charged to the door. "We have a feast to attend and a house to build." As he passed the old woman he stopped to whisper to her and touch her cheek. A glow appeared in her tired eyes.

Out in the cool evening air Wolverine spoke to the people crowded around him and conveyed Old Chief's message. Without hesitation, everyone who could help to rebuild the longhouse or provide supplies wanted to participate. The plan was to leave early in the morning by foot, while those with ropes, baskets, and bark would travel by canoe.

Most of the night was spent preparing for the building—and for the feast that would follow.

As soon as the morning sky turned to gold, crowds gathered at the edge of the river for the long walk. People carried packs slung over their shoulders or on their backs, with deerskin tumplines across their foreheads. Others filled the canoes waiting beside the river. Willow and Otter couldn't paddle with raw hands, so they walked back through the woods with Wolverine. The broken bow hung around Willow's neck.

As the sky brightened they filed through the forest, protected by warriors and the strength of their numbers, singing songs as they went. Wolverine walked at the front of the group, with Turkey Vulture, Willow and Otter following close behind. Some of the younger children darted in and out of the trees picking puffballs for the feast. Whenever they found an over-ripe ball they squeezed it, spraying tiny clouds of dust at each other with screams of delight.

For no apparent reason, Wolverine came to an abrupt stop and raised his arm. The others froze in their tracks. He stepped cautiously to a tall pine at the edge of the ravine, not far from the trail. Sticking out of the trunk at eye level was an arrow with coloured feathers. Wolverine knew instantly that they weren't the feathers used by the people who lived in his area, so he signalled the elders to join him and inspect it. They talked in hushed voices. He then looked at Otter and Willow and signalled for them to come close.

"You passed by here yesterday?"

"Yes, in the late afternoon," replied Willow.

"Did you see this arrow in the tree?"

Willow and Otter looked at each other in wonder. "This arrow wasn't here," replied Otter. "We would have seen it."

"This is where we saw the buck," said Willow. "I fell on the bow right there," he said, pointing to a scuff mark on a rock. "And another rock crashed down the ravine. You can see where it rolled over the saplings."

Wolverine touched the tree where the arrowhead pierced the bark and a drop of sap that had trickled down from the wound like blood, still soft and sticky. He announced what was obvious to everyone. The arrow was an enemy arrow, shot into the tree the day before. He followed the projection of the arrow back into the forest where he stopped in a small grove of cedar trees and looked at the ground. Seeing that the dry, reddish-brown cedar sprigs that

Enemy Arrow on the Trail

covered the ground had been ruffled by the footsteps of one or two people, he called to Willow.

"Stand where you were just before you fell on the bow. Everyone else," he said raising his voice to a yell, "stand well back."

Willow stood still beside the scuffed rock while Wolverine took an arrow from his quiver and loaded his bow. He pulled the string back.

"Now fall where you fell yesterday," he said. Willow immediately dropped beside the rock, clutching the pieces of the bow he had fallen on before.

Wolverine's fingers slipped off the bowstring and the arrow shot through the trees over Willow's head and into the pine tree, a hand's width above the other arrow. Willow looked up at the arrow and then at Otter, who stood with his mouth open, his eyes wide.

Wolverine marched purposefully back to the others. Standing directly before Turkey Vulture, he said in a low voice, "How can we talk to the enemy about peace when they send cowards to hide in the trees and shoot at our young warriors?"

Turkey Vulture looked at Otter and Willow and then responded to Wolverine. "This is why we need peace among the nations. We can't go on attacking our brothers—on either side of the Beautiful Lake."

Wolverine turned to the clan leaders. "We must continue to strengthen our nation and defend against the enemy. We'll leave guards on the island to watch for invaders while we're away. It's a full moon tonight so they won't likely attack, but we know there are spies near. The rest of us will stay close together."

He raised his bow to the sky and signalled to the others to follow.

"Keep your eyes wide open! We have friends who need our help." Instead of a loose group, they now walked in close formation. Wolverine and the clan leaders led, the women and young people followed in the middle, and a group of warriors guarded the rear with weapons ready. They walked silently through the forest until they came to the open fields surrounding the village on Thunder River, where they broke formation. The youngest children charged to the village gate, screaming greetings to the sound of barking dogs, while the warriors followed behind carrying their gifts.

The village was as active as an anthill on a hot summer day. People came from every direction carrying poles, bark and logs for the longhouse, funnelling small loads through the main gate and passing poles and logs through a narrow gap that had been opened in the palisade. Sounds of chopping could still be heard far in the distance, coming from every direction.

Willow and Otter walked in the main gate with Wolverine and the clan leaders to the cheers and calls of everyone in the village. The building frenzy stopped as the two groups of neighbours mingled and laughed together. Wolverine and Old Chief grasped hands with the respect of old friends who had been through many battles together.

"We must speak," said Wolverine. "There are enemy warriors in the area and they almost put an arrow through your grandson's head—the one named Willow."

Old Chief looked at him with alarm. "Where is the boy? Willow? Willow?" he shouted, twisting his neck around like a turtle. Willow, who was standing behind Wolverine, stepped forward.

"I'm here, grandfather."

"You're not hurt?" demanded Old Chief.

"No, but I broke your bow."

"And Otter? Is he all right?"

"I'm fine," said Otter, who appeared from behind Willow.

Old Chief threw his sinuous arms around them and sang a quiet song of thanks—one usually sung when warriors returned from battle—as Wolverine watched silently. When Old Chief had finished singing, Willow spoke.

"I fell on your bow, Grandfather," he said, holding up the broken fragments.

Old Chief looked long and hard at the bow he had held in his hands for so many years. During many tense nights before battles, he had stared at its carved cats in the firelight, wondering if he would survive the next day. Sometimes the cats looked so real he thought they were moving. This was the bow that had earned him the reputation as a great hunter—and now it hung in pieces. He took it from Willow.

"This bow has seen and heard many things," he said sadly. "We have grown old together, and now we are brittle." He laughed to himself and turned to Willow and Otter, glowing with pride. "The important thing is that you are both here and safe.

"Come with me and we will eat together."

As Old Chief passed the fire pit he untied the bowstring and placed it gently on the smouldering coals, where it curled and twisted in the heat before igniting in a flash of smoke and light. He took the carved remains of the bow with him. As they all walked past the scorched earth where the fire had been, they could hear the howl of a wild cat deep in the forest on the far side of the river.

– CHAPTER THIRTY-NINE –

A Celebration

A light frost fell on the ground during the night, covering the grass and leaves until the warmth of the rising sun chased it away. Soon after, Old Chief sat in his favourite place with the sun's rays on his face. He was anxious to speak to Turkey Vulture. He had heard about the peace talks among the People from Across the Lake and he wanted to know how it would affect his people. Before long, Wolverine and Turkey Vulture arrived to sit with him.

Wolverine began by telling Old Chief about the arrow in the pine tree. He then urged him to gather all the warriors from the northern shore of the Beautiful Lake and from other nearby lakes to attack the enemy in retribution for the attack.

Turkey Vulture remained silent. He knew this wasn't the time to speak of peace.

"We must speak more about this when it is dark," replied Old Chief. "There is so much to consider."

When everyone had eaten, the work on the longhouse began again. The Bear Clan and the Wolf Clan had the most difficult work. They placed four poles flat on the ground, side by side, with the middle poles six paces apart and the outer ones two paces apart. The centre pair was taller than the others, so the roof would be

— *A Celebration* —

higher in the middle. Nimble fingers from both villages then tied shorter poles across the four long poles to hold them in position.

When the frame was finished, the builders cried out for help. "Frame rising!" they shouted and everyone nearby ran to help them—or watch the excitement.

The crowds carried this huge frame over to where it would be lifted upright, and as soon as it had been moved, another group of builders started laying out poles for the next one. The base ends of each of the four solid poles were positioned over deep holes in the ground.

Next came the dangerous part of raising the frame. With the children standing back and watching from a safe distance, Moose gave the signal and the roof end of the frame was lifted to shoulder height and propped up on short poles. Little by little, the builders replaced the short poles with longer ones and the frame began to rise into position.

At the base of the frame, the heaviest members of the village had the risky job of sitting on the rising frames to keep the bottom ends of the poles firmly over the holes. Teams of muscular men pushed against the frames to make sure the ends didn't slip out of place.

"Get ready everyone!" called Moose. "This is the hardest part. If the ends slip out of the holes while this frame is being raised, it will shoot forward like a four-pronged spear—and the other end will crash down like a deadfall trap. We all need to be careful. No sudden moves!"

When Moose shouted, the frame was lifted to the height of a man's head. Longer poles were jammed under the end of the structure to support its weight.

"Lift!" bellowed Moose. Using the poles, the builders now pushed the frame to the height of one man standing on the shoulders of another man.

"Again!" he called in a hoarse voice. The men at the high end strained to push the frame until it was almost standing upright.

"Now for the fun," yelled Moose, turning to the crowds behind him. He knew that raising a frame was part building and part spectacle. Everyone watching the event knew the danger involved and most had seen at least one accident when an uncontrolled frame slipped from its position. Moose knew the danger too, and he basked in the cheers when each frame was raised successfully into its final position.

"Watch now," cried Moose, as he lowered his arm. "Push with all your strength!" Every muscle in every builder strained to push the frame upright. It groaned as it moved into position and, with a sudden jerk, dropped straight into the deep holes—all four poles slipped in at once. The crowd screamed and cheered as the men on the opposite side of the frame pushed to hold it in place—until the frame finally stopped moving. When they stood back the crowd cheered again, praising the builders. Moose beamed with pride.

By late afternoon several frames were standing in a long row, joined together by horizontal poles tied tightly into place. And by the time the sun began to set on the far side of the river, Moose and Old Chief stood beside the huge skeleton of the longhouse. They talked proudly about the work that had been completed that day, with no mishaps or injuries.

"Tomorrow we'll start to put the skin over the bones," said Moose. "We have enough cedar bark to cover most of the house and some elm for the rest. We had trouble stripping the bark after such a dry summer. It's much easier in the spring when the sap is flowing."

"Everything is easier when the sap is flowing," replied Old Chief with a smile.

Moose laughed at Old Chief's wise words. "You're right, my friend. I would hate to have to skin a tree as old as you." Old Chief nodded in agreement.

"The men from the Turtle Clan had to travel far up the river to find enough cedar bark for the house," said Moose.

"Every year we have to travel farther to get what we need to repair the houses," observed Old Chief. "When we move the village again, we will have to move far from here."

— A Celebration —

They slipped out through a small hole in the palisade and walked to Old Chief's usual resting spot. From this high plateau they could see the sun sparkling on the water and every creature moving below.

"This is my favourite place to sit. I will miss looking down the river valley. I fear I'll never find another view that compares with it."

Willow ran across the open space toward Old Chief and stopped at his side.

"Turkey Vulture says he would like to speak with you," he said breathing heavily. "He asked me to see if he could meet with you now."

"This Turkey Vulture is a puzzle," said Moose. "He looks as fierce as an osprey, but he has the peaceful song of a robin. I don't know what to think of him."

"Those are my thoughts too," said Old Chief. "We should listen to his song more closely and find out."

Old Chief put his hand on Willow's arm. "How are your hands, grandson?"

"They're better now."

"Already? Let me see them." Old Chief unwrapped the binding to reveal Willow's badly injured hands. Moose grimaced at the sight of the raw skin.

"Does it hurt?" Moose asked.

"No. Not any more."

"Good," said Old Chief, as he replaced the binding. "You can tell Turkey Vulture that Moose and I will meet him here at my favourite place. Bring him over and then go to see the old woman about your hands."

On the way back to Turkey Vulture, Willow met Loon returning to the village from the trading trip with his father.

"Come with me while I give a message to Turkey Vulture," said Willow. "He's from the river at the end of the Beautiful Lake. He talks about strange things and wants us to be at peace with the People from Across the Lake."

Loon stopped in mid-stride.

— *Enemy Arrows* —

"Peace with our enemy?" repeated Loon in astonishment. His feet appeared to be planted in the ground like the roots of a tree, but he swayed like a sapling in the wind. "If we're at peace with our enemy, who will we fight?"

Laughing at his own silly question, he continued. "We'll have raiding parties against the bears? Or maybe we'll be at peace with the bears too. We'll be at war with the butterflies!"

"Come and ask him yourself," said Willow, chuckling at the images of warring butterflies. But he wondered—was Loon right to doubt the talk of peace?

Turkey Vulture was staying in the longhouse of the Deer Clan at the far end of the village. They found him sitting with two elders beside a fire, smoking his clay pipe. The bowl of the pipe was a miniature head with eerily realistic features and eyes that appeared to stare back at anyone who looked at it.

Willow stood near the fire until he and Loon were invited to speak with the elders. "My grandfather would like to speak with you," he said to the visitor. "When you're ready I'll take you to him."

Turkey Vulture emptied his pipe in the fire then picked up his tobacco pouch and squirrel skin cloak. He stood up slowly. The eyes of the elders followed him as he approached Willow and Loon.

"Take me with you, my young friends," said Turkey Vulture. "The young will guide the old," he said, looking back at the elders.

They crossed the dark spaces beside the longhouses. Only a few dwindling fires lit the way through the village and a light breeze carried the smell of smoke through the cool night air. Most people would soon be inside their longhouses.

Loon couldn't hold back his curiosity. He had thought of the right question to ask, but the words didn't come out as he planned.

"Why do you want us to be friends with the people who attack us?" he asked.

Turkey Vulture looked at him in the faded light and raised his eyebrows. He had heard the question many times, but never was it asked so bluntly. Instead of answering his question directly, he decided to answer Loon's question with another question.

— A Celebration —

"Do you like being attacked?"

"No."

"Do you think other people like to be attacked by you?" he continued, as they walked through the dusk.

Loon hesitated for only an instant. "They must," he replied. "Or they wouldn't do it to us."

"Is it their attacks that make your warriors attack them?" asked Turkey Vulture.

"Yes," said Loon emphatically. "We have to get revenge when they sneak across the lake and kill our people. We know how evil they are."

"If they stopped attacking you and your people, would you leave them in peace?"

Loon was unable to answer a question that sounded like surrender.

"It will never happen," Loon said. "We've always been their enemies—and they'll always be ours."

"You want to be a brave warrior when you are older," said Turkey Vulture, more as a statement than a question.

"I'm a brave warrior now," replied Loon firmly.

"There is my grandfather sitting with Moose," said Willow, pointing to Old Chief's place above the river.

Turkey Vulture paused to thank Willow and Loon. Then he spoke slowly before leaving them.

"I am speaking with your elders, but my message is for you. You are the future of your people. I know many young warriors across the lake. I've lived with them and can see they are the same as you. It's not right to kill each other. It is madness!" he said, raising his fists.

Turkey Vulture breathed deeply before continuing in a calm voice.

"One day there will be peace between our people and the People from Across the Lake, as there is now peace among the five nations across the lake. If you strive for peace, you will have it—but if you do nothing you will always have war."

"You know the people on the other side of the lake?" asked Willow.

— Enemy Arrows —

"You know *the enemy*," Loon interjected.

"I know many people from across the lake, but I call them my friends."

Turkey Vulture turned and walked over to the sitting place. They watched him until they heard the welcoming voices of Old Chief and Moose.

"He doesn't make any sense to me at all," said Loon, as they headed back toward the longhouses. "It's not right to kill our enemy!" he laughed. "Mad to kill the people who attack us!" He shook his head, as if to clear his ears. "I think he's spent too many lean winters eating tree bark," he joked.

With a sudden burst of laughter, he picked up a rock and hurled it at the palisade, making a loud crack. Instantly the dogs began to bark. "Or too many days in the hot sun," he continued between bursts of convulsive laughter.

"Loon," said Willow in a voice without laughter. "What if he's right?"

"What?" hooted Loon. "You've been eating bark too!"

"I have to see the old woman about my hands," said Willow, as he ran off toward her longhouse, leaving Loon standing in stunned silence.

– CHAPTER FORTY –

The Scales of a Fish

The next day, by the time the first rays of light had illuminated the eastern sky far above the River of the Dawn, the builders had begun to tie bark on the frames of the new longhouse. It was a job anyone could do. They started at the far end of the longhouse where the thin poles had been buried in the ground to form a wall. Narrow saplings were tied in place at waist height. Beginning at ground level, women and children hung slabs of bark on the poles while the oldest women twisted strips of bark into twine. It was a perfect time for exchanging stories with the visitors from the River of the Dawn and the nimble tongues kept pace with the fingers tying slabs of bark in place.

When they had completed a row along the bottom, they started on the next row up. Each row hung over the one below like the scales on a fish. Sometimes the women sang together about the spirits of the river and the sky and the bravery of women defending their village from invaders. They sang of building and rebuilding. The work and the singing and the stories continued throughout the day.

At the far end of the longhouse, Willow and Otter watched Loon and other young warriors scramble over the frames high above the ground to lash the roof poles in place to form an arch like a turtle shell. When the poles were stable they began the dangerous work of tying bark to the poles to form the roof. With his injured hands, Willow could only wander beneath the structure pointing out gaps in the bark covering. He saw others climbing through the frames and he shuddered at the memory of scrambling over the burning roof—a painful thought as fresh and raw as the injuries to his hands.

It took days to complete the roof and cover the entire structure—all but the four holes left for the smoke to escape. Slabs of elm bark beside the open holes were attached to long, thin poles, so they could be pulled over the openings when it rained.

On the final day the inhabitants of the newly built longhouse had a feast to thank the people who had worked so hard to rebuild their home. Since they had little food left, they relied on the generosity of their clan members and neighbours. Some guests brought pots full of stew, while others carried baskets of fresh fish from the river.

Old Chief had nothing left from his own stores, but he was able to serve his guests from his own special harvest of corn. He loved to eat it almost as much as he loved to share it with his friends. The day before the feast he had returned to the swamp to find the submerged basket filled with the tiny ears of corn he had left there in the summer. The corn had marinated in the stagnant swamp all summer long and was now ready for the soup pot. He proudly served fermented corn soup to everyone who came to help. It was one of the finest gifts he could offer to show his gratitude, and his guests were honoured by the pungent gift.

Many who came to the feast brought gifts to replace what had been lost in the fire—baskets of corn, squash, beans, dried fish, furs and robes made from every animal in the forest, as well as tools, pots and bowls. Soon the longhouse was restocked, ready for the feast. Old Heron, Orchid and the women of the longhouse stood at the door to welcome the guests and thank them for their many gifts. The response was always the same. "We help each other."

As the guests filed in to admire the new longhouse, Old Heron and Orchid looked at the large crowd of people. Orchid took a deep breath through her nostrils.

— *The Scales of a Fish* —

"There is something magical about the smell of a newly-built house," she said. "New houses are so bright inside, and the cedar is so fragrant."

"And the mice are gone," replied Old Heron.

"Yes, the mice are gone!" laughed Orchid. "That's why it's so quiet."

"But they'll be back," said Old Heron. "We'll hear the munching again before dawn. Perhaps one day we will learn to eat the mice that eat our corn—just as we eat the turkeys that take so much. Then we'll never be hungry!" She threw her head back and held her thumb and forefinger together above her open mouth, as though she was holding a mouse's tail.

All night long the feasting and dancing continued. Sounds of songs and drums echoed across the fields and into the forests until the moon disappeared behind the trees.

At dawn only a few old people stirred. Old Heron added wood to the fading fires in the longhouse, trying not to wake those who slept where they had collapsed in an exhausted heap. Willow, Otter and Loon woke up late, after the sun was high. They spent the day on Thunder River fishing from their old canoes with a net strung from one to another. It was a relaxing way to fish after a night of strenuous games and dancing and they knew they had to conserve their strength for another night of celebrations.

"Old Chief has called a meeting of the clan leaders and elders tonight," said Otter.

"I hope he doesn't tell Turkey Vulture about it," said Loon. "He'll want to speak about his wild ideas."

Willow checked the net for fish and threw it back into the water. "I think he'll be there," he said.

"Then I'll be somewhere else," said Loon. "The elders will have to meet without me," he said with a laugh.

"I can't imagine us as elders," said Otter.

"Why not? Why do we have to be old to be elders?" asked Loon. "Why can't we start our own meetings of elders who are still young? I think we could make good decisions, just like the elders who are old."

"I agree with you now," said Otter. "But I might not agree when I'm old."

"But do you think we'll ever be elders?" pondered Loon. "When I was trapped on the shoal of that northern lake, I thought I'd never see the sun again. I was sure I'd never be an elder."

Otter inhaled quickly, as if he were about to fall into cold water. "When I was swimming under the ice looking for the hole, I thought I'd breathed my last breath. Even when I came through the hole, I thought I was frozen. I couldn't pull myself up. There are so many things that can stop us from being elders—bears, ice, enemy arrows, fire. I wonder how anyone can live that long."

"That's what I felt when I was falling into the river after my flight," said Willow. "It wasn't far to fall, but it took such a long time before I hit the water. And I remember thinking about all the things I was going to miss when I was hunting in the stars. For one thing, I'd never get to fight a battle with my friends."

"You can fight with us any time," laughed Loon.

"I mean *fight the enemy* with my friends. We'll do that together, and when we're old we'll talk about our battles around the fire—if we're alive."

"This talk is scaring the fish away," said Otter. "Let's be quiet for a while."

All afternoon they fished lazily on the river in the warmth of the autumn sun, no longer straining themselves with difficult thoughts or deeds. But despite the quiet calm of the day, they all wondered how long it would be until they were in battle together.

– CHAPTER FORTY-ONE –

The Unsettling Song of Turkey Vulture

The elders began to gather at Old Heron's new longhouse at dusk. Willow and Otter sat in the shadows behind Old Chief, where they could listen to the speeches without being noticed. As the elders and clan leaders arrived for the meeting, they talked quietly, waiting for the meeting to begin.

Old Chief smoked the ceremonial pipe beside the fire. When he inhaled, the eyes lit up and thick smoke rose to the roof of the longhouse, out through the holes, and up to the flickering stars.

At last, he placed his pipe on a rock and stood up. The others became quiet. He chanted in a low voice, speaking words of praise to the spirits of the sky and the river. He lit a clump of tobacco on the fire and walked around, spreading the sweet-smelling smoke through the longhouse as he moved. Then he sat down again beside the fire.

"We're here tonight to talk about peace," he said, looking at the stony faces of the elders. "Not the ordinary peace we have with our friends, but peace with our enemy." He looked over to Turkey Vulture, as he repeated the words. "Peace with our enemy."

There was a low murmur from the elders—quiet enough to be respectful, but loud enough to be heard. Turkey Vulture sat motionless, unaffected by the sound or the message it conveyed.

"I welcome Turkey Vulture as our guest. He has come from the Wide River of Many Islands and he'll speak to us about his hopes for peace."

Turkey Vulture stood up and scanned the longhouse from one end to the other. Not a single person escaped his penetrating stare. Dressed simply in a loincloth and deerskin leggings, he wore only a string of bear claws on his bare chest. His hair was in two braids, each wrapped in strands of deerskin with grouse feathers among the strands. Long earrings of coloured shells hung from his ears. His sweeping eyes fixed momentarily on Willow and Otter, as if to repeat that his message was for the young.

"We are very fortunate," he began in a soft voice. "We live beside the water and take what we need from the lakes and rivers. Our land produces crops, berries and fruits and the animals give us meat, furs, and bones. We take only what we need. The spirits treat us with kindness—and our lives are good.

"I have travelled far in every direction and I've seen people in faraway places. They've built nations for themselves with their hard work. Some are more prosperous than others, but none compares with the prosperity we have in our nations. Our nations are strong—and our people are strong.

"How did we come to live in this place that is the envy of all others? Did we fall into it as the rain falls from the sky, not knowing where we would land? Or did our ancestors stumble upon it, as a blind man stumbles through the night?

"No, my friends, we didn't stumble on what we have now. Our ancestors built these nations with their hands and their thoughts. They created a way of life that they have left in our care. We tend it like we tend our forests, our rivers and our fields, and then we pass it on to our children. We will leave it in their care."

Turkey Vulture glanced over at Willow and Otter in the shadows of the longhouse. He scanned their faces before he continued in a more forceful voice.

"We build our nations as we build our houses—strong and well protected. Nation building begins with a plan in the same way that house building begins with a plan. The tall poles in the framework of our nations can be found in our villages and in our clans. These strong ties join our people from different villages together. The framework can be found in our strong Chiefs and War Chiefs, in our councils, in the treaties we have among our own people, and in our laws. We know what kind of payment must be made to the family of a person killed by another, and we realize that a payment is better for our people than revenge. Revenge leads to more revenge. This understanding is part of the framework of our nations."

Turkey Vulture paused to scan those who sat quietly listening to his speech before he continued.

"We cover the frames of our houses with bark to keep them warm and dry. When the bark falls off, we repair it. A different kind of bark covers the framework of our nations to keep our people safe within. We have treaties with our allies from other nations. Many of us can recite the treaties—trade treaties and safe travel treaties. We send our envoys to spend time with our allies to strengthen our ties and ensure the peace, and if some of this bark falls off, we repair the damage to our nation as quickly as we can.

"Finally, we surround our houses with palisades to protect ourselves from our enemies. We protect our nations in the same way, by drawing boundaries at the edges of lakes and rivers that act as palisades around our nation. We attack any enemy who crosses the boundary—and we delude ourselves into thinking it protects us. But it doesn't, because our attacks on their nations bring their attacks on our nations, and on and on."

Some of the clan leaders and elders adjusted their positions, as though they were suddenly uncomfortable.

"Revenge leads to more revenge," Turkey Vulture repeated. "It's a lesson we learned when the Great Turtle first came to this land. We don't seek revenge against people who live in our home because we know that retaliation destroys a home. It drains away the laughter—the joy—so the home becomes nothing more than a shelter.

"But we haven't learned that revenge against our enemy also causes us grief. The result is always the same—grief for them and for us. Why haven't we grasped this?" He let the question hang in the air, blending with the smoke that surrounded them.

"The People from Across the Lake are building a new structure to leave to their children. Their five nations are meeting together, so they can form one nation. They say they'll be like five arrows tied together. One arrow might be broken easily, but five arrows together cannot. If they're successful, the peace will prevent fighting among their five nations and they'll keep their palisades in place only to guard against attacks from us.

"Is it time to settle the differences with our enemy the same way we settle differences within our community? Would our nations be stronger? Will the nations we leave to our children be stronger without attacks and counter-attacks?"

Again he paused to ponder the questions.

"When we build a longhouse, we mark the shape of the structure on the ground. Building a peace begins the same way. If we want to have peace with the enemy—as we have now within our own nation—we'll need a plan. We can build a peace if we have the will. I ask you to consider the implications of the five-nation alliances—not only for our enemy, but for ourselves. I urge you to consider the path of peace for ourselves and our children."

When Turkey Vulture sat down silently beside the fire, Old Chief responded to his speech without standing.

"Our friend is courageous to speak these words," he said. "He knows his ideas are difficult for us to accept. We have been subjected to so many cruel attacks from our enemy for so many generations that it has become a way of life for us. Still, his ideas are sound. We work hard to keep the peace with our friends because we are peaceful people—as peaceful as the chipmunks in the woods. They do not harm any other animals. But if they are attacked, they become ferocious. When we are attacked we do the same. We must fight hard to survive the constant attacks from the enemy."

Wolverine had listened respectfully to the words of Turkey Vulture and Old Chief. When Old Chief finished, he rose to speak.

The Unsettling Song of Turkey Vulture

"My views on this peace proposal are well known. Though Turkey Vulture speaks eloquently, his idea of peace with the enemy is madness. It is madness of the worst kind, because it gives the illusion of being right. The words of Turkey Vulture carry us along like the current in the river above the Great Falls. We follow his words effortlessly as his idea pulls us along, but by the time we see the danger, it's too late to save ourselves. We're carried over the falls and smashed to bits in the turbulence below.

"Of course we want peace, but we can't have it with this enemy any more than we can have it with the mosquitoes. They're incapable of peace. They live to pierce us with sharp things and draw our blood."

Wolverine stared at Turkey Vulture with dark sunken eyes. Deep lines crossed his face, like the ravines in a forest.

"If we follow this madness, we'll lose everything we have—our lands, our waters, our sky, and every creature in them. We can never forget that the People from Across the Lake want to drive us from our land. They may talk of peace. They may even agree to peace treaties. Perhaps there will be peace for one, two, or five generations, but long after our bones have been mixed together and buried in the ground, when our palisades have rotted and disappeared into the soil, they will attack. They will drive our people from our villages and take everything we have.

"I agree with Turkey Vulture and Old Chief. Peace is undeniably better than war," Wolverine continued. "It may be easier for us to have peace while we are alive, but when our spirits are hunting in the vast forests among the stars, will our grandchildren's grandchildren be driven from this land by their trusted 'friends'—the People from Across the Lake? Who among us is prepared to sacrifice the existence of future generations for the convenience of peace during our own lifetime?"

Wolverine searched the longhouse for anyone who was willing to make that sacrifice, but no one moved. No one spoke. After a long silence, the leader of the Deer Clan added his voice in support of Wolverine.

"The only way we can have peace is to chase the enemy far into the forest. We need to go to their villages and burn them down. Drive them out of their lands before they have a chance to drive us from ours. And if we chase them far enough, they'll never come back to threaten us.

"We can build a nation of peace, but that's the only way to do it."

Brown Bat, the adopted warrior, swooped out of the shadows of the longhouse and stood uncomfortably as though waiting for permission to speak.

"I have something to say," he said, looking nervously at Old Chief. A few of the clan leaders frowned at him. The leader of the Wolf Clan signalled to him to sit down, but he didn't. He waited for Old Chief to raise his hand before he spoke.

"I don't usually speak at gatherings like this," Brown Bat said. "I don't believe it's my place to be involved in the decisions that involve the People from Across the Lake. Some of you would agree." There were words of agreement throughout the room, but he ignored them and continued, looking to Turkey Vulture.

"Those who know me know that I spent the early part of my life among those people. I was born across the lake in a village like this and the people who lived there were like the people who live here. They do all the things we do. Even their language is like ours.

"I've been living with you for most of my life. I have a family, like all of you, and I hunt and trade beside you. My children are close friends with your children. The only thing I won't do with you is attack the People from Across the Lake. Why not? Because I don't see those people—the people who raised me and cared for me when I was a child—as the enemy. I can't see them as brutal animals, the way you see them. I couldn't fight them or injure them.

"When I was young I was taught to fear you," Brown Bat said. "I say 'you' when I think back to my childhood. I was taught by my clan chief that you were dangerous, bloodthirsty killers, who wanted to drive us from our land. When I was captured by your warriors, I thought I was going to be gutted alive like a salmon, but I soon learned that you were the same as my people, and when I was adopted into this village, I learned how kind and welcoming you are. I have lived as one of you and now I've become one of you. One day our bones will be buried together. I know from living on both sides of the lake that we are the same people. We want to live in peace as they do. We want to raise our families and hunt and trade and celebrate the beauty of our land—and to be left alone. Just as they want to be left alone by us.

"Wolverine talks of the 'madness' of peace with the enemy," Brown Bat added. "I talk of the madness of this war. Why do we fight with people so much like ourselves when we could have peace? *That* is the madness." Brown Bat smashed a clenched fist against the palm of his other hand, and then he disappeared back into the shadows.

– CHAPTER FORTY-TWO –

The Ice Jam Breaks

The sound of Brown Bat's slap echoed in the longhouse. Otter whispered to Willow before anyone else spoke. "My head is bursting. Let's find Loon and tell him about this." They slipped quietly out of the longhouse and soon found their friend playing a game with other members of the clan in another longhouse. A strained look appeared on his face as he shook painted pits in a wooden bowl.

"Loon," called Otter. "We have to tell you what happened!"

"Not now," Loon answered without looking. "This is the big throw of the night." He shook the pits until he was ready and then, with a flourish, bashed them against the floor of the longhouse. The pits rattled inside the wooden bowl before coming to rest with all five pits showing their white sides—not a single dark side among them. He let out the scream of the conquering warrior.

"The spirits are with me tonight!"

One of the other players handed him a finely flaked stone knife. "Enjoy this until I win it back," he said to Loon.

"I'll enjoy it for the rest of my life," laughed Loon. "Next time we'll play for fingers—you can't win them back!"

He danced in circles around the other players, waving his new knife, until Willow and Otter led him outside into the dark night.

"We have to tell you about the speeches," said Otter. "I thought I knew all about peace with the enemy. Now I don't know what to think."

"I'll tell you what Turkey Vulture said," continued Willow. "He said, 'I have travelled far and I have seen people in faraway lands. They've built nations for themselves, but none compares with the prosperity we have in our nation. Our nation and our people are the strongest.'"

Willow began to recite the speech almost word for word, but soon noticed that Loon wasn't listening. Instead, he was looking past Willow into the longhouse, watching the dancers and listening to the music, his feet moving with the rhythm of the drum. Finally he raised his hand and Willow stopped speaking.

"I think I've heard this speech before," Loon said with an uneasy smile.

"There's much more," said Otter, eager to recite the rest. "Turkey Vulture said, 'We build our nations the way we build our houses. Some people in distant lands . . .'" Again, Loon raised his hand and moved close to Willow and Otter, looking upward into their eyes.

"I am having a great night tonight," he said. "The spirits are with me. Did you see what I won?" He held the knife up between them. Abruptly, his laugh disappeared and he spoke in a strange tone. "I know we'll never have peace with our enemies—and I don't want it. I want to fight them and drive them away. I want a chance to show them how strong I am."

Loon reached up and put his hands on his friends' shoulders. He looked past them toward the lights and sounds of the longhouse and the dancers jumping high in the air. "You can talk about this if you want, but I'm going to dance tonight—until my legs fall off."

Then he pinched their shoulder muscles until the two young men winced, and disappeared among the writhing mass inside the longhouse. Willow and Otter stood silently in the darkness outside, watching the dancers and listening to their laughter.

— *Enemy Arrows* —

"We could go back and hear some more of the speeches," said Otter. The sound of a turtle rattle could be heard above the laughter and singing.

"We could," agreed Willow. "Turkey Vulture said his message was for us." They stood silently, trying not to sway to the beat of the drum in the cool night air. The moon hung above the trees on the other side of Thunder River.

Willow began moving his feet to stay warm. "Or we could dance until our legs fall off," he said with a grin. Otter returned the look. As though struck by the same bolt of lightning, they charged into the longhouse among the throngs of leaping dancers, some beautifully decorated in multi-coloured swirling feathers, jangling silver beads, and glittering shell jewellery. Drums, rattles, and scrapers competed with the laughter that filled the huge space from one end to the other. Above them all was Loon, leaping as if to reach the rafters. The piercing sound of his familiar loon call could be heard over the din, calling out to Willow and Otter to join him.

During the darkest part of the night Willow left the longhouse—before his legs had fallen off—and headed across the village toward his own loft. On the way, he saw a solitary figure sitting beside a dying fire, with bear teeth hanging from around his neck. When he walked closer, he saw who it was.

"Your speech made my head spin," said Willow, as he stood awkwardly on the other side of the dim light.

"I said it was for you and your friends, Willow," replied Turkey Vulture.

Willow nodded. "Can I sit with you?" he asked.

"I'm a guest in your home. You can sit wherever you like."

Willow sat on a log and stared into the low flames, glancing occasionally at Turkey Vulture, who waited patiently for him to speak.

"I want to ask you something that's hard for me to say," he began at last. Turkey Vulture looked at him expectantly until Willow continued. "I have thoughts that plague me. Whenever they come into my heart I chase them away. I can't imagine putting them into words, but I have to." He looked anxiously at Turkey Vulture.

"Ask me what you want."

"Can I ask you a question you will never repeat to anyone else?"

"You don't need to fear that," replied Turkey Vulture with a smile. "I'm a negotiator between warring nations. My life depends on keeping secrets."

"Did you know my father, Gray Fox?" he asked.

"No."

Willow moved closer to Turkey Vulture and spoke in a low voice. "Then I won't destroy his memory by telling you this." He hesitated before he continued. "You won't repeat this?"

"Have no fear, my friend."

The ice jam that had been holding back Willow's thoughts broke open with a deluge of stories and images and questions about battles and adopted prisoners. He told Turkey Vulture about his father's death and the Wanderer's daughter with her false message from his father, and his feelings about being the son of a traitor. As Turkey Vulture listened, Willow repeated what Shrike had said to him about his father's last battle and finally, in a desperate voice, he confided that he didn't know what to believe.

"I can see why you don't want to dishonour your father by repeating this lie to people who knew him. Words are like birds in a basket. Once they're out, they can't be recaptured."

"It would cause too much pain to repeat this," Willow said. "I couldn't do it. What would my grandfather say? And my mother would grieve all over again. What would my friends think?"

"If it were true, would you tell Old Chief or your mother?" asked Turkey Vulture.

Willow thought before he answered this difficult question, which generated such hurtful thoughts. He could feel his spirit twisting and writhing within him and his stomach tightening into a knot.

"I don't know," he replied. "If it were true, I'd have to decide, but I can't think about that now. It's too painful."

"I can see this uncertainty has weighed heavily on your spirit," said Turkey Vulture. "You have to know whether Oriole's words are true or false, and I may be able to help you find out."

"How can you do that?" asked Willow.

"I'm going to visit my friends on the far side of the lake this winter to resume the negotiations—there's still some hope, faint though it may be. I should be back early next summer. When I'm there, I'll ask about your father and find out if he's alive or dead. You'll know when I return."

Willow stared into the fire. "I'm not sure which answer I want to hear, but I have to know."

"There's nothing more you can do. Put this question out of your thoughts until I return."

"I'll try, but when I see the Wanderer's daughter . . . I want to hide."

"You can hide for now if you like, but when I return, you'll be able to answer her with the truth," said Turkey Vulture, as he lifted himself to his feet. "It's time for me to rest before the sun comes up. I hope your spirit settles soon."

He disappeared into the darkness, leaving Willow to wonder what he would eventually learn from the enemy.

"I can't wait that long," the young warrior said to himself, covering his face with his scarred hands.

– CHAPTER FORTY-THREE –

Under a Giant Spruce

Old Chief sat inside by the warm fire as the brutal winds of winter rattled the newly built longhouse and tore at its thin bark covering. When the strongest gusts shook the tall building, dried corn hanging from the cross beams swayed in unison like eel grass in a shallow stream. Old Chief watched wisps of smoke rise until they were scattered by the wind circling near the smoke holes and mixed with the snowflakes blowing into the openings.

Later that afternoon, Willow, Otter and Loon entered the longhouse covered from head to toe with snow. They had been hunting in the blizzard since dawn, but returned with nothing. Like ravenous coyotes, they scooped some watery stew out of a large pot next to the fire and sat down beside Old Chief to eat.

When they had finished, Willow told his grandfather about their trip. They had seen no tracks in the deep snow. All of the animals had taken shelter and any old tracks had been buried. There was nothing to hunt in a storm. Old Chief adjusted a large stump on the fire until higher flames lit up the smoky longhouse.

"I need help," he said, with mischief in his eyes. "I need three young warriors who are brave—not afraid of the cold sting of winter."

"You probably want warriors who have killed a bear," said Loon, pretending to search the longhouse for such hunters.

"Oh, yes," answered Old Chief smiling. "At least one bear."

"Do you need warriors who can swim long distances in ice-covered water?" asked Otter.

"I don't ask the impossible," replied Old Chief. "But if there were such a person, I would take him with me."

"You might encounter an enemy ambush," said Willow. "Will you need a warrior who can duck out of the way of unseen arrows?"

"Do not be foolish!" said Old Chief. "I'll never find anyone who can do that."

Loon couldn't stand the suspense any longer. He jumped to his feet. "When do we go?" he cried.

"Be calm, Loon," said Old Chief patiently. "This is not the way warriors behave." Loon sat down again, slightly humbled but barely able to contain his excitement.

"Where will we go?" asked Otter, as coolly as he could manage.

"We're going to the village by the Bottomless Lake with a large load of corn," said Old Chief. "I've heard worrying stories recently about food shortages in the village, so we must help them get through the winter."

"How do we get corn there at this time of year?" asked Willow.

"It won't be easy. The lake is about to freeze. We'll go by canoe as far as we can and then travel inland along the creek to its end, and then by sled. I've asked Lynx to come as well. We'll load the canoes in the morning and leave before the sun is high."

Old Chief could see the anticipation in their eyes. He knew they were excited about going to the Bottomless Lake and he savoured their joy. "Then you will come with me?"

Loon almost leapt to his feet again, but he held himself back.

"We'll come with you," he said in his most restrained voice.

Lynx began to prepare for the trip at dawn. He selected two sleek, new canoes and covered the interior cedar ribs with bearskins to keep out the numbing cold—knowing that the chill of the icy water races through birchbark with the same speed as fire. He then draped the seats with beaver pelts to spread over the paddlers' knees. After choosing two old canoes to carry the loads of corn, he tied them to the new ones, ready for launching.

The travellers brought baskets of corn down from the village on two sleds, which would be used to transport the precious food from the river to the village at the Bottomless Lake. Each basket was placed carefully in the cargo canoes and covered with deerhides. The sleds and five pairs of snowshoes were strapped securely in place on top of the hides.

Before long a small group of people gathered at the snowy shore to help with the loading and see the travelers off. Orchid chanted a song to the spirits of the Beautiful Lake about snow falling into frigid waters, wondering where the snowflakes went when they disappeared. She asked the spirits to take as many snowflakes as they could devour, but not to take the young men of the village. Then she whispered some tender words to her father, Old Chief, and held him close before she said good-bye.

While Loon waited in the front of one canoe, Old Chief climbed into the centre and covered himself with beaverskins, singing happily as he waited for the trip to begin. Lynx slipped effortlessly into the back and pushed the canoe from the snowy shore without letting his winter moccasin touch the water.

Willow and Otter paddled the second canoe out into the river, where the current swung it around toward the Beautiful Lake. The old cargo canoes, battered but with the dignity of age, followed, riding low in the water from the weight of the corn.

When the four canoes reached the mouth of the Thunder River, the morning sun was high above the lake and not a breath of wind stirred the surface of the icy water. It was as calm as a frozen lake—and almost as cold. Old Chief pointed to mountainous shapes on the western horizon.

"Look at those clouds," he said "They are sure to bring deep snow—up to your chin."

Lynx laughed. "Then we'll run down a deer on our snowshoes, like we did when we were young."

"You can run. I'll follow in the sled," said Old Chief, pulling the furs around him. "I'm too old for that."

They paddled through the day over the placid waters of the Beautiful Lake until the sun sank toward the western horizon, turning the unearthly clouds into fire-coloured peaks. At last they turned the canoes up the slow-moving creek leading toward the Bottomless Lake—only to find the creek was frozen solid.

They unloaded the canoes at the mouth of the creek and turned them upside down under a giant spruce tree. Before long they had strapped the baskets of corn onto the sleds and were walking over the icy creek hauling the sleds behind them with ease.

"The moon will be full tonight," said Old Chief. "At least until the snow clouds block it out."

It wasn't long before the full moon rose in the eastern sky, illuminating the trees and turning the snow a brilliant blue. When the creek disappeared into a tangle of thorn bushes, they laced on their snowshoes and plodded through the forest along a narrow trail. Old Chief wanted to reach the village before the heavy snowfall—and he could see the giant clouds creeping steadily across the starry sky.

Long before the clouds obscured the moon, the snow began to fall—minute specks of ice glittering in the moonlight. They knew they had to move quickly to reach the village before the trail disappeared and their direction was lost in the snow.

"Take a rest for a while, my friend." said Lynx, signalling to Old Chief to sit on the sled. Once Old Chief had climbed reluctantly on the sled and covered himself with bearskins, Lynx signalled to Loon to push the sled from the back—and they were off again. Willow and Otter followed in their tracks, hauling the other load.

The snow fell hard. By the time they reached the base of the cliff where the disastrous deer hunt had taken place the year before, Old Chief had almost disappeared under a covering of white. The night was so dark and the downfall so heavy that Otter and Willow could barely see the tracks in the snow—yet Lynx kept going. Finally, Lynx stopped near a slope and asked Old Chief to get to his feet. They were going to leave both sleds behind.

— *Under a Giant Spruce* —

The climb up the steep slope toward the village was difficult at the best of times. Lynx found a path up the lowest part of the slope and made his way to the top. Old Chief followed close behind him, stopping from time to time to rest while the others waited in his tracks. The chunks of ice clinging to their freezing eyelashes were beginning to blind them, so Otter held on to Willow's robes, while Loon held on to Otter. They followed as close to Old Chief as they could and rested whenever he did.

Lynx was the first to reach the plateau where the village was located. He could smell wood smoke and quickly followed the scent to the palisades. Somehow the dogs sensed their presence and were soon howling to announce their arrival. Lynx called out to let the villagers know they were friends and a group of warriors immediately appeared to guide them to the village.

Soon the weary travellers were sitting as honoured guests beside a warm fire in Porcupine's longhouse, filling their empty stomachs with hot soup and smoked fish. Old Chief announced he had brought two sleds full of corn, which they had left at the bottom of the cliff.

"We'll get it in the morning," said Porcupine, speaking slowly and deliberately. "There isn't a living creature outside tonight that would eat it or take it away. It's safe where it is."

Porcupine sang to the spirit of the sky for making the snow so deep. He knew that hunting would be good if they could find a deer or a moose. With their snowshoes on, no animal could escape them, except the near-invisible snowshoe hares, which were as white as the moon and could run across the surface of the deepest snow.

The blizzard continued in the moonless night, while the chiefs sat beside the fire, catching up on the news since the summer hunt and the tragic death of the Deadfall Hunter. They spoke about the peace talks among the People from Across the Lake and the increased danger of attack from a united enemy. Old Chief repeated Turkey Vulture's speech from memory. As the night passed, they reminisced about battles from long ago and before long, Willow, Otter and Loon were asleep.

The snow fell all night and continued through the next day. Before dusk the sun appeared from beneath the clouds at the horizon, illuminating their undersides in brilliant orange and then disappeared from sight beyond the Bottomless Lake. The stars seemed to shine more brilliantly than ever after being hidden for so long, lighting the snow with a shadowless glow. The forest was as silent as the sky.

Dawn brought a brilliant white sun rising in a sky the colour of a robin's egg. The full magnitude of the snowfall could be seen in the sparkling light of morning—trees laden with deep mounds of snow on every branch and twig, cedars bent to the ground, and the hard edges of broken rocks buried beneath beds of white powder.

The clear skies also brought a biting chill from the north, forcing the animals to hide deep in caves or hollow trees.

As the sun climbed higher the village chief called his warriors to retrieve the sleds and baskets of corn. With snowshoes strapped on, Lynx walked across the deep snow to show where they had left the loads, followed by Willow, Otter and Loon. A few young dogs tried to keep up with them for a while, but the snow was far too deep and they soon returned to the longhouse fires. Old Chief remained inside with the other elders.

They followed the trail away from the village and down a ravine to the stream. When Lynx reached the place where he left the sleds he stopped and looked around him. The night had been dark when he left the trail, and the snow was blinding. He couldn't see them anywhere.

"The snow has swallowed our corn," he announced.

The warriors from the village laughed at his joke, but they couldn't see the baskets or the sleds.

"We'll have to dig for it," said a warrior from the village. He snapped the top off of a thin sapling, stripped off the branches and began to poke it into the snow, listening to the sound it made when it hit the rocks and roots buried below. The others in the group did the same and soon the entire group was poking into the white depths. Sometimes one of the warriors bent down to dig, but without success.

Loon was the first one to hit the hidden corn. He poked his stick into the thick snow and heard the muffled sound of a crumpling basket.

"Here it is!" he yelled. "The snow may have swallowed it, but we'll pull it out of the entrails."

The others rushed over to help him dig. Once they were uncovered, the sleds rode easily on the surface and the relieved group pulled them up the hill to the village. Cold air seared their lungs and their breath rose in thin clouds through the still air. Ice formed on their fur robes and around their faces as they panted up the hill.

Old Chief was beside the fire talking with Porcupine and the elders about shifting alliances, when the villagers brought in the snow-covered baskets. Everyone praised Old Chief for his generosity, but, as always, he waved away their thanks, saying he could not have done anything without the assistance of Lynx and the young hunters. He said he was just an old man who took pleasure in helping his friends—a man who looked to the spirit of the sky as the source of everything good.

Though food was scarce in the village, it was a time to celebrate—if not to feast. The next few nights were spent dancing beside the fire in the finest furs and decorations—and the young men showed their strength and prowess by leaping high over poles and walking on their hands, springing from their hands to their feet and back.

The young women danced with the same intense energy in a blur of decorated furs, gleaming hair and multi-coloured feathers, but no decoration compared with their bright eyes and white teeth as they flashed their radiant smiles throughout the longhouse.

Outside, the bitter cold lasted for four more brilliantly clear days and nights. When the clouds reappeared on the western horizon and the deadly cold lifted, Old Chief announced it was time to leave the Bottomless Lake to return to Thunder River. They would leave at daybreak.

— *Enemy Arrows* —

In the morning Old Chief sat regally on a sled wrapped in fur robes, while the elders of the village gathered around him to sing their songs of friendship and gratitude. Lynx and the young warriors exchanged farewells with their friends and then they were off across the deep snow, down the hill to the base of the deer-hunting cliff, and along the frozen stream to the Beautiful Lake.

Gray clouds scudded across the sky from the west and a stiff wind blew, drifting snow over the path in front of them. Old Chief sat low on the empty sled to avoid the icy wind.

Suddenly Lynx stopped on the trail and held his hand up in the signal for 'silence.' The others immediately crouched down and waited.

"Tracks crossing the stream," he said quietly, without turning around. "Moose tracks—and they were just made."

– CHAPTER FORTY-FOUR –

Laughing at Death

"Loon and Otter," he shouted. "You stay with Old Chief. Take the sleds down to the canoes. Willow, come with me. We're going to run this moose down."

In an instant Lynx cut a sapling and stripped off the branches. He sharpened one end into a point to make a deadly spear and then dashed into the forest on his snowshoes, following the moose tracks. Willow quickly grabbed a dead branch and ran after him.

The moose tracks led up a hill, through a grove of oak trees still covered with brown leaves, and past a stand of bent cedars. On a ridge overlooking the stream, they saw the stately animal in the distance, struggling through the deep snow. Lynx stopped to wait for Willow.

"There it is," he said. "From here it looks like a male—it's shed its antlers by now—too big for a female."

From the top of the ridge, Lynx noticed the lake and pointed to it.

"I don't see any whitecaps," exclaimed Willow. "There's a strong wind here, but it must not be blowing on the lake."

"The lake is frozen," said Lynx with a grin. "Frozen with black ice!"

— *Enemy Arrows* —

They ran after the moose on their snowshoes. By this time it had heard their voices and smelled their scent. It began to leap through the deep snow—like a deer leaping through brush—but in no time they had caught up to it.

Lynx ran beside the frightened beast, shouting loudly to force it toward the lake. As it veered in that direction through the snow, steam shot out of its huge nostrils and its chest heaved. They chased after it, yelling and beating their poles on trees to keep it moving toward the shore. Finally, the exhausted animal stopped and whirled around at its attackers. It lunged at Lynx, forcing him to step backward on his snowshoes and fall on his back in the snow. Willow immediately jumped in front of the moose, waving his stick and shouting until it turned again and continued its slow escape toward the lake.

By the time the hunters had driven the moose to the shore of the frozen lake, it was exhausted. It could only step slowly through the snow—but when it came through the cedars and saw the open space, it tried to leap again. As the weakened creature approached the lake Lynx rushed at it and in one skilful movement drove his spear behind the rib cage and deep into the moose's heaving chest. It fell with its big head on the frozen lake, blood oozing from its fleshy lips and spreading in a steaming, scarlet pool over the black ice.

Lynx squatted down beside the moose to catch his breath as the wind howled around his ears. Willow collapsed in the snow beside him. Far across the frozen lake was the mouth of Thunder River—straight downwind from where he sat. Lynx jumped up.

"We have to get Old Chief," he shouted. "No time to rest."

They set off along the shoreline toward the mouth of the stream where they had left the canoes and found Old Chief, Otter and Loon sitting on a sled beside the buried canoes. They had pushed both sleds all the way to the lake. Old Chief moved slowly, with his head down. He had the exhausted look of a warrior returning from an unsuccessful attack on the enemy.

"We're too late for the canoes," yelled Loon. "The lake is frozen."

"We know," said Willow. "We chased a moose there. It's lying with its head on the ice."

"You got the moose?" asked Old Chief, with a spark of interest returning to his eyes.

"Yes. It's a fat one—and not too old," said Lynx. "It will make a feast!"

Lynx moved close to Old Chief. He slipped his hand out of his mitten and put it on the older man's neck. "Your eyes are empty, my friend, and your neck is cold. Are you well enough to make the trip home?" Old Chief hesitated before he answered.

"I want to sit beside my fire," he replied. "I'll have to make the trip home." He looked out toward the frozen lake. "Come with me now," he said weakly, "I'll make sure we reach home safely."

Lynx poked the ice with the pole and found it to be as thick as his leg. "It will hold," he said. "Let's put the sleds onto the ice. We'll be back to the village in no time. The canoes will stay here."

They pushed both sleds to the edge of the frozen lake. Away from the shelter of the trees the wind blew strongly, driving thin wisps of snow across the surface. They followed the shoreline, where the deep snow met the black ice, until they saw the dark motionless shape.

Old Chief rose slowly from the sled and shuffled across the ice to admire the animal. He opened its mouth and pulled the warm tongue out of the way to examine the teeth.

"It is no more than two years old," he said. "It will be very good to eat." He took some tobacco from his fire pouch and sprinkled it near the moose's head, but the strong wind swept it away instantly. He sang a song while the others stood patiently in the cold wind. When he was finished, they dragged the animal across the ice and heaved it onto the two sleds standing one beside the other. Then they lashed the sleds together and tied their snowshoes to the sleds. Old Chief sat beside the moose with his robes wrapped tightly around him.

Lynx turned his face into the wind to tell its exact direction. He saw the sun low above the horizon. Far across the ice in the opposite direction was the mouth of Thunder River.

"Push it out," signalled Lynx in the wailing wind. They moved the sleds effortlessly across the smooth ice, away from the shore, as the wind whipped around them. A smile flashed over Old Chief's face when he realized what Lynx was doing.

"Get it going now!" screamed Lynx. They pushed the sleds in the direction of the wind.

"Now jump on!" he yelled.

With a sudden gust, the wind caught the sleds, shooting them across the ice like an arrow from a bow, snapping their necks backward with the force.

"Yaaaahhhhhhhhh!" yelled Willow and Otter over the sound of Loon's uncontrollable laughter. The shoreline flashed past in a blur and they held on to each other, laughing and screaming. Lynx stood at the back on the sled runners, trying to steer them in the right direction by dragging his moccasin on one side and then the other. Old Chief stared straight ahead with his eyes opened wide and a grin on his face—but the laughter was contagious. He soon joined the young hunters, laughing wildly at the thrill of speeding faster than the birds.

On they flew across the flawless black ice, gaining speed until the sound of the wind faded away. Willow noticed that his hair no longer blew around his face.

"We're going as fast as the wind now," said Lynx in the still air. This made the others laugh even harder.

"We don't need feathers to fly anymore!" shrieked Loon. He held his arms out straight, as though he were flying, making Willow and Otter laugh louder and Old Chief hold his ribs.

"Stop!" cried Old Chief.

"We can't stop until we hit something," shouted Lynx.

"I mean stop laughing," pleaded Old Chief. "I'm laughing myself to pieces."

— *Laughing at Death* —

"He's falling apart!" gasped Willow, holding his stomach. "So am I!"

Loon was bent over on the moose, trying to regain his breath, when he saw the moose's head shaking as the sled raced over the ice, its bulbous lips wobbling back and forth. The young warrior collapsed into hysterics.

"Look," he choked, pointing to the moose's bouncing head. "Even the moose is laughing!"

Old Chief threw his head back, gasping for breath. His chest heaved. Tears streamed down his cheeks and he pressed his mittens against his heart.

As the broad bay at the mouth of Thunder River sped toward them, Lynx shifted his weight to point the sleds at the frozen river. When he reached the opening, he swerved the sleds up the valley. But, unlike the smooth lake ice, the ice on the river was covered in deep snow and they slowed to a walking pace. The wind howled past them from the direction of the setting sun.

"Time to push again," said Lynx.

They jumped off the sleds, strapped on their snowshoes, and pushed up the river while Old Chief sat slumped against the moose. Before long they were back at the edge of the river where the trail led up the steep hill to the village.

"My ribs are aching," said Otter.

"I laughed myself apart," answered Willow. "It was like flying again."

"Let's go back and do it some more!" shouted Loon.

Lynx helped Old Chief up the hill to the village. He couldn't speak. He dragged his snowshoes along the snow, stopping often to rest. When he finally reached the longhouse, he collapsed on a bearskin beside the fire. Old Heron rushed over to see him.

"Old Chief is not well," Lynx said quietly to her.

"What happened to him?" she asked.

"We made him laugh," replied Lynx.

"Laugh?" she blurted. "How can that hurt anyone?"

"He laughed very hard," answered Lynx. "Harder than any man should laugh."

Old Chief slept through the night until late the next morning. When he woke, he couldn't lift himself from the bearskin by the fire. He asked Old Heron to call for the other clan leaders. When they arrived they propped him up against a post and stuffed beaverskins behind his back. Willow sat beside him. The clan leaders saw from the pallor in his face that he was gravely ill. He gazed at them through glazed eyes and spoke in a voice like a whisper.

"My brothers and sisters," he said slowly and deliberately. "I see you through mist that isn't there. I watch your mouths moving, but I hear you from far away." He took a strained breath. With a loud crack, a log on the fire exploded, spitting glowing hot coals through the air. A burning ember landed on the back of Old Chief's hand but he didn't move. Willow quickly reached over and brushed it off. The smell of seared flesh spread through the air—a smell that told the clan leaders more than Old Chief was able to say.

"I'll soon be with our ancestors in the sky," he continued. "But I want to see my people one last time before I go. I ask you to take me to them." The clan leaders looked at each other with distress in their eyes.

"You will see your people," said Old Heron. "You will see them tonight."

Old Chief closed his eyes and lowered his head. "Tonight," he repeated. A smile came to his face. Willow knew it was too late to speak to his grandfather about the lies he had heard from the Wanderer's daughter, and the scorching pain of words not spoken added to his unspeakable grief.

That day the women of the longhouse dressed Old Chief in his finest attire under the watchful eye of Old Heron. Wren adorned his hair with eagle feathers to show his status as a great warrior. Orchid draped a wolverine robe over his shoulders, and pendants of precious rocks and silver and copper hung from his neck. Old Heron tied bracelets of brightly coloured beads around his arms.

— *Laughing at Death* —

As the sun set, Old Chief sat in adorned splendour on a loft in the centre of the longhouse, where everyone gathered. Large slabs of moose meat were being roasted over the fires and pots of stew warmed beside the coals.

All through the evening the villagers filed past Old Chief giving their farewells, as the old women cried softly in the shadows. Willow approached Old Chief.

"Grandfather," he said. Old Chief opened his eyes and smiled.

"Willow, my son . . . my brother," he said quietly, between laboured breaths. "We have always known the same spirits. When I see you, I see myself. I hear my words coming from your lips. Your light once shone from my eyes." Willow didn't know how to respond.

"I'm proud to be like you," he said.

"I will live on through my descendants—as you will," said Old Chief. "We will both be brave."

Willow took a deep breath. "We'll be brave," he repeated. "But we will miss each other. You've been a good friend to me."

"And you have been a good friend to me," said Old Chief. "We will see each other again in the sky—and we will both be at peace."

The words ripped through Willow like lightning through a tree, shattering his composure. His eyes filled with tears and his throat became choked. How he longed to have one more day—a few more rays of light—to speak to Old Chief and ask him about the thoughts whirling around inside of him.

But it was too late. He stood up to leave with his head down and his hand over his eyes.

Orchid threw herself on Old Chief, wailing and sobbing. She had already said her final words to Old Chief.

"Don't go father!" she begged. "Don't go yet."

Old Chief looked at her tenderly. He tried to raise his hand to stroke her hair like he had when she was young, but it wouldn't move.

"You are the most beautiful flower in the forest," he said. "It is now time for me to say my last words. Will you help me, my daughter?"

Old Heron rose to her feet and signalled to the people in the longhouse that Old Chief was going to speak. They moved in closer to hear him, and when everything was silent again, he began to speak in a low voice.

"My people, these are my last words to you. I have tried to live bravely, and I will die bravely." He looked up through the roof to the sky above and continued.

"It has given me joy to live among you. Our people are strong and generous. We take care of each other. We live in the most beautiful, most abundant land anywhere on the Great Turtle's back, surrounded by beauty from the moment we come from our mother's body until we die. We have the trees and the water and the sun—cornfields in summer and snow in winter. No people have ever had a better life than we have now. And no one will ever have a better life."

Orchid choked back her tears. She reached over to Old Chief with a bowl of water and wet his lips, before taking a drink for herself.

"My own life has been filled with pleasure. My family and friends have given me endless joy. I have felt the warmth of sharing with others and helping them to flourish. Even in times of sadness and pain, I have known the thrill of intense feelings. I am grateful to each of you.

"I leave the movement of the sun through the sky," he said, turning to Willow. He looked at the grieving faces of the villagers surrounding him.

"I leave the great forests and the birds and animals in them. I leave the flowers and soft sand beaches on summer nights—the touch of a loved one. I leave Thunder River and the Beautiful Lake and all the fish in them. I ask you ... *I beg you* ... to cherish them as I have and to care for them always, as they have cared for us."

Old Chief lowered his head and sat in silence. The longhouse was still, except for the sputtering fire. He looked up with a faint smile on his weary face.

"He is a happy man . . ." he whispered, with the slightest trace of a smile, "who dies . . . from too much . . . laughter."

His head fell back, his smile faded, and his eyes closed. Orchid cried aloud and collapsed on her father. The silence of the longhouse gave way to cries of anguish from all directions. Willow stood silently beside Old Chief showing no emotion, as his grandfather would have expected.

Before Old Chief's body was cool, a group of men and women from the Deer Clan bent it into a crouching position and wrapped it in the finest mink and wolverine furs. Outside the longhouse, the dogs sensed Old Chief's death and began to yowl in the moonlight, as a strong wind blowing through the leafless trees filled the forest with a mournful wail.

The following day, the women of the Wolf Clan met in secret to decide on a new chief. Old Heron's suggestion was accepted by all of the clan women, and Brown Bat was called upon to lead the village. Though he was not born in the village, he was respected for his humility, his clear thinking, and his uncanny ability to understand all points of view.

Three days later, Old Chief's remains were placed in a bark box and taken to the resting place of the dead, near Old Chief's favourite sitting place. Far below, Thunder River stretched into the distance on its way to the Beautiful Lake. The box was hoisted onto a platform high above the ground, where it would remain until the Feast of the Dead.

– CHAPTER FORTY-FIVE –

Time Alone

Willow knew it was time to be alone. It had been a long winter with feasts and celebrations, but the death of Old Chief weighed heavily on his spirit. He had spent too many dark days and nights in the smoky bedlam of the longhouse, listening to the sounds of babies crying and old people moaning from the pain of broken teeth. Late one night a dog chased after a squirrel, upsetting pots and baskets as it tore through the house. It was time to go.

He met Orchid in the doorway, where she was talking to Toothless Hunter. They both stopped and stared at him in surprise. He was dressed for winter with his high moccasins, a beaver cloak, long sleeves, leggings and a bearskin robe. His quiver, arrows and fire pouch hung from a strap slung over one shoulder, along with a small clay pot.

"Where are you going?" his mother asked.

"I'm going away. I'll be back before the moon is full," Willow replied.

"Don't go," she said, grasping his arm tightly. "Stay for a while longer—it will soon be time to collect the maple sap."

"I have to go now," he said. "I can't stay any longer."

"Oh, stay until it's warmer," she pleaded. "You can't be on your own in the middle of winter."

— *Time Alone* —

"I have to go," he repeated, moving past her.

"You're too young to do this," said Orchid in desperation, still holding his arm. She turned to Toothless Hunter for help. "Tell him he's too young to go off on his own."

The old man squinted at Willow through cloudy eyes. He thought about his time alone, so long ago. He remembered the days without food, the fear he experienced hearing strange voices in the dark empty forest—and the cold. But most of all he remembered the elation he felt when his guardian spirit came to him. He held Willow's other arm and peered into his eyes.

"Be brave in the night," he said in a hushed voice. "They come at night."

"He is too young!" cried Orchid.

"And watch out for the enemy," said Toothless Hunter, as he went inside the longhouse.

"My friends are waiting for me, mother," said Willow, putting his hand on her hand. "They're over there by the gate."

Orchid shook her head sadly and let go of his arm.

"I hope I see you again," she said, her voice choking with anguish. "If your dreams tell you to go back to your village, turn around and come home."

"I will," he answered, as he headed to the village gate. Orchid ran into the longhouse.

Otter and Loon were waiting by the village gate, eager to speak with him.

"I don't know why you're doing this in the winter," said Loon. "We're going to have to dig you out of the ice somewhere—if we ever find you."

"You'll find me," laughed Willow. "I am not going any farther than that tree." He pointed to a tall oak just outside the gate.

"You can be alone and still enjoy the company of your friends," said Otter.

"That's what I'll do when I go away!" joked Loon.

"Wish me strength," said Willow.

"You have strength and courage," said Otter. "We know that better than anyone."

"I should be back by the next full moon." He raised his hand in the sign of 'good hunting' and set off across the frozen fields. Otter and Loon watched him until he was out of sight, not knowing whether to pity him or envy him.

Willow followed the river north under a cloudy, windless sky, listening to the music of the river where water had broken through the ice. He heard the sounds of blue jays shrieking from the cedars and red jays whistling from the pines scattered over the vast open spaces surrounding him. He felt the peace and serenity that came from being away from noise of the village. He had been too close to too many people for too long. Now he could breathe and listen to the birds without hearing the chatter of humanity and sleep undisturbed in the silence of the endless forest.

As he wandered along the river, Willow saw the tracks of deer, but he didn't follow them. There was no need to be burdened by food on this journey, or by anything else. He followed the river until dusk and then found a place sheltered by cedar trees from any wind that might come up during the night. He gathered some short sticks of dry wood and soon had a fire going. Beside the fire he built a lean-to of branches covered with bark and leaves that was just big enough to keep him warm and dry. When it was completed he crept inside, wrapped himself in his bear robe and savoured the cold serenity of the night. There would be no dogs scratching by his fire that night and no infants screaming nearby. There was only stillness and peace—the pure, breathless silence of the moon and stars that never make a sound. Before long he was asleep with his bow and quiver of arrows beside him.

During the night he woke up shivering to find a dark pile of smoking coals where the fire had been. He struggled to add more small sticks to the coals without getting out of his warm shelter and blew on them until flames reappeared. When the fire was going again he threw thicker branches into the flames and wrapped himself tightly in his robe. Still feeling a chill, he moved closer to the fire and stayed there until the sky began to turn gray in the east.

There is a special kind of hunger that comes in the hour before sunrise, when the sky is dull and cold and the ghostly shapes of the night are beginning to turn into trees again. Willow added more wood to the fire to camouflage the sickly hue of the pre-dawn light, and before long the emerging trees were bathed in a dancing yellow glow, making him feel safe and warm inside. He turned over and fell asleep again, trying to forget his hunger.

When he awoke the sun was shining brightly above the trees, directly into his lean-to. Almost blinded by the light, he crept out of his shelter in his bear robe and stood facing the warm rays. The fire had burned down again, but he didn't need it anymore. It was time to move on. Grabbing his clay pot, fire pouch, bow and quiver from the lean-to, he headed north again through the trees.

He hadn't gone far when he noticed prints in the snow the size of his hands. At first he thought they were bear prints, but when he looked more closely, he saw they belonged to a wolf—with the back paws stepping where the front paws had been. A large male wolf had been near the lean-to. Willow took his knife from his fire pouch and followed the tracks into the woods, where the wide prints joined with the tracks of a female wolf and young pups. Altogether he counted six sets of tracks. All but the large wolf had stayed in the woods during the night.

Willow was alarmed by the fact that he hadn't heard a sound while he slept. Good hunters can *feel* danger approaching. He left the wolf tracks and kept heading north, walking on the ice of a narrow stream until he reached some low hills covered with giant maples and oaks. There he found a clearing beside the water—a perfect place to make his camp. Working slowly, he cut saplings to build a frame and covered it with bark to make a small hut overlooking the clearing. On the south side, he made an opening to allow the warmth of the sun to pour in. It could be closed at night by placing a large sheet of bark across it. In the centre of the hut he built a small fire and lined the floor with a thick carpet of cedar boughs. As the sun was setting he gathered dry wood and brought it inside where he knew he would be safe and warm.

By the time the sun was below the horizon, his new home was complete and it was time to rest. He covered the opening with bark and sat inside by the fire—hungry and tired, but warm.

He began to think that the fasting had heightened his senses. He could see the faint light of the moon through the smoke hole in the roof and smell the fragrant scent of cedar. He even thought he could hear an owl in the distance, silently swooping down on its prey, but that's when he realized he must be imagining things. Soon the hunger pangs would fade, as they had many times before when he had gone without food, and then he would forget about eating. Instead, he could think about being alone and stare at the stars in the endless open sky.

The wolves began to howl after sunset. Willow could hear their voices coming from every direction. Some were low and sombre, while others were high and playful. Long drones echoing through the hills were interrupted by short yelps. As the night passed he could clearly make out the different wolf voices. Trying to fall asleep, he remembered that the sound of wolves at night had always made his bones feel cold, no matter how much wood he put on the fire.

In the morning Willow sat by the opening of his hut until he was warm. Then he wandered aimlessly through the forests and across the frozen streams in search of something. He wasn't sure what he was looking for, but he had felt emptiness inside since his grandfather's final words. Perhaps he would encounter a spirit to guide him, the way other warriors had found divine powers to watch over and protect them through life. He had listened to the elders describe their invisible guardians many times and had heard warriors calling to them before battles.

Every evening he gathered armfuls of dead branches from the forest and filled his hut with firewood for the long night. Most nights he could hear the sound of the wolves in the distance, but he also began to hear other strange sounds. One night he heard footsteps outside his hut—but saw no tracks in the morning. His thoughts were becoming sharper and more vivid from lack of food, though he knew it was taking him longer to gather wood and build the fire each night.

The noises always started in the darkest part of the night, when the air was still and the moon had sunk below the horizon. One night a thin crust of icy snow covered the ground and again Willow thought he could hear the crunch of footsteps near his hut. He pulled the bark covering from the opening and looked outside, but could see nothing in the darkness. He grabbed a burning branch from the fire and threw it outside. Flames sputtered as it spiralled through the darkness and landed on the snow in a burst of sparks that lit up the night, illuminating dark forms skulking into the darkness.

He threw more wood on the fire to keep the flames high and punctured the bark covering of his hut, so the flames could be seen from the outside. No animal would come into an enclosed space where there was a fire—though an enemy warrior wouldn't hesitate. The spirits would come in whether there was a fire or not.

Willow remembered what Toothless Hunter had said to him before he left.

"What did he mean?" he wondered. "Who comes at night? What do they want?"

The night passed slowly, with sounds of scuffing in the icy snow outside his hut. Willow didn't sleep, despite his exhaustion. He kept the fire going until the first signs of light appeared through the holes in the bark. When he looked out the shadowy forms had vanished, and he soon fell asleep by the fire.

Late in the day he woke up to the sound of rain falling on the bark roof. He crawled out of the opening to find the ground covered with slush where the thin snow had been. At the edge of the nearby stream, he saw soggy snow drifts collapsing under their own weight into the water.

Willow walked through the rain with his robe wrapped around him, trying not to notice the stench of wet bearskin. He was becoming weak from hunger and faint from lack of sleep. Out of nowhere, he could hear the sound of footsteps behind him. He turned around quickly to see the tip of a gray tail disappear behind a bush, a stone's throw away.

– CHAPTER FORTY-SIX –

The Warm Breath of a Wolf

Willow grabbed an arrow from his quiver and slipped it on the string of his bow—all the time trying to hold his robe around him. Then, with bow in hand, he backed away from the fleeting tail and followed a nearby stream. The rain had been falling for most of the day and the frozen stream was swollen with slushy brown water rushing over chunks of ice, cutting into the banks.

By now the gut bowstring was soggy and loose from the rain. If he had to shoot at a predator, or the enemy, his arrow would just bounce off—if it could reach its target. How he wished he had Old Chief's bow, with a string made from the neck skin of a snapping turtle. That stayed taut even if it fell into the water.

Willow turned around often to see if there was anything following him, because his senses told him that eyes were watching him. He doubled back in a circle deep into the woods and then returned to the stream where he had seen the gray tail. There, on the wet ground, he saw the tracks of a small wolf following his footprints. With a cautious eye on his own tracks, he walked on along the high mud banks overlooking the rushing stream, as the rain came down in torrents and the water continued to creep up the steep sides.

A loud crash behind him caused Willow to drop to his knees on the wet ground. He turned to see the walls of the stream not far

— *Enemy Arrows* —

away tumble into the rushing water and oily mud—just as the edge he was crouching on lurched and then collapsed into the muck. He rolled away in time to save himself and looked behind him for predators, but saw nothing—and no longer felt eyes on his back.

He backtracked to see the destruction caused by the collapse. Mud and broken branches had spread across the water. Staring at the debris on the ice, he noticed a wisp of gray fur. Beneath him on the edge of the bank was a young wolf hanging by one paw, limp and still. It had been caught when the earth beneath its feet gave way and its paw was now wedged between two roots protruding from the mud. There was blood dripping on the ice, not far from the swelling water.

Willow crept closer to see if the wolf was alive. Its paw was badly injured and there were gashes in its leg where the desperate animal had tried to free itself by gnawing the leg off. But it hadn't lived long enough to escape on three legs.

The rain came down harder than ever as the exhausted young man stood beside the water, wondering about the wolf. It may have been stalking him. Perhaps if the earth had not collapsed under its feet, he would now be in its jaws. Then Willow had an idea. Though the wolf was small, it had a thick coat that would make a good robe, if it was properly skinned. He decided to cut off the trapped leg, drag the body to a flat spot and skin it before heading back to his hut.

As Willow leaned over the swirling water, about to cut the leg off with his knife, he realized that it would be easier to cut through the roots to free the carcass instead of the bone. He reached down, grabbed the wolf's free leg, and sliced at the closest root until it broke. When the injured leg was free he hauled the limp, bloody body up the slope and dropped it in the slush.

This would be the first wolf Willow had skinned by himself, but he knew what to do. He lifted the wolf's neck to cut its throat and bleed it, but hesitated with his knife in position to admire its strong, sharp teeth—those of a wolf in its first winter.

As his mind wandered in the fog of fasting, thinking about the wolf's short life, he saw one of its eyes open and roll back in its head before closing again. In a reflex action he dropped the animal on the ground and stood back.

The young hunter wasn't sure what to do. Had he actually seen the eye rolling, or was the lack of food making him imagine things? He bent down again, held the wolf's head in his hands and shouted, but it didn't respond. Then he clapped his hands above the wolf's ears. Still it didn't move. So he picked up his knife and separated the fur on the wolf's neck, but once again the eye moved—and the other one opened.

Both eyes wandered around in the wolf's head and came to a stop, fixed on his own eyes. The young creature's upper lip pulled back to show its teeth as it made a feeble growling noise from the back of its throat. Then its eyes rolled back in its head and the eyelids closed.

Rain continued to fall from the low, gray clouds as the light began to fade. It was time to get back to the hut. Willow lifted the wolf from the wet ground and threw it over his shoulders. The head and forelegs dangled down one side of his drenched bear robe and the back legs and tail hung down the other. He picked up his bow and quiver and set off toward camp.

The place was just as he had left it, with no new tracks visible. Willow pulled the bark away from the opening and dragged the limp wolf inside. It lay still on the ground beside the dwindling woodpile. He made a small fire and went to gather more wood for the night. Most of the snow had been washed away by the rain and the wood on the forest floor was too wet to use, so he broke dead branches from the trees and carried them back to his pile.

Inside, the wolf lay motionless where he had dropped it—oblivious to the fire. Throughout the night, Willow checked it by putting a smoking twig next to its nostrils, and saw that it was breathing enough to make the smoke swirl in rhythmic patterns.

— *Enemy Arrows* —

Willow lifted the wolf from the wet ground and threw it over his shoulder.

Willow didn't hear any howling that night. He sat by the fire watching the limp animal and the chills of the day disappeared. After piling more branches on the fire, he slept undisturbed for most of

— The Warm Breath of a Wolf —

the night. Once, when he woke up to add more wood to the fire, he thought he saw the wolf's wounded leg twitch in the dim light, but he fell back to sleep. The young animal's eyes were still closed and Willow hoped it was too weak to attack him.

In the dreary morning light the wolf was still lying where Willow had placed it and its wounded leg continued to twitch. Willow cleaned the blood from a gash on its head and then dribbled water into its open mouth. The animal licked its lips and swallowed the water without opening its eyes.

For two days the wolf lay still while Willow gave it water and cared for it. As he watched the wolf in his hut, he was overcome by confused thoughts about the meaning of the events which caused him to have a fierce animal *inside* his shelter. His hut was built to keep dangerous animals *away*—but now it was home to a ferocious predator. When he slept his dreams were filled with visions of himself walking among a pack of wolves while they circled him, round and round until his head spun and he fell to the ground from dizziness. Still the wolves circled.

On the third day, the young predator opened its eyes for an instant before they rolled back into its head. Its injured leg continued to twitch. Willow sat by the fire until he couldn't stay awake any longer. He knew he had become weak from hunger and cold. His thoughts were jumbled and his body cried out for food. By this time his dreams strayed into his waking thoughts. One became the other. He thought of his village and the warmth of the longhouse, the winter feasts and the taste of maple sugar.

Somewhere between his dreams and his thoughts, Willow pictured himself walking through the gate of his village, where his young sister ran to him and threw her arms around him. The rest of his family and friends gathered beside him, offering him warm soup and deer meat. Most of all they gave him the warmth of their company. There he lay by the fire, listening to the familiar sounds of the longhouse that he missed so much.

The rain stopped during the night and faded into a freezing drizzle as the cold weather returned. In the morning Willow crept

— *Enemy Arrows* —

out of his hut and found an icy world. Everything that had been wet before nightfall had frozen before sunrise. Icy branches crackled and clattered as a light breeze blew through the hard-coated trees. The ground was frozen again.

The sun rose bright and clear, its brilliant light scattering among the ice-covered branches.

Willow sat facing the sun on a log in front of his hut, thinking about his beloved village on Thunder River. He thought about his family and his close friends, Otter and Loon. Most of all he wondered what would happen to him when it was time to do all of the things his father had done. Would he be brave in battle like his father, travelling long distances to destroy enemy villages? Would he be able to defend his own village when it was being attacked? What would happen if he was injured in battle and couldn't hunt? What if he was captured?

Painful thoughts churned inside him. Would *he* allow himself to be adopted if he was captured? Would he become one of the enemy—one of the people who attack and burn his own people's villages? No, he would never be a traitor! Once again, Willow grew angry thinking of what Oriole had said to him. He would fight to his last breath—and he knew his father would have done the same.

Willow picked up a rock and threw it against a birch tree, leaving a deep gash in the bark. He faced the sun with closed eyes and felt its warmth on his face. This time his thoughts wandered to the People of the Lakes and the kindness he had experienced among them. He wanted to travel to the north again. Perhaps he could stay for a winter and hunt with them. He wondered if he could be an envoy of his people again. Would he be known and respected by people from faraway lands? Would he be seen as a wise man when he was old? Would people come to him for advice, the way they had flocked to Old Chief?

He wanted to be known as a generous man, able to take care of people who could not provide for themselves. Would he be that kind of person? His thoughts ran wild like fire through a dry forest, but he felt he wasn't ready to make any decisions yet. Now, he wanted to hunt with his close friends—to do what he loved most. These other thoughts were too difficult. It was so much easier just to be free with Otter and Loon.

His mother had told him that he would probably live apart from his friends. They would scatter like seeds when they found wives, as his father had done. They might each go to different villages to be with their wives' clans—but that wasn't what Willow wanted. He might find a wife after many years had passed, but she would have to be from his own village. Why should he have to go away? There were strong, beautiful young women in his own village.

But Willow's thoughts were interrupted when he had the cold feeling of being stalked. When he opened his eyes he saw the largest gray wolf in the forest—with its eyes fixed firmly on him. It was close enough to leap on him in one bound. With piercing yellow eyes surrounding vacant black dots, it stared through him, as though he were a thin sheet of ice.

He froze, unable to move even if he had wanted. From the corners of his eyes, he could see dark shapes prowling through the trees, close to the ground.

The giant wolf snarled in a way that caused the trees to shake. Willow could see its enormous teeth and knew that a wolf that size could crush his skull in one bite. Then, moving silently, several other wolves came out from behind the trees and stood behind the giant. Still the young hunter didn't move.

A gray female began to howl directly behind him. It was the high, piercing sound he recognized from so many nights ago. All of the other wolves joined the howling at once and the sounds echoed through the cold air and resonated throughout the forest. The leader stood silent and rigid as the others wailed around it, and Willow knew it had come to hunt him. He felt like a rabbit staring at an arrow hurtling toward him, although dying quickly from an arrow would be far better than being crushed by those hideous teeth and ripped apart by a pack of hungry wolves.

– CHAPTER FORTY-SEVEN –

A Message to Heed

Then the giant animal moved toward him in slow, measured steps. Still Willow couldn't move. When it was beside him it threw its huge head back and released a howl that would frighten the dead. Willow could feel the beast's warm breath on his face and the force of its voice vibrating through his chest like the skin of a drum. The other wolves howled behind it, but their calls were lost in its deafening wail.

With Willow immobilized by fear, the gray monster moved past him and pushed its enormous body against the side of the hut until it lurched and toppled over. The young wolf lay in the open beside the remains of a fire—its head raised and its tail beating weakly on the ground. With its sharp teeth the beast carefully grasped the young wolf by the fur on the back of its neck and lifted it to its feet. It wobbled on three legs, holding its injured paw above the ground, then slowly hopped toward Willow on three legs. As it passed him, sitting on the log like a frozen frog, it turned its head to him, curled up its lip to show its teeth and growled from the back of its throat. Then it limped into the forest with the other wolves.

Willow turned around to see the huge gray beast with its leg cocked, peeing against the remains of his hut. The stench of warm urine spread through the air, as the great wolf scuffed the ground

— A Message to Heed —

with its back paws, throwing massive clumps of wet earth on the ruined hut. Then it let out another deathly howl and loped silently into the forest.

For two cold days and one miserable night Willow followed the stream to the river and then finally to his village. His strength had given out. When he approached his home he saw three women gathering sap from the sweet maple trees. After calling to them in a weak voice he collapsed on his face in the mud. Instead of enjoying the triumphant return he had imagined, he was carried through the village gate by the three women and several young boys.

In the darkest part of the night he woke up beside the fire. His mother sat next to him on a bearskin.

"I didn't think I'd see you again," Orchid said, trying to hide the anguish in her voice. When she saw him raise his head slightly, she gave him hot soup to drink. He had a few swallows and went back to sleep.

For two full days Willow lay beside the fire recovering his strength. Otter and Loon came to see him, but he didn't want to talk. He sat glumly staring into the flames, refusing to say anything about his time alone.

"Leave him for a while," Orchid said to his friends. "He'll talk when he's strong."

On the third morning Willow opened his eyes to see Moose sitting by the fire with a hot bowl of soup in his enormous hands. He passed it to Willow and held his head forward so he could drink.

"You left suddenly," he said.

"I had to go," replied Willow.

"I know," said Moose. "I've felt that too. I see you made it home without any tooth marks on your body," he continued. "You did better than I did." He showed Willow the scar on his leg where he had been bitten by a bobcat when he spent time alone. Willow listened, but he didn't want to talk. Moose told him the story of the bobcat and how he had met his guardian spirit.

"Tell me," said the Moose in a low voice. "Did you see your spirit?"

Willow looked into his eyes and shuddered uncontrollably. "An enormous wolf with yellow eyes came to me. It was as close to me as you are now and it howled so loudly—so horribly—that I couldn't move. I could feel its breath on my face. If it had something to tell me, I don't know what it was. I was too terrified to hear any message."

"Tell me what you saw and heard," said Moose.

"I saw snow and rain. I felt hunger and cold and exhaustion. I heard wolves howling all night. I looked for my spirit, but I didn't see it." He turned his eyes back to the fire.

"Where did you hear the wolves?" asked Moose.

Willow told him about the young wolf dangling on the bank of the stream and that he'd seen its eyes move when he was about to cut its throat. He described how he had kept the young wolf beside the fire and given it water. With a trembling voice he described how the giant wolf had howled in his face and knocked his hut over—and peed on it.

"It peed on your hut?" repeated Moose.

"And scuffed dirt on it too," said Willow. "Is that what guardian spirits do?"

Moose sat silently by the fire with a look of astonishment on his face, trying to make sense of the great wolf's actions. As he thought about the wolf, he removed his deerhide cloak and hung it on a loft behind him. He stirred the fire with a charred poker. In time, he spoke again to Willow.

"Sometimes their messages are hard to understand. This one is a puzzle. But it seems the wolf was speaking to you, and showing you something important."

"What was important about peeing on my hut?" asked Willow.

Moose laughed. "I'm not sure. Perhaps it was showing you how to live your life," he said thoughtfully.

Willow was mystified.

"It may have been showing you what it had learned as the chief of the wolf pack—how to lead your people and protect them from harm—and guard your territory from enemy invaders. You were in

— A Message to Heed —

his territory. He could have ripped you apart, but instead he let you live. Why would a wolf let you live?" Moose wondered aloud.

"I don't know. I cared for the young wolf. All it did was snarl at me," answered Willow.

"The giant wolf rewarded you for your generosity in caring for the weak. Perhaps it was trying to show you the difference between strength and needless violence."

Willow was speechless.

"Come with me," said Moose. He helped Willow to his feet and found a wolfskin robe for him to wear. Though he was still weak, Willow followed Moose out of the longhouse into the daylight. The young warrior stood blinking in the bright sun until he could see Otter and Loon playing stickball in the wet snow near the village gate. He didn't move or call to them.

"Some people go through life without a guardian spirit," said Moose. "Others take time to recognize their spirit and understand its message. You should take time to think about this in case the wolf had more to give you than the pee on your hut."

Willow pulled the wolfskin robe tightly around his shoulders. Without a word he shuffled across the field to join his friends. As he neared them, the Wanderer appeared from between the longhouses, followed by his daughter. They had paddles in their hands and heavy packs on their backs and were also heading toward the gate. Willow stopped where he was, slightly out of sight.

"Safe journey!" said Otter as the Wanderer passed.

"We'll see you when the leaves are red," answered the Wanderer with a wave of his paddle, as he neared the gate.

"You'll have plenty of time to practice your dancing," sang Oriole. "Maybe you'll be able to keep up with me next time!" Her eyes shone in the brilliant light of the spring morning and orange feathers fluttered around her throat.

"We're still sore from last night," joked Loon, as he collapsed in the snow.

"And if you ever see your friend again, tell him I want to talk to him," she said as she was about to leave.

"You can tell him yourself," said Otter, pointing at Willow.

Oriole whirled around like a dancer and walked toward Willow, her piercing stare immobilizing him like a bird held on its back.

"Are you still a snapping turtle?" she asked quietly.

Her voice was soft and melodic, but it had the same effect on him as the howl of the giant wolf. He looked at her, unable to speak. At the same time, he noticed the look of determination in her eyes and saw how easily her strong shoulders held her heavy pack. She had the solid stance of someone who had endured many long portages.

"Do you still hide in your shell?"

Willow didn't reply. He wanted to ask her so many questions about the message and the man she said was his father. He wanted to know how she could twist his spirit into knots by telling him something that everyone knew was false. Most of all, he thought about Turkey Vulture and the answer he would bring in the summer. But before Willow could say anything, the Wanderer's voice boomed from the other side of the palisade. Oriole yelled a few words to her father that only they could understand and then spoke quietly to Willow—so only he could hear.

"I hope you're out of your trance by the time we return in the fall. There's something you and I have to talk about—before it's too late. I think you know what it is." She took a step to leave, but stopped long enough to shift her heavy pack. "Poke your head out of your shell," she added before she turned and disappeared through the gate.

Loon and Otter raced over to Willow, who stood bewildered in the wet snow with the wolfskin wrapped around his shoulders.

"What was she saying to you?" demanded Loon.

"What was it?" echoed Otter, grabbing Willow by the shoulders.

"She's bewitched," Willow replied meekly. "She talks to the dead."

"What dead? Who?"

Again, Willow couldn't bring himself to stain his father's memory by repeating what Oriole had said. "I can't tell you."

"You *can't* tell us or you *won't* tell us?" asked Loon.

"I can't tell you . . . what's in her mind."

Otter and Loon stared at each other in disbelief and then back at Willow. With a shrug, Otter released Willow's shoulders and stood back. "We're your friends, Willow. You have to tell us what's troubling you." Otter waited patiently for him to respond. "If you can't tell us now, you can tell us when you're ready, but you have to tell us."

"When I'm ready," Willow repeated.

The three warriors stood awkwardly until Loon broke the silence by throwing his stick to Willow. "Can we play some ball until you're ready? I'm getting cold standing here."

They spent the rest of the day lobbing the ball between them. With each shot Willow could feel the thoughts of Oriole and the giant wolf fading into the depths of his memory, like fish disappearing into the darkness of the Beautiful Lake. Every leaping catch made his spirit soar once again. He was with his friends in his own village, with a stick in his hand and a ball speeding toward his head.

– CHAPTER FORTY-EIGHT –

War Mask

Once more, the seasons changed from spring to summer. The early summer sun set round and red like an enormous drop of blood above the western horizon. From their camp on the island, it appeared to be setting directly on the village at Thunder River.

Willow, Otter and Loon had been fishing in the bay between Thunder River and the River of the Dawn. They had camped for the night beside the beach on one of the outer islands, where the wind blew from the Beautiful Lake through the willows and birches. When the sun went down the breezes kept the mosquitoes away.

A large trout hung over the fire, suspended on a green stick pushed through its gills. The three friends sat nearby waiting for it to cook over the blowing flames.

"The Great Turtle is moving," said Willow. "By the next full moon the sun will be setting over Old Chief's summer-sunset tree. Then the Turtle will shift and it will begin to set closer to the lake again, little by little."

"Did you see the Turtle when you flew over the river?" asked Loon with a wide grin.

"No," laughed Willow. "I wasn't high enough."

"Then how do we know it's there?" continued Loon.

"How do we know the sun will rise in the morning?" asked Otter. "How do we know the moon will ever return?"

Willow poked a stick through the skin of the trout to see if it was cooked.

"I don't know how we know," said Loon, turning to Otter. "Tell me how you know these things."

Otter threw some more branches on the fire before he responded. "We know the sun will rise because it has always risen after the night. It's always been that way—for our ancestors and for us. The moon always follows the same pattern, too. We've seen it all our lives. I don't know where the sun and the moon go when we can't see them, but I know they'll return. " He looked at Loon patiently.

"The Great Turtle has always been there," Otter continued. "Everyone knows that. I can't see it, but I can see what it does. It changes the seasons from summer to winter and back to summer. Do you actually worry that the sun won't rise tomorrow? Are you afraid you won't live to see the sunrise?"

"No," replied Loon, with a mischievous smile on his face. "I expect to live to see the morning sun. I just like to worry you!" He leapt to his feet, as Otter lunged at him, grabbing Loon by the legs. They wrestled in the wet sand by the beach and into the shallow water. Otter pretended to push Loon's face into the water until Loon squirmed out of his grasp, gasping for air and laughing—once he had enough air to make a sound. With the sparring over, he threw himself down by the fire, dripping on the dry sand. Otter emerged from the lake with a threatening, bloated face and spat a mouthful of water at Loon.

"You're like a toad—spitting at your enemy!" yelped Loon, throwing a handful of sand at Otter.

"This fish is ready," said Willow, lifting the steaming trout from the fire and placing it carefully on a piece of driftwood. "Fill your stomachs!" He carefully split the fish in two parts, starting at the back fins, and then stripped out the spine and ribs. They devoured the delicate flesh while they lay on the beach, gazing up at the low clouds drifting across the darkening sky.

"If you two feel like fighting, you should paddle across the lake to the enemy," said Willow. "There won't be a moon tonight. You could bring back some prisoners."

"Will you do that with me, Otter?" said Loon, holding his friend's arm. "You're not afraid are you?"

"No, I'm not afraid," replied Otter. "But I don't want to die yet. If we go alone we'll be killed."

"Then we'll go on the next raid with the other warriors," said Loon.

"Yes!" yelled Otter.

"We'll burn their villages!' cried Loon.

The thick blanket of clouds drifted across the lake, turning dusk into darkness without the moon or stars to light the way. Beyond the circle of light from the fire, nothing could be seen. While Willow slept, Otter and Loon talked into the night about the battles they would have with the enemy when they finally joined a raiding party. After they had exhausted themselves with their imaginary battles, Otter put another branch on the flames and they fell asleep.

The fire had burned down to a few luminous coals when four ghostly figures appeared from the darkness. They stood beside the dying fire, looking down at the three motionless shapes. One of the figures signalled to the three others and they drew their knives from their sheaths. Slowly they moved across the sand toward the sleeping bodies with their weapons held out in front of them. Silently they crouched, each one putting a cold stone blade near the neck of a victim. The other figure threw a branch on the fire and sparks lit up the sky. That was the signal.

As the young warriors sprang upright, the invaders grabbed them by the hair and screamed horrifying noises into their ears. The three struggled at first, but with sharp knives digging into their necks they soon realized they were overpowered. They knew it was better to submit—with a chance of escaping later—than to fight and meet certain death. It was over quickly.

The invaders turned them on their chests with their faces in the sand and lashed their arms behind their backs, before hauling them by their hair to three trees standing close together, where they were tied firmly. By this time the fire was burning high again, lighting up the beach and the strangers.

Out of the darkness emerged several canoes filled with enemy warriors who leapt on to the beach and went over to inspect the captives. Some spat on them. Others jabbed at them with knives, inflicting cuts on their shoulders and chests. One slit Otter's broad chest from his collarbone to a nipple, leaving blood trickling from the wound like sap from a gouged pine tree.

A large man with several war feathers in his hair moved close to Otter. Above his loincloth he wore a protective jacket made of split cedar strips and his face was painted in a hideous mask of death. Otter had never seen anything as terrifying as this enemy warrior with his battle dress and war paint. The warrior waved the others away with a slight movement of his arm and he pressed his face close to Otter.

"What village are you from?" he asked. Otter could barely understand the language he spoke. The warrior's voice was distant, as though he was speaking inside a cave. Otter looked away and spat at the ground. The warrior yelled an insult at him and pierced the skin on his chest with a knife. Otter recoiled with shock, but showed no sign of pain.

"You are a brave boy. You will die bravely."

He moved over to Willow and held his knife against his neck.

"Tell me what village you are from—or you will die with your friend."

Willow kept silent. The warrior pressed his knife against Willow's neck.

"We are from the village on the River of the Dawn," blurted Loon in an attempt to mislead them. He tried to look brave, but his body quivered like a moth with singed wings. "The river is at the end of the bay." He jerked his head in the direction of the river.

"Yes," said the enemy warrior. "That makes things easier. We are going to destroy your village." He moved back to Willow and studied his face in the light of the fire.

"I've seen you before," the warrior said. Willow shook his head. "I know your face." The warrior moved around Willow to look at him from all angles. "How do I know your face, if I've never seen you?"

"Some people say I look like a dog," said Willow.

The warrior smirked. "And you do. We'll see if you're as a brave as a dog."

The warrior rejoined the others and spoke to them in a hushed voice. They moved toward the beach where they continued to speak. A tall man with black and red paint on his face drew a map in the sand by the light of the fire and they all squatted down to poke at the lines and have their say. The captives couldn't hear them—and they could not be heard.

"If I escape, I'll kill a few of these fiends before they get me," said Loon.

"No," said Willow. "We don't want to see that."

"The first one to escape must run and warn the village on the River of the Dawn," said Otter, his blood congealing on his chest. "If they're warned they can defend themselves."

"Then they'll send a runner to our village," said Loon. "Our warriors will rush over and destroy these wicked dogs."

The enemy warriors looked over at them. The largest one lumbered over and spoke to Willow again.

"Your village will be burned to the ground tomorrow," he said with a frightening leer. "Some of your people will die and the ones who get away will starve in the winter. We will avenge your merciless attacks on our people and answer your cruelty with even greater cruelty." He moved behind each of them to tighten their ropes and then joined the others beside the fire.

As the night dragged on, Willow pulled and pushed at the ropes around his wrists and felt them getting looser as he worked them. He watched the warriors beside the fire, and they watched him. Over the rustling sound of the ropes that bound him, he could hear Otter and Loon struggling to loosen their knots.

With the twang of a bow spring, Willow's ropes came apart in his hands. He raced to Otter and tried to undo his ropes, but they were too tight. He was about to leap past him to untie Loon's ropes when one of the warriors shouted at him and jumped to his feet. Willow ran into the darkness, feeling his way through the trees with the sound of enemy warriors chasing after him, yelling loudly and breaking branches as they searched for him.

Without a sound he moved through the trees and across the island toward the bay where their old canoe was pulled up on the beach. He found the white bark of the canoe in the darkness and groped in the sand until he found a stick to use as a paddle. With one strong step, he launched the canoe and paddled silently into the black void.

In the distance he could hear the shouts of the enemy warriors who searched for him on the island. He couldn't see anyone pursuing him in the darkness across the bay and didn't hear the sound of any other paddle. Slowly the sounds of his pursuers faded into the distance. When he reached the far side of the bay he slipped quietly out of the water and ran along the marshy shore to find the trail leading north. He stopped and stood silently, listening for the sound of footsteps. He heard nothing but the sound of his own breathing and the pounding in his chest.

Only a few stars were visible through the scattered clouds. Willow knew the narrow trail leading north, where it crossed the trail between Thunder River and the River of the Dawn, close to the place where he had been shot at with an enemy arrow. As he ran he thought he heard footsteps following him. When he stopped to listen, the footsteps stopped. The forest was silent, but each time he moved he heard the sound of something behind him. He cut into the woods to throw the pursuer off of his tracks and again the footsteps followed him through the trees. Willow knew almost every part of the forest, but his pursuer seemed to know it as well as he did. He wasn't sure if there was a person or an animal chasing him, but he was certain there was something.

With his body trembling from fear, he went back to the trail and followed it toward the one between the two villages. There he stopped behind a large pine tree and waited in the darkness for his pursuer to pass, holding a rock the size of his fist to bring down upon the creature when it passed. He waited. There wasn't a sound.

He could hear the flutter of bats' wings as they swooped past him, and the sound of peepers in the wetlands, but no footsteps. Alone in the darkness, he wondered whether his pursuer had lost him in the dark, but as he stepped back onto the trail he was grabbed by the neck and forced to the ground. Once again, he felt the cold edge of a stone knife at his neck.

"Don't struggle," said a voice in the darkness. "I don't want to hurt you."

Willow recognized traces of the accent of the People from Across the Lake. "Who are you?" he cried.

"Listen to me carefully," said the voice. "You've been tricked by the warriors from across the lake. You are going to warn the wrong village."

"I'm going to warn them—even if I have to kill you on the way!" shouted Willow, struggling to free himself.

"You're not in a position to make threats," said the voice. "Stop struggling and listen to me. I don't want to use this knife on you."

He jabbed Willow on the shoulder, leaving a narrow gash, and Willow stopped struggling.

"The warrior tightened your friends' ropes, but he loosened yours. He and the others *wanted* you to escape—so you would run to the River of the Dawn and warn them of an attack. They knew those people would send a runner to the village on Thunder River for help. Most of all, they wanted the warriors from Thunder River to leave their village and race to the River of the Dawn."

"And we will defeat your people!' yelled Willow defiantly.

"Defeat my people," repeated the voice sadly. "My people. We are all the same people. We defeat ourselves with this shameless killing."

Willow found these to be strange words from an invading warrior.

"Listen to me," said the voice firmly. "The attack will be on the village at Thunder River, not the River of the Dawn. You must understand. They will attack when the warriors have gone to help the other village—lured away to fight a battle that will never take place. You can't let that happen!" he said emphatically.

"You must go to Thunder River and warn them of the attack," continued the voice. "I will let you go, but you must warn them."

"You're trying to trick me now," said Willow forcefully. "You want me to go to Thunder River and warn the wrong people. You want them to send a runner to the River of the Dawn for help, and when their warriors have left, you'll attack. I heard your chief say he would destroy the village on the River of the Dawn. I won't help you with your twisted plan."

"I don't want to see any village destroyed," said the voice firmly. "This madness has to stop."

"Why should I believe your talk of peace?" Willow asked. "You're an enemy warrior holding a knife to my neck."

The voice was silent. The knife still pressed against Willow's neck and a strong hand held him down. In the dim light, Willow searched the forest floor for the rock that dropped from his hand when he was ambushed. He didn't move and his captor kept him still. Far in the distance, Willow heard a wolf howling at the coming dawn. It was the sound of the giant gray wolf that he knew too well.

As suddenly as the knife had been pressed against his neck, it was released. Then the hand that held him relaxed its grip. As he raised himself to his feet, Willow grabbed the rock. He turned around to face the enemy in the bleak light of dawn and hurled the rock, striking the man in the eye. It was a blow that sent his enemy staggering backward. He fell against a pine tree before collapsing in a bed of needles, with blood gushing from his wound. As he lay stunned by the impact, Willow lunged at him, wrenched the knife from his clenched fingers and held it firmly against the man's blood-splattered neck. He looked at the deep gash above the man's eye. His eye had disappeared. It looked as though it had been knocked out of his head.

The injured man opened his good eye to see Willow. He felt the knife against his neck. His good eye rolled back like the eye of the young wolf. He blinked and shook his head, as a man between wake and sleep.

"You're a fighter," said the man, raising his hand toward his eye. Willow jabbed him with the knife. He lowered his arm.

"And you are a prisoner," said Willow.

"You must warn my people of the attack," said the man.

"Warn *my* people?" cried Willow. "Your people are attacking my people!"

"They were my people once," said the man. "The village on Thunder River was my village—long ago. I had a wife and a daughter and a son. You must warn them."

Willow looked at the man in the faint light. He had a scar on his back and a tattoo on his chest in the shape of a running deer. His eye was badly injured and scarred beneath the fresh wound.

His heart pounded in his chest and his hands began to shake uncontrollably. In that instant his worst fears were realized. Oriole's lies were true. His father was a traitor.

"Then you are Gray Fox," he said without showing any trace of emotion.

"I was Gray Fox . . . in another life," he answered. "Now, I'm called Muskrat."

"Muskrat," repeated Willow despondently. "Then you are a traitor—and I am the son of a traitor."

"The son of a trait . . .?" he stammered. "You are my son? Willow?" Muskrat turned to look at him, but Willow held him firmly with a knife against his throat.

"Let me look at my son," he begged, but Willow refused to release his grip.

"I was your son . . . before you went to live with the enemy . . . before you became a traitor."

"No, Willow. I'm not a traitor," pleaded Muskrat. Blood oozed from the wound in his eye. "I'm a man who was adopted instead of being tortured to death. You must understand what I have endured—so I could see my people again."

"My mother grieved for you," replied Willow. "She still grieves for you."

"I tried to send you a message, Willow. You must believe me."

"I don't believe you. You betrayed your own people."

"I could never betray my people," he protested.

"You're betraying your own people now—telling me their battle plans."

Muskrat looked at the ground. A look of anguish came over his bloody face and his body convulsed. "I don't want to see any more bloodshed," he said. "Go and warn our people of the attack or they'll be killed. The next time we meet, it will be as friends."

"We won't meet as friends," said Willow, getting to his feet. "You're my enemy and my prisoner. If I could, I'd take you back to my village as my prisoner. Maybe someone would adopt you—or you'd be tortured to death as a traitor. I don't know. But I can't drag you along with me. I have to warn the village where your evil chief is going to attack."

"This is not how I wanted to greet you, Willow," cried Muskrat, holding his head in his blood-covered hands. "Not with weapons aimed at each other. Not this way." He moaned like a wounded moose and fell backward into the leaves.

Willow turned in the dim light and headed north. His father called to him, but Willow couldn't hear what he said. He stopped in the silent forest, listening to his own breathing and to the mournful sounds coming from Muskrat. Once again, he could feel the giant wolf's warm breath on his face.

He raced through the forest along the trail he knew so well, as though he had wings. Before the sun had risen he reached the main trail between the two villages. In one direction was the River of the Dawn. In the opposite direction was Thunder River. He knew that on one river or the other an enemy war party would soon be slicing through the water in elm canoes, closing in on its target.

– CHAPTER FORTY-NINE –

The Silent Muskrat

The enemy warriors left the islands shortly after dawn, leaving Otter and Loon with blood flowing from their wounds and their hands tied to trees behind their backs. With their faces painted in frightening images, the attackers made their way along the sand beaches of the islands and across the bay to the mouth of the Thunder River, where several canoes were already pulled up on the eastern shore. As the sun climbed in the sky they hauled their own canoes onto the beach and smashed all the birch canoes to prevent their enemy from chasing them. Then, with the morning sun sparkling on the waters of the Beautiful Lake behind them, they followed the ridge north toward the village.

As the enemy neared the village on Thunder River, their War Chief looked for signs of movement along the shore. If his plan had worked, Willow had made his way to the River of the Dawn to warn of the impending attack and a runner had been sent to the village on Thunder River for help. By now, the warriors from Thunder River were running through the forest to fight a battle at the River of the Dawn—a battle that would never take place—and the rest of the people in the Thunder River village would have retreated behind the palisade, protected only by old men and women with weapons.

The Silent Muskrat

First the invaders would burn down the palisade and then they would destroy the village. The enemy War Chief saw no signs of movement on the river and he told his warriors that the plan had worked. The war party approached the village from the trail overlooking the river. Trees opened onto broad cornfields stretching into the distance, and on the far side of the cornfields the warriors could see the village palisade. No one was in the fields. The enemy warriors put arrows in their bows and ran toward the main gate of the palisade to attack.

From a platform at the top of the palisade Moose, the War Chief, looked through the slats in the walls, watching the enemy invaders rush toward the village. His face was streaked with soot and he was armed with a bow and a quiver full of arrows. A pile of rocks lay on the platform by his feet. Willow stood silently beside him among the best archers in the village. Old Heron was ready with an arrow in her bow and several more in the hands of Wren, standing beside her. They squatted silently behind the barrier. On the ground below them, young boys stood beside pots of water ready to douse fires set by the enemy.

Most of the warriors waited inside the village walls at the winding entrance to the village. Brown Bat and others held long, sharp poles ready to ram through the slats in the entrance walls at any enemy warrior who tried to rush through. From where he stood, Brown Bat could see flashes of light and colour through the gaps in the palisade as the enemy charged, and he heard the familiar war cries he had learned as a child.

Lynx and other warriors stood at the entrance, ready to pursue the enemy in retreat. Everyone remained silent, waiting for the signal, as the enemy approached the village walls.

Far below on Thunder River, a blue heron waded slowly downstream through the placid waters along the shore, twisting its head slightly from side to side to locate its prey, oblivious to the surging fighters on the plateau above. When it spotted a minnow swimming upstream, it froze mid-step with one thin leg raised and then slowly, imperceptibly, lowered its leg and stood silently in a still pool of water, eyeing the minnow, watching, waiting, with its head close to the surface and its bent neck ready to lunge.

With a suddenness of a striking heron, Moose shot his head above the wall and yelled—and the village erupted in a thunderous roar from every direction. Rocks rained down from the palisade, scattering the invaders with the dull thud of stone on flesh. Arrows flew through the air from the length of the palisade wall, striking the enemy warriors as they fled in panic. As always, Old Heron's arrows hit their targets. Shouting rose in every direction throughout the palisade. From the village high above Thunder River, fierce war cries rocked the valley.

Then out through the village gate charged Lynx with the fastest warriors in pursuit of the retreating invaders. They ran until they were within range of the attackers, stopped to shoot and then were off again.

Two enemy warriors hid in a gully close to the village. They waited until Lynx and his warriors were out of range of the protective arrows from the village—and then counterattacked, leaping over the ridge and shooting a volley of arrows. When Lynx was hit in the arm he signalled to the others to continue pursuing the main group of enemy warriors. Then he dropped his bow and fled back to the village entrance with the two invaders close behind him.

As he approached the village, he was hit again by an arrow—this time in the leg. He collapsed in the field and tried desperately to push himself through the long grass toward the village with his other leg. The two enemy warriors closed in on him with their bows, ready to finish him off.

With the speed of a beating wing Brown Bat flew out from the village gate and raced toward Lynx with his knife held high above his head.

"Run!" he yelled at the enemy. "They're coming after us!"

The two enemy warriors stopped in their tracks and stared at him. From the platform high on the palisade wall, Moose watched Brown Bat running toward the enemy.

"Run!" repeated Brown Bat. "I'll finish off this filthy dog!" The words he used were not often heard in the village at Thunder River. They were the ones used by the People from Across the Lake.

Moose shouted to the warriors below and they ran out of the entrance across the field after Brown Bat. At that instant Brown Bat fell on Lynx with his knife held high above his head. His clenched fist came down on Lynx's chest, once, twice, three times until Lynx lay still. Brown Bat jumped up and ran toward the two enemy warriors in the direction of the river, flapping his arms and shouting at them to run.

"The dogs are after us!"

The two enemy warriors spun around and raced ahead of him. They disappeared over the lip of the hill and scrambled down toward the river, but the instant they were out of sight Brown Bat turned around and raced back to Lynx. The warriors from the village ran toward him with their bows ready to shoot. Brown Bat knew that treason in battle meant immediate death, so he grabbed Lynx by the arm and in one quick movement yanked him to his feet. The village warriors stopped short. Lynx was still alive and there was no blood on his chest. They aimed their arrows at Brown Bat, but they didn't shoot for fear of hitting Lynx.

"Go after the enemy!" Lynx shouted at his comrades. He leaned on Brown Bat's shoulder. "He's one of us. Go!" He waved his good arm in the direction of the river where the two warriors had gone. "Get them!" he shouted. The warriors ran past Lynx in pursuit of the enemy, over the ridge and down to the river.

"You fooled everyone," said Lynx, teetering on his good leg. Brown Bat nodded. He supported Lynx, as he hobbled back to the village, listening to the distant shouts. Lynx stopped when they reached the village gate and held on to Brown Bat's shoulder, while the barricades were removed.

"You even fooled me for the flicker of an eye," Lynx said with a trembling voice. Again Brown Bat didn't respond.

"You risked your life," said Lynx.

The village erupted in a thunderous roar from every direction.

"You would do the same for me," said Brown Bat. They wound their way through a narrow gap in the entrance to the village.

"You called me . . ." began Lynx hesitantly, "you called me . . . a filthy dog."

Brown Bat smiled and shrugged his shoulders. "You would do the same for me."

"I would, my friend," Lynx answered with a weak smile. "So I would."

Moose jumped down from the palisade and raced toward a group of his warriors. After urgent words and frantic arm-waving between them he called for the Beaver Clan to go after the enemy, taking as many canoes down the river as they could paddle, then he shouted to the rest of the warriors to pursue any straggling invaders who were heading to the lake.

The wild-eyed fighters surged forward in a crowd armed with bows, arrows and quivers to chase down the retreating warriors, screaming ferociously as they ran. Young boys, delirious with excitement, followed behind them far in the distance to watch the battle, shaking pointed sticks in the direction of the retreating enemy and yelling in high-pitched voices.

Joining the others, Willow raced beside Moose, trying desperately to keep up with his long strides. Willow watched him closely, following every movement. Never had he seen Moose run so quickly—with such an intense look in his eyes.

This was the battle Willow had been preparing for since he was a child, and his senses were in a heightened state of alertness. The skills he had learned playing stickball came to him in a vibrant rush. He could read the slightest movements of the warriors flying beside him, turning and rolling together like a flock of sparrows, without words or signals. He felt wings on his feet as he pursued the enemy, and could see the battle spread out before him, as though he were looking down from the sky. He sped through the fields and woods beside Moose, clinging to him like a shadow.

The shock of the unexpected onslaught left the enemy warriors in disarray. They fled down the trail to the Beautiful Lake toward their waiting canoes while Moose and the others shouted loudly and showered them with arrows, causing them to trample one

— *Enemy Arrows* —

another. Dogs barked madly at them, nipping at their legs and tripping them as they tried to escape. Dead and wounded fell on the trail or rolled down the cliff into the river below.

Leading the retreat was the large man wearing a protective jacket and feathers in his hair. When he turned around in terror to see Moose and the approaching warriors, Willow saw the same hideous mask he had seen on the island. Once again he heard the man's cruel, threatening voice: "You are a brave boy. You'll die bravely." Willow's stomach twisted in knots as he recalled the horror of being a prisoner, and he wondered in the confusion of the battle what the man in the mask had done to Otter and Loon.

When the enemy warriors reached the mouth of Thunder River where they had left their canoes, they found some had been punctured by the hail of arrows and others had been destroyed by guards hidden in the woods beside the river. A few shattered wrecks of canoes with broken ribs and loose wings of elm bark flapping in the breeze drifted over the water like wounded geese amid the ripping sounds of arrows plunging into the lake.

Enemy warriors who tried to escape along the shore were intercepted by archers and forced back along the beach, trapped on the shore like deer at the edge of a cliff—unable to go forward or back. In desperation, they formed a small knot and held their ground on the sand, shooting back as many arrows as they could.

Moose signalled for their warriors to stop the chase just out of range of the enemy arrows. They spread out in a curve, surrounding the invaders, and prepared for a final attack.

"Stay behind me!" Moose shouted to Willow, as the enemy arrows fell nearby. The War Chief stood up to shoot and his arrow was followed by a barrage that rained down upon the cringing enemy. By this time, the fleeing warriors had run out of arrows, apart from those that fell from the sky. As Moose moved closer, they ran in panic into the lake, crowding into the few remaining canoes, overloading them almost to the point of capsizing.

When the huge man with the protective jacket tried to climb into an overcrowded canoe, he fell back into the waist-deep water and disappeared beneath the surface. The warriors in the canoe tried frantically to escape. Those with paddles tried to use them in the crush of bodies. Others pulled at the water with their bare hands.

The large man emerged from the water and lunged after an escaping canoe. As his friends tried to pull him into the overcrowded canoe without flipping it over, the man was struck with an arrow in the side of the neck. Blood gushed from the wound in quick rhythmic spurts into the churning water. When he turned to face his pursuers, a look of terror shone though his war mask. It was the look of a man who knew his plans had failed and he had reached the end. He staggered toward the shore, holding his neck in a futile attempt to stop the bleeding, screaming like a wounded wolverine until he fell face down into the shallow water.

Down the river raced the Beaver Clan with a swarm of canoes ready to pursue the enemy across the Beautiful Lake. They stopped at the beach long enough for their own warriors to leap into the boats before racing after the escaping warriors. With only a few men in each canoe, they would soon able to catch the overloaded canoes.

A crowd formed at the beach where Thunder River emptied into the Beautiful Lake, yelling at the fleeing invaders. Willow quietly moved away from the others, as painful memories began to flood over him—of his capture, his escape through the forest, and his agonizing meeting with Gray Fox. It was not the way he had wanted to meet his father again—if he had been alive.

He was also overcome by the lingering screams, the smell of sweat and blood, the taste of fear in the air, and the raw brutality of his first battle. This was nothing like stickball after all. It was a dizzying blur of sound and movement where the only goal was to kill or be killed. With the sudden pain coursing through his veins, he fell on his knees and retched violently in the sand, lost to the battle around him.

With the canoes disappearing into the distance, the yelling from shore began to fade and before long the beach was silent again, except for the sounds of redwing black birds. A group of warriors from the Deer Clan captured the wounded and took them back to the village. Another group from the Bear Clan set off to find Otter and Loon on the islands.

Orchid was distraught at Willow's news that her husband was alive. His reappearance from the dead threw her into a state of despair, but she demanded to be taken to the place where her son had left him. Moose and Willow went with her, escorted by eight warriors fresh from the battle, eager to fight again if they found any stragglers in the woods.

Willow found the place where he had left his father—where the pine needles on the forest floor were splattered with blood—but he was gone. Moose followed the trail of blood through the woods until he came to the bay. On a narrow beach they found footprints and the mark left by a single canoe. Moose turned to Willow and spoke quietly to him.

"Your father saved our village," he said, as though speaking of a spirit. "He was always the strongest and the best. We owe him our lives."

"I thought he was a traitor," said Willow, his voice choked with confusion. "I wish I had seen his true spirit."

"You did see his true spirit," replied Moose. "You believed his warning."

"How could I injure him?" asked Willow. "With a rock!"

"You struck an enemy warrior to defend yourself and protect your people," Moose answered, clutching Willow's arm tightly with his giant hands. "You could not have known."

As the sun moved across the sky several canoes appeared in the bay, gliding over the shimmering water toward the beach. Otter and Loon were slumped in the first two, not moving. When they reached the beach, they sat quietly while the other warriors stepped out to guide the canoes onto the sand.

Low voices talked about the strange reappearance of Gray Fox, as Willow went over to his friends. He saw immediately how badly they'd been beaten and cut with sharp knives. The spark of life that was always in his friends' faces had disappeared. Instead, they looked at him with haunted eyes. With effort Otter sat up straight in the canoe, but his strong chest was now bloody and hollow, and his face betrayed his pain.

"We were brave," he said in a trembling voice.

Loon stared blankly into the water. The late afternoon sunlight shone from behind him, casting his wavering shadow on the pebbles and sand beneath the shallow water. Moving patterns of reflected light from the rippling waves danced across the lakebed and over his shadow, making it disappear and reappear with the rhythm of the waves. His spirit had deserted him. He didn't have the strength to speak.

– CHAPTER FIFTY –

Feast of the Dead

The celebrations began as soon as the warriors returned to Thunder River. It was a time to rejoice at the defeat of the invaders and to sing praise to the spirits who had guided them to victory. This had been a triumph for the entire village—not only for the warriors who had chased the attackers back to the lake and the daring fighters who had risked their lives to punch holes in the enemy canoes, but also the brave archers on the palisade and the children who gathered water to put out fires. Everyone could eat, sing, and dance together. There had been few injuries and no deaths among their people.

Willow's fear of being reviled as the son of a traitor vanished when he was led into the village as the son of Gray Fox, the hero who had returned from captivity to warn of the attack. The young warrior was also praised for his quick thinking and strong actions in battle. Although he said nothing to the others, Willow knew that the spirits had guided his decision to warn his people of the attack and he was thankful they hadn't misled him. He was aware that his life—and the lives of his people—would have been different if he had chosen to accept the lies of an enemy warrior over the true word of his own father, and he shuddered when he thought how close he had come to warning the wrong village.

— Feast of the Dead —

This feast was like no other. Salmon and whitefish from the lake were added to the cooking pots with strawberries and cattail roots. Deer and geese were roasted over open fires. Young girls chewed kernels of corn into a thick paste to be mixed into succulent corn bread. The events of the day called for special treats.

Never had the dancing been more exuberant. Young and old leapt and whirled with the special, almost uncontrollable energy that comes from a victory over the enemy. It was the dance of the fearless, the dance of the invincible. And the singing had never been louder. Strong, proud voices drowned out the pounding drums and the noisy rattles. They sang as if to display their power to the spirits in the sky, with colourful lyrics of revenge against the People from Across the Lake.

The only one who didn't celebrate was Loon. He sat silently in the middle of the festivities watching patterns of light from the fire dancing on the walls of the longhouse. He had always been known as the most enthusiastic dancer in the village and there he sat, motionless and mute, leaning against a basket like an old man.

Three enemy prisoners covered with scrapes and bruises were tied to posts in the centre of the village for all to see and the villagers hurled insults at them and dumped waste at their feet. Blood dripped from the chest of one prisoner, though he stood bravely against the post with his head held high as the summer wind blew his long gray hair from his face. Even surrounded by reeking waste, he carried himself with dignity while the others slumped listlessly against the posts, enduring the jabs and taunts of young boys until Brown Bat chased them away. He hovered close enough to protect the prisoners from abuse, but not close enough to be seen as one of them. He knew he could only protect them for so long because the cries for revenge were getting louder as the days passed.

On the third day after the battle, when the celebrations were over, Brown Bat called a meeting of the clan chiefs on the plateau overlooking the river. They gathered as the sun was setting. He asked the War Chief to speak of the battle.

"We have defeated this attack on our village," said Moose, looking around at the many proud faces. "The enemy warriors who managed to escape will spread stories of our skill and bravery among the People from Across the Lake. They'll be afraid to return." He hesitated, knowing as well as the other chiefs that the enemy would not be defeated by one battle. "But they will return," he continued. "They'll return to avenge their defeat and conquer us. That is their way. We must take steps now to protect ourselves.

"This time the spirit of the sky saved us by sending a messenger to warn of the attack. If we hadn't been warned, we would have suffered enormous losses. Our village would have been burned to the ground. Next time, we may not have a warning."

The clan leaders listened carefully to the words of the War Chief. "We must prepare the village for future attacks. Our palisades must be expanded and strengthened. Our lookout towers must be built higher. We must have scouts along the shore at all times of the year to watch for enemy invaders. When they come again we must be ready."

The leader of the Fox Clan rose to speak. His long hair was tied behind with a thin strip of snakeskin. "You know my thoughts. I've expressed them before. There's no sense in strengthening this village. It has outlived its natural life. It was time to move even before the enemy attacked and now there's no time to waste. The village is too close to the lake—too close to the enemy. They can sneak up on us, as they did a few days ago, and attack us before we can defend ourselves. This time we had a warning, but the strange events that led to that warning will never be repeated. The next time we'll be ambushed by the enemy if we stay here.

"We should move far up the river to get away from the threat of an invasion," the leader of the Fox Clan continued. "Some place where there are forests of uncut trees for firewood, plentiful bark for our houses, fresh soil for our crops.

"Next time the enemy will attack us with the rage of a forest fire. They will destroy us if they catch us by surprise. Now is the time to go to a place where we'll be safe."

Feast of the Dead

The leader of the Wolf Clan spoke next. His words came slowly and thoughtfully. As always, his speech was brief. "Those of us who have tried to attack the enemy villages know how difficult it is to ambush them. They build their villages far up the rivers and watch them carefully. We should learn from them."

"I agree," said Moose after a long silence. "The best way to defend a village from attack is to build it far up the river. There are too many spies near the lake. War parties easily invade our villages. We can't live near its shores any longer.

"I'll miss being close to the Beautiful Lake, the islands, and the bay. I'll miss the sand dunes and the beach at the mouth of Thunder River, but I won't miss the enemy attacks. We must go to the new site we have been preparing far up the river—and we must go now."

The speeches continued until after dark and into the warm summer night. Finally Brown Bat summarized what everyone had agreed. They would move the village that summer and the harvest would be taken to the new village. It would require a huge effort to build as many longhouses as they could before the winter.

"Some of the bark and poles from this village can be used at the new site," said the leader of the Loon Clan. "We can move almost everything we have."

"Not everything," said Old Heron.

"No," said Brown Bat, sombrely acknowledging what everyone knew already. "We can't move the burial place. We'll have to leave the bones of our dead here."

"It is time for the Feast of the Dead," said Old Heron.

"And it will have to be done soon," said the leader of the Deer Clan. "We have a village to build before the snow comes."

"The full moon has passed," said Brown Bat. "We'll have the Feast of the Dead on the next full moon. We can send out messengers with invitations right away." The other elders agreed. The preparations for the Feast of the Dead would begin at dawn.

As soon as he woke up, Moose went searching for Willow, Otter and Loon. He found them talking in the open field outside the palisade. Loon sat in the grass beside them. Moose called out and signalled for them to come to him quickly. Willow and Otter knew immediately that something exciting was about to happen. They lifted Loon to his feet and hurried toward Moose with their listless friend in tow. When they reached him at the village gate they were breathless with anticipation.

"I need your help," said Moose. "There's so much to be done." He told them about the decision to move the village farther up the river. He explained that they would have to bury the bones at a Feast of the Dead. Otter started to jump up and down where he stood. He knew there would be more memorable nights of feasting and dancing. They had all heard about the Feast of the Dead many times, but were too young to remember the last time it had been held.

"You three can take a message to Wolverine," Moose said. "Tell him that the Feast of the Dead will be held at the next full moon. Everyone in his village is welcome. Stay together and listen carefully for sounds of danger. It's possible there are still enemy warriors in the forests, but I think they've fled in terror. Our scouts have found no one." Willow and Otter looked at each other, silently recalling their last trip to the Village of the Dawn.

"I'll be going to the village by the Bottomless Lake to spread the news. Be back in two days if you can," said Moose. He glanced at Loon and saw a faraway look in his eyes.

"Loon," Moose said calmly. Loon looked up at him. There was an echo of pain in his eyes. "Are you well enough to make the trip?"

"Yes," he replied with a distant voice.

"Good," replied Moose. He studied Loon's face again and then turned to Willow and Otter. "Go to your house and get your bows. Get Loon's as well. I want to talk to him. Meet us back here."

Moose put his hand on Loon's arm and the young warrior turned away without saying anything.

"Loon," Moose said. "Try to look at me. You've been through a terrible experience." Loon looked down at his feet. "Try hard, Loon. Try hard to look at me. You know I'm your friend."

"I will," said Loon, slowly lifting his head.

"You have endured what many brave warriors could not. You behaved with honour." Loon gazed past him and stared vacantly across the fields. Moose continued. "You were wounded—and your spirit was broken. Both take time to heal."

Loon looked back at Moose. "How long will my spirit be broken this way?" the young man asked. "I'm haunted by the enemy day and night. I can't go anywhere without fearing them, because I couldn't endure any more pain. It nearly killed me. What kind of warrior am I now?"

"You're the bravest kind," replied Moose. "I don't know how long it will take, but I know you will heal. Spend time with your friends. Do the things you love to do—and you will heal."

"Will my spirit come back?" Loon asked weakly.

"It will come back."

Willow and Otter returned with the bows and quivers and they were soon on the trail to the village on the River of the Dawn.

"Watch out for each other," shouted Moose, as they disappeared across the fields.

They ran slowly to conserve their strength. Otter was in front and Willow at the back. From the middle, Loon watched nervously for signs of movement. They stopped only once for water from a spring, and by the time the sun was high they had arrived at the hill overlooking the wide valley of the River of the Dawn, with the village on the far side.

When they reached the village this time, they were taken immediately to see Wolverine, who stood waiting for them outside the palisade looking down at the river below.

"I heard there were three brave warriors running through the forest," he said with a generous smile. "I should have known it was the three bear hunters from Thunder River. Come and sit with me and share our food." He offered them some watery corn soup from a pot beside the fire. When they had finished eating he turned to Willow.

— *Enemy Arrows* —

"Tell me about seeing your father. Tell me everything you can remember. You know that your father and I grew up together. Like everyone else, I thought he was dead."

Willow told him the entire story about his father and how he had fought him to stay alive. Wolverine listened closely. When Willow described how he had struck his father with a rock, Wolverine's eyes filled with tears.

"How could you know it was Gray Fox?" he asked, wiping his eyes with both hands. "How could you know?"

Willow continued with the story to the final defeat of the enemy. With each word Wolverine became more and more distressed. Then he turned to Otter and asked for *his* story. Otter described his capture by the enemy and how he was tortured before being rescued. He showed Wolverine the knife wound across his chest.

"You were very brave to withstand that," said Wolverine, rubbing his head anxiously. Finally, he turned to Loon and asked him to describe what he had seen, but Loon couldn't answer. He just stared into the fire at the light on the flickering coals. Wolverine didn't press him. He had seen that look before in the eyes of warriors captured by the enemy.

"I almost forgot!" blurted Wolverine, slapping his thigh. "Turkey Vulture's envoy was here a few days ago with some messages. He said Turkey Vulture won't be coming back for a while. He said the peace proposal has failed—as we all knew it would—and he asked me to pass on a message to the three bear hunters of Thunder River. I have no idea what it means."

– CHAPTER FIFTY-ONE –

The Trust of Brothers

"Let me see if I can get it right," said Wolverine. He looked to the sky, trying to recall the message before he continued. "Yes, I have it. '*The turkey vulture has lost its feathers—it no longer flies. The song of the oriole is true and clear.*' Or did the oriole lose its feathers?" He paused for a moment. "No, no, turkey vultures don't sing. I had it right. That's the message exactly as I heard it."

Otter looked mystified. Loon's thoughts were somewhere else, but Willow smiled to himself.

"Anyway, you must have other important news," said Wolverine.

"We have a message from Moose," said Otter. "He invites you and your village to a Feast of the Dead on the next full moon."

"A Feast of the Dead," repeated Wolverine. A frown came over his face as he pondered the meaning of the message. "Does this mean you are moving your village?"

"Yes," replied Willow. "The elders say we're too close to the lake, so we have to move the village into the forest—far away from the enemy."

"And what will become of us?" Wolverine asked himself. He stood up quickly. "Rest and eat all you can. I must speak to the elders about this news." He disappeared inside the village gate.

Willow looked at Loon and shook his head.

"Are you going to be well again, Loon?" he asked.

Loon looked up from the fire with a start. "I don't know."

"We haven't heard you laugh since the battle," said Willow.

"I think terrible thoughts. I've forgotten how to laugh."

"Forgotten how to laugh?" repeated Otter. "You'll never forget how to laugh!"

"Do you remember when we rode across the ice with Old Chief?" asked Willow. "You remember how we flew at the speed of the wind and how Old Chief laughed?"

Loon looked at his friends. A faint smile appeared on his face. He felt glad to be with them again.

"Do you remember how the moose laughed with the rest of us? How its lips wobbled and its head bounced?"

Loon's shoulders shook gently as he remembered the moose's bulbous lips flopping up and down. He could feel the memories of happy times soothing his troubled spirit. One day he might be able to laugh again.

On the quiet trail back to Thunder River at sunrise, Willow told Otter and Loon about the message from Turkey Vulture. At long last he disclosed what Oriole had said about his father and how Turkey Vulture had offered to help him find out if it was true. Otter stopped in his tracks to listen, as if the effort to make sense of what Willow was saying left him no strength to walk. Loon stood behind him, looking straight into Willow's eyes. The pain of his own distress had disappeared from his face.

"That's what's been gnawing at you!" shouted Otter. "Why did you keep that from us?"

"I couldn't tell you in case it was a lie," replied Willow. "And I knew it was a lie."

"You knew it was a lie?" repeated Otter.

"I thought I knew . . ." Willow said awkwardly. "And I couldn't let anyone think my father was a traitor—and I was the son of a traitor. I couldn't do that."

Loon elbowed his way past Otter, grabbed Willow by the shoulders and stared at him with a look of sudden recognition. He spoke firmly but respectfully, as though he were speaking to Old Chief.

"We're your friends, Willow—your brothers. You can't keep these things from us. We could see your spirit was broken and wanted to know why. We wanted to know so we could help you. Brothers take care of each other."

"He's right," added Otter, with a force that bordered on outrage. "We trust each other and we're alive today only because of that. When we fight the enemy again we have to know that we *can* trust each other. We *have* to know that—or we won't come back alive."

"You're right," replied Willow, slapping a mosquito on his forehead with the palm of his hand. The blood-filled insect burst, leaving a smear of blood on his face. "But what would you have done? What would you have said if I'd told you my father was one of the People from Across the Lake?"

Otter and Loon exchanged glances, each waiting for the other to answer.

"Would you have believed me?" Willow asked.

They answered in unison, Otter saying 'Yes' and Loon saying 'No.'

"Would you have thought he was a traitor?"

This time Otter answered 'No' and Loon replied, 'Yes.'

"Would you have thought of me as the son of a traitor?"

Loon released Willow's shoulders and stood waiting for Otter's response, but Otter wasn't sure what to say. Instead, he looked back at Loon, waiting for him to reply to a question that had no believable answer. Loon said nothing. Before he uttered an answer, he pointed his finger toward the trail behind Willow.

"Look out!" he shouted, ducking his head. Willow and Otter dove for cover in the undergrowth and scrambled into the forest on their knees. The breathless silence of the forest then erupted with Loon's high-pitched laugh, broken only by his haunting loon call as he raced down the trail toward Thunder River.

"Our Loon is back," said Otter, creeping out of the bushes and brushing the sticks from his hair.

— *Enemy Arrows* —

Willow wiped blood from a gash on his knee. "Loons can stay underwater for a long time, but they always come up for air."

"Let's feed him to the dogs!" cried Otter.

"When we catch him!" yelled Willow. They charged down the trail after Loon, shouting and laughing as they went, and before long the forest was silent again.

News of the Feast of the Dead spread through Thunder River with the speed of a spring flood. Everyone in the village had friends or family in the burial place. The souls of their relatives would finally be released to make the dangerous journey to the Land of the Dead—and those who made the journey across the stars would spend eternity hunting and fishing in peace. Everything possible would be done to help them on their journey.

The elders selected the site for the final burial of the bones. It was in the open field outside the palisade at the end of the plateau—where Old Chief used to sit and watch over the river below with the Beautiful Lake far in the distance. From that place, Old Chief could see the first faint traces of green on the buds of spring and the first specks of red on the autumn leaves. Now, with his final burial, his spirit could watch the canoes gliding up and down the river forever.

The young warriors arrived at their village covered with leaves to find a large pit dug in the place where Old Chief used to sit. They had never seen such a hole. It was deep enough for one man to stand on another's shoulders without being seen, and it was too wide to be crossed by the best jumper—no matter how fast he ran or how high he leapt.

Before long the three were helping Moose build a circular platform around the outside of the pit, topped with narrow cross-poles pointing toward the centre. The poles had to be strong enough to hang the many presents that would be displayed by each of the clans before burial—before the bones of their loved ones would finally be mingled for eternity.

Guests started arriving that day from the surrounding villages. The bodies of dead relatives were then taken down from the raised scaffolds inside the palisades, where they had rested since the last Feast of the Dead so many years ago. Orchid asked Willow to help her with the body of her mother, who had died just after Willow was born. Together they gently lifted the fur-wrapped body from its platform and placed it on the grass, where Orchid removed the tattered robes from the body and scraped the bones clean—singing her mother's favourite songs as she worked. Next, they gathered the bits of fur and sinew in baskets and burned them in a fire, before wrapping the clean bones in beaverskins decorated with beads and shells from far away. These were taken to the longhouse and left on the loft where Orchid slept. It was good to have her mother close to her once again.

The body of Orchid's father, Old Chief, was also taken down and wrapped in new robes. When they were ready Moose placed the remains on a small wooden platform and, with the help of Lynx, carried them to the large pit where they were left with the other bones on raised platforms, away from the eyes and teeth of animals.

The feasting began when all the dead had been cared for and prepared for the journey to the stars. Orchid and Moose gave a feast in honour of their long-dead mother and Old Chief. The speeches and gift giving lasted until dark, and then the dancing began. From every longhouse and every shadowy corner of the village came the sound of drums and rattles and the wailing voices of mourners.

The dancing lasted until dawn and this time Loon joined in, though not with his usual brilliance. But by morning he was blowing in his cupped hands, making the shrill sound of a loon—to his own delight and the cheers of his friends.

– CHAPTER FIFTY-TWO –

Mingling the Bones

The day dawned cloudy and windless and a light drizzle began to fall. Before midday Orchid carried the bag containing her mother's bones outside the longhouse and spread them carefully on the ground. She and her sisters mourned their mother one last time. Their cries of sorrow mixed with the sounds of grieving coming from every longhouse in the village. The drizzle continued through the day, covering the village and everyone in it with tears from the spirit of the sky.

In the middle of the day Orchid put the bones back in the beaverskin bag and carried them to the scaffold surrounding the pit, along with the gifts that had been given to honour the dead. The gifts were strung on the poles of the circular wall for all to see. It was a time to show the wealth of the clan and the respect they had for their dead.

Orchid then took the wrapped bones and hung them on the cross poles at the top of the wall. When the bones were comfortable and respectfully settled, she and Moose stood on top of the scaffold and called out the names of their dead. Next the elders of the clan announced to the villagers who among them would receive the many gifts collected in the names of their loved ones. Gifts for Orchid's mother and Old Chief were given to Orchid and

— Mingling the Bones —

Moose and their sisters, and friends of their mother, as well as to Willow, Otter and Loon and the many others who had helped to bury them. In the evening the mourners lined the bottom of the wet pit with the finest beaver robes. The body of Old Chief was carefully lowered to the bottom. Then some old kettles were placed in the burial pit for the use of the dead. When this was done, the mourners made fires around the circular wall and spent the night quietly in their presence.

The young warriors sat together under the platform out of the rain, speaking in whispers.

"I'm glad this doesn't happen often," said Loon.

"Death is a part of life," replied Otter. "We have to deal with it."

"One day we'll be rushing across the stars on our way to the Land of the Dead," said Willow. "We'll all be there together and we'll hunt forever."

"We can enjoy ourselves without any fear of laughing ourselves to death!" said Loon loudly.

"Not so loud," said Otter, making the sign of silence.

They talked late into the night and fell asleep in the grass beside the fur-lined pit.

Fog shrouded the village in the darkest part of the night, but as the sun rose bright and clear, the mist lifted from the dew-covered fields and climbed toward the sky like the spirits of the dead. When the sun's light reached the tallest poles around the pit, the mourners moved forward with their bags of bones, crying and shouting again for the dead. Moose and two clan leaders climbed down into the pit beside the wrapped bodies. Once they were in position, the mourners emptied the bones from the beaverskin bags where they were mingled together in a huge mass. There, in that pit, they would be together forever.

Bright Star watched the ceremony from a distance, with tears streaming down her face at the thought of Deadfall Hunter buried alone in a distant village. She knew the bones of her husband had not been mixed with those of his people because he had died violently in a fall from the cliff. No one in the village would dare to anger the spirits by burying his bones with the bones of others.

She understood, but she couldn't bear the thought of her husband being left alone throughout eternity while his friends and relatives hunted together. Seeing the look on Bright Star's face, Moose thought how hard it must be for her watch others being honoured while her husband was so far away.

When all the relatives had been buried, Moose, Brown Bat and the clan leaders pulled the beaver robes over the bones and climbed out of the pit. Then they covered the pit with poles and wood from the circular wall, and pushed the sandy soil back in place. Once the ground had been smoothed over to form a low mound, Orchid and the other women mourners sprinkled corn on the top as food for the souls of the dead.

In the heat of the midday sun Moose and the other mourners drove stakes into the ground around the burial place, built a roof to shelter the souls of the dead, and covered it with bark like the roof of a longhouse. When it was completed, the mourners said their parting words to their dead and returned to the village to honour them one last time.

By now there was only one prisoner remaining at the village. The others had been taken away in exchange for their own people being held prisoner across the lake, or had died of their injuries. The gray-haired prisoner was still lashed to the post by himself, standing in waste. Though he was getting thin and weak, he still carried himself with dignity.

Moose went to him with a pot of water. He spoke to the prisoner respectfully and the courtesy was returned. Moose then held the pot to the prisoner's mouth while he drank. As he was finished, the captive lowered his head to Moose. When Moose reached for his knife, the prisoner tensed his muscles and took a deep breath. With one quick movement Moose sliced off the ropes and led him away from the foul-smelling sludge where he had been standing and, without ceremony, delivered him to Bright Star.

— *Mingling the Bones* —

"This man will take care of you, Bright Star," said Moose. "He's now one of us."

Bright Star inspected the prisoner from his head to his stinking feet. His gray hair was matted and caked with dried blood. He wore only a tattered loincloth and his legs and feet were covered with muck. Though he was old, he appeared to be strong. Bright Star spoke to him and he responded with gratitude, so she led him down to Thunder River where he could wash the filth from his body.

Willow left the village by himself before dawn the next day. He knew it was a special morning. He was not far from the village when he heard Wren's voice behind him, and he turned around to see his sister racing down the path after him.

"Can I come?" she cried. "Can I come with you?"

He smiled and waited for her to catch up. Then they walked together along the path toward the Beautiful Lake.

"Where are we going?" she asked.

"We're going to the Turtle's Back," he replied. "Today is a day to see amazing things."

Wren's eyes widened with excitement. "What are we going to do?"

"You'll see," he answered. They walked along the trail toward the orange horizon singing together until Willow suddenly stopped. Beside the path was a patch of strawberries covered with morning dew. On the other side was another small patch, where Old Chief had scattered a handful of ripe berries a year earlier.

They picked some to eat and then Willow buried a few in the grass farther along the path. "Next year there will be more," he said to Wren.

"There are enough here for a feast," she replied, holding his arm tightly.

"We'll stop again on the way back," he said. They walked through the woods until they came to the Turtle's Back. On the top of the mound was Old Chief's empty turtle shell, which Willow pressed against his chest, thinking once again about his times with Old Chief. They stood there looking out toward the lake.

"There are the islands," said Wren, pointing across the distant bay.

She turned toward the river. "There is the mouth of Thunder River. Oh, this is the most beautiful place I know! We can see forever from here. I feel like a bird looking down at everything."

Willow sat down on the Turtle's Back with Wren close beside him.

"Do you see that tall pine tree above the other trees?" he asked.

"Yes," she answered.

"If you watch carefully, you'll soon see it catch fire."

"This is such an exciting place!" she said. They sat together looking at the lake and the river below. Willow showed Wren the thirteen scales on the back of the turtle shell and told her how she could count the thirteen moons between one spring and the next. He then counted the twenty-eight tongues along the edge of the shell and told her how she could count the time between one full moon and the next.

In a sudden flash of colour, a sliver of radiant gold light shone from behind the pine tree. "Look!" said Willow pointing to the pine tree. "It's on fire!"

Wren clutched his arm and held it close to her. "Willow," she said with a knowing smile. "That's the sun."

"No, it really is!" he said, trying to make her leap to her feet as he had done when he had first seen the burning tree.

"It's the sun, Willow."

After basking in the glow of the rising sun, she stood up again and held her hand out to Willow. "Let's go back to the village now," she said with the voice of a songbird. "There's so much to do."

– CHAPTER FIFTY-THREE –

Hunting in the Stars

And so much was done. Through the summer and into the fall, the old village was dismantled and a new one was built, far away from the Beautiful Lake—far from the reach of the enemy, far from the cornfields and Thunder River. Only the bones of the dead remained. The new village was constructed beside a stream flowing north into the Great Swamp, on a flat area with sandy soil and endless hardwood forests.

The village on the River of the Dawn was abandoned, too. Wolverine and his people joined in the new village or moved farther north to join villages near the Lake of Islands.

The new longhouses were as large as the old ones and when the snow came, they were full of corn, squash and beans harvested from the fields beside Thunder River and carried overland by sleds. Orchid and Wren found a loft in the centre of the longhouse, where they kept a pot of corn stew close to the fire. Sometimes they added fish or meat. Old Heron continued to watch over the longhouse as though there had been no change.

The three young warriors would often return to the abandoned village above Thunder River to sit where Old Chief used to sit. It was late in the fall when they saw the Wanderer's multi-coloured canoe appear on the river, loaded to the gunnels and covered with beaverskins. They went down to the river to greet him and his daughter.

Oriole stared at Willow when he grabbed the front of the canoe and guided it to shore. Once again Willow could hear the sound of her voice when she had called him a snapping turtle and could hear her laugh.

"Where are the friends who always come to meet us?" asked the Wanderer, stepping lightly from the canoe into the murky water. "Have they forgotten us?"

"Only a snapping turtle to welcome us," said Oriole.

"Where?" yelped the Wanderer, leaping onto the shore.

Oriole and Willow couldn't hold back their amusement. Somehow her laugh seemed less threatening than it had before.

Once they were safely on shore, the young men told the astonished travellers about the enemy attack and described the new village that was built so far away. They took the travellers past the covered burial mound and then up the trail to see the abandoned village. The Wanderer walked through a wide gap in the remnants of the palisade and stood where the village had been. He held his arms out in front of him while he stared at the empty space. "This is not how I remember it."

Oriole gazed at the empty place where so many lives had been lived, without saying a word.

Before long Loon had made a fire and they ate a meal of corn and dried fish. Willow told them every detail about the attack on the islands and Otter described what had happened when he they had been captured, showing the scars on his chest. Oriole grimaced and looked away. Loon tended the fire, still unable to talk about his horrible ordeal. Willow told of his escape and his encounter with his father.

Finally Oriole spoke to him.

"I wish you had let me give you the message from your father," she said softly.

"Where?" yelped the Wanderer, leaping onto the shore.

Willow stared into her dark eyes. They were kind and honest eyes. He wondered how he could have been so hostile when she attempted to pass on his father's message.

"But I didn't. I was a turtle, as you said," he answered, looking into the fire. "We can't change what happened." The Wanderer nodded in agreement.

Oriole touched Willow's arm and the orange feathers from her bracelet brushed against his bare skin. "I've known your father all my life and he was always kind to me." She smiled, showing her bright eyes and strong teeth. "You should find him."

"Find him?" replied Willow. "How could I find him? He's gone. He didn't return to his own people—and he'll never be able to go back to the enemy."

"We can find him," said the Wanderer quietly. "Unless he's hunting among the stars, we'll find him. We go everywhere and speak with everyone we meet."

"Come with us," said Oriole, putting her hand firmly on Willow's arm. "You can change what *will* happen."

"Yes, come with us," said the Wanderer. "When we find him, you can meet as friends."

Willow didn't know how to respond. He'd had no thoughts at all of meeting his father, either as an enemy or a friend. Instead of answering the Wanderer, he looked to Otter and Loon.

"We're your brothers, Willow," said Otter.

Loon leaned over to Willow and grabbed his shoulder. "If you go, we're going with you."

Willow turned to stare once again at the view of Thunder River that Old Chief had loved so much. How he wished he could tell his grandfather what had happened and hear what he had to say. But it was too late. Instead, he recalled Old Chief's words when Willow had been determined to fly over Thunder River: "You are a brave warrior and bear hunter. You make your own decision."

He turned back to his friends and then smiled at the Wanderer and his daughter. "We are warriors and bear hunters. We'll go with you."

ACKNOWLEDGEMENTS

So many people have helped to get this book off the ground, each offering support in his or her own way. I owe them all a huge debt of gratitude. Here are a few of the many people who have made this book about the Wendat Nation come to life.

The late Bruce Graham Trigger, OC OQ FRSC, author of *Children of Aataentsic, A History of the Huron People to 1660*, for his groundbreaking research and for inspiring generations of Canadians to learn more about the Wendat people.

Prof. John Steckley, anthropologist, author of *Words of the Huron* and adopted member of the Wyandot tribe of Kansas, for his advice, his unique historical perspective and his kind words of encouragement (in the Huron language).

Tom McNeely, the brilliant Canadian illustrator and writer, whose long experience in recreating scenes from Canada's past has been invaluable.

Zack Curcija, Cultural Interpreter, Crawford Lake Conservation Area, scholar and outstanding outdoorsman of European, Metis and Algonquin-Anishnabek ancestry, for his thoughtful review of the manuscript and his many practical suggestions for improvement.

Marianne Fedunkiw, Ph.D. for her careful and meticulous editing of the manuscript in its nearly-finished state, and for her skillful suggestions to make the words flow.

— ACKNOWLEDGEMENTS —

Monica Bodersky, artist and editor, who patiently helped me to hew the first drafts out of solid rock.

Joyce Morris, Lillian Madunic, Linda Robinson and Jean Turner of Gardiner Roberts LLP, for their enthusiasm and their assistance in making the manuscript readable, and George Hatzipantelis for his photographic and technical expertise.

A. Britton Smith, MC QC LLD, my esteemed uncle, war hero, writer and historian, and his dear wife, the late Sally Smith, both of whom read an early draft of this manuscript and provided excellent suggestions and endless encouragement. Brit was instrumental in making the illustrations appear on these pages.

My three wonderful daughters, Charlotte, Jane and Meg, who loved to hear bedtime stories as children about the First Nations of Canada, and without whose boundless support as adults this story would still be an idea in my head.

My dear mother, Ann O'Hara, artist, poet, editor and teacher, for her suggestions on the early drafts of this manuscript and her unflagging encouragement, but mostly for passing on to her children, grandchildren and great-grandchildren her own great love of the outdoors and the beauty of nature.

My creative siblings and their spouses, Kathleen, Doody, Dennis, Jill, Tony, Chris, and Catherine, all life-long lovers of the outdoors and most as comfortable in a canoe as they are on dry land, for their enthusiasm from the first wisp of an idea. Eternal thanks to Kathleen for her painstaking edits of several early drafts of the manuscript and gratitude to Doody, Jill and Chris for reading drafts and providing their positive suggestions.

Susan Winfield, who took our three children to see the reconstructed village at Crawford Lake Conservation Area too many times to count and provided a home where her family could thrive.

The Iron Men, Tom Dutton, Paul Sinel and Eric Murphy, for the many unforgettable canoe and cycling trips we shared, and particularly Eric for his unending encouragement as we independently weathered the challenges of taking an idea from inception to publication.

Anne Gniewek, who gave me the strength to cross the finish line.

Finally, thanks to my many good friends and relatives who listened patiently to my tales about creating this book, wondering to themselves when they would ever see it. Here it is!

ILLUSTRATION CREDITS

All original illustrations in *ENEMY ARROWS* are by
Tom McNeely

The battle image was inspired by an illustration by Lewis Parker
in *Life in a Longhouse Village* by Bobbie Kalman
published by Crabtree Publishing Company

**View full colour illustrations at
www.enemyarrows.com**

COVER DESIGN

Cover designs by
Elaine Kehler, Kehlermedia

FURTHER READING

Benn, Carl. *The Iroquois in the War of 1812.* Toronto: University of Toronto Press, 1998.

Bial, Raymond. *The Huron.* New York: Benchmark Books, Marshall Cavendish Corporation, 2001.

Bruchac, Joseph. *Children of the Longhouse.* New York: Puffin Books, 1996.

Champlain, Samuel de. *Algonquians, Hurons, and Iroquois: Champlain Explores America.* Dartmouth: Book House Press, 1567-1653.

Engelbrecht, William E. *Iroquoia: The Development of a Native World.* Syracuse: Syracuse University Press, 2003.

Gidmark, David. *Birchbark Canoe: Life Among the Algonquin.* Willowdale: Firefly Books Ltd., 1997.

Jenness, Diamond. *The Indians of Canada.* Toronto: University of Toronto Press, 1932.

Jury, Elsie McLeod. *The Neutral Indians of Southwestern Ontario.* London: London Museum of Archaeology, 1974.

Kalman, Bobbie. *Life in a Longhouse Village.* St. Catharines: Crabtree Publishing Company, 2001.

King, Thomas. The *Inconvenient Indian: A Curious Account of Native People in North America,* Toronto: Doubleday Canada, 2012.

Latourelle, René, S.J. *Jean de Brébeuf's Writings*, (translated by William Lonc, S.J. and George Topp, S.J.): published by William Lonc

McClintock, Walter. *Old Indian Trails*. Boston: Houghton Mifflin Company, 1923.

Mann, Charles C., *1491: New Revelations of the Americas Before Columbus*, New York: Vintage Books, 2011.

McMillan, Alan D. *Native Peoples and Cultures of Canada*. Vancouver: Douglas & McIntyre Ltd., 1995.

Morse, Eric W. *Fur Trade Canoe Routes of Canada: Then and Now*. Toronto: University of Toronto Press, 1969.

Raffan, James. *Bark, Skin and Cedar: Exploring the Canoe in Canadian Experience*. Toronto: HarperCollins Publishers Ltd., 1999.

Rajnovich, Grace. *Reading Rock Art*. Toronto: Natural Heritage/Natural History Inc., 1994.

Ray, Arthur J. *I Have Been Here Since the World Began*. Toronto: Lester Publishing Limited and Key Porter Books, 1996.

Rogers, Edward S. and Smith, Donald B., eds. *Aboriginal Ontario: Historical Perspectives on the First Nations*. Toronto: Dundurn Press, 1994.

Sanderson, Frances and Howard-Bobiwash, Heather, eds. *The Meeting Place: Aboriginal Life in Toronto*. Toronto: Native Canadian Centre of Toronto, 1997.

Sioui, Georges E., translation from French by Jane Brierley. *Huron-Wendat: The Heritage of the Circle*. Vancouver: UBC Press, 1999.

Steckley, John L. *Words of the Huron*. Waterloo: Wilfred Laurier University Press, 2007.

Trigger, Bruce G. *The Children of Aataentsic: A History of the Huron People to 1660*. Montreal: McGill-Queen's University Press, 1976.

Warrick, Gary. *A Population History of the Huron-Petun, A.D. 500 – 1650*: Cambridge University Press, 2008

Williamson, Ronald F., ed. *Toronto: An Illustrated History of the First 12,000 Years*. Toronto: James Lorimer & Company Ltd., 2008.

EXPLORATIONS

Canadian Canoe Museum, 910 Monaghan Road, Peterborough, Ontario
Canadian Museum of Civilization, 1 Vimy Place Pvt., Ottawa, Ontario
Crawford Lake Conservation Area, 3115 Steeles Avenue, Milton, Ontario
Ganondagan, 1488 Victor-Holcombe Road, Victor, New York
Golden Lake Algonquin Museum, Golden Lake First Nations Community, Golden Lake, Ontario
Huronia Museum, 549 Little Lake Park Road, Midland, Ontario
Iroquois Indian Museum, Box 7, Caverns Road, Howes Cave, New York
Lawson Site, 1600 Attawandaron Road, London, Ontario
Longwoods Road Conservation Area, 8449 Irish Drive, R.R. #1, Mount Brydges, Ontario
Musée Huron-Wendat, 15 Place de la Rencontra, "Ekionkiestha'", Wendake, Québec
Museum of Indian Archeology, 1600 Attawandaron Road, London, Ontario
Native Canadian Centre, 16 Spadina Road, Toronto, Ontario

New York State Museum, 222 Madison Avenue, Albany, New York

Petroglyphs Provincial Park, 2249 Northey's Bay Road, Woodview, Ontario

Rochester Museum & Science Center, 657 East Avenue, Rochester, New York

Royal Ontario Museum, 100 Queens Park, Toronto, Ontario

Saint Marie Among the Huron, Highway 12 East, Midland, Ontario

Sainte Marie Among the Iroquois, 6680 Onondaga Lake Parkway, Liverpool, New York

Whitchurch-Stouffville Museum 14732 Woodbine Ave Gormley, Ontario

WEB SITE

www.enemyarrows.ca

Printed in Canada